EMPIRE OF PAIN

J.L. BECK

Copyright © 2023 J.L. Beck

Cover design: Haya Designs

All rights reserved.

No part of this book may be reproduced in any form or by any electronic or mechanical means, including information storage and retrieval systems, without written permission from the author, except for the use of brief quotations in a book review.

For all the readers that gave Callum and Bianca a chance. I'd have no one to write stories for if no one read them, so thank you. For reading and falling in love with these characters just as I did.

CALLUM

"What's in the crate?"

I can hardly hear Romero's voice over the thundering beat of my own heart. My fingers grip the edge of the box for dear life as I stare down at the contents.

Words refuse to come.

My brain short circuits. I can't comprehend what I'm seeing.

Images come to me in flashes, one piece at a time.

Green eyes that once flashed dangerously, that used to burn with contempt. Now they see nothing, their vacant stare looking right into the deep confines of my soul. A bullet hole is directly between them. I force myself to look away from Amanda's face, and down to the body in her arms. In her arms is my daughter —*our* daughter. Her head rests against her mother's bloody shoulder, appearing as if Amanda had rocked her to sleep.

It's a grotesque parody of motherhood that only a truly sick, heartless cretin could put together. Amanda is seated with her back against the inside of the crate, with her head tilted backwards and her eyes staring lifelessly at the ceiling. A trickle of blood trails from the hole in her forehead and down her nose before drying there.

I've seen many terrible things in my life. Images that have haunted me for days after, robbing me of sleep. The result of violence brought on by greed. The aftermath of explosions, gun battles, death. But this? This is unfathomable.

I can't accept it. Something inside me refuses to accept what I'm seeing as one precious second after another passes by. I can't move. I can't breathe. It's real, even if I don't want it to be. Amanda is dead. It's only when Romero jostles me and reaches into the crate that I snap back to reality. Every ounce of information comes rushing in, assaulting me from all sides.

Tatum.

They might have killed her too.

Romero's choked cry rings in my ears. "No!!" He reaches into the crate, taking Tatum's limp body into his arms. Her skin is pale, a drop of dried blood trails down her temple from a patch of blood-matted hair on the side of her head. The ugly bruises circling her arms portray someone bigger and stronger holding her tight. I have no doubt she would've fought.

"No, Tatum, wake up. Wake up." I manage to rouse myself in time to take her legs and lift them over the edge of the crate before Romero lowers her to the floor.

I take a knee beside them and press an ear to her chest, listening for a heartbeat or any sign to let me know she is still alive. Everything moves in slow motion. Countless moments flash before my eyes, as fresh and clear as if it was only yesterday they took place.

Her first steps, toddling across the floor with her chubby arms extended outward, reaching for me. She knew I would catch her and hold her when she fell.

Her first dance recital, wearing a pair of angel wings with glitter in her hair, and the way she smiled at me that day was like I meant the world to her.

There was glitter stuck to her skin for days afterwards.

The one year for Halloween when she insisted on dressing as a pirate even though all the little girls her age wanted to be princesses.

My daughter wanted me to black out her teeth and draw stubble on her cheeks, and I did it. I did it even though I had a hundred other things to handle. I did it because even then, I was all she had and because she captured my heart the second we locked eyes for the first time, and as her daddy, it was my job. I would have done anything for her.

Her chest is barely moving, but I hear the soft intake of air in and out of her lungs. That's all I need to know to keep me motivated.

"She's breathing," I announce, and the touch of my fingers to the inside of her wrist reveals a shuddering pulse. All the air leaves my lungs, the pressure in my head making me light-headed. Relief floods my veins. She has a pulse, but that doesn't mean anything. "We need to get her to the hospital now."

I couldn't keep her safe, could I? The one thing she needed most, it was beyond me. I let her down. Failed her. What kind of father was I if I couldn't even protect my own daughter?

Romero's gaze collides with mine, eyes wild, his features frantic. Placing his trembling hands on both sides of her face, he peers down at her. There isn't so much as a fluttering of her eyelids to show she feels his touch. My thoughts are everywhere, my mind an endless fishbowl. There's something missing. Something that bangs like a gong, vibrating at the back of my skull.

Bianca.

"Where's Bianca?" I yell into the vast space. My head swings back and forth, my eyes searching in vain for her. The sick fucks who did this cleaned out the warehouse, taking everything besides the bloody crate and the bodies of a few of my men who are now being gathered, together, and dragged across the floor.

"What the fuck are you doing?" I bellow, making them all stand at attention. "Where is Bianca?"

Their expressions all mirror confusion. "We did a perimeter check, Sir. There's no one else here, at least that's alive."

My heart sinks into my stomach. Lower and lower, it falls until I swear it feels like it's going to jump out of my chest.

"Find her!! Look again!! I want you to search every inch of the property," I order, my voice frantic, my mind racing.

Romero meets my gaze. "She's not here. If she were, they would've told you by now."

"She has to be. Where else could she be?" I can't breathe. I can barely speak. First Tatum. Now Bianca.

It's not possible. They didn't take her.

"Find her!" I'm nearly shrieking, and I know, even in the haze of frenzied horror that I'm closer to losing my grip than I ever have been. The room spins around me, and I try to breathe, but it doesn't feel like I'm getting any oxygen into my lungs.

Where is she? Where did they take her?

"Boss, I know you're worried about Bianca, but we need to get Tatum to the hospital *now*. Someone hit her in the head. She could have… swelling or something worse."

I wheel around, prepared to tear his head off, only to find Romero gently gathering Tatum into his arms, cradling her the way she was cradled in her dead mother's arms. *Amanda.* She's dead. Still, the reminder doesn't allow me to feel anything. I'm numb, cold from the inside out. Think, think. There's a storm raging in my head that I need to calm. I can't afford to lose my grip on reality when my daughter needs me. *They all need me.*

Rationally I know he is right. Tatum might have sustained injuries that we cannot see. "Get her in the car," I order Romero before shouting to the men. "I want the entire area searched for any signs of Bianca before you dispose of the bodies."

"Save their phones," Romero calls out. "Bring them to me at the hospital."

In my heart, I know they won't find anything. There won't be a trace of my little bird. If this was about killing her, they would have left her here for me to find. It's what I would have done in their position, whoever they are. If I wanted to break a man down, if I wanted to strip him bare and hit him where it hurts, I'd have killed the only two things he loved more than his empire, money or life.

If this was about proving a point, they'd both be dead. This wasn't that. No, they took her somewhere else, somewhere hidden and the mess they left here was a hint at what's to come if I don't play along with their game. I know the tactic, have even done it myself a time or two, but I'd never involved innocent lives.

Stepping outside, finally free of the coppery stench of blood hanging heavily in the warehouse, I clear my head and steady my resolve. There is no time for breaking down, no time for blaming myself, or asking what I could have done better. That can come later, once I have Bianca back, once I know Tatum is okay.

First, I need to focus my attention on my daughter, who is now being loaded into the back seat of the car. I slide in on the other side, cradling her head in my lap while Romero jumps behind the wheel.

"Wake up, sweetheart," I murmur, stroking her cheek with a shaking hand. "Come back to me. Please. I can't lose you."

"I'll fucking kill them all," Romero grunts, cutting the wheel, tires squealing as we make a sharp right. The car nearly fishtails, but he manages to maintain control, weaving in and out of traffic once we hit the main road.

"Try not to kill us first," I bark over the blaring of horns, holding her firmly to keep her from sliding off the seat. He doesn't say a word, but he also doesn't slow down either.

Fuck around and find out. Those words are burned into my brain, taunting me. I know I said I'd try not to think about how this is my fault, but it's hard when you're holding your daughter's lifeless body in your arms, and you know she wouldn't be here in this situation if it wasn't for the man you are, for the dark and dangerous life you live. Somehow, I had overlooked the threat. I allowed her to go off alone—I never should have, no matter how much she ranted and raved about me being overprotective. Making up excuses in my mind, I thought I was doing the right thing. Giving her space to breathe, to heal.

Yes, look how she's healed.

Unconscious and half dead, the blood from her hair and scalp stains my slacks. She came so close to her bright, brilliant light being snuffed out. Thinking about the future, I can't say she'll be the same. After everything she's been through and endured. How far can a rubber band stretch before it snaps? A different kind of fear grips me, then. Physical wounds can heal, but emotional wounds...the brain can become your worst enemy if you allow it. I can't help but ask myself if she witnessed her mother dying. After everything, this might be the final nail in her coffin. The prospect of her never recovering makes me sick.

"Do you know anyone at the hospital? Can we call to let them know we're coming?"

He lifts a hand, pointing. "We're basically here." Now that he's said it, I notice the red and white emergency sign a few lights beyond where we have to stop for cross traffic. He leans on the horn, but it's no use. He can't stop the cars moving in both directions in front of us.

"As soon as she's taken care of, we need to start making calls." We've lost precious minutes that could have taken Bianca further from me. Who would be dumb enough to do this? It doesn't matter who it is. All that matters is finding her and ensuring she's okay.

"If Amanda had her phone on her, one of our guys will grab it," Romero grunts in frustration before leaning over the wheel in his eagerness to move. "It could also have the answers to our questions."

"Give me your phone." He has everyone's number programmed into his contacts, and once he hands me the device, I scroll through the list and stop at the first of the men we left at the warehouse. I press the call button for Bobby. I bark into the phone as soon as he answers, "Amanda's cell. Have you found it?"

"It wasn't in her purse—which they left under the body," he explains. "It also wasn't inside, and it's not in her pockets."

"Her car, it has to be there. Search the vehicles, too. Get me an update as soon as possible."

"Of course, boss," he replies and I end the call.

Romero swings the car into the emergency room lot, pounding the horn with his palm as he races for the doors. By the time the car squeals to a stop, a pair of paramedics are jogging out of the ambulance bay.

"She needs to be seen immediately!" I shout once they open the door closest to me. "All we know is that she has a head wound."

"Let us take it from here." One of the men practically pries her body from my arms. I don't know if I'm going to live through the pain that's cutting into the muscles of my chest. It burns, the skin fileting back, leaving my still-beating heart vulnerable. I'm vaguely aware of Romero pulling away to park the car while I jog behind the paramedics rushing Tatum to an empty bay in the emergency room.

A middle-aged nurse places herself between my daughter and me, pushing a laptop on a wheeled stand and blocking my path. "I'm going to need her information to enter into the system," she informs me while a team of doctors assesses Tatum.

"Look, can't this wait?"

"I need a name and a date of birth for her ID bracelet, along with insurance information and any known allergies."

There's a crazed animal in me, fighting to break loose and paint the tiled floor with blood. Think of Tatum. Tearing into this hospital won't get her help any faster. "Jane Doe," I growl.

She looks up from the screen, frowning. "Excuse me?"

"You heard correctly. Her name is Jane Doe."

Straightening slowly, she murmurs, "Sir, do I need to call the authorities?"

"I don't think so and, honestly, I would rather you didn't."

"You're telling me you don't know this girl's name? Exactly how did she come to be injured? Or are you unaware of that, as well?" The snippety attitude she's giving me is the last thing I need, and it needs to end now.

"Listen to me very carefully." My voice drops to a whisper as I lean over the top of the computer screen until she has no choice but to lean back. "I don't care what it takes for you to do it, but this girl's name will not be recorded. It could be dangerous for her if someone were to call and ask if she's been brought here." Not that I see that happening, but I can't afford to take any more chances. "Suffice it to say she is my daughter. I found her this way, and I don't care how many tests you need to run—or what anybody around here requires in order to keep their mouths shut. Is that clear?"

"How do I know you aren't bringing her here after losing your temper?"

"If I was, do you think I'd come in with her and risk being blamed?"

"Sir, you have no idea exactly how often that very thing happens." She glances over her shoulder to where Tatum is. I should be in there with her, damn it. "I could have security escort you out and acquire her side of the story once she's conscious and doesn't have you standing over her."

This isn't working. Would they really throw us out if I don't tell her? Can I risk it?

The idea takes my voice down to a murderous hiss. "Listen to me. The people who did this to her, they're dangerous and don't give a fuck about anyone else except themselves. There's no saying that they might not decide to show up here to finish the job. I will not risk leaving her vulnerable. Now stop questioning me and enter whatever the hell you need to in that computer, or I'll find someone you love, then make sure you had wished you'd stopped asking questions and done your goddamn job."

Her lips draw into a thin line, but her skin grows pale, giving way to a slight trickle of fear. "I've been threatened before," she whispers.

"Never by somebody so prepared to follow through." I make a point of checking out her name tag. "Cecilia Miller. What a nice name. Nice wedding ring, too," I add with a glance at her left hand. "Mr. Miller has good taste. Let me guess, 2.5 kids, a big house with a picket fence. It would be a real shame if something happened, now, wouldn't it? Do your kids have any close family? Do you think they could live without their mother or father?"

Her chin quivers before she makes a strangled choking sound while questioning whether I mean what I'm saying. Whatever she sees on my face convinces her. She gives me a short nod before clearing her throat. "Jane Doe it is," she whispers while a bead of sweat rolls down her temple.

Romero finds me when I'm finished, barking orders into his phone before jamming his finger at the screen to end the call. "We're gonna find them," he whispers, watching as Tatum is treated through an opening in the curtain. "We're going to find them, and when we do, they're all fucking dead."

"Way ahead of you," I murmur, already imagining the pain I'll inflict. "After we get Bianca back."

"It might be a good idea to call him."

I know who *him* is, and it's the last thing I want to do. *Fuck me.* It's a good idea since I need as many people as possible to search for her. Charlie has years of experience tracking people, but he's her father. He's going to kill me, or worse, lose his mind. Bianca is all he has left, and if he thinks she might be dead... Well, I can only imagine the fury that he'll unleash. There will be no stopping us, and the hell we will rain down on these people if anything happens to her.

"I'll call Charlie," I tell Romero.

"I know you don't want to deal with him, but maybe he can help."

I sigh, "Yeah, maybe, or he'll kill me. At this point, it doesn't matter." If anything happens to Bianca, I won't be able to forgive myself.

Bianca's home number is already stored in my contacts. I never imagined her father being the person I'd be calling if I ever had to call that number. My hand trembles as I bring the cell to my ear after hitting the green call button.

"Hello," Charlie's deep voice fills my ear.

"Charlie, it's Callum." Closing my eyes, I whisper, "I need you to meet me at the hospital. We have a problem."

BIANCA

My body trembles. My teeth chatter together, the only sound filling the small space. Is this what shock feels like? I can barely think of anything except what happened.

Is Tatum okay? What did they do to her? I couldn't see what happened, but I will never forget the weight of her limp body across my legs. It's where she fell after she slid down my body. And that terrible sound. The sound of bones crunching together. Shattering into tiny pieces.

The shivers worsen when I start to dive deeper into my thoughts. *Focus.* I can't continue to think like this, not if I'm going to get through this. I'm still alive, and that means something.

I have to do this, for the baby. If for nothing else, I have to survive for my baby's sake. And for my father, who's already lost enough, and Callum. *Oh, my God, where is he? Does he know what happened?* I'm sure by now he knows what's happened and that I'm missing.

I'm not sure how much time has passed, but it's dark outside. The small window cut into the cinder block wall tells me that. Hours must have passed since they took us from the garage.

Time doesn't matter. I know him. He'll come looking for me.

A sharp pain radiates through my stomach and I curl into a tighter ball on the cot somebody left me on when we arrived. It's filthy and smells like mildew, but it's the only piece of furniture in the small, dark room. Something is dripping somewhere, a leaky pipe maybe, but I can't see it. The rhythmic *plink plink plink* is almost soothing.

After a few deep breaths, I settle enough to focus on the pain. It's not cramping, thank God. I don't know much about pregnancy yet, but I doubt cramping would be a good sign. It's more like nausea; not surprisingly, fear and dread will do that to you. My stomach is knotted, and I barely contain the scream of rage threatening to tear its way out of my throat when my thoughts drift back to Callum again. I can only imagine how frantic he is right now. The thoughts he's having. I have no idea what they did with Tatum. What if they killed her and left her body there for him to find?

We only need this one. That was one of the last things Amanda ever said. My God. I'm reminded again that she's dead. Just like that. I would never have called her my favorite person—she went out of her way to drive a wedge between Callum and me by getting inside my head. She called me filthy, ugly names. She dragged out the divorce for ages, all so she could make Callum miserable, and she was a terrible mother. So much of Tatum's toughness is a defense mechanism. She built a wall around her that got thicker with every ignored call, every missed meet-up, every skipped holiday. Regardless of those things, it doesn't mean I'm glad she's dead. No matter how many times I replay those ugly, terrifying moments, there's no convincing myself of any other outcome. She was a shadowy figure in front of me, then there was a gunshot, and her silhouette disappeared.

I have no idea who shot her or if she was working with someone. The voice that spoke wasn't familiar. The only thing I could tell was that it was a man whose name was never spoken. He shot somebody else after Amanda—I don't know who, but I heard something heavy hit the floor—before somebody else picked me up and carried me out. The pillowcase stayed firmly in place until we reached this small, filthy room, and even then, I didn't get a good look at the man who carried me in. The room was too dark, and all I could do was try and protect myself for fear they'd kill me too.

I blink slowly and stare at the rust-stained metal door across from the cot. The very thin strip of empty space between the bottom of the door and the floor is enough to reveal light on the other side. There has to be somebody out there, right? Guarding me, at least. They wouldn't leave me alone if I'm supposedly valuable.

My chest aches, my heart thundering loudly in my ears. They're going to use me to get to Callum. That much, I can put together, even while lying here on the tail end of shock.

The puzzle pieces fall into place. Whatever was supposed to happen, Tatum was never supposed to be involved. Did they bring her here, too? Maybe they figure they'll get more from him that way. I can only assume this has to do with money. Amanda probably found somebody desperate for cash and convinced them to go through with this. I already saw what she did to Lucas. There's nothing she isn't capable of.

Was. Past tense. Oh god. This has to be a nightmare. It can't be real.

However, the stink of mildew is very real. The nausea twisting my stomach. The uncontrollable shivering. I couldn't have imagined the sound of something hitting Tatum's head. It was too sickening. Is she still alive? Did they kill her to send a message, the way they killed her mother? If she's dead, how am I supposed to live without her? What will I do without my best friend?

Calm. All these what-if questions are twisting me up tighter and tighter. I force myself to take deep breaths, filling my lungs thoroughly. I can't let myself think that way. I need to get out of this—whatever *it* is—alive, so I can't give in to the panic. It might even be possible to do that until a shadow blocks out the light coming in under the door.

Staring at that shadow, I press my back to the cold wall. No matter how hard I listen, I can't make out more than mumbling on the other side. Who is on the other side of that door, and what do they plan to do to me? My heart seizes at the click of the lock. *Please, don't let them hurt me or my baby.* I sit up quickly, causing my head to swim. Ignoring the dizziness, I draw my knees to my chest and wrap my arms around them, trembling while I wait for the door to open. I wonder if they're drawing it out to scare me.

If they are, it's working.

The door creaks as it opens, and at first, the light streaming in from outside the room blinds me after spending so long in the dark. I have to squint and turn my face away while a man enters. "Getting some rest? I'm sure you need it in your condition."

I recognize the voice from earlier, but still don't know who it belongs to. The memory of what he's capable of and how easy it was for him to do it leaves me fighting against the need to run and scream. I have to be careful.

"Where is Tatum?" I whisper, blinking hard as I turn my face toward him again. My vision starts to adjust, and now I can make out his dark hair with its touch of gray, as well as his angular face.

"How sweet," he murmurs. "More concerned for your friend than you are for yourself. What a shame her mother wasn't more concerned for her—but then she was blinded by greed and hatred, sadly."

His eyes. I remember those icy eyes staring at me from across a table while his son reacted in horror thanks to the fork sticking out of the back of his hand—the venom and rage in those eyes.

"Jack Moroni," I growl his name. And now it all makes sense, at least partly. He and Callum weren't on good terms when that dinner ended. I haven't thought about him since then, really, thanks to all the shit that went down afterwards.

"Bianca Cole. I'm honored you remember me."

"How could I forget?" When he snickers, I demand, "Where is Tatum? Seriously. What did you do to her?"

"Seriously?" He looks over his shoulder to the thug standing behind him. There's a gun jutting out from the man's waistband. I'm not stupid. I know it's a silent threat. "Well. Callum certainly hasn't taught you how to threaten people properly."

"What did you do to her?" It takes everything to fight back the tears threatening to choke me. I will not let this man see me cry. He's nothing. A coward who can't fight a man face-to-face, so he has to kidnap a defenseless girl.

He strokes his sharp jaw, lips pursed. "You know, it all happened so fast. I can't quite remember."

There's no way to keep my chin from quivering. "You're a sick fucking bastard!!" I seethe.

"I've never been called that before.." Again, he looks over his shoulder, this time sharing a snide laugh with one of his men.

Tatum. This is my fault. If she hadn't been with me, she'd be fine right now. I wouldn't have to imagine her dead body lying beside Amanda's in some random building.

"If you killed her, I swear to God…" Emotion chokes me before I can finish the thought. What would I do anyway? Kill him? Kick him in his shin? How could I possibly do any of those things with an armed man standing a short five feet behind him?

"You'll, what?" he taunts. "What would you do if I killed your little friend the way I killed her mother?"

What would I do? The answer is nothing. I can't do a single thing, and this asshole knows it. I grit my teeth and clench my fists, fighting back the anger. If he did kill her, at least Tatum heard in the end how Amanda didn't want her to be part of this.

She must have heard the fear and anger in her mom's voice when she first discovered us. At least she has that little piece of knowledge. That her mom, even as selfish as she was, still tried her best to protect her in the end.

There's still a chance she's alive. I remind myself. Jack hasn't confirmed he killed her, and I'll hold onto that until I know for sure. Nausea grips me hard enough to bring tears to my eyes. Somehow I manage to blink them back.

"In fact..." Jack's amused expression hardens. "Your little friend ended up the way she did, thanks to that nasty mouth of hers. You might want to take a lesson from her and watch what you say, or you'll get the same treatment she did."

A chill runs through me at the memory of that sound. Even the gunshot that killed Amanda doesn't make me shiver like that. "Why are you doing this?" I whisper. "Is it because of what I did to your son?"

"Come on, you're a smart girl. Do you truly think I'd go through all this trouble because you jabbed Dominic with a fork?" His smirk sets my teeth on edge.

"Why, then?" I mimic his smirk, looking him up and down while I do. "Let me guess. Amanda twisted you around her finger the way she twisted my ex-boyfriend? She must've offered you something great."

"She didn't twist shit," he snaps. It doesn't take much to shake him up—I make a mental note to remember that. I don't want to be the next person with a bullet in her head.

"No? Then tell me this wasn't her idea. She's one of few people who know I'm pregnant, and she told you. The two of you concocted this little kidnapping scheme together."

"She didn't concoct a thing," he informs me in a deceptively smooth voice. If I didn't know better, I'd think he was a calm, rational man. I might even make the mistake of finding him charming. He's skilled at putting on an act, that's for sure.

He folds his hands in front of himself, smiling faintly while standing over me. "Poor Amanda was the typical greedy woman who thinks they're smarter than they are. She made the mistake of believing she was in the driver's seat when all she did was give me the ammunition I was looking for. Fucking with the man's business wasn't enough to make him pay for insulting me. He needs real motivation to make things right."

I can't believe I'm asking this question, "What will it take to make things right?"

He lifts a shoulder encased in a dark suit. Nobody looking at him for the first time would have a clue as to what he's capable of. "I'm not quite sure yet. Amanda wanted to dangle the baby over his head to squeeze every cent she could out of him, but I'm not particularly interested in cash."

When I raise my eyebrows, he chuckles. "You've got me there. Money is good. But making a man regret his choices is much better. And I intend to make Callum regret insulting me to all of our business associates."

"How are you going to do that?"

He sighs as he tips his head to the side. "You'll find out when the time comes. For now, you have nothing to worry about."

"Why is that?"

"If he loves you as much as he supposedly does, he won't hesitate to give me what I want. I'm sure you'll be out of here in no time."

He's loving this, savoring it like a fine wine. Watching my every reaction and barely bothering to hide his glee. "And I know that I said this didn't have to do with my son, but since you brought it up, maybe the next time you want to stab a man for brushing his hand over your leg, you'll think twice. Look at what your actions have set into motion. All of this because you couldn't control yourself."

I know this is nothing but an intimidation tactic, and I'm feeding right into it by responding. Only I can't stop the words from coming out.

"Your son was groping me, and I told him to stop."

"So you say."

My skin grows hot as blood rushes in my ears. I can't let him get to me. I can't make it that easy for him, but damn it, there's not much that gets under my skin easier than being deliberately misunderstood. I doubt he even misunderstands me—no, he knows what his son did. However he doesn't care. It's all the same in the end.

"Now that you mention it." He lowers his arms to his sides, and from the corner of my eye, I notice his hands tightening into fists. "I'll have to see to it that you regret your decision, as well. You both have a habit of reacting without thought."

This son-of-a-bitch. How fragile must your ego be to make you do something like this? The bitter heat in my chest threatens to crawl up my throat and flow out of me like lava.

Go fuck yourself, you piece of shit. I want to say it, snarl it, scream it. But this isn't only about me. I believe Callum loves me, no matter what Jack thinks. He's going to find a way to get us out of this, and the least I can do is stay alive until he does.

I can't give this guy a reason to lose his temper.

"Anything more to say?" He waits but gets nothing while I bite my tongue hard enough to taste blood. "I didn't think so."

Jerking a thumb toward the man behind him, he continues, "You'll get food and water. *Eventually.* Do yourself a favor and don't bother screaming or yelling for help, nobody here cares and the walls are thick. All you'll do is annoy my men, and we can't have you upsetting yourself. Not in your condition."

Do not react. Do not.

Somehow, I manage to keep it together while he saunters from the room and lets his thug close the door. I even wait until the shadows under the door disappear before I allow myself to break. Soon there's deafening silence shattered only by the painful thumping of my heart.

He wants to use the baby against Callum. It's not easy to believe anybody could be so cruel, but then I witnessed him possibly killing a girl in front of her mother, so I guess he's capable of a lot of things.

What if he wants to keep me hidden until the baby is born? What if he takes the baby—

Stop it. Tatum's voice rings loud and clear in my mind, almost as if she's in the room with me. She'd be screaming, kicking, and threatening to flay these guys alive if she was here. I can't do the same if I want to protect my baby and stay alive for the people I love, yet that doesn't mean I should drive myself crazy by letting my thoughts wander in such an awful direction.

I have no choice but to keep it together. Callum will find me, *us*. As I lie down again, curled in a ball, the coldness seeping into my bones, all I can do is hope he doesn't take too long. Because with each second that passes, I find myself cracking just a little more.

CALLUM

"Where the fuck is he?" The asshole's voice carries down the hall and directly into my ears. *Fucking Charlie.* Only he would come storming into the hospital like the fucking Calvary at a time like this. What a sanctimonious prick.

I'm barely out of Tatum's room, when I find Charlie Cole marching down the hall, his cheeks red, his gaze murderous, looking like he just stepped out of the shower when I called—his dark hair wet and raked away from his forehead. I notice he's wearing sweats and a pair of slides on his otherwise bare feet. Two nurses make the mistake of crossing the hall at the same time and are nearly steamrolled in his attempt to reach me. Of course, the man's too busy glaring at me with rage to notice.

He's my last concern once I catch sight of the taller man walking behind him. His officer badge gleams treacherously back at me from the lanyard hanging around his neck.

Yeah, fuck no.

"Absolutely fucking not," I warn, holding up both hands before pointing at the stranger. "I will not have cops involved in this."

Charlie stops short, his scowl deepening, "I didn't have him come to be a cop. He's a friend."

"Apologies, I came right from work," the man offers a tight-lipped smile. "Ken Miller."

"I don't give a shit what your name is," I snap. "And I don't care if you didn't call him to act as a cop. I don't want the cops involved, on duty or off duty. This could have horrible ramifications for everyone involved." I'm incredibly close to reaching my breaking point and can't be held liable for the blood that will be spilled if I end up going on a murderous killing spree.

"Where is she?" Charlie demands, as if suddenly realizing why I called again.

"If I knew, I would tell you, wouldn't I?"

"I could have ten cars out there looking for her right now," Ken offers, clamping a hand on Charlie's shoulder. I have to wonder if these two idiots heard a single word I said.

"No," I growl, shaking my head. "Going to the police isn't an option."

Charlie's eyes bulge out of his head, "How can you say you give a shit about my daughter but refuse to get the authorities involved? They could be looking for her instead of standing around like you are right now."

I take a threatening step forward, barely remembering who he is and what he means to Bianca. All I can think about is how I should kill him for speaking in such a disrespectful manner to me. He doesn't have even the slightest understanding of how deep my love for her goes and that the only reason he's still breathing at this point is because of her love for him.

"He could be right." Ken holds Charlie back when it looks like he's going to be stupid enough to lunge at me. "It might complicate things if we go to the authorities."

"This is your fault." Charlie spits, his eyes are red-rimmed, and fresh tears fill them. "I told her what to expect being with a man like you, but she went ahead anyway, didn't she? She let you destroy her. Being with you puts her in danger, possibly costing her life."

The thing is, there's nothing I can say to defend myself. He's absolutely right. This is my fault. If Bianca wasn't involved with me, she'd be living a carefree normal life. Living with a boyfriend who works at a nine-to-five job, looking forward to spending time with friends over the weekend. Maybe planning a vacation somewhere or saving up to buy a house. She could have a simple, quiet life free from the danger our involvement keeps putting her in. None of those thoughts really matter though, because, damn it, she's mine and I'm not letting her go.

She belongs to me, with me. I can't accept the idea of us not being together, not even now, when Romero has done nothing since Tatum went down for scans except to call in every favor owed to him by everyone in his extensive network of colleagues.

"Okay, let's take this one step at a time," Ken suggests. "Start at the beginning. What happened?"

Though my instincts tell me to brush him off, this is not the time when I can afford to alienate anyone who might be able to help. And if he's going to calm Charlie down and keep him thinking rationally, he's someone I need to have on my side. Even as I find myself grinding my molars, I do my best to provide a clear, honest answer to his question. "A text I received—we received," I amend, jerking my head toward Romero. He's pacing the large room, muttering instructions into his phone. He's every bit his cold self, except there's a little more worry in his features now.

Pulling my phone from my pocket, I show the men the text.

"I would ask who you pissed off," Charlie sneers, "but I'm sure we don't have the time to go through the entire list."

My fist involuntarily becomes a ball that I want to smash against his nose. *Asshole.* "It might surprise you, but there aren't many people I consider my enemy. The list of people that are stupid enough to go to those lengths has become less and less over time."

"Is there anyone in particular who you've had a falling out with recently?" Ken asks.

"Are you kidding? Somebody like him? This could be anyone," Charlie groans, holding his head in his hands as he turns away. I watch along with Ken as his entire body shudders with rage, his clenched fist raising as he slams it into the wall hard enough to leave an indent.

"Pull yourself together," Ken urges him. "You won't be of any help if you hurt yourself."

"This is because of you!" Like a light switch being turned off and on, Charlie loses it. He lunges at me, throwing a punch before Ken can stop him. He's too worked up, and the swing is wild, only making contact with my shoulder before I drive him backwards into the wall he just dented.

The breath leaves his lungs all at once, but he recovers quickly and snarls in my face, spit flying. "All you'll ever be is a fucking cancer that destroys everything it touches! Why couldn't you leave her alone? She might be too young to understand, but damn it, you're not! You know better!!"

"I know that," I agree, my voice low as I back away. Ken takes my place, and good thing, because I might have to break the bastard's neck if there isn't space between us. Bianca loves him. I have to remember that.

"If you truly cared about her, you would've pushed her away! There's no hope of her ever being safe or happy when she's with you!" Charlie shoves Ken out of his way almost violently. Apparently he's still itching to wrap his fingers around my throat and squeeze the life right out of me.

"Do you honestly think I haven't told myself those same things? That I should've walked away and denied our attraction. That she would be better off without me. Do you know how much guilt a man can heap on himself in a heartbeat? As soon as I knew she was gone, I told myself all of the things you've said and more."

"Then how the hell are you still breathing?" his lip curls into a snarl. "How? How can you live with yourself? How are you still standing here? I would have thrown myself out of a fucking window by now if I was you. What if she dies? Can you carry that on your conscience? Huh? Knowing that you're the reason she's dead."

Similar to a rubber band pulled to its limits, I snap. I've tried to be strong for her sake, but I can't be strong anymore. Charlie's eyes bulge when I pin him to the wall and close my hands around his throat. With gritted teeth, I snarl, "If she dies, then you might as well put a bullet in my fucking heart because I'll die, too. It might be difficult for you to believe, but I love her, too. I don't care if you're her father or not. My love for her doesn't change. I know that what I do and who I am puts her life at risk. Once I have her safely back in my arms, I'll do whatever it takes to ensure this doesn't happen again, so don't assume you know anything about my feelings for your daughter–because you don't. I'm here because she needs me, and I won't stop searching for her until she's back in my arms."

"That's enough, both of you," Ken scolds us as he somehow manages to pry me off his friend. "This isn't helping."

"You're right about one thing," I tell him while he rubs his neck, glaring at me. "I deserve it all, every lick of pain and sadness. Every broken bone, bruise, and bullet. I deserve all of the bad, but Bianca and Tatum." My voice cracks with raw emotion, "They don't deserve it, and neither does your grandchild."

His face becomes ghostly white, and the haunted look in his eyes reappears. I ponder for a moment if the confession shocked him too severely. I understand the feeling. I went through the same thing back at the warehouse when I first found the contents of that crate.

"I don't think I heard you…"

"No, you did. I said your grandchild. Bianca is pregnant."

"No!!" he groans, then sags against Ken, who holds him

upright. "It can't be true. Bianca is too smart to do something like that."

"No matter what you think or how you feel," I continue, ignoring his emotional outburst. "It's true. She's pregnant, so if you don't think this is tearing me apart, ripping my heart to shreds, I don't know how else to prove it to you. Do you need to see me bleeding out? Would that satisfy you? Make you understand how important this is?"

At the other end of the hall, the elevator doors slide open, and the sight of my daughter's pale, motionless form on the wheeled bed pulls me from the conversation. I try to distract myself from the tubes in her arms, but it isn't easy. I hate seeing her like this and, even more, knowing she is here because of me. She will be devastated when she discovers the bald patch on the back of her head where ten stitches now reside. I forget all about Charlie and our conversation and sprint across the space to greet the nurse.

"The results haven't come back yet," the nurse tells me just as I reach them. "I know you want answers, but it will take some time."

"What if she doesn't have time?" I demand, walking beside the bed and grabbing onto her frail hand.

"Mr. Torrio, her pupils are normal size and responsive," the nurse assures me. "There's no reason to believe she sustained severe injury. There's a chance this is nothing more than a concussion, and that's something that will resolve itself in time. All we can do is wait for the test results and the doctor to confirm."

She could've died today, and there would've been nothing I could do to stop it. That's how fast it could've happened. One single instant, and everything could've changed. "Hang in there, baby," I whisper, clutching her hand. "I'm going to make them pay. Don't you worry."

"Boss." Romero enters the room and thrusts his phone my way, "It's Costello."

Of all fucking times. I grab the phone and bring it to my ear. "Sebastian, I really don't have time for this right now."

"Oh? You don't have time for our meeting this evening?"

Releasing Tatum's hand and walking out to the hall, I whisper, "Listen. Things... things are about as bad as they could be right now." I can't afford to hold back now. He might be able to help me somehow, and even if it means showing a sliver of weakness, it's worth the cost if it brings Bianca home safely.

"What's that beeping in the background? It sounds like you're in the hospital."

Observant kid. "We're at the hospital in town."

"Is everything okay?" He seems interested, yet an intelligent man knows he's merely digging for information. Quickly as possible, I give him the rundown, hitting on the important parts for the sake of time. "I'm sure my ex-wife had something to do with this, although I don't know who she was working with. Romero has eyes and ears on it, so hopefully we'll have an answer soon."

A glance into the room shows Romero seated at Tatum's side. I don't think he's blinking, staring at her with an intensity I've never seen from him. "My money is on Jack Moroni."

"I'll ask around, see if there's been any chatter. Please, let me try to help."

I don't have a choice but to accept, do I? No less than my entire life hangs in the balance. My daughter, my unborn child, and the woman I love. They need me. I can't afford to fall apart the way Charlie is, swinging from grief to rage to helpless horror and back again.

"Thanks. Let me know if you hear anything," I mumble into the phone and hit the end key. I grip the device in my hand, squeezing it tighter than necessary. Somewhere out there is the woman I love, and she's at the mercy of someone menacing because of me.

I'll never forgive myself if I lose her, if I lose our baby.

Finding her isn't an option.

If I have to, I'll burn the world to the ground to bring her home.

BIANCA

*J*ust when I thought I'd been through the worst that a person could ever possibly go through…you know, after everything that happened with Lucas, all the ups and downs I went through with Callum, losing mom, and watching my father fall apart. All of those things have left invisible scar tissue running through my body, brain, and heart. That scar tissue however isn't thick enough to protect me against the shame that's now coating my insides with a sticky residue.

"Do you really have to watch me do this?" As if pissing and shitting in a bucket in the corner of the room isn't bad enough. That alone would be horrifying and degrading without an audience keeping tabs on my every move.

The thick-necked thug standing with his back to the closed metal door barely offers a sneer in response. The room is no longer dark thanks to the bare bulb glowing overhead, but I'd prefer the darkness. At least then, the darkness would hide his vulgar expression and the cold glittering of his beady eyes.

"Aren't you going to respond?" I demand, standing beside the bucket, trying like hell not to look inside, because these assholes refuse to empty it.

"Yeah." His lips turn up into a full-on, nauseating smile. "I was actually just thinking about how I can't wait till the boss says it's okay for us to get to know you better."

My stomach churns when he reaches down and grabs his crotch through his jeans. Like I needed a visual explanation.

"I'd think long and hard about that because the moment you put a hand on me, is the moment you'll end up losing that hand," I vow, meeting his gaze.

"You're a real big talker, but I don't see anyone coming to rescue you yet. A smart girl would learn her place around here before talking shit like you are."

My biggest concern is keeping myself alive. I don't know how long these guys will treat me decently—not that there's anything decent about watching me relieve myself, which I have no choice but to do while they watch me do it. I'm both ashamed and embarrassed, but I have to be strong the way I know Callum would need me to be.

Somewhere out there, he's looking for me, and the only thing I can do is keep it together until he gets here. I refuse to let Jack think he's won. That thought alone keeps me from shattering into a million pieces. I'm not going to give him that type of satisfaction. He thinks he's dealing with a weak, fragile flower. Except I'm not a flower. I'm a Queen and given the opportunity, I'd kill him and anyone else I have to in order to save myself and my baby.

"Satisfied?" I ask once I'm finished peeing.

"I'll be a lot more satisfied when the boss loosens up the rules." He's even breathing heavier than before, the noise making my stomach churn. It takes a certain kind of sickness to get off on the despair of another individual.

"Hey, remember what I said. I doubt I would be breaking any woman's heart by castrating you. In fact, I'd probably be doing them a favor." My panic rises when he turns toward the door, and I blurt out, "Where is Jack? I want to see him."

"It's a real shame you don't call the shots."

"I'm serious. I want to talk to Jack."

"So am I." He lets out a malicious laugh before leaving the room, swinging the heavy door back into place with a thud before the lock clicks into place.

Now that I'm alone, I can let the mask fall. Putting on a front is exhausting, and the exhaustion only gets worse with every visit from these assholes. No matter how hard I try, there is no fighting back the fear that races through me. It isn't easy to ignore the doubt tickling the back of my mind now that a full day has passed, and it's dark all over again, signaling the end of another day. So much time has passed, and Callum still hasn't found me. I know he's trying—I believe that to the depths of my soul—but that doesn't mean he's anywhere close.

How much longer until they're no longer satisfied following Jack's rules, which probably aren't going to be strictly enforced anyway. These do not seem like patient or smart men, for that matter. They're bored, probably irritated that they have to be here to guard me.

Eventually, they're going to want some entertainment, something to make it worth their time. Humiliation appears to be their favorite tactic at the moment, because, of course it's more fun to hurt me than it is to watch paint dry, and I'm sure Jack enjoys knowing I'm being humiliated. Instead of lying back down on the dirty cot, where springs poke at me no matter how I position myself, I throw my arms over my head to try to loosen the stiffness in my muscles.

Being in this cold, nasty place isn't helping any. I finally came to the conclusion that this is some basement, but to what building, I'm not sure. I can reach the window enough to know it's painted shut, but I can't see much of anything besides the sky when I look through it.

The frame to the cot is heavy, but not so heavy I couldn't drag it across the room and stand on it to get a better view. The only issue is that I don't need any of the men in the hall hearing me. I'm sure it would make a terrible screeching noise, dragging the rusted metal over a concrete floor. If I was only concerned about myself, I would still try it. They might slap me around a little, but I could handle it, but there's more than just myself to think about now. I guess I don't need to see outside that badly if it means risking another life to do it.

I peer down at my gross attire, wishing I could take a hot shower and wash away the events from the last twenty-four hours. It's challenging to keep my head on straight when I feel soiled and uncomfortable.

I'll do it for you, little one. With one hand resting over my belly, I breathe deeply and almost instantly regret it when the smell of waste reaches my nostrils. I gag, barely keeping myself from vomiting.

What I wouldn't give for some fresh air.

"Soon." I rub at my still-flat belly. "Soon, this will all be a distant memory."

I do whatever I can to think happy thoughts, but the minutes tick by slowly, and soon all I'm left with are the memories of what took place in that warehouse. I blink back the fresh tears forming in my eyes. I'm tired, so very tired, in every way possible. Sleep evaded me last night, and all I could do was stare at the strip of light under the door, dreading the possibility of a shadow darkening it again, wondering who would come for me next and if they were going to hurt me to send a message to Callum. There's still that possibility hanging over my head. The longer it takes for him to give Jack what he wants, the more frustrated and desperate Jack will become. Thus the more strained his temper will get, and the thinner his patience with me will be.

In the end, Callum will never give him what he wants. Men like Callum don't back down. Jack all but stole the queen chess piece off his board. To Callum, this is much more than business. This is personal, a declaration of war.

I don't know how much time passes, but soon the lock to the

door clicks again. I glance at the bag of fast food that sits untouched on my cot. Lunch, they called it. The fries were so old they'd gone hard by the time they reached me. Breakfast wasn't too bad, a foil-wrapped sandwich that was still warm, so I'm not too eager to eat. At least not yet, although I get the feeling it isn't dinner that they'll be delivering.

I expect one of Jack's men to come walking through the door, but I'm surprised to find the snake himself. The expression I give him is dissatisfaction at best. He's in yet another suit, his polished shoes so shiny I can practically see my reflection in them. Suddenly I feel even dirtier.

"I hear you were desperate to have my attention for a few minutes." His nose wrinkles, his gaze sweeping the room. "Rather unpleasant of a smell in here, isn't it?"

"Yeah, the second I got a whiff of it, the only thing I could think of was you."

His icy eyes gleam like a kid's on Christmas morning, like he's enjoying this, while his thin lips twist into a vindictive grin as he takes a step closer to me. My heart stutters, and for one terrified second, I'm sure he's going to hurt me–his hands are balled up into tight fists, and he's preparing to strike. There's nobody here to stop him from taking his hate for Callum out on my body and nobody to tell him he's taken it too far.

Fear slithers down my back, but I swallow it down and steel my spine, forcing myself to look forward, while holding my chin high. I want to cross my arms over my head and brace myself for what's coming, but I will not give him the satisfaction of watching me cower. He snorts softly after dragging the tension out for moments that might as well be an eternity. "I can see why Torrio is so smitten with you. Some men enjoy a sharp-tongued bitch to tell them all the things they secretly think about themselves."

"Are we talking about you, or Callum?"

His smile widens, and though the satisfaction in my chest

builds, I know I'm skating on very thin ice. "Keep it up, girl. You'll soon learn I don't shy away from hurting women who deserve it."

"Oh, I believe that."

"Is the food I'm providing you not good enough?" He tosses a dirty look at the guard, who slipped in behind him, the same one who watched me pee earlier. "It's rather disrespectful not to eat what is given to you, don't you think?"

"It's ice cold and looks like somebody scraped it off the floor of their car."

"Do I need to remind you how important it is that you eat?"

I know how important it is, but this is my only way of fighting back. I can't thank them for the tiny scraps they give me. Maybe it's stupid, being this stubborn, but it's all I have. "By all means, take a look at it and tell me if you think any of it is edible. It was just as bad when it got here as it is now."

"Go ahead, keep this little charade up as long as you like. Starve yourself for all I care, but soon, you'll discover this isn't a joke. I'm willing to do anything I have to do to reach my end goal. When it comes time for us to leave this place, we'll take you elsewhere. I can keep this going for months—until your baby is born, even."

I grit my teeth against the simmering, indignant rage burning a hole in my stomach. *How dare he?* I can't lash out. I can't show him the anger because losing control also means risking the fear coming forward. I won't do that. He won't get the satisfaction.

All I can do is concentrate on keeping my face blank and my voice flat. It takes everything in me to keep from shaking as he studies me. "We both know this won't be going on that long," I mutter through clenched teeth.

Cocking his head to the side, he inspects me like a bug under a microscope, "Do we? Eventually, you're going to figure out this wasn't a decision made on the spur of the moment. We could leave this very minute, and any work Callum has done to locate you would be for nothing. I could move you again and again, from location to location, and there is nothing you, or even him, could do about it."

He's telling the truth. I know it, and can feel it in every word he speaks. He didn't go through all this trouble for nothing. He moves closer until his polished shoes nearly touch my feet, and I force the fear down until it's nothing more than a tight knot in my belly. I don't know everything. However, I do know he needs me, alive and well, if he intends to get whatever it is he wants from Callum, and I hold onto that knowledge knowing it'll keep me alive.

"Make no mistake, I'll take that baby from you the moment it draws its first breath, and you'll never set eyes on it. You'll never know what happened to it, and you'll get to spend the rest of your pathetic life wondering and worrying."

My chest is so tight, I can hardly breathe. Panic snakes around my body, tightening around my ribs until I'm sure the pressure will crack them. "He's going to kill you for this," I whisper, looking up at the man looming over me. "I hope you know that, you worthless piece of shit."

Any last hint of the human mask he wears slides away to reveal the cold lizard underneath. "Don't think I'm above closing your mouth the same way I closed your friend's." As if on cue, the man standing at his elbow cracks his knuckles.

Stupidity is what I would call my next move, but I'm already past my breaking point. A bubble of laughter escapes my lips. It's the most bizarre, unthinkable reaction possible, but there's no helping or taking it back once it's out.

"I'm sorry," I manage before another laugh bursts out of me. "It's just... What is this? Did somebody script that for you? And you," I add, waving a hand to the thug. "How many times did you practice cracking your knuckles to get it to happen just like that?"

Jack nods only once, and like magic, pain explodes across the left side of my face. The force of the slap makes my head snap to the side, and I cover my cheek with my hand—it's hot, burning, followed by the acidic taste of blood in my mouth. I shouldn't do it. Shouldn't say anything else, but I never did know how to keep my mouth shut.

"Pathetic. You can't even do it yourself," I mutter, glaring at Jack while his image blurs, thanks to the tears in my eyes. "What kind of man makes his goons do all the work?"

I should have expected it this time, but I'm surprised when my head snaps back again, the pain blooming on the right side of my face now. The force of the second blow makes me fall backwards and onto the cot, squashing the bag of cold food beneath me.

"That's enough," Jack grunts. "We can't have her bruised and bloodied. Gag her and tie her up."

My head is spinning, but somehow I manage to get the words out, "You need me, and that alone is what will keep me alive, because if you wanted me dead we both know it would've already happened. You want something out of this, and you're going to use me to get it."

"There's a huge difference between keeping you alive and keeping you content, and you're going to discover exactly what that difference is," Jack sneers, his looming image hanging blurrily above me. By the time the world starts to come back into focus, all I can make sense of is the tearing sound of tape. I struggle against the man's grasp as he easily flips me over, pulling my arms behind my back and pressing a knee into my lower back to keep me in place. I'm dizzy, and my face aches. Although I still fight, because not fighting means giving up, and I refuse to do that.

"He's going to kill you all, and I'm going to laugh watching as you bleed out," I growl, my voice partially muffled by the cot. Once my hands are secured and tied with tape behind my back, the asshole rolls me over. A scream rips from my throat but is soon muffled behind the duct tape he slaps against my mouth.

"For some reason I thought you were smarter than this." Jack shakes his head, "Now, stop wasting your energy and put on your best acting." Dipping a hand into his pocket, he pulls out his phone. The desire to thrash and kick at him consumes me, but a pearl of more profound wisdom in my head holds me back. I can't continue to act out.

Those couple of slaps made me dizzy. Even as angry as I am, I can't risk getting hurt or putting the baby in danger with stupid behavior. I can't let myself lose control. Instead of kicking him in the ass, I recoil backwards when he holds up the phone like he's taking a picture. *Only he isn't.* He's taking a video, smiling down at me as he leans closer. What a sick bastard. He's making a video that he's going to send to Callum. I know he is. It's the joy pouring out of him like an overflowing sink that confirms it.

"Here she is," he announces, not bothering to disguise his voice. "Torrio, I'm sure you've discovered by now that you're missing something... something beautiful and fragile. A true temptation. I'm sure you're aware of how easy it would be to break her, and what good is a toy if it's broken, right?" My throat burns with all the vile words I want to scream at him. "Don't fret, we're taking good care of her. Yet I won't lie, she's a bit of a hassle, and as you know my patience lasts for only so long. Soon I won't have an option but to start sending you pieces of her. One by one. Perhaps I'll start with her tongue."

I shouldn't cry. I don't want Callum to see me like this, but the thought of the rage that will consume him when he sees this and hears the terrible things Jack's saying makes it impossible for me to hold them back. No matter how much I try to blink them back, I can't. Hot tears leak from the corners of my eyes and roll down the apples of my cheeks, soaking into my hair.

"I'll cut the bullshit. Torrio, you're going to give me what I want," he continues. "Or I'm going to take what you love, and more."

He pulls the phone back, chuckling. "Good work, sweetheart. Was it all acting? Because I won't lie, you truly look pathetic. It's going to drive him crazy." A moment later, he dons a satisfied grin as he watches it back. The sound of his voice echoes off the walls making me want to barf. "Sent. We'll give him a little time to think it over before setting the terms."

A little time? What does that mean? The question tears at my heart like razor blades.

"Do I leave her this way?" The guard asks, while Jack heads for the open door.

He glances back at me over his shoulder. "Yes. Let her spend the night this way, and maybe she'll come to value how she was being treated. Perhaps by morning, she'll be a bit more agreeable."

Behind the tape, I release an enraged scream that sounds more like a pathetic groan. Anger rips through me, and I continue to scream long after the men are gone, venting everything I've locked away for the sake of seeming strong.

There's no use in pretending now. There's only mourning for the pain I know Callum will suffer as soon as he sees that video. Is this what real love feels like? Wanting to protect the people you love even if you're the one that is suffering? My heart breaks for Callum, for myself, and for the baby since I don't know if anything will be the same after this.

CALLUM

*L*ava burns through my veins, threatening to turn me to ash. I can't make my brain catch up with what my eyes are seeing. No matter how many times I watch the disgusting video, I can't believe it's true, and maybe that's because I don't want to.

My grip on the phone tightens. "I'll kill him. I will fucking kill him."

"That's Moroni's voice," Romero murmurs, watching the video on his own cell phone. Once again, the message was sent to both of us, almost like he was afraid we'd miss it.

"Yeah, it is." And all the recognition does is heighten my rage. I should have known. I should have known all along. Sabotaging my business wasn't enough for him. He had to take things a step further. Deep down, my gut said he might have had something to do with this. Only with no warning signs, no shipments being messed with, no problems or chaos, nothing was pointing us in that direction. I can't wrap my head around it.

Romero flinches when I pick up the small vase full of flowers on Tatum's table. I unleash all my fury into tossing that vase. It collides with the wall, sending glass and flowers everywhere, but it doesn't ease the ache in my chest. It doesn't make me less angry.

"I know you're upset, but Tatum doesn't need this. What if she wakes up and that's the first thing she sees?" His gaze swings to Tatum, who is still sleeping soundly the way she's been for the past two days. I know he's right, but at this point I don't give a fuck. I want to rip the entire room apart.

"That fucker is dead," I grunt, my teeth clenched. "Him and every last one of his men. I won't rest till they're dead."

"I already sent the video to have it analyzed in case we can pinpoint where it was recorded," Romero says, his voice cold as steel.

That's great but it does nothing to help Bianca now. She needs our help now, not hours from now when Romero will inevitably get word there's no way of tracing the video's location. The thought of the inevitable outcome pains me, my heartbeat skyrocketing to a dangerous pace. I can only imagine how terrified all of this has made her, for herself, and the baby growing inside of her.

Our baby.

Jack made this personal, and now the only thing that will serve as proper payment is his dead body at my feet. *I want blood. I need it.* There's no hope of venting my rage.

Nothing is going to make this better. I step out of Tatum's room and into the visitor's suite beyond it, making sure to close the glass door behind me before kicking a chair across the otherwise peaceful space.

Rage swirls through me, and I clench my fists tightly. The overwhelming urge to destroy this room and the next sinks its claws into my mind. He tied her up and put tape over her mouth. He touched her, hurt her. Though the pain is enough to make my chest burn, I force myself to watch the video again. That's the least I can do for my little bird. She's suffering because of me—I can be strong and witness this again.

Seeing her lying helpless on a thin, filthy mattress sets off a screaming in my head. Bile rises up my throat, but I force myself to study her, to memorize every bit of what's been captured. She's in the same work clothes she wore after leaving the house yesterday, and they seem to be in one piece. No tears or anything like that. A promising sign—they haven't roughed her up.

There's no bruising on her legs, either, and thank God for that. No blood, no scratches. Jack must have convinced his men to keep their hands off her. I'm not stupid enough to think that will last forever, which only intensifies the screaming in my head until I can hardly hear myself think.

He goes in close on her face, the asshole, ensuring I get a good look as she starts to cry. There's a lump in my throat that threatens to choke me, but I continue watching, tracing the path of her tears as they cut down her cheeks, leaving mascara streaks behind—a face that's too red, and not from emotion. There's what looks like a handprint on her right cheek.

So they haven't left her entirely untouched. It's been one hour since the video was sent. I can only fathom what they could be doing to her now. My brain conjures up all kinds of thoughts and images that I can't stomach. *Think, damn it.* The most important thing is that I don't lose my cool. I cannot fracture right now. Forget what I suspect or fear. *What do I know?* I know it was Jack Moroni who made the video—he didn't bother trying to disguise his voice, but then why would he? This wasn't going to be a secret forever. Eventually, he planned to reach out to me, as there was no way he did all of this for nothing.

He's a stupid, heartless bastard who isn't stupid enough to take things too far. He'll menace her, make her cry, and rub it in my face, but knowing he was working with Amanda, it means he knows Bianca's pregnant. Which means he knows what's at stake. He hasn't confirmed that, but I can't imagine this being about anything else.

He thinks he's finally found my Achilles' heel; he's not wrong.

That alone is what will keep my little bird safe, at least for now. He wouldn't risk her losing the baby, because it would mean losing much of his leverage. Knowing Jack, he wouldn't want a sick girl on his hands, either. Not that he'd care, but it would inconvenience him. At the end of the day, he's a businessman. He wouldn't want to risk an expense like that.

All of this weighs heavier and heavier on my shoulders. The door leading from the hall opens, and I expect it to be a doctor or a nurse, but instead, it's one of my own men. "Sorry, boss. I, uh, wanted to bring the phones over for Romero. He said he wanted to take a look at them."

The way Nathan's eyes dart around the suite, it's clear he's not sure how much he can get away with saying.

"We're alone," I confirm. "I thought somebody would've brought them over by now." What a blur it's been. I barely know which way is up or who's coming and going.

"Sorry, we've been pretty busy," he explains. "They left a real mess back there, although we got it cleaned up." I'm sure the memory of having his nose broken when he mouthed off to me is a lot of the reason why he seems so hesitant now.

"This type of thing would've been much more useful yesterday." He doesn't need to explain it to me. Normally, Romero would have reminded someone that he gave an order which hadn't yet been obeyed. *This is not a normal situation.* Even when I told him to go home and shower, he refused to move from Tatum's side.

"I'm supposed to protect her. I already failed her once. I won't leave her again." That was his only explanation, and I didn't ask for more. At the heart of it, we're a lot alike. That's probably why we work so well together—and why it's so easy for him to push my buttons.

"Can I..." Nathan gestures toward Tatum's room, looking pained as he hesitates before opening the glass door leading inside.

"Go ahead, go in and give them to him."

Nathan's engaged in quiet conversation with Romero on the other side of the glass when the door to the suite opens again, and this time it's Charlie. I told him to go home and stay there and that I'd update him when I had more information. Clearly, he doesn't care what I have to say.

Instantly, my stomach sinks. He doesn't know about the video, and I don't plan to show it to him. It would kill him to see her that way—it nearly killed me. He might not be my favorite person, but we're both fathers. I would hope he'd grant me the same courtesy if it was Tatum being held by a fucking maniac.

"Any news?"

It's a good thing lying comes so naturally to me. "No. Nothing's changed, though we're closer to narrowing down our list of suspects. One of my guys brought the phones from the warehouse in, and I'm hoping we'll find a little more information on one of them. I told you I'd call you if I had any news."

"I don't take orders from you." He grumbles, "And how is Tatum?" He goes to the door, his shoulders slumping further when he finds her condition unchanged.

"The doctor is confident she'll be fine. She just has a lot of healing to do and is tired from all the meds and the concussion. She did manage to stay awake for a minute or two but passed out again pretty quick."

"That can happen sometimes," he murmurs, watching her through the glass door. "Back in the day, when I was working cases, we sometimes had a victim like that. We'd need to talk to them, but they couldn't stay conscious long enough to talk. It's sort of the brain's way of escaping reality—that's what the doctor told me once."

"She's definitely seen enough to make anybody want to escape." My poor girl. How will I ever make this up to her? It would take the rest of my life, every single day, and even then, I doubt it would be enough. I'll never forgive myself, and I wouldn't blame her if she never forgives me for leaving her vulnerable to the darkest aspects of my world.

We both step aside when Nathan leaves Romero alone again. He nods briefly to Charlie and me. "I better get back to the house."

"Yeah, keep your phone on you and contact me immediately if anything changes." He gives me a nod and disappears out of the room.

"How many people do you have on this?" Charlie asks once we're alone again.

"Every man I have employed, plus all of Romero's contacts—which means half the city."

"And nobody's found anything?"

Again, my thoughts go back to the video. "I have reason to believe Jack Moroni is the man behind this."

"Yes, the name sounds familiar. You used his name before when you were trying to narrow the list down."

"He wanted to arrange a marriage between Tatum and his son, and of course I didn't go for it. He's been fucking with my business ever since, but I never imagined… I mean, I couldn't have thought it would end this way."

"No, I'm sure you didn't think that." There's that sharpness I'm used to hearing from him, appearing right on schedule.

Only for Bianca's sake do I bite my tongue. Much more of this, and I'll bite it off. "To be fair, I doubt he would have done it if it hadn't been for my ex-wife approaching him. She needed somebody with money and muscle in her corner."

"I'll tell Ken," he announces, pulling out his phone. I sort of wish Ken was here, since he's the only calming influence in this situation. He manages to keep Charlie from going over the edge and isn't so quick to let his emotions cloud his judgment.

"Are you familiar with the name Jack Moroni?" he barks into the phone and begins to pace like I was earlier. "Well, Callum tells me it's looking like he's the one behind this. Do we have any idea where his people hang out?" He doesn't seem to notice that he used the word *we*, as if he still has a job in the department. I guess some habits are harder to break.

"Okay, good. Do that and get back to me." Charlie orders, and then hangs up the phone. "I'm going to meet up with Ken and try and get some more intel on Jack and his men."

"Alright, keep your phone on you, and let me know if you discover anything that might be beneficial." He nods and leaves the room without another word.

Holding the door open to Tatum's room, I ask Romero, "Can we get a list of any of Moroni's properties? It only makes sense he'd be holding her at one of them."

Usually, Romero would've already thought about this. He might already have a list of properties for me to look through. Who knows. All he can do now is lift his gaze from the phones, his eyes rimmed with dark circles. "I'll make a call and get a list together."

"Anything on the phones?"

"Here." He wears a grim expression as he holds one of them out to me before typing on his own device. "It's hers. They set it so you only need a pin to unlock it—four zeros."

One day, I might have it in me to look deeper through her messages, but for now, I only need the last text she ever sent. It was part of a long thread of messages between her and a contact labeled *JM*. I don't have to guess whose name those letters stand for.

Amanda: I'll be at the warehouse at 5:30. I can't wait to see the look on that little slut's face once she finds out what's coming to her.

Romero stands, his eyes wide as he stares down at the phone he's examining. "It was Booker."

I'm too involved in hoping Amanda burns in hell to register his meaning. "What?"

"Booker. He was one of the guys we lost at the warehouse." He holds the phone out for me to read something on the screen. "He'd been texting Amanda for months—and she's not the only one whose name is in here."

"Dominic Moroni," I murmur, scanning the messages between them. The puzzle is slowly coming together, and the image it creates turns my stomach. "He's who we need to track down. He's in on this."

"On it." Romero turns away from the bed to type something into his phone while I move up beside my daughter. She whimpers softly and the sound is like a knife cutting through my heart. Even when she was conscious, her babbling made no sense. She's underwater, lost in her trauma—a sinking ship.

"It's okay, sweetheart," I whisper, leaning down to brush my lips against her clammy forehead. "We'll get revenge. I promise, they'll pay for what they did."

But first, I need to get my family back.

The memory of Jack's snide and gleeful message is like kerosene poured over my already blazing fury. *Laugh it up while you can, you bastard. I'm coming for you.*

BIANCA

Nighttime is the worst, it's when the coldness seeps into my bones, and the despair causes me to believe Callum will never come for me. I try to keep my spirits up, but even I know I was not cut out for this cruel darkness of this world.

Sleep never finds me, and my body is a mass of knots by the time the lock disengages. My entire body stiffens, the breath in my lungs stills, and panic bubbles to the surface, giving way to worry on which guard I'll have to face this time.

Will this one decide he doesn't want to follow Jack's orders?

The door swings open slowly, and the sound of choked gagging fills the room before I even see a face. I know it's not one of the guards, and it's not Jack, but I recognize him immediately.

"It smells like a fucking sewer in here," Dominic gags, his gaze sweeping the room and stopping once it lands on me. The instant flash of recognition sends a wave of dread ripping across my skin.

Why does it have to be him?

"Is this not the funniest thing in the world? I bet you never guessed you would find yourself in this position?" His cruel cackle rings in my ears. "Wouldn't it have been easier to be friendly during that dinner? It's sad how unforgiving the world can be. Look where it got you. Practically marinating in your own shit."

There's nothing for me to say, not that I could say anything that would be understandable with the tape over my mouth.

He goes to the window and tests it, cursing quietly when he finds the frame painted shut. "That can't be safe, but then again, we can't have you trying to escape, now can we?" When he turns his attention back to me he lets out a snort. "What am I saying? You're not going anywhere, not like that, at least."

I want to scream, to let out all my rage, but the best I can do is grumble internally to myself.

Dominic shakes his head, "Not that it matters but you'll be glad to know my father sent me to check up on you and remove your restraints, only if you've decided to behave yourself?" Shooting a knowing expression toward the partly open door, he says, "I don't think he trusts those guys."

I wouldn't believe he cared regardless, but the almost giddy tone of his voice tells me everything I need to know. It wouldn't bother him in the least bit if every single one of them took advantage of me—for all I know, he might watch as they do so. Nausea twists my empty stomach, and it only worsens the closer he comes to me.

I try not to recoil, knowing that's exactly what he wants, but it's hard not to when your body wants to override your brain. "Relax," he murmurs, pretending to be concerned when it's obvious he's getting off on my fear. "I'm a friend in all this. Frankly, I think my father took things too far. He's old school, though, while I believe there's always a way to work things out peacefully."

What is the point of this? If he's trying to sweet-talk me into complying, it's not working. Not when I know that every word coming out of his mouth is a blatant lie.

"Let's free your arms," he suggests, wincing in a mockery of sympathy. "I'm sure you can't be comfortable." He shakes his head,

"It's a shame they left you like this all night? These men are savages. I can't believe they'd let you suffer like this."

He's not wrong about that, but I'm not fooled by his charade of sympathy. He doesn't feel a lick of empathy for me. Part of me wonders if Jack sent him to play the good cop. It's almost degrading that they'd assume I'm stupid enough to believe that.

"To think, this all could've been avoided." He leans over me, crouching, and again my stomach threatens to revolt. This time it's thanks to the proximity of his crotch to my face. "I apologize for all of this. My father is a bit of a hothead. Not surprising since he doesn't take well to insults. Callum made a fool out of him. That kind of thing isn't so easily forgiven in our world."

I'm barely paying attention to a word he says since the acidic touch of his hands on my skin is so off-putting. No amount of soap or water will remove the dirtiness of his fingers from my skin.

"Just looking for the top layer of tape," he murmurs, a false attempt at explaining why it's taking so long. I avert my gaze from his crotch and look at the dirty brick out of the corner of my eye. This nightmare can end at any point and time.

"You know, now that I think about it, I do have a knife. I guess I could use that instead." Without rising, he reaches into his back pocket and flicks the knife open, the steel of the blade coming within inches of my cheek. My heart lurches out of my chest, and I choke on a gasp. *Asshole.* He gives me a little grin as if to say he knows I'm terrified of him.

Now I'm grateful for the tape covering my mouth, since I'm not sure I could keep my thoughts to myself. *This fucking coward.* I hope he's having fun, making sure I know who's in charge because when this is all over and it's time for revenge, the only person laughing will be me. Callum would eat him alive if he were here.

But he isn't here, is he? He still hasn't come. I blink back the stupid tears in my eyes at the thought. Now is not the time to let my fear screw with my head. I don't know what's taking so long, but I can't give up hope.

"There we go. This will only take a second. Try to stay still," he adds with a snicker. I hope I get to kill him myself; I really do. His father is sick, but this guy is a complete psycho. Who gets off on a helpless woman being tied up, and held against her will? This man, obviously.

I hold my breath when the cold blade touches my wrist. He hesitates, as if deciding whether to cut into my skin or not, before choosing to slice through the tape. I don't dare move for fear of the blade slipping—accidentally or otherwise. He loves this, I know he does. I can tell from the rapid breathing and the telltale twitching in front of my face. He's actually getting hard, the sick fuck.

Even that doesn't matter once the tape breaks and my arms are free. Immediately pain zings up my limbs and across my shoulders. I try hard to bite back the groan in my throat, but I can't help it. It's a mixture of pain and relief all in one.

"I bet that hurts," he frowns, perching himself at the edge of the mattress. Even with my arms screaming in pain as blood starts flowing back through them again, instinct forces me to inch away from him until there's nowhere else to go.

"Don't be rude. I'm not going to hurt you." The way his frown deepens, it's like he's actually offended.

My arms are in no condition to yank the tape from my mouth—they're still stiff, with a pins and needles sensation racing up and down them.

"Hmm, I think I like you better this way." The bastard sighs softly while his eyes rake over my body in a way that makes my skin crawl. I'm fully clothed, and somehow he makes me feel naked. "Gentle, quiet. Submissive. You can't run your mouth with that tape over it, and you know better than to try to fight back. You have too much to lose now. "

The hint of a smile tugs at the corners of his mouth and makes my veins fill with ice. "It's a good thing I'm not one of my father's guards now, isn't it? I heard them talking out there. Saying there's nothing stopping them from filling you up with their cum, when they finally get the chance to take your pussy, because you're already pregnant. Can you believe how disgusting some people are?"

Disgusting like you, yes.

He reaches for me, his hand closing around my ankle. I can't help but whimper while revulsion makes me flinch. "Relax. I'll tell them you belong to me and that they're forbidden to touch you." Fingers dance up my calf, pausing at my knee. "I'll just need something from you in return to make it worth the hassle. A small upfront payment, if you want to call it that."

Revulsion turns to something more profound, hotter, as he begins a slow trip up my thigh. He's not going to stop. This isn't just a game. His intentions are clear, yet so are mine. Before I have time to make a plan or even deliberately fight back, I pull both legs in, draw them to my chest and kick them out as hard as possible. My feet land against his chest, the impact hard enough to knock him off balance but not enough to throw him to the floor.

"You fucking bitch," he snarls, reaching for me. His fingers wrap around my ankles squeezing to the point of pain. I let out a pitiful scream before his fingertips dig deep into my skin, forcing my thighs apart. I want—no, need—to fight. I have to protect my baby. I have to fight back, only I'm helpless. "I try to be nice to you and now see what that gets me. Nothing." I let out a scream muffled by the tape covering my mouth. *Don't cry. Don't cry.* "What an ungrateful bitch. Maybe that's been the problem all along. Perhaps you don't want me to be nice. Maybe you want me to take from you."

I want to be strong, but I feel myself breaking, parts of my soul splintering.

"Dominic." A voice echoes through the room. It's like magic. The second he hears his father's voice, he releases me. By now the blood is flowing through my body, and my arms are finally working, at least enough that I can manage to scramble to the back corner of the cot and wedge myself in it.

"What the hell do you think you're doing?" Jack questions angrily. "You were told to keep your hands off her."

"She fucking kicked me." Of course Dominic plays the victim, pressing a hand to his side like I actually did some damage. *I hope I did.*

"Then you shouldn't have gotten close enough for her to do it," his father snaps. Before he leaves the room, Dominic shoots me an irritated glare. I swear there are a thousand promises of pain in that singular look.

"Until next time." He grins.

The second he's gone, I gather up the rest of my courage and pull the tape from my mouth. Fiery hot pain sizzles across my lips and cheek, though I ignore it. "Am I being fed this today?" I ask. My throat feels scratchy, and I could go for a bottle of water, but it's doubtful I'll even receive that at this point.

"That will depend solely on you. I've given you a place to sleep and provided you with food. I make certain you're unharmed, and all I get is an attitude and ungratefulness tossed my way. Why would I want to be generous if I get nothing except disrespect in return?"

Generous? This is his idea of generosity?

A venomous response rests on my tongue, although I keep it to myself. There's no point in pissing him off further. He'll feed me if he wants to. I'm at his mercy and he knows it.

"Can I at least have some water?" I won't beg. I'm not that desperate yet.

"I'll think about it," he tosses the words over his shoulder and walks out, slamming the door shut behind him. I'm alone once more, though I'd prefer that to being nearly raped and attacked. Placing a hand to my trembling lips, I do my best to calm myself. Since I'm alone and don't know when I'll have the chance again to do so in private, I roll off the cot and empty my bladder into the bucket. I would sigh with relief if the rest of my situation wasn't still so grim.

How much longer will it be before this is over?

That question repeats like an endless echo in my mind while I force myself to lie down with one arm curled under my head. This will all end eventually, right?

* * *

STARTLED, I awake in a daze, my eyes still heavy with sleep. I peer up at the window and can see it's nightfall. Goodness, I must've slept most of the day, too overwhelmed and drained to do anything else. I rub the sleep from my eyes and twist around on the cot. A strangled shriek rips from my throat when I hear what sounds like gunshots echo through the small space.

My heart's in my throat as I climb off the cot and rush to the door, pressing my ear to the cold steel in hopes that I'll hear what's going on the other side. There's shouting, a lot of it, followed by more shots. Louder this time. *They're getting closer.*

Could it be Callum? *Oh, God, please, but only if he's safe.* I can imagine him out there, doing something crazy to rescue me. He would risk his life in a heartbeat for my own, but living without him isn't an option, so I need him to be safe.

Silence. It's that eerie silence that shows me what it means to truly be afraid. *Please, please, let him be okay.* Every second that crawls past in silence makes my imagination go wild. No one is coming for me. I'm going to die trapped in this stupid room beside a bucket of pee and poop.

All there is quiet, until there isn't. The lock on the door clicks. I take a step back as hot tears spill onto my cheeks, my feelings caught between hope and dread. My lungs burn as I hold my breath. It seems like an eternity before the door creaks open, and at first, I can't believe it's him. I tell myself it's my imagination, that it's all a dream, but it's not.

"Callum?" I whisper his name, afraid he'll evaporate into the air if I speak too loudly. This is real, as real as the heat of his body clashing with mine as he wraps his arms around me, as real as the strength of his embrace and the pounding of his heart against my ear as he crushes me to his chest.

"Please tell me you're okay?" The anguish in his voice rips through me.

"Yes, I'm okay. Exhausted and emotional, but I'm okay." My voice is raw.

Callum peers down at me, his gaze penetrating. I've missed that look. The one that says he'll do anything to make sure I'm his forever. "Fuck all I want to do is hold you in my arms. However we aren't safe, not yet. We still have to get out of this place. I took out a few of Jack's men, but I know there's more coming." I breathe him into my lungs; relief like I've never felt before encompasses me.

"I don't care. All that matters is that you're here." Cupping me by the cheeks, he presses his lips against mine. He breathes life back into me, making my worries and fears crumble. I'm whole now that I'm back in his arms again. The kiss breaks far too soon and I sag against him, wishing we were out of here already and safe within the walls of the mansion.

"Of course, I'm here. I've spent every second searching for you. I wasn't going to give up, not until I had you back in my arms. I love you. The moment I opened that crate, and you weren't inside with Tatum, I about lost my mind."

The mere mention of Tatum makes my heart clench. "Is… Is Tatum okay?" I have to force the words, since I'm afraid to know the answer.

"Physically, yes. Emotionally we don't know yet," he soothes, petting my hair gently. "And I wish we had more time to talk, but we need to get out of here before more men arrive." He releases me and turns, blocking me with his body. "Stay behind me and keep close. I don't know how bad it will get and I don't want to lose you."

I nod and push away the terror threatening to claw its way out of me. I just want this nightmare to end. We step out of the dark and dingy cell and into another room. The lights above are bright, and I must rely on Callum to lead the way until my eyes adjust. They do so just in time for me to get a look at a man slumped against the wall. A splatter of blood on the cinder blocks marks the spot where he was standing when he was shot in the head.

Somewhere in the back of my mind, I recognize him as the guy who cracked his knuckles and later slapped me until I was dizzy. The perverse impulse to laugh is almost too much to ignore, but there's no time. We round a corner, and another pair of dead men greet us. Adrenaline pulses in my veins when the sound of footsteps ring out up ahead of us.

"Stay back." Callum shoves me around the corner an instant before an ear-piercing gunshot sounds, followed by another.

Callum falls back beside me, breathing hard, his gun hitting the floor before I understand why. The blood that starts to bloom like a crimson flower on his blue shirt gives me my answer. "No, no," I whisper, staring in horror as the blood spreads through the fabric. No, this wasn't supposed to happen. I can't lose him like this, not after everything. Instinct drives me to press my hand to the wound to help stop the bleeding.

"Flesh wound," he grunts, raising an arm to wipe away the sweat beading against his brow. "I'll be fine, I promise."

"Torrio," Dominic's voice taunts from down the hall. "You're not giving up that easily, are you? If so, I'm disappointed. I won't lie, I expected more from you."

He shot Callum. He spilled his blood. Fear and anger make it hard for me to concentrate on the next step. If we don't move, we're sitting ducks, but where else can we go? Back to the cell?

"What do we do?" A panicked whisper escapes me while blood

continues to flow from his wound. No matter how much pressure I apply, I can't make it stop.

"Go," he grunts. "Run. Get out of here."

"But I don't know where we are!"

"Car's... outside," he groans through the pain. "Hurry. All that matters is you and the baby."

"Come on!! I was just starting to have fun," Dominic yells. The heavy click of his footsteps grows louder the closer he gets. We're as good as dead if we don't get moving.

"You have to go," Callum urges.

"I'm not leaving you."

"Bianca..." Dominic taunts, his voice light, singsong. "I'll make you a deal. Come with me without a fight, and I might spare your baby daddy's life."

Closer. He's getting closer, and every footstep heightens my panic until I can hardly hear anything other than my own racing heartbeat.

"Come out, come out," Dominic croons. "We both know what you need to do if you want him to live. I'm going to count to five. You show yourself before I reach five, and we'll be on our way. Otherwise? You'll still come with me, but you'll also have his death on your conscience. What's it going to be?"

"Run," Callum insists, his hands shoving me away before pointing down the hall. "There's a back door. There will be somebody out there, watching the door. Hurry, go."

What do I do? I have to protect the baby, but I can't leave him here. I refuse. I love him too much to do that. I know what I have to do, even if I don't believe I have the strength to do it. I'm tired of running. Tired of crying and being afraid. None of those things will end this.

The bulge above Callum's ankle catches my attention, and I pull up his pant leg to find a knife strapped there. "What are you doing?" he demands when I pull it free.

What am I doing? Maybe the stupidest thing possible, but Dominic won't take anything else from me.

"Fine," I yell, and adjust my hold on the knife, my clammy palm making it problematic to get a good grip. I hide it at my side, hoping to use the element of surprise to my advantage. "I'll come out. Just please, don't hurt Callum. Promise me."

"I promise." He can't even be bothered to sound serious. "He'll be fine. Just come with me, and all of this will end."

You can do this. You're strong.

I suck a shaky breath into my lungs. "Okay."

Callum reaches for me, however it's a failed attempt at stopping me when I gently but firmly push his hand away from my leg. There is a very good chance this could end badly, but it's my only hope. I've never fired a gun in my life, and I wouldn't trust myself to do it now, but a knife? That's a different story.

With the knife hidden behind my back, I step around the corner. No going back now. Dominic is only a few feet away, and when he spots me, he lowers his gun. "See? Things are so much easier when we work together as a team."

"Please… don't hurt him." I take a small, tentative step toward him. I have to play the damsel in distress. Let him see my fear, and weakness.

"If I kill him, we get nothing. You're what we want." With the agility of a snake, he strikes, his hand wrapping around my forearm and pulling me close.

Close enough for me to sink the knife deep into his stomach, which is precisely what I do. Without blinking or thinking too much about it, I tighten my hold on the butt of the knife and put every ounce of pain and anger into thrusting the knife right into the soft flesh of his stomach.

At first, he doesn't even notice a smile still sitting triumphantly on his face. It doesn't take long for surprise and shock to cross his features. Most likely finally feeling the pain, he looks down to find the handle of the knife jutting out of him. It's my turn to smile, and I do so when pulling the knife from his stomach. Just as quickly as the first time, I stab him again, ignoring the blood that seeps onto my hands.

"What the fuck?" The gun drops to the floor and he stumbles backwards, placing a hand on his stomach. Blood starts to absorb into the fabric of his t-shirt and he looks at it with disbelief. "You... you fucking bitch!!" he growls, and I reach for the gun, picking it up with my bloody-trembling hands.

I turn it on him and put my finger near the trigger. I've never shot a gun before or have even considered killing someone, but I now understand why Callum did what he did. There was never a time when I wouldn't do what I needed to protect those I loved.

"Fuck you," I whisper through gritted teeth, watching him slide down the wall at his back, his hand wrapped around the knife. "You take one step towards me and I'll blow your fucking head off."

His shirt soaks up the blood like a sponge, a bloody smear following him as he slides down the wall. Running on adrenaline alone, I walk slowly back towards Callum.

"You'll pay for this!!" he snarls, his features twisting in pain. I ignore the threat and slip back around the corner.

CALLUM

*I*t's the ultimate torture, sitting helplessly against the wall while blood runs out of you and everything goes quiet. The acrid odor of gunpowder fills my nostrils—that, and the coppery smell of blood. Gunshots ring out on the other end of the basement, and someone, somewhere, moans in pain. The sounds overlap until I'm sure my skull will crack.

"Bianca," I whisper, but my voice is lost in the chaos echoing through the halls between rows of rooms like the one I just pulled her from. Seconds stretch out until they feel like hours, and every pump of my heart means more blood loss, but all I care about is her.

What did she do? Where did she go?

I lean over, wincing as I stretch, and finally close my fingers around my Glock, pulling it closer. Fuck this. I'm not waiting for him to kill her. She needs me, and I'd rather die protecting her than against this fucking wall. I'm halfway to my feet when all at once, my little bird appears in front of me. She's wide-eyed, her entire body trembling. Relief takes the strength out of my legs for a heartbeat, making me lean against the cinder block wall for support.

"What—"

She shakes her head, wrapping an arm around mine. "Dominic's down, but he's not dead. Just wounded. We need to move quickly."

She's right. We should move, get out of here, and never look back. I have what I came here for, and she's in one piece. That needs to be enough, but somehow, it's not. Maybe it's because I read some of the messages he sent one of my crew detailing what he and his father planned to do with Bianca that makes me thirsty for revenge. How they were going to use her to milk me dry and convince me to sign over most of my businesses before either killing her or waiting for the baby's birth before selling them both on the black market.

Those messages are burned into my brain; now they're all I can see. "He needs to die."

"No. We need to go. There will be another time for revenge." She tries to pull me toward the back door I told her about earlier, but I round the corner she disappears behind to confront the man who joked about selling her.

He's holding the knife that still juts out from his stomach. She sank it up to the hilt. *Good girl.* My little bird is becoming a phoenix rising from the ashes of her suffering. I find the bastard panting, his skin a grisly white.

"You pathetic piece of shit." I raise the gun, smiling down at him.

"Wait. Wait!" He holds up one blood-coated hand, pleading for the mercy he would never have extended to Bianca. Oh, how I want to savor this moment. I'd love nothing more than to drag this out, to keep him alive the way I did Kristoff. To torture him until he begs for the sweet release of death, only for me to keep him alive anyway, lingering on the invisible line between misery and oblivion until his heart can't take the strain anymore.

This isn't about anything as low-level as money. I wouldn't bother holding him for ransom. No amount of money, property, or power would be enough to save him from me. This is revenge.

"Dominic!" Gunshots ricochet ahead, and I shove Bianca behind me to protect her. There's only one man that voice could belong to. *Jack.*

"Dad!" Dominic whines. It's a pitiful sound. "Hurry! She fucking stabbed me, and he's going to shoot me."

I should blow his brains out for the hell of it, and would if it wasn't for the bullet that whines past my ear. It brings me back to my senses in a hurry. There will be another time to end his pitiful existence, where I can draw it out and make it worthwhile. Right now Bianca is all that matters, her and the baby. Even my blood loss and how the world starts to go fuzzy and blurry around the edges don't matter half as much as getting her to safety.

"You got lucky, you son of a bitch," I hiss an instant before another bullet passes me. This time, lodging in the cinder block above my head. I've already pressed my luck as far as it'll go.

"Let's go." As always, my little bird cares more about me than herself. "You've already lost so much blood."

"I've had worse," I whisper, leading her to the door which opens to the rear of the building. I can't remember when, exactly, but this is not the time to split hairs. I hear Jack behind us, shouting at his son. And, for one blood-chilling moment, I imagine him coming after us rather than sticking to his son's side.

It's enough to make me cast a look over my shoulder, expecting to find Jack glaring at me in the fluorescent light flickering faintly overhead. It wouldn't surprise me to find him there, his gun aimed at my head.

"You fucking bitch!" he screams, his words bouncing off the unforgiving surfaces of the basement. "I should've ripped your fucking heart out, you cunt!"

"Don't!" she urges, pulling me by the arm. I didn't even realize until she did it that I faltered. As if my subconscious was about to turn me around and send me down the hall to paint the walls with the brains of both men the way Jack painted that crate with Amanda's brains and blood.

We burst outside together, the light from the rising sun paints the sky an array of pinks and oranges. I don't think I've ever seen a more beautiful sunrise. Strange how that's the first thought that comes to mind. I might have lost more blood than I realized—my head feels heavy, and the black car waiting for us with its headlights on and doors open seems to be a million miles away.

"Boss!" I don't know who it is that calls out to me. I only know that one of my men catches me before my knees hit the ground.

"Get her... to the car..." I'm so fucking weak. She doesn't need to see me like this. It'll only make things worse. "Jack and Dominic are still in there. Dominic's wounded." A second guard takes off at a run, his gun drawn. I doubt he'll catch up to them, but I hope that if he does, he shoots to maim rather than to kill. I want the pleasure of ending their pathetic lives myself.

"Callum?" Bianca's at my other side, clinging to me despite my blood staining her clothes and snow-white skin. "Don't you dare die on me. I didn't go through all of that just for you to die. Stay with me, please!!"

"Yes, ma'am." A weak smile stirs my lips upward, and before I know it, I'm in the car. A groan of pain passes my lips, and I hate that I'm so weak I can't hold myself together.

Bianca tumbles in after me and presses her face to my shoulder. "Callum... oh, my God..." Anything else she tries to say is lost to her broken sobs, each so powerful they make her body heave against mine. I hate that she's crying and that I'm partially the cause of her pain.

"You're safe now. Everything is going to be okay." Wrapping my left arm around her leaves my right hand free to press against the bullet wound on my side. The bleeding seems to have slowed but hasn't yet stopped.

"No, it's not. You're bleeding out." There's dried blood on my hand though I touch her cheek anyway, marveling at how she's here. I have her back. I can touch her, hear her sweet voice, feel the warmth of her body against mine. That's a good thing, too, since I'm suddenly shivering.

Fuck. I'm going into shock.

"My phone's in my pocket." I lean over, grimacing, breathing deeply to stave off the darkness threatening to overcome me. She pulls it out. "Call Romero. Put it on speaker."

She does as she's told, and a moment later, his voice fills the car's interior. "Is it done?"

"We have her. She's here."

A question quickly follows his sigh of relief. "You sound bad. What's the situation?"

"He was shot," Bianca blurts out, her voice trembling. "He lost a lot of blood."

"Shot... in my right side," I explain through clenched teeth when the car hits another bump. "I think it went through clean, but I lost a lot. I need you to alert the staff. I'm going to need help when we arrive."

"Five minutes," I hear from the front of the car.

"What about you, Bianca?" Romero asks.

"I'm fine. They didn't hurt me."

"She'll need a bed," I insist, ignoring her shaking head. "And I want an ultrasound done ASAP. Whatever it takes. We need to make sure the baby's okay."

"I'll have it arranged by the time you get here. I already got a call from Isaac–he went back in, but they were gone. He said there was a trail of blood leading out to the front lot that ended next to an empty parking space. They got away."

I knew it, of course, but hearing it chills what blood I have left. "It was impossible. Jack was firing on us, I had to get her out of there–"

"Nobody's blaming you," he insists, cutting me off. "You did what needed to be done. But rest assured, we'll find them. The more they run, the more I want them."

Somewhere along the line, this became personal for him. "I know we will." My head touches the back of the seat, and I sigh. Now that the emergency is over and Bianca's here, there's less adrenaline to keep me alert. My eyes drift closed, and my limbs become heavy.

"Callum?" I blink my eyes open to find Bianca leaning over me, her face filling my awareness. *Her sweet, beautiful face. Like an angel hovering over me.* "Stay with me, okay? We're almost there. Stay awake. Don't leave me."

"I will... never... leave you..." Even if it feels that way. My eyelids have never been so heavy, and holding them open takes every ounce of strength I possess. They begin to close on their own in spite of my struggle to keep them open. "It's going to be okay. We'll all be okay."

"We're almost there!" the driver shouts. "Stay with us, boss."

"Callum, please." The last thing I sense is the touch of her lips against mine.

Even if I die here and now, I couldn't think of a better way to go.

BIANCA

I hate how hospitals smell, though it's heavenly compared to what I spent the past few days smelling. It's so... clean. We didn't even stop at the ER—I'm already in my own room, just as Callum is. A room I wish I was in right now.

"Where is Callum? Is he alright?" I pepper the nurse with questions as soon as she walks in.

"Miss Cole, I already told you that he'll be just fine." I'm sure the nurse is tired of me asking that by now, even as she hides it pretty well while hooking a bag of saline up to the port in my arm. "He's being stitched up as we speak."

"But he's okay? Are you sure?"

She offers a warm smile and pats my hand. "I'm fairly sure, and I'll check on him once we're finished here with you."

"I'm fine." Now that I had an ultrasound to ensure the baby was okay, I only care about Callum. I might as well be talking to a wall for all the good it's doing. Nobody understands how important it is for me to know he's safe. Either that, or they're placating me because the news is terrible, and nobody wants me to know yet. Maybe if I start screaming, somebody will drop the act and be honest with me.

"You're dehydrated and need to eat something. We have to be sure you're taken care of as well." While she chides me, she takes my blood pressure. "The most important thing right now is making sure you stay calm. Your blood pressure is a little higher than I'd like."

Easy for her to say. "I'm trying."

"We'll give the saline some time, and someone from down in the cafeteria will bring up the meal you requested. All you have to do right now is rest."

"What about Tatum? My friend." I really wish Callum was here with me. I'm entirely in the dark, and I hate it. "Where is she? I have to see her."

A male voice answers that question. "She's in a suite upstairs."

I crane my neck and look around the nurse— I never thought the sight of Romero would bring happy tears to my eyes.

"Hi," I whisper.

He offers a faint grin. "Good to see you alive and well." He and the nurse exchange a look, and suddenly she's in a big hurry to leave the room. I can understand why—he's pretty intimidating, even to me. I can't imagine how much worse it would be for a stranger to face his dark, intense energy for the first time.

"How is she?" I ask.

Once he reaches the side of the bed, it hits me that he's the one I should be more concerned about. I wonder if he's slept at all in the days since we were kidnapped. "She's doing better, just not talking much. She stares out the window most of the time. She did perk up when I told her you were here, and that you were safe."

Thank you, God. I'll never forget what it felt like, her weight suddenly landing on me. I was so sure she was dead. "I have to see her."

"You'll get to see her. But first, you've got to take care of yourself. Meaning you should eat something before I take you up."

Did everybody decide to treat me like a child once I was rescued? It's like they're all working from the same script.

"Truthfully, they weren't that awful to me. I'm not in bad shape. Dehydrated and exhausted, yes, but it could've been much worse."

It's rare to see him smile—not that there's any lightness or humor in it. It's more like he's trying not to snicker at me. "They weren't *that bad* to you?"

"You know what I mean. They didn't, like, beat me or anything."

"Tell that to the bruises on your face."

"I haven't looked at myself in the mirror."

He touches his fingers to his own cheek. "It's not that *bad*. Just a little bit here and there." He switches to the other side. "Looks like you got slapped."

"That's because I did."

"Other than that, you look like you could use a shower, but that's it. No offense."

"You look like you could use one, too," I retort. No, he wasn't being critical, but I'm tired, frustrated, and sick of the condescension I've received from almost everybody since arriving at the hospital.

"I'm sure you're right," he admits while rubbing a hand over his scruffy cheek. "Since Tatum is awake and you're back, I might be able to grab one."

"Has my dad been here?" I whisper.

"He's on his way. I called him to let him know you're here, and safe."

"Thank you, for everything. I'm sure this hasn't been easy, and you look like you've been through the wringer."

"I've endured worse, believe me. I'll check in with Callum and then tell Tatum you'll come up after eating something." He heads for the door but doesn't make it out before it flies open. My father rushes into the room, barely glancing at Romero after bumping into him and heading straight from me with his arms outstretched.

"Oh, my baby. My girl." If I didn't know better, I would think he is trying to crush me with how tight his hug is.

"It's okay, Dad. I'm okay. Everything is fine," I assure him.

"You're alright?" Finally, he releases me and I can breathe. He takes my face into his hands and examines me himself. "You were held hostage for days. How can you say you're fine?"

"Well, every test they ran said I'm in good shape, and I won't argue with test results. Dehydration is the worst of it."

"Have you eaten? Damnit, I should've brought you something."

"Dad, please, relax. It's okay, you didn't have to bring me anything. I asked to have some food from the cafeteria brought up."

He nods, studying my face. "Are you sure you're okay? What did they do to you? Did they hurt you?"

My head aches at the idea of explaining any of this to him. "Dad, I'm exhausted. And I don't think I have it in me to rehash the whole story." His face falls, and that expression stirs up guilt, so I add, "They didn't really hurt me. For the most part, they left me alone. I was in a tiny little room by myself."

"So no one... tried to take advantage of you?"

My skin crawls, and I can almost feel Dominic's hands on my ankles when he forces my legs apart after I kick him. I don't want Dad to see what his question does to me, so I shake my head with as much of a smile as I can muster. "Honestly, it was scary, but it wasn't as bad as it could have been. Callum got there before things took a dark turn."

"Yeah, he's a real hero," he says sarcastically. It's not that I didn't expect the anger, the way he slides right into his typical attitude toward Callum. It still hurts to see it, though. Is this how it's always going to be? Torn between the two of them, wanting them both to be happy no matter how miserable it is for me?

"He is," I insist. "He ran right into the chaos to save me and ended up getting shot and risking his own life to get me out."

He shakes his head just when I think he's about to come

around. "There wouldn't have been any need for that if it wasn't for the way he lives his life. Don't argue with me," he grunts when I open my mouth, prepared to do just that.

"He almost died for me. I don't know what else you want from him."

"Not only for you."

There goes my heart, stuttering at his words. "What do you mean?"

"He did it for the baby, too, didn't he?"

"Oh." Suddenly, I'm too tired to sit upright, so I lean against the raised bed with a sigh. "Surprise?" I offer in a whisper. This wasn't how I envisioned him finding out, but there's no keeping it a secret anymore.

"I'm glad you can joke about it."

"I didn't want you to find out this way." I pick at my thin blanket, suddenly nervous to look at him.

"I'm surprised you wanted me to find out at all."

"You're my father. Of course, I was going to tell you. Although it's still so early."

"Don't give me that bullshit," he scolds.

"Even now, you're going to be this way?" I slap a hand against the bed, releasing some frustration. "You come running in here and almost squeeze the life out of me after I was missing for days, then give me this attitude."

Silence falls between us while he sits with his gaze downcast. "What do you want me to say?" I finally whisper. "I didn't plan it. Sometimes, these things happen."

"Now there won't be any escaping him. Whatever future you had planned, it's now tied directly to his."

"How can I make you understand? I don't want to get away from him. I want to be with him."

"I know." I can think of only a few times in my life when I saw the look that's on his face right now. A look of disappointment and sadness. He will never understand what not having his approval does to me. It looks like this is the way life will always be. Carrying the weight of his disappointment on my shoulders even when I know Callum is the only man I will ever want.

It's a relief when a knock on the door interrupts us. "Come in," I say, and the door squeaks open as a staff member brings in a tray of food. The aroma of bacon and sausage leaves me practically choking on the saliva that floods my mouth. The second the tray is set on the wheeled table near the bed, I pull it closer, then manage a mumbled apology before practically shoving my face into the plate. The first taste of salty bacon is enough to bring tears to my eyes. Nothing has ever tasted this good.

Shuffling footsteps at the open door grab my attention from my feast in time to find Callum slowly walking through the door. Now the bacon might as well be sawdust, because nothing else matters. He's here. He's alive, and he's walking—even if it's slow going.

"Should you be walking around?" I ask, while my heart skips a beat. He looks about as well as I would expect anyone to look after being shot, even though, at this moment, he is the sweetest thing I've ever set eyes on. Even while wearing a hospital gown over his slacks.

"They say movement is good for healing." He tries to hide a wince as he makes his way across the room. Dad doesn't get up from his seat on the edge of the bed, and all I can do is roll my eyes and hope he doesn't plan on acting childish for the rest of his existence. He doesn't have to like my choices, but he should respect them.

"I told you we'd get her back." The two of them stare at each other for a silent eternity, while all I can do is look back and forth and hope they don't decide to get into a fight. Callum's looking a little pale, and his voice is not as strong as usual, but the electricity crackling through the room tells me he wouldn't back down if Dad goaded him.

It's Dad who blinks first. "Thank you for bringing her back

safely." It doesn't do much to ease the tension, but it warms my heart anyway. He's trying. I have to give him credit for that.

Callum's scowl deepens, and I hold my breath, waiting for him to ruin the moment. Instead of smarting off, he only nods with a soft grunt before directing his attention to me. "How are you feeling?"

"Better, now that I've eaten. I really want to go upstairs and see Tatum?"

"Would it make a difference if I said you need to get some sleep before you do that?"

"Not really." I look from him to Dad, who doesn't seem much happier with my response. "Please?"

"Fine, but afterwards, you're going to rest," Callum orders.

I barely hold back from rolling my eyes. "Sure, Dad, whatever you say." I realize the mistake I've made as soon as the words leave my mouth.

* * *

Yup, she's exactly the way Romero described her: sitting up in her bed, staring out the window. She's not blank-faced, the way I'd assume she'd look if she was in shock. People in shock don't look like they're deep in thought and pissed off about it.

She doesn't acknowledge me entering the room with Callum close behind me. I wonder if she's like this with everyone, shutting the world out completely. She's alive, though, and I can't help but tremble with relief at that knowledge.

"Tatum?" I whisper.

Her head snaps around, and I can't help but notice, even in all of my relief, how pale and unhealthy she looks. I'm sure the harsh lighting in the room doesn't help things, but no amount of fluorescent light could create the haunted look in her eyes. Even when she wells up with tears and offers a shaky smile, that look doesn't go away.

"You're really here? It's not the pain meds messing with my head?"

"It's really me." I shake my head when she notices the IV bag I'm wheeling around. "Just saline. No big deal. I'm okay."

"Thank God." She reaches for me and I sit on the bed, placing my hands in hers. "I've been so worried and scared." My knuckles are practically grinding together with the way she's squeezing, however I simply grit my teeth through it.

"I'm here, and everything is going to be okay." I mean, I don't know if that's true or not, but I need to believe it. Sure, Jack is still out there, and so is Dominic, but right now, it has to be enough that we're together and safe.

"The baby?" she whispers with a catch in her voice.

"All clear. They gave me an ultrasound, and everything looks good. All is where it should be.."

Callum joins us, slowly lowering himself into a chair on the other side of the bed. I'm glad she was so distracted by my presence that she didn't notice him slowly walking or how careful he needs to be. I can't give him shit for refusing a wheelchair when I did the same, yet he does need one much more than I do.

"How are you feeling?" I ask the most obvious question.

She lifts her shoulder. "I don't know. How am I supposed to feel? The pain meds help, but everything else is numb."

I wince. "You're still feeling pain?"

"Only the worst headache of my life," she grunts through clenched teeth. "Feel like someone is beating a gong inside my head."

"The doctor said that should improve within another day or two," Callum points out in a gentle, understanding tone. I'll never get over the way he softens around her. "It won't be forever."

"Yeah, I guess my skull is as thick as you always said it was." She tries to grin at him but comes off more like a grimace.

Stroking the backs of her hands with my thumbs, I murmur,

"Hey. You don't have to be strong right now. It's okay to be weak, to have moments of sadness."

"I don't know how else to be." She looks me straight in the eye, intense, unblinking. "I overheard Romero mention Jack Moroni on the phone, so I know he was behind this."

"That's right." His smug, sneering face flashes in front of me and now I'm the one squeezing her hands for dear life.

"That was her, I heard. Wasn't it? That was my mother."

I can barely breathe. Only Tatum could blindside me like that. But what am I supposed to say? I can't lie. *What did you expect Bianca?* I guess I figured they had talked this over by now, but then if she only woke up for good overnight, they wouldn't have had the time. And if her condition was kind of touch and go, I'm sure Callum wouldn't have wanted to heap that sort of trauma on her.

Callum clears his throat and places his hand on her arm. "I'm sorry, sweetheart. You weren't in any condition to talk about what happened. I wanted to wait until you were ready."

"Then it's true, isn't it?" Her delicate features flood with color, and her chin quivers.

My heart breaks for her and for what this will do to her. She was unstable before, although now... Now I'm sure she'll fall off the deep end.

"She was there," I whisper, sliding a warning look Callum's way. Just because she knows Amanda was there doesn't mean she assumes she's dead. We can't drop that on her all at once.

As it turns out, we don't have to. "Well, what did he do to her? She was pretty pissed I was there. Did he hurt her? Is she here in the hospital too?"

Fuck. I have to say something. I wish I could find the right words. Callum is just as lost as I am, sputtering, his features pinched like he's trying to contain his emotions.

"Just tell me." Any trace of hope is gone from her flat voice. "Just tell me already! I can take it." Silence. I try to find the words, only they just won't come. She blurts out a soft, bitter laugh. "It's not like she was ever much of a mother, anyway."

It should be Callum. I know it, and the look he gives me says he knows it, too. "Sweetheart, I'm so sorry, but she's gone... I wish there was a way I could have prevented it. I really do."

I watch as she takes a deep shuddering breath before letting a single tear roll down her cheek. "That's what I figured. I don't know why, but I genuinely wanted it to not be true."

"Sweetie, she was your mom no matter how she acted. It's only natural that you care about her." It's more than a little awkward trying to hug her with a tube in my arm and tubes in hers, but somehow I manage to do it without dislodging anything. Eventually, she scoots over so we can share the bed. She rests her head on my shoulder, her tears slowly leaking from her eyes and getting caught by my thin gown.

Meeting Callum's gaze over the top of her head, I see the anguish in his eyes. No, he won't miss Amanda any more than I will, but his daughter is suffering, and the Moroni men are still walking free somewhere. I should've jammed that knife into Dominic's heart.

"Can you stay here with me?" Her mumbled tear-choked question takes me by surprise, though it shouldn't. I wouldn't want to be alone at a time like this, either.

Callum answers for me. "We'll work something out. There's plenty of room in here for another bed." That's putting it mildly—I've been in hotel rooms smaller than this.

"I won't leave," I promise, holding her a little tighter. "I'm here for you, always and forever."

CALLUM

Pain. One of the most inescapable emotions in life. It's an experience you learn from at a young age, when you touch the hot stove or fall down and skin your knee. It's your body's way of telling you something isn't okay, or check this out, or stop what you're doing—a protective mechanism of sorts.

In my life, I've experienced many bouts of pain, physical and emotional, but nothing compares to the pain you feel seeing your child hurt and knowing there is nothing you can do to ease that pain. I've never been what anyone would call a helicopter parent, hovering over Tatum, watching every choice she makes. That is, until now.

While watching my daughter walk up the front steps of our home while half a dozen guards keep a watchful eye out for threats around the building's perimeter. I can't afford to take any chances, not with both her and Bianca back under my roof.

"Take it easy," I urge. "Slow down."

Tatum rolls her eyes at me over her shoulder, which I take as a good sign. "Dad, I have a concussion. I didn't forget how to walk."

"I know, but you need to take what the doctor said seriously.

Too quick movements could cause you to lose your balance, and hitting your head again will not help you recover any faster."

"My balance is fine." Pausing inside the doorway, she turns to me, giving me her best glare. "I'm begging you. Please, lighten up. You're the one walking around with a bullet wound in your abdomen. If there's anyone you should be worried about, it's yourself."

Bianca steps in like a beacon of hope, offering a gentle but firm response. "Come on. I don't know about you, but I miss sleeping in a regular bed and not having a nurse come in every twenty minutes to check on me." Taking Tatum by the arm, she offers me a look of sympathy. Is there something wrong with me trying to make sure my daughter is okay?

I wish she would let me help her, but she's as stubborn as a mule.

As glad as I am to watch her walk down the hall again, with Bianca at her side as they head to her wing, my heart sinks. No matter how much I tighten my grip, she's like quicksand slipping through my fingers. How can I help someone that doesn't want my help?

We continue through the house, and every step I take leaves me feeling relieved. I didn't know how much I missed being here. "It's good to be home."

"That it is," he agrees, sticking close to my side.

Too close. "Afraid I can't make it to my office alone?"

"Did I say that?"

"You don't have to." I make a point of taking a giant step to the left to place more distance between us. "I can practically feel your breath on the back of my neck."

"Remind me later not to ask if you need any help changing your bandages."

"I wasn't going to ask for help."

"No, of course not. Why would you accept anyone's assistance?" Sarcasm drips from his response. It's only once we've reached my office that he exhales loudly, rubbing at the back of his neck, giving off a frustrated energy. "I have to say it because it's eating me up inside, but I feel like if I was there, you wouldn't have been shot."

"You don't know that." It never occurred to me that he would see things that way. "The best place for you was to be at Tatum's side."

"I understand that, but you could've died. Does that not make any bells go off in your head?"

"Of course it does, yet there wasn't any other option. If it makes you feel better, you can help change my bandages." I smirk to lighten the mood.

"Sorry, the window of opportunity is closed." At least he's grinning when he looks my way. "I haven't wanted to bring it up since there were more important things to discuss—Bianca and Tatum and all that, but what are our next steps?"

"To find and kill Jack, and his son." The answer is simple. Jack and his son will pay for fucking with what is mine.

"He's gone deep into hiding. I've been checking with my contacts around the clock, and nobody's seen or heard from him. I even checked local hospitals—if she sank that knife as deep into him as you said, I'm sure he needed more assistance than some paid under-the-table doctor."

"It's almost poetic," I sigh. "Though it would have been better if she'd stabbed him in the balls, that prick. She might've spared the world the possibility of there being another Moroni one day."

"If we take him out, and I mean soon, we'll eliminate that possibility as well."

"That means we have to flush him out somehow—both of them. Any ideas on how to do that?"

"Nothing aside from the usual. I haven't been thinking strategically, let's put it that way." That makes two of us. "Set one of his warehouses on fire, burn his house down, find his men, and send him photos of their torture, that kind of thing. I'm not sure that would do it, either. Not if he's that determined to stay hidden."

The temptation to go along with the idea is almost too strong to resist. I would love to bask in the warmth of a fire if it was Jack Moroni's life burning to cinders. My pulse races, my fists tighten, and I want to find the nearest book of matches.

"That will be what he expects," I point out, not gladly. "Nobody wants to destroy his existence more than I do, but we have to play it smart. We can't rush out, guns blazing. We could end up walking into a trap or miss our chance, and who knows if we'll get another. We've got one opportunity." I watch as he absorbs my words, and I notice his shoulders rising, the tension in every muscle. "Romero. I need you with me on this. I can't have you going rogue."

"I have no intention of going rogue. I'll do whatever you think is best. You're the boss."

"I don't like it any more than you do," I assure him. "I probably hate it a hell of a lot more. I want him to pay more than anything, but acting without thought isn't going to get us what we want. The snake has to poke his head out eventually. We'll get him the moment he does."

"Right." He turns away from the window, and if I didn't know better, I would think the snarl he wears was directed at me. The sky behind him grows darker by the moment. It's been several long days, and we all need a minute to catch our breath and get our shit together.

"I was thinking of reaching out to Costello," he suggests. "But I wanted to check with you first. Since the relationship is still somewhat new, I wasn't sure if that would be the right move."

"I think it's a great idea. He won't be looking for anything from Sebastian." As far as I know, Costello is unaware of our dealings. "Yes, we'll reach out to him. He seemed eager enough to be of help when Bianca was missing."

"Not that he was accommodating in the end," he retorts, a little sour.

"As it turns out, we didn't need him to be. We had everything we needed. It was only a matter of time before we put the pieces together." Too much time. Time Bianca should have been with me, not trapped in some stinking hellhole. Yes, it could have been worse, but she didn't deserve to experience a moment of what she did.

"I'll reach out to him and set up a time for a meeting." I don't bother trying to hide the way I look him up and down. "As for you, why don't you go home, get some rest in your own bed, and get your head on straight. We'll dive back into this tomorrow."

"But—"

Ultimately, there's no option but to let him see my frustration. I've been trying to hide it, reminding myself how difficult it's been for him, how little sleep he's gotten, and how he's beaten himself up more than once. First, it was blaming himself for leaving Tatum unprotected, and now he blames himself for my getting shot. I can't have him falling apart, not when I rely so heavily on him.

"No *buts*," I snarl. "That was a fucking order. Go to bed. Get some sleep. You'll be able to think better in the morning. You're no use to me as you are now."

His jaw clenches, though he's smart enough to keep his thoughts to himself before stalking from the room, jamming his fists into his pockets. His footsteps echo like gunshots down the hall until they fade to silence with the closing of the front door.

Slowly, I rise from my chair, groaning as I do. I consider going upstairs to the bedroom, but instead, my feet lead me to the door separating the main house from Tatum's wing. It's closed—not unusual—but I have to ask myself whether or not to open it. I can't shake the feeling that somewhere deep down inside, Tatum blames me for all of this. It could very well be my guilt manifesting itself in projection, and at the end of the day, it was her mother who set this up, not me, but we don't think rationally when we are in a crisis, and what she's going through qualifies as that. I grip the door handle and twist the knob opening the door, only to find Bianca on her way out of Tatum's bedroom. The way she moves—tiptoeing, holding a finger to her lips when she spots me—tells me Tatum must be asleep.

She confirms this in a whisper once she draws closer. "She went straight to bed. I know how she feels. It's impossible to get a good night's sleep in a hospital."

"Then let's get you to bed, too." I have to laugh at the raised brow of suspicion she gives me. "I'm grateful for your confidence in my abilities, but that's the last thing on my mind for once."

She frowns, "You must really be in bad shape, then."

"Not in bad shape. Just extremely sore and not in the mood to tear my stitches."

"I don't want that, either." She slides an arm around my waist, her touch gentle, careful, and I drape an arm across her shoulders. There is something incredibly right about this, the two of us ambling toward the stairs, together. When I think of how close I came to never having this again… It's a pain intense enough to eclipse anything I've experienced until now.

As we walk, Bianca speaks again, "Would it be rude of me to offer an opinion on Tatum?"

"You know her better than I do," I point out with no small amount of anger that I try hard to cover. It isn't her fault my daughter doesn't want to talk to me.

"I think it might be a good idea to bring a therapist here, to the house. This way, she can't shut down the idea. Tatum's in a dark place." She sighs heavily, almost despairing, her head touching my shoulder. "I hate seeing her like this. It's such a helpless feeling knowing the only person who can bring her out of this is herself."

"And what about you?" We reach the landing and turn toward the bedroom.

"Honestly, I'm okay. I really am." Bianca does her best to assure me. However, I wouldn't be surprised if she was lying to save making me feel guilty. As we enter the bedroom, I spot the bag of

EMPIRE OF PAIN

supplies the hospital provided: gauze, tape, and alcohol wipes. One of the men must've brought it up here.

"Do you need help with this?" she asks, lifting the bag from the nightstand.

"You wouldn't be changing the subject, would you?" With a smirk, I take the bag, shaking my head. "It'll be a cold day in hell when I accept help to change my bandages."

"Whatever you say." She purses her lips, and to my surprise, she trails along behind me as I walk toward the bathroom. "What?" she questions, noticing my curious expression.

"You don't want to watch this, do you?"

"I thought I would hang around and talk with you." When she bites her lip, those familiar worry lines appear between her brows, and I realize this is what she needs. This is our first time being truly alone since before she was taken—the hospital doesn't count, especially with the ever-present threat of a nurse or administrator strolling in at any time. I can't pretend I don't crave her nearness with every fiber of my being.

"Be my guest." I set everything up on the vanity while she closes the lid to the toilet and takes a seat.

"Does it hurt?" she asks once I've removed my button-down and revealed the bandaged wound on my side.

"As much as you would expect a bullet wound to hurt."

"I'm sorry." She frowns.

"Bianca." Setting everything down, I stare at her in the mirror. "Let's get one thing straight: *you are not to blame yourself for this.* I would think it's obvious by now, but I have no problem reminding you that I would take a hundred bullets for you if it meant sparing your life?"

"Don't say that, please. I almost lost you once before. I don't want to think about you taking any more bullets, least of all for me."

"It's the truth, Bianca. Your life is much more valuable than mine, and I will do anything to ensure you're safe and taken care of."

"That's your opinion." Her lips set into a firm line, and she lowers her gaze to the floor. I get the feeling there's something on her mind, something she might not have been comfortable sharing before now. She's had days to think things over, and it's taken every scrap of self-control to give her the time and space she needs to work through it. I can't revert to demanding things from her when she isn't ready to share. I can't scare her off. "That was the worst part, honestly. When I knew you would find out I was missing, that Tatum was missing, and there was nothing I could do to help you. That was easily the worst part."

I know the feeling, since the ugly scenarios my imagination insisted on spinning up were enough to test my sanity. "What else? I mean, what else did you go through? You can tell me. It's important for you to talk these things out, too, just like it is for Tatum."

"I don't know. I knew in my heart you would come for me. I knew you were doing your best. But he..." The hair on the back of my neck rises, and it isn't easy to be gentle and give her time to find the words. Instinct makes me want to demand, to grill her, and get every last detail out of her in hopes of pulling together a way to punish that bastard.

"What did he do?" I have to ask after several teeth-grinding moments of silence.

"He said he would take me somewhere else and hide me. He said..." Her voice catches, and I don't even realize I'm holding my breath, waiting for her to speak till my lungs start to burn. "He told me he would keep me until the baby was born, then sell the baby, and me, if he didn't get what he wanted from you."

Calm. Be calm. She needs you to keep it together.

"He said that to you?" Not that I'm surprised. I'd expect a man like that to terrorize an innocent woman with the threat of selling her child. I'm just angry that she was spoken to like that. I can only imagine the way that made her feel.

Her head bobs up and down. "Is it wrong that I wish he was dead?"

"Absolutely not." And now I very much wish I'd stuck around and blown that fucker's head off. He was going to sell my child. My heir. He would've trafficked my little bird, and then he would have held it over her head for months, making her dread the arrival of what was supposed to be a gift.

My blood pressure is nearly through the roof, and everything around me becomes hazy while my mind is flooded with rage and my body with adrenaline. Jack needs to die.

What am I doing, going to bed? I need to be working, finding him, making him pay.

Rational thoughts replace the rage. I need to be with Bianca just as much, if not more. I need her touch, her presence, to remind me that she's safe. *Mine.* She is what matters, her, and Tatum, and the baby. *But will I ever have another opportunity like the one I had in that apartment basement?* There's no way of knowing, but I can't let the need for revenge make me lose sight of the most important things.

"Good." She raises her head and meets my gaze in the mirror. "Because I really hope you find him and kill him."

That's exactly what I intend to do. I'm going to find him. I'm going to make him hurt for what he's done. I'm going to make him beg for death.

BIANCA

I don't know what's wrong with me today. Everything is back to normal. The baby is okay, and I *should* be happier than ever, except I can't seem to stop my eyes from leaking.

If I didn't know better, I would think I have PMS. I'm that emotional and uneasy, hanging on the edge of tears while I sit around the house and try to keep myself occupied. Callum's understandably busy, working like crazy with Romero to track down Jack and Dominic. I'm not about to get in the way of that. I want those bastards dead.

Whoops, there go my eyes again, filling with tears and blurring the article I'm reading on my tablet about the ways stress can affect pregnancy. I need to believe there won't be any adverse effects on the baby after what I experienced. No matter how many times I remind myself of all the women in the world who deal with stressful jobs every single day, busy family lives, or any number of other stresses while pregnant, it's not enough. I'm still anxious, and worried.

I wish I had killed Dominic when I had the chance. I should've stabbed him to death. One wound for every time he made my skin crawl while touching me in that filthy room. One for every nasty remark, every time he pushed his crotch into my face.

It still wouldn't be enough.

And it's knowing they're still out there somewhere that frustrates me to the point of tears. My best friend is locked in her bedroom, unable to bring herself to talk to anybody but me—even then, it's like pulling teeth to get anything more than a few words at a time out of her. She's retreating into her shell again and is sinking deeper whenever anyone tries to pull her out. It's the most scariest, helpless feeling and, ultimately, those monsters are walking around free somewhere while we carry the emotional and physical scars of their actions.

My hand trembles as I reach for the herbal tea on the nightstand. It isn't fear sending tremors through me, or frustration. It's anger. I'm angry, and I'm even angrier that I have a reason to be angry. I hate them for what they've done to all of us. For how they've changed me. I don't recognize myself. Who is this woman so bloodthirsty for revenge?

I'm still mulling that over and sipping on my tea when the bedroom door opens slowly, like the person doing the opening is being extra careful not to be noisy. My heart swells and for the first time in hours, I smile.

"I'm still awake," I call out.

A moment later, Callum appears in the doorway. "It's late," he murmurs. If I didn't know better, I'd think he was scolding me. Not that he wouldn't, but he should know better than to waste his time by now. I'm a big girl.

"It is." Setting the cup and tablet aside, I glare at the clock before raising an eyebrow. "And here you are, finally leaving your office a little after midnight."

"Pregnancy is making you even more of a handful than you were before." He grins, taking a seat next to me, before slowly bending down to place a kiss against my belly.

The caress of his lips is soft, almost reverent, and I melt into the mattress. Nobody would guess he's the sort of man who can be both gentle and kind. A man who makes me feel absolutely worshiped.

I can't resist running my fingers through his soft, dark hair. "Are you as tired as you look?"

"I'm alright." His soft sight tells me otherwise. "This isn't the first time I've burned the candle at both ends. I'm used to the lack of sleep."

"Are you getting any closer to finding him?" Lifting his head, he peers up at me. A flash of guilt flickers in his eyes, and suddenly I wish I hadn't asked. "Actually, I'm sorry, that was stupid. I shouldn't have asked. If there's one room of the house where you should be allowed to close the door on all our problems, this is one."

"If you want to talk about it, I'm happy to." Sitting up, he takes off his tie and starts unbuttoning his shirt.

"It's late. Let's talk about it tomorrow." I sit up, then push myself onto my knees behind him. I can't explain this sudden, all-consuming desire to touch him. To be closer. I've finally figured out what was missing all day, why I've been so edgy and emotional.

Him. I was missing him, his touch, and his familiar spicy scent. Something about it makes my toes curl, and this heady need builds low in my belly. Possessed with need, I bury my face into the crook of his neck and breathe him in. I place my hands on his shoulders, and I swear something loosens inside me. It's like a knot unraveling.

It's been too long since we've had sex, and I crave his closeness. There's something so sweet and simple about pulling his shirt off once it's unbuttoned, revealing the intricate ink and muscles that move beneath my fingertips as I trace the dark lines of his dragon tattoo.

"How was your day?" He turns his head, and I lean in for a kiss before pressing my lips to his bare shoulder. The groan of pleasure he releases zings straight through me. "You have no idea how good it feels to have your lips on me. I've missed you so much. Missed your touch and your scent. It was unbearable torture without you."

"I know." I continue to pepper kisses along his shoulder and the back of his neck, then massage the tight muscles with my thumbs. "Today was long, but I kept myself occupied. Sheryl was nice company. I asked her if she'd teach me some of her recipes. I love cooking and want to be able to make some of the things she makes for you, that you enjoy."

He reaches back and covers my hands with his. "This is what I want. This is what I've had in my head from the beginning. Having you here, waiting for me at the end of each day. Something sweet to look forward to after all the ugly, filthy shit I wade through."

"You mean you want me to hang around the house all day and be available to you whenever you snap your fingers?"

"What's so wrong with that?" When I dig my nails into his flesh, he lets out a husky laugh. "What? I'd like to keep you barefoot and pregnant and chained to the stove. So long as the chain is long enough to reach the bedroom."

"You're a chauvinist pig," I protest over his laughter.

"Okay, okay, fine." He smirks at me over his shoulder, and the soft light from the nightstand dances over his chiseled features, turning him from the dark, dangerous villain to the kind, compassionate man I've come to know. "That's a line I heard from my old man when I was a kid. All I want is you here. All the time. Where I can see you and touch you and remind myself you're real. That I didn't dream you up."

"You didn't dream me up." The scruff on his cheeks rubs against my palms when I take his face into my hands. "I'm real, and I'm here. I might give you shit, but my biggest joy is being right beside you."

"I love you." The words shine from within him when he smiles, warming me like the sun on a soft spring day. Gentle, yet necessary for life. For my life, anyway.

"I love you, too." The words don't come close to expressing how I truly feel. How much I need him, how whole he makes me. How his kiss unlocks something in my core, something hot and greedy and strong enough to make my breath come fast.

A sizzle runs up my spine when his tongue probes my lips, then slides into my mouth. He takes his time, kissing me slowly, exploring me while my nails sink into his firm shoulders. My hunger for him isn't the kind that fades away when I get a taste. It only grows more potent, like his kiss is gasoline poured on the fire blazing in my heart.

He breaks the kiss to lift my t-shirt over my head and tosses it on the floor. When he stares at my body—nostrils flaring, mouth open to allow for his harsh breathing—a flush creeps up over my neck and into my cheeks.

"Perfect," he whispers, running a finger from my collarbone down to my navel. Goosebumps pebble my skin before he eases me back until I'm lying against the satin-covered pillows.

Taking my breasts, he molds them in his hands, pushing them together. His tongue sweeps over my nipples until I lift my hips, beckoning him between my legs. I need him, right now. "Callum... yes..." I whimper while my fingers run through his hair and scrape over his scalp. He groans and shudders as his tongue moves in wet circles, teasing my nipples into taut peaks.

After tempting me, he finally closes his lips around one and sucks, flicking the sensitive tip until my head spins and all I can do is moan his name. My arousal continues to build, the juices from my pussy running down my thighs until they soak into the sheets. All for him. He's the only man who could do this to me.

I'm panting by the time he releases my nipple with a soft pop. Then he's moving his lips, blazing a skillful trail down my torso, making my muscles flutter beneath his lips. "I've missed your body," he whispers, and the hot breath fanning against my flesh makes me shiver. "I've missed the way you melt beneath my fingertips and moan my name."

I part my legs to make room for him between them, and he releases an animalistic growl. "And the way you smell..." Another growl rips from him as he lowers his head and drags the scruff of his cheeks along my inner thigh. There's no resistance when he peels away my soaked thong to drag his tongue over my smooth, swollen lips.

I jerk my hips forward and let out a gasp of pleasure. "Yes... yes, more of that...Callum!!"

He flattens his tongue against my pussy and takes his time devouring every inch of my skin, before finding my tiny clit. It's complete bliss, that first flick of his tongue. Lightning bolts of pleasure ripple through me, and I lift my hips greedily in anticipation of the next lick.

"Fuck, little bird. Spread those legs wide. I want to see this pussy, *my pussy*," he orders in that deep voice of his where I can't help but do as he says. I'm exposed and at his complete mercy, and nothing has ever felt so right. "I'm obsessed with your cunt, Bianca. I want to eat it all fucking day, to swallow every drip of cum and do it all over again. Morning, noon, and night I'd spend between your thighs so long as you keep that pretty pussy on my tongue."

"Your mouth is filthy," I groan. The words are barely out of my mouth as he descends on me, his tongue lapping up my juices before focusing on my clit. He makes quick strokes against the sensitive bundle of nerves and suddenly I'm breathless.

My heartbeat thunders in my ears, my muscles tense, and every fiber of my being is fixated on reaching the end. I'm so close, so fucking close. "Callum, oh god!!" I manage to gasp before moaning again, and again, while Callum's tongue drives me higher and higher until... until...

My voice breaks and there's nothing to do but scream silently, letting the waves of blissful pleasure crash over me. Somewhere in the back of my mind I'm afraid of the intensity and the way it goes on, stretching out thanks to the way Callum continues eating me like a man starved. I can't control the sensations coursing through me as the orgasm drags on, growing more powerful.

Callum only lifts his head when my silent screams turn to tears. "Shit. Bianca, what's wrong? Did I hurt you?" he asks, crawling up the length of my body. There's deep concern etched across his features when I pry open my eyes to find him looking down at me.

I shake my head as hot tears roll down my cheeks. "No. I'm sorry. I can't stop the tears from coming. I don't know what's wrong with me." It's so ridiculous that I have to laugh at myself even as my body coughs with sobs. I can't control my emotions.

Is it the baby? Or just the fact that my life's been so hectic and unpredictable lately?

Callum answers the question before I can voice it. "You needed that release," he muses, wiping my cheeks with his thumbs.

"I guess I did." The intensity is dying down now and I feel sort of stupid, yet he continues to stare at me with adoration.

"I've never made a woman come so hard, she cried."

"There's a first for everything." I wind my arms around his neck and press into him, my lips on his. The tangy taste of my arousal explodes against my tongue, and there's something incredibly erotic about tasting yourself on someone else. Callum quickly works his way out of his pants and boxers, leaving himself bare. His cock is rock hard—the slight brush of my hand against his dripping head stirs a rumble from deep within his chest.

"Do that again, and I might just come on the mattress."

"We can't have that now, can we?" I tease.

Braced on his knees, he lifts me by the ass and tugs me forward. "There's an all-consuming hunger that can never be sedated that lives inside me when it comes to you. No matter how many times I claim you or how much I taste you, it never feels like it's enough. I want more, need more." The hunger shines in his eyes, and he grips my legs, lifting them and gently pressing them to my chest.

"I need you, fuck me, Callum. Claim me." I sink my nails into his thigh.

This position leaves me completely vulnerable, every inch of my pussy exposed to him. He shifts forward on his knees, and his thick cock slips through my wet folds. I shiver, the sparks of pleasure that zing over my skin at the simplest of touches.

"What type of man does it make me to want to destroy your pussy, to fuck you until you're screaming, begging, and pleading for me to stop." Peering down between my legs, he watches, his gaze never wavering, as he guides his thick shaft into my pussy. "What type of man does it make me, Bianca?" he whispers, his eyes meeting mine.

"It makes you mine." I gasp. There's nothing like the first few seconds when he sinks deep, stretching me to my limits, filling me with every thick inch. It's amazing how after all the times we've had sex I still have a difficult time taking him.

"So tight and perfect. Your pussy was made for me, little bird. Made for me to sink into, again and again, to fuck, and kiss, and tease. All mine."

Leaning over me, he presses my knees to my chest and grips my hips, fucking me slowly, plunging deep, before pulling himself out. Watching himself as he does it, worshiping my body with every stroke. *Is this what making love feels like?*

Unreadable emotions flicker in his eyes, and my soul ignites into a blazing inferno.

"Callum..." All I can do is moan his name, the pleasure building like bricks in my lower belly.

Swiveling his hips, he presses against something profound and all-consuming. "So good, so fucking perfect. The way your muscles clench around me, holding me inside, tightening over and over. You want to come, don't you?"

"Yes, please… Please let me come." I'm panting, and yet his pace remains the same.

"Soon, little bird, so soon. We'll come together." He grits his teeth, his grip on me tightening. I'm close, so close. I lift my hips, needing more, any bit of friction to push me over the edge. Callum notices this and pulls out of me completely. I'm about to ask him what he's doing when he grabs me, flipping me onto my belly. The air swooshes out of my lungs, and I peer at him over my shoulder.

"What?" I hiss, irritated because I was so close to coming.

"Get on your hands and knees. I'm going to spank this pretty little ass while I fill your cunt with my cum."

I don't even blink and move into position quickly. Callum moves behind me an instant later, his fingers press into my skin, and his cock slips back inside me. *Home.* We both let out a satisfied sigh, and he starts to fuck me again.

His touch moves from my hips to my ass, where he squeezes the globes individually, messaging them. "I can't wait to fuck your ass again."

"Oh god!" I press back against him, meeting his strokes, the pressure in my core rising with every thrust and slap of his balls against my clit.

"Fuck, you're close, aren't you, little bird?" His hand comes down on my ass cheek, the sting of pain only pushing me closer to the finish line. "Your pussy's so good. So fucking good and tight." Another slap lands against my warm skin, and the tension becomes unbearable. I'm a bowstring close to snapping.

My body jerks against his. "Callum…" I cry out, and he spanks me one more time. The painful sting against my skin sends pulses of pleasure straight to my core and, like a star close to destruction, I explode. My body gives out on me and I sag against the mattress, every muscle in my body tightening.

"Such a good fucking girl, coming on my cock. Squeezing me so tightly." Callum praises, his thrusting coming faster. "You're going to make me come... fuck I'm going to fill your tight cunt." The desperation in his voice barely meets my ears. "Tell me you want it. Tell me you want me to fill your cunt with my release."

"Yes, yes!! Give it to me," I beg, my hands fisting the sheets.

Callum pounds into me, my body moving up the bed with each hard stroke he delivers. "Jesus fucking Christ. I can't get enough of you, Bianca, and I don't think I ever will." He roars and explodes violently as the orgasm slams into him.

His cock jerks deep inside of me and I feel the warmth of his release spread through my core. He gathers me into his arm, his cock still deep inside me, and rolls us to our sides. Nuzzling his face into my neck, I let my eyes drift closed. *Safe. Protected. Cherished.* When the haze clears and reality comes back into focus, all the fear, fretfulness, and uncertainty are gone. I remember who I am and where I belong. There's nothing that could ever come between us.

No matter how hard the rest of the world seems to try.

CALLUM

Things are starting to look up, which leaves me wondering when the other shoe will drop. I'm finally starting to move without too much pain, and whatever lingering pain there is is much more manageable with the help of ibuprofen.

If it wasn't for the fact of Jack and Dominic Moroni being out there somewhere, mocking me with their very living and breathing, I'd have to say life is pretty good. I have a lot to be grateful for, and I am, though it doesn't feel like anyone is truly safe with them still out there.

I can imagine Jack sitting back and laughing—even if he didn't get what he wanted and all his efforts were for nothing. He didn't get a single cent out of me and had no control over my businesses. All he did was nearly lose his son.

If only I were naïve enough to think he won't try again, however I'm too jaded to believe that. A man like Jack will not rest. He'll want revenge for Dominic's injuries and for the men he lost. He's like an arsonist who wants repayment for the damage he caused. None of this would've happened if it hadn't been for him setting things in motion.

Him, and Amanda.

The thought of her makes me rub my temples, leaning back in my chair with a weary sigh. After imagining so many times how simple it would be to end her life and rid me of her permanently, it seems I should be relieved. Even grateful. She'll never darken my doorstep again. There will be no more threats. No meetings with lawyers. No insults toward Bianca.

Instead, I have my daughter to worry about—the trauma of losing her deadbeat mother in such a violent way. Never getting closure. I can't pretend to understand why she cares about a woman who never cared about her, yet it's clear she does. That's all that matters.

Romero should be wrapping things up on that front as I sit here in my office, reviewing candidates to replace the men we've lost. According to him, these guys are the best of the best. Then again, Booker was supposed to be one of the best back when he first joined my crew, and where did that get me? He acted as Amanda's spy for months. Considering the nude photos she sent him, I don't have to ask what she used to bribe him.

There I was, thinking a generous salary would be enough to keep my men loyal to me. Turns out loyalty *can't* be bought.

When my cell buzzes, I expect it to be Romero calling to let me know he's on his way from the crematorium, where Amanda's remains were taken after being removed from the warehouse. It took the regular payment amount, but I am confident about the guys working there. This would hardly be the first time we've sent business their way—the kind the public can't and will never find out about.

Unfortunately, it's not Romero whose name flashes across the screen. I sit up a little straighter, my impending headache forgotten. "Sebastian. I've been meaning to call you."

"I understand. You've had plenty on your plate, and I take it everything turned out as well as it could?"

"We're home safe and sound, and with the exception of a few sutures to my side, all is well."

"I'm glad to hear it." He clears his throat, then takes a prolonged pause while I wait to see what this is really about. It wouldn't be like him to call and see how I'm doing. No, we don't do that type of thing in my line of work. He wants something, or at least has something he feels he needs to share with me. I won't prod him. Let him be the one to make the moves.

"I'm in the neighborhood and wondered if you had a few minutes for a one-on-one. Understandable if you aren't. I know you're getting things back in order, so if it doesn't work, maybe we can choose another day?"

I close my eyes, clenching my hand into a fist. "Not at all. As I said, all is well. You're more than welcome to stop by."

"Great. Ten minutes, work?"

"I'll be waiting." What choice do I have? If I say no, it's as good as admitting any weakness, and the worst thing you can do is let someone know when you're weak, even if you really are. Besides, I want to keep this relationship warm and friendly. I might end up needing him somewhere down the line and can't afford to alienate an ally with so many loose ends.

I'm pulling on my suit jacket when Romero's footsteps echo down the hall. He stops short on rounding my doorway, sizing me up. "What did I miss?"

"Why do you assume you missed anything?"

"You're in 'meeting mode'." I raise my brow, and he continues, "Call it an energy that fills the air."

"Costello's on his way over. He called a minute ago. He wants to have a conversation in person. What it's about, I don't know." I pretend not to notice the sour expression he gives me, instead nodding to the small, brown box he holds in one hand. "Tell me that isn't what I think it is."

"Let me explain."

"This had better be good, because I can't come up with many reasons why you would bring my ex-wife's ashes into this house.

You were supposed to leave them there to be disposed of, or did you forget that part?" I crane my neck, peering behind him.

His jaw ticks, irritation bubbling to the surface, though that's the thing about Romero: he's smart enough to take a breath before responding. "I wanted to give Tatum the chance to decide whether she wants them."

"You're fucking with me, right?"

He blinks, his expression unmoving. "Would you rather tell her the ashes were lost and there's no hope of getting them back? I have to wonder if you even discussed this with her. Does she know her mother was cremated?"

"Alright, fine, you win. But it's damn morbid, if you ask me."

"That's your opinion," he reminds me. "She might not feel the same, and if she doesn't want them, she can… I don't know, scatter them or whatever it is people do. She deserves to have a choice in the matter. She wasn't a great mom, but she was her mom, nonetheless."

How does he manage to make me feel like an asshole when it comes to my own child? The pride I need to swallow comes damn close to choking me before I mutter, "You're right. I didn't think about it. All the bad blood between us… Amanda hasn't been much more than an enemy for a long time, you know that."

"And you know you don't need to explain anything to me. I've been here through all of it."

Note to self: have a discussion with my daughter about the remains of her late mother. I'm sure this will be easy for both of us.

When Henry calls from the front gate to alert me to Sebastian's arrival, Romero makes a point of going to his office. "You're not going to sit out the entire meeting, are you?" I call out.

"No. I'm setting these somewhere safe." And something tells me Romero is in no hurry to meet up with him, anyway. I've never known him to be so openly averse to any of our associates. Normally he's cold, emotionless. Although, lately, he's shown more and more of the boy he was back when I first took him in.

He does have a point, though. I don't need a box of ashes on my desk when Sebastian walks in. I'd rather they not be in my house, at all, honestly. I'm not about to develop a soft spot for the woman now that she's dead, especially when she caused me nothing but misery till the very end.

It sounds cruel, but she got what was coming to her. I can stifle my true feelings for Tatum's sake, but when I'm away from her, there's no pretending Amanda was more than a waste of oxygen.

Pushing out of my chair, I walk to the entrance to greet my guest, walking as smoothly and quickly as possible. The last thing I want to give off is the impression of weakness—maybe it's childish or makes me a stereotype, but I'll be damned if I slow down or show discomfort. Especially in front of some cocky young kid.

I've opened the front door and am stepping out onto the brick patio when Sebastian's car pulls around the courtyard. As before, he is not alone, his driver remaining behind the wheel while two guards exit the vehicle, scanning the area from behind their sunglasses despite the severely overcast skies.

It's a show of power that I give zero fucks about. Sebastian emerges, raising his own sunglasses before lifting a hand in greeting.

"It's good to see you," I greet, offering a firm handshake before ushering him into the house. "Especially under better circumstances." Thunder rumbles in the distance, signaling an oncoming storm. "We'd better get inside before the sky opens."

"I'm glad everything turned out alright. Your daughter's okay? And Bianca?"

"Everyone is doing fine."

"What a relief. And Moroni? I've heard he's gone underground."

"Yes." I grit my teeth as we walk side by side. The sound of the man's name is like a match dropped in a pool of gasoline, turning my gut into a raging inferno only vengeance can tame. "I heard the same. Why do I feel like that's part of the reason you're here?"

To his credit, he laughs, giving me a sheepish expression. "Am I that transparent? Really, I thought I was better than that. I need to up my face game."

I know better than to think he'll accept, but I offer him a drink once we reach my office. He refuses, unbuttoning his jacket before taking a seat. It's a little early for me, too, so I grab a bottle of water and take my usual seat.

"Where's your guy?" he asks, eyes darting around the room. "I thought he came with the room. Part of the furniture or something."

And he'd rip your head off if you dared say that in his presence. Clearly, we've begun to drop the formalities. "He'll join us shortly."

"Ahhh! Okay, well, as I was saying, yes, Moroni is a big part of why I wanted to talk to you. I'm as committed as ever to helping you take that bastard down. It was one thing when he wanted to screw with your business, but he changed the stakes by attacking your loved ones. He deserves to suffer for that."

"I'm sure you understand without being told that I agree. I have every intention of finding him and ending his miserable life as soon as possible. If you could offer assistance, I would be more than grateful, but I want you to know that I want to be the one to kill him. He needs to die at my hands and no one else's."

Romero chooses that precise moment to enter the room, offering Sebastian a short nod. "We've been discussing our common enemy," I explain.

"And how I'm willing to commit resources to helping you find him—and end him." Sebastian glances from me to Romero and back again. "In exchange for a slice of the Moroni pie."

At least he's straightforward. I'm tired of this performative dance, the false joviality. "Exactly how big a slice?"

"Not so big it would choke me, yet big enough that it makes it worth my while."

Romero perches himself on the corner of my desk, facing Sebastian. "And exactly what do you plan to contribute here?"

"For one thing, I have men on the inside. Men who are close to Moroni's closest associates. They know the ins and outs of his private life and how to get to him. I also may be able to pick up some intel on any properties Moroni owns off the books. Where he could be hiding his son while he recuperates, for instance."

This time, his smile isn't sheepish but rather approving. "Word is, he was stabbed with something a lot bigger than a fork this time."

If only she had planted that knife in his heart, the prick. "Shit, word does get around, doesn't it?"

"No. It doesn't." His eyes flash while a wolfish smile plays at the corners of his mouth. "Like I said. I have people who know people, and if I know your girl stabbed that fucker in the gut, and that, that kind of information doesn't hit the streets, what else do you think I can discover?"

Dammit. I hate to admit it, but I'm intrigued. The problem now is getting Romero to believe he's as good as he claims.

"Give me a list of the businesses you want, and we'll come to an agreement. I'm willing to be generous," I add. Romero's shoulders jump, but he otherwise conceals his reaction. I have no doubt he'll chew me out later, but I'll be damned if I give a shit. I don't need the extra income and would gladly burn everything Moroni owns to the ground so long as he was inside and burned right along with it. This kid can take over the entire Moroni network for all I care. What Jack operates is small beans compared to my own work.

"Excellent. I knew we could—"

He's cut off by the desk phone's double ring. I snatch the receiver from the cradle, irritated at being interrupted. "What?" I snap at Henry, who's calling from the gate.

"Torrio!! Let me the fuck in! We have some things to discuss!"

"Sir, I'm not sure what to do." The poor old man's voice shakes while Charlie continues ranting and raving in the background.

"Callum? Callum!" Bianca bursts into the room, breathless, with Tatum on her heels. "My father. He's on his way, and he's furious about something. He wouldn't tell me what it is."

Of all the fucking times. I have to avoid Sebastian's steel gaze as I turn my attention to Romero, whose face is a stony mask, as he gets up from the desk and strides from the room. "I'll take care of it."

Bianca's mouth falls open in dismay. "Take care of it? What does that mean?" Before I can stop her, she spins on her heels and follows him, Tatum tagging along behind her.

Henry's still on the phone. "Sir?"

"Let him in," I sigh, because anything else will only end up causing more trouble. I wouldn't mind seeing him break his neck ramming the gates, but that would only cause Bianca pain, and my little bird has endured enough of that.

Sebastian rises, buttoning his jacket with his lips pursed. He's wearing an expression I can only describe as *better you than me.* "I didn't mean to interrupt whatever domestic dispute is happening here."

"Could you wait here, please?" I ask, rising from my chair.

"I would, but I want you to know that if he jumps out of that car screaming threats, my guys are going to get in his face." *Shit. He's right.* He takes off in front of me, trotting down the hall, while I follow behind. The man is lucky he's Bianca's father, or I would have shut him up permanently a long time ago.

"Torrio!" I hear from out in the courtyard. Sebastian left the door open when he walked out, so there was nothing to block the sound of squealing brakes and a slamming car door.

"Charlie, come on, be smart, don't do this." It's Ken, and for once it doesn't seem like Charlie is listening to the voice of reason. By the time I step outside, I find Bianca with her hands raised. She's trying to keep her father from storming into the house while

Tatum and Romero stand off to the side. Sebastian's men have their guns drawn, but Sebastian quickly waves them off as he approaches them.

"There you are." Charlie bares his teeth at me from over Bianca's shoulder, spit flying. "You bastard. After everything you put her through, I discover this?"

"What are you—" The question dies in my throat when I identify what he throws at my feet. A small device, easy to overlook—and forget. *Damn it, I forgot all about it.*

"Care to explain that?" he screams.

His face is deep red, verging on purple, and sweat beads at his temples as it rolls down his face. He'll have a stroke if this keeps up much longer. "Want to tell me how that ended up where I found it?"

"Dad, what are you talking about?" Bianca casts a terrified look my way before gazing down at the camera. "What is that?" I glimpse at Romero, who clearly understands we fucked up and forgot to plant the camera in her room. *How could we forget?* I mean, it's understandable after everything that's happened, but it's just another mistake, another thing to push him over the edge.

"Since Torrio appears to have lost his voice, let me explain to you what that is. It's a hidden camera," Charlie informs her. "A camera that was hidden in your damn room." Shaking his head in disbelief, he continues, "How do you not see this? This is what he does. He tells you he loves you, but it's not love. It's control. He wants to own you, Bianca." His eyes glitter with hatred over his daughter's shoulder. "Tell me I'm wrong. Lie your way out of this one, Torrio."

Bianca bends and picks it up, holding it in her hand. "Callum? Is this true? Did you put this camera in my bedroom at my dad's house?"

Fuck me. This is what happens when the lies mount, and the secrets you do your best to keep buried become exposed.

"I was clearing some things out," Charlie tells her. "I found it on the bookshelves. It was pointed directly at your bed. I don't know how you did it," he snarls, his eyes back on me, "but I know it was you."

"Charlie, you need to calm down," Ken tells him, taking him by the arm.

An arm he yanks away, snarling. "No. I need to break every fucking bone in this bastard's body for what he did. He's never going to change," he insists to Bianca. "This is what love is to him. It's lies and control. Manipulation. Come home with me."

I want to tell him he's wrong, but he's not. In the past, all I wanted was to be able to control Bianca, to make sure she couldn't leave me, and parts of me still have a deep-rooted desire for that, because the thought of losing her kills me, but I'm trying to do better, be better, and I refuse to let Charlie think he can tell her what to do.

"She's a grown woman, capable of making her own choices," I remind him.

"I wasn't speaking to you."

"I don't care. Bianca is old enough to make her own choices. I know it's difficult, but you must learn to respect that."

"The only thing that matters to me is her safety, and if that means getting rid of you, then I will. I'll fucking kill you," Charlie growls—before lunging at me, pushing Bianca out of the way in his frenzy. She catches herself before falling, letting out a cry of dismay. I reach for her, but a fist connects with my jaw before I get to her.

Pain pulses across my chin. I don't want to hurt this man, not in front of her. Even if my instincts scream for me to defend myself, the most I do is shove him back. "Enough of this."

"What? Don't tell me you won't fight me like a man?"

"Don't do this!" Bianca begs, and her voice is the only thing keeping me centered while Charlie takes another swing.

"Dad!" Tatum cries out, rushing for me before Romero wraps an arm around her waist and pulls her back.

"Charlie, that's enough," Ken yells and tries to place himself between us, but all that does is piss Charlie off more, and he shoves him out of the way like he's nothing.

"This is all you'll ever have with him!" Charlie insists. "Don't you see? Armed fucking men standing out in front of the house. This isn't freedom. This isn't a life! You have so much potential, you have a bright future ahead of you. Why are you wasting it on him?"

"Boss, let me take care of this," Romero growls, and I find Tatum shaking her head at him when I glance their way.

"No." No, I don't want him to take care of this. Because, goddamn it, the man is right. This isn't a life for her. She deserves better. I've done so many things to keep her with me, to keep her close, all because I can't live without her. And what can I offer? More of this? Sitting in my office, negotiating a deal that will lead to a man's murder—out of revenge for what that man did to her. What I allowed to happen, all because she's associated with me.

The memory of the cell in which they held her keeps me from fighting back when Charlie lands another hit. His fits come quickly, landing repeatedly, driving me to my knees. Bianca lets out a terrifying scream before she starts to plead with her father, only he doesn't listen. It could be that he doesn't hear her, too intent on finally ending me the way he's always wanted to do, or he just doesn't give a fuck.

"Stop, Dad, please stop!" She tries to put herself between us, to shield me, but I shake my head, spitting out blood from the corner of my mouth, well climbing to my feet.

"Let him have what he wants," I insist, swaying, moving her aside as gently as I can. "Let him hurt me, let him have this, because he can't have you."

That did it. That hit him harder than my fist ever could. Something overtakes his features. I can't tell what it is, horror? Disgust? Or maybe it's a realization—cold, hard truth. Yeah, I bet that's a hard pill to swallow.

He pulls his fist back, eyes blazing. "You fucking—"

Fireworks explode in my head when he makes contact with my jaw. A perfect punch all around. I fall back, this time landing on my side while the world spins like a merry-go-round. I roll onto my back, and the first drops of rain from the storm that's been threatening with rumbles all morning begin to hit my face.

"Dad, no! Don't!" It's Bianca's yell that warns me, but there's no preparing for the burst of fresh agony that renders me breathless once Charlie's foot makes contact with my side. Fucking Christ. Pain burns across my flesh and deep through my muscles.

My stitches. He tore my fucking stitches.

He's going to kill me. He won't be satisfied until I'm dead.

Considering I've never been anything but a curse to his daughter, I deserve this.

BIANCA

My biggest nightmare is taking place right before my eyes. I can't get my feet or body to move fast enough as I frantically throw myself between them again, shielding Callum's body with my own. I immediately notice the splotch of blood on his shirt and follow the trail oozing from his split lip, then his nose and the cut above his eye.

He's bleeding.

The memory of racing through that basement while Callum was bleeding out makes my heart race painfully, pumping adrenaline throughout my body.

He took care of me. I have to take care of him.

"Stop! Now!" I scream the words with every last bit of strength I have. Silence surrounds me, and I glare up at my father, who stands over me with his fists clenched. The knuckles of his right hand are already turning a sickly black and blue. He stumbles backwards, his shoulders heaving with every breath, while drops of sweat glisten against his skin. "You've made your point!"

Romero rushes to Callum's side, and Ken grabs hold of my father, tugging him back, away from Callum. "I'll take him upstairs," Romero grumbles, pulling Callum to his feet, wedging himself under his armpit to keep him upright. "I'll check his wound, but I'm warning you, he might need to be stitched back up."

"I'll be up there as soon as I can." I nod to Tatum, whose eyes swim with unshed tears as they ping-pong between us. She's weary of leaving me alone with my father, but I don't need her here. I'm not scared of him. "Go ahead. I'll take care of this."

I vaguely recognize the stranger hanging around the dark sports car with another man. "You should probably go too," I tell him. Barely bringing myself to look at him, the humiliation of what my father has done twists my organs, making it difficult for me to feel anything other than shame.

"Everything okay here?" There's an edge of concern to his voice, though I don't need the stranger's pity or worry.

"Whatever meeting you had with Callum is over now. I'm sorry for the interruption. I'm sure he'll reach out soon to reschedule something."

"Are you sure you're okay?" he asks again, and I'm so frustrated I could scream.

"I'm fine, and everything here is fine. Please leave." He gives me a slight shake of his head, probably questioning the balls of steel I must be carrying to order around a man like him. As he climbs into his car, I notice him peering over at Dad and Ken; they are in a heated argument. At least they aren't punching each other. Yet.

Once he starts to back out and turn around in the driveway, I march down the steps and shove my father with both hands. "How dare you?" I hiss, flicking back a few raindrops that land near my eyes. "What the hell do you think you're doing?"

"He installed a damn camera in your bedroom, to spy on you!! What do you think this is about? What's it going to take to show you what a mistake this all is?"

"You're right, that was wrong of him to do," I agree. Still can't wrap my head around it, but then again, I can't wrap my head around any of this. "And I'm going to talk to him about it.

However, coming here and attacking him isn't going to change what happened. It isn't going to change anything!"

He rolls his eyes, snickering. "Oh, you'll talk to him."

"What do you want me to say? Huh? You want me to pack up my things and come home with you? Is that it?"

"That is exactly what I want you to do." As he speaks, he keeps shaking out his right hand. It's clear he's in pain, but I can't pretend to have any sympathy for him. Nobody made him do any of this.

"That's not going to happen, and I can't believe you would do this." My chin quivers and tears blur my vision. "How could you?"

Thunder rumbles all around us, even shaking the ground, while he glares at me. "You're not serious, are you? You're not going to stay here, even after knowing what he did, are you?"

"I know for damn sure I'm not leaving with you after what you just did. Did you ever think what that would do to me? Do you ever actually think about me at all, and the impact your actions have on me? I know you're trying to do what you think is right, but this… this is…" All I can do is shake my head in disbelief.

His face crumbles with despair. "How could you even ask that? You're all I think about. All of this is about you."

"Are you sure it isn't about you, too? I told you that you were right already, that what he did was wrong, and I will talk to him about it, but that's not good enough for you. I will get to the bottom of this, but damn it, you don't get to come over here ranting and raving and beating him when I beg you to stop. And that's what bothers me the most, Dad. I begged you to stop, and you wouldn't listen to me. You don't care how much this hurts me. All you want is revenge."

Maybe I'm finally starting to get through to him. His breathing slows, and some of the tension drains from his face. "He broke into my home and placed a camera in your bedroom. He deserved to get his ass kicked for that."

"Did you know he took a bullet for me? Of course, you did.

You were at the hospital, but who cares about that, right? Who cares that he's healing from a wound in the very place you had to kick him. Don't tell me that was accidental. He took a bullet to save my life, and all you could think to do was kick him right where you knew it would hurt the most."

"You wouldn't have ever been kidnapped, or in a situation to be shot at, if it hadn't been for him!" He tosses his hands into the air while blurting out a laugh. "Nothing I say gets through to you anymore. He's completely destroyed you. I don't even know who you are anymore."

"No, the problem is you never knew me at all."

Ken backs away, shaking his head. "I shouldn't be here for this." He's right; he shouldn't be. I'm tired of pretending anything about this is normal. I'm tired of trying to be polite, tired of trying to do the right thing just to keep the peace. I'm tired of trying to make everyone else happy. It's exhausting, and truly, the only person who loses is me. I'm an adult who's old enough to make my own choices.

"Can I remind you of something that happened not very long ago?" When all he does is lift his chin, I continue, "Remember when you called that landlord and told them I wouldn't be moving in? Remember that? Remember when you made that decision *for* me? When you made a fool out of me without even considering my feelings? Remember when you thought you knew so much better than I did?"

"Don't even try to compare me to him. There's no way you actually think that what I did came anywhere close to what he's done."

"Oh no, but it is. You only did that because you wanted to protect me and keep me safe. I get it. I don't have to agree with it, but I can at least understand where you were coming from."

"What's your point?"

"My point is, he's just like you. Maybe, just maybe, that's why you hate him so much."

"Don't try to put us in the same box," he warns, holding up a hand. "I'm nothing like that man. You don't get to twist around the past until it looks the way you want it to look. You know damn well what I've had against him for all these years."

I'm angry. Angry at my Father. At Callum's past actions. I'm angry that I have no control over my own life, and I'm done being a doormat for others.

"Let me put this in the simplest terms for you. It's none of your damn business. You're not even a cop anymore. Why make taking him down your life's mission? What is it about him that makes you so bloodthirsty for revenge? Is it because you didn't like that he got away with the things he did?" I sigh in defeat.

"How many other people get away with those same things? Why didn't you go after any of them? If you ask me, it doesn't necessarily have to do with what he did or *didn't* do that's got you angry. You grew obsessed with the need to pin a crime on him, and you became obsessed with making him pay because no one ever has, so you wanted to be the first."

My father's lips press into a firm line, and it looks like he wants to say something, but I shake my head.

"If he put a camera in my room, it was because he wanted to see with his own eyes that I was safe. I can't pretend I understand why he thought that was a good idea, but I do understand his reasoning. Just like I understood yours even though I was furious with you at the time. You violated my trust and my privacy just as much as he did. And if you can't see that, then I don't know how to make you."

"I should press charges."

"Can you prove it was him? Can you prove any of this?" When all he does is sputter, I shake my head. "You should know, of all people, you have to have proof. The fact is, you don't know when that camera was placed there. And you don't know why it was there, to begin with. But, okay, sure, press charges. Make all of this even worse."

I can see that I'm getting through to him as much as he wants to ignore every word I say. He is determined to live in his own twisted mind where I'm being held here against my will, and that my life is over because I love Callum.

"Dad, I love you," I whisper, "but you're going to lose me if you refuse to let me live my own life. I'm not asking you to agree with my decisions, although I am asking you to respect them. I'm an adult, not a little girl anymore. You're going to be a grandfather, and you're out here beating the crap out of a man who happens to be my baby's father. Stop and take a look at yourself. Is this who you want to be? Because, right now, you are not the father I remember."

"I just..." He puts his palms to his forehead, tipping his head back with closed eyes. "I just can't lose you, too. Don't you get that? I don't want to lose you to this violent world he lives in. You came so close this last time. What happens the next time someone comes after you, or the time after that? Because when you are close to a man like him, the attacks will *never* stop. His enemies want to get to him, and they're going to do that by using you, and the baby," he adds before I can open my mouth. "Telling me you care about that child in the same breath you tell me you want to stay with him, it doesn't add up, Bianca."

I cross my arms over my chest. "Callum is doing everything he can to keep us safe. I trust him."

I've seen him look defeated more times than I even want to count in the past few weeks alone. However, nothing tops this, the way he hangs his head and almost seems to whither down inside his clothes. His shoulders hunch, his back stoops a little, and I get a flash of the old man he'll be one day. One day soon, if he doesn't clean up his act and get himself back on track.

I realize I'm part of the reason why he hasn't done that yet, and the guilt I feel is almost crippling, but no. I'm not responsible for his happiness or who he is. I'm not going to spiral out of guilt anymore. He chose to come here today, and all he did was drive a wedge between us. If he chooses to drink his life away or make other bad choices, they are *his* choices. Just like my choices belong to me and nobody else.

"I think you should go home," I tell him, my voice trembling with sadness and grief. Grief for everything he's going through, and for the distance between us. *Mom would hate to see us like this*, is I want to say, but that would be too cruel, so I don't. Although it weighs on my heart as I watch him back away.

"Please, Bianca. Please know that I only want what's best for you. You and the baby will be much safer back at the house. Away from his enemies and the dark, violent world he lives in. Nothing is keeping you here. You don't have to stay."

"Your right," I agree. "I don't have to be here. Only that's just it, I want to be. This is where I belong."

His jaw works slowly, his eyes welling up with tears. He has more to say, I'm sure, but he just gets in the car. Ken looks saddened when our eyes meet, and I raise a hand to wave goodbye, shuddering to think what would have happened if he wasn't here—then again, it's not like he did much to keep Dad from making a complete ass of himself.

The rain's starting to come down harder now, and the thunder booms louder and more frequently, so I duck inside before I get drenched. Tatum comes running from the kitchen with an ice pack in one hand when she hears me close the door. "Jesus Christ. Are you all right?"

"Physically, yes. Emotionally I feel like I got punched in the heart. I'm sorry for what just happened."

"Don't apologize for your father. You didn't do anything wrong."

Didn't I? It seems like no matter what I do, I feel like I'm failing. "I'm going to go upstairs to see how he's doing. Are you okay?"

"You think that's the first time I ever saw somebody punch my dad?" It's her shaky laugh that worries me. She's already going through so much, and right now she looks like a pale imitation of the girl I went to school with, shared secrets with, and did all the things best friends are supposed to do together. She was always the ballsy one, the loud, brassy kid whose shadow I could hide in. Now it's like she's hiding from herself inside that shadow, a turtle trapped inside its shell. "None of this is your fault, so don't blame yourself. Shit happens."

"Do you want to come up with me?" I start for the stairs, looking at her over my shoulder.

"No, I don't think that's a good idea. You know what the sight of blood does to me." She hands me the ice pack. "You should take it to him. I'll make something to eat." I watch her walk away and already my heavy heart feels heavier, like someone's tied a brick to it. There's this invisible wall between us now. We're still friendly, cordial, and all that. However, instead of talking to each other, we're talking through a plexiglass wall, causing some of the words to be lost. I don't know how to get us back to where we used to be. Maybe we'll never be the same.

As I reach the bedroom, Romero's on his way out. "Turns out he's tough as nails and will manage to survive. Just a little bit of seepage."

"Oh, thank God. I would hate to have to take him back to the hospital."

"After everything that just happened…"

"If you're wondering if I'm okay, the answer is yes." I interrupt, giving him a lame smile that probably looks more like a grimace.

He must see right through it because his brows draw together and his eyes narrow. " Okay, well, in case you were wondering… I mean, about the camera…"

I shake my head before he can inform me of what I already know. "I already know, and I'll save you the embarrassment. We don't have to talk about it, and I honestly don't want to either."

"Fair enough. I'll be downstairs if you need anything."

I give him a nod. I knew it had to have been Romero as soon as

Callum and him looked at each other. I've seen that look before. These men have a boatload of secrets between them. I shudder to think about the things they've done.

"I'm fine." It's the first thing Callum says to me when I enter the bedroom to find him stretched out on his back. What I'm looking at conveys a different story: he's stripped down to his boxers, his head propped up on pillows, and his eye starting to blacken under the cut Dad gave him.

"Tatum was going to bring you this." I hand him the ice pack, which he places over his eye.

I have so many questions.

Why does he do what he does? Why did he think the camera was the right thing to do? Why didn't he ever tell me about it? How much of my privacy did he invade, exactly?

The one at the forefront of them all is the one that pours out of me first. "What would possess you to let my father do that?" I ask, sitting on the bed next to him. Romero must have taped a new piece of gauze over his wound, since it doesn't look like there's any more blood coming through... yet. *What if he's hurt worse than we suspect?*

"What do you mean? Are you asking why I let him knock me on my ass?" His speech is a little slurred thanks to his split lip, although that does nothing to affect the sarcasm in his voice.

I nod, "Yes! You didn't even try to defend yourself, and don't you dare tell me you did it to protect me."

"Maybe..." He forces a deep breath into his lungs and winces like it hurts, but continues, "Maybe I knew I deserved it."

"No! Don't do this."

Shrugging, he says, "He's right. About the camera, about the way I'm ruining your life. I know you deserve better than all of this. You, Tatum, everyone in my life. No matter what I do, I end up hurting the people I love the most. So yeah, I think I deserved an ass kicking."

My heart aches in my chest. I refuse to allow him to believe the things he's saying. "Listen to me. For one, I'm with you because I want to be. After all, life without you is utter misery. For better or worse, we belong together, and fighting against the inevitable is a waste of time."

"He made several valid points out there. You know he did, even I can admit that."

"If you are so bad for me, why am I here?"

His jaw tightens, the muscles jumping as his lips draw into a thin line. "Because it's like you said: it's a waste of time trying to pretend you don't belong with me. No matter how hard I try to keep you away for your own sake, that only seems to make things worse."

"And because you want me to be here, right?"

"What do you think?" His hand finds mine, wrapping around my fingers and squeezing tight. "I love you. Nothing is going to change that. Not even your crazy father."

"I love you, too. *That's* why I'm here. At the end of the day, this is where I belong."

Rather than grill him about the camera, I kick off my shoes and crawl over him, settling in on his good side. Despite everything, there is a sort of peace when I lie down beside him that I've never felt anywhere, with anyone else. It's like something in my soul clicks into place when I rest my head on his shoulder, and he drapes an arm around me, pulling me closer.

Whatever happens in this world, we can always come back to this—the two of us, together, which is all that truly matters. I want to believe that, yet somehow I can't. Because downstairs is my best friend, who seems more lost than ever, and out there somewhere are the men who almost ended our lives. On top of all of that, my dad might never speak to me again.

I can't pretend our being together hasn't upended my life, but I do know that it's worth it. With Callum's love wrapped around me anything seems possible.

CALLUM

"Are you sure they're open?" I ask, knowing the answer already.

It's adorable how she bites her lip, frowning as she gazes out the window toward the restaurant. "They look closed. Do we have a reservation?"

She means it, too. That's what makes it so easy to love her. How she never expects anything, her lack of worldliness. There's no greed or demands. She never expects anything from me, and being with someone like that is refreshing. Especially when all my life, every single day, there has been someone expecting something from me.

"We have a reservation. Don't worry, little bird." Taking out my phone, I place a call to the owner to let him know we've arrived. It's not another minute before he appears on the other side of the glass door to unlock it for us.

"You know how important it is that we stay safe, which means flying under the radar." I lift her hand, brushing my lips over her knuckles. Her skin is smooth and so fucking soft. "I hope you don't mind, but you won't be able to show off how absolutely

EMPIRE OF PAIN

stunning you look tonight—at least not to anybody except a few staff members."

There's no denying how stunning she is in the sleek, black dress that molds to the perfect curves of her hourglass figure. My mouth waters, and I want to rip it off her and feast at what's beneath. I don't know what gets my dick stirring more: the way she looks or knowing how soon she'll start to swell with evidence of the life I put inside her. If she weren't already pregnant, I'd be doing everything I could to knock her up.

"How did you manage this?" Bianca gives me a superstitious look.

I shrug, "Connections. I know the owner, and he was happy to close down the restaurant tonight for us. Well, have the entire place to ourselves. It'll be an intimate, quiet dinner."

"That's awfully nice of him."

"He didn't do it out of the kindness of his heart, but believe me, I made it worth his while." The money spent to rent this place out was a drop in the bucket. There's no price tag when it comes to spending a quiet evening out with Bianca, while also knowing she's safe and protected at the same time.

Bianca lifts a hand and places it against her chest. "I... I can't believe you went through all this trouble... for me."

"Don't act so surprised. If anyone deserves this, it's you. A nice quiet evening spent together, with food and your smile, is worth any cost." Leaning in, I press my lips to her tempting mouth; her full pouty lips are painted a glossy pink.

The smile she wears, and the twinkle of joy in her eyes while swiping her thumb over my lips to wipe away the smear, leave me wanting to bask in its warmth, like a cat sunning itself in a window. I could live inside the warmth that her joy provides.

"Let's go. I'm starving." She waits inside the car, while I climb out, taking care to scan the area as I walk around the vehicle. There's a pair of guards behind us in a car of their own who nod to me as I pass—they'll be waiting outside the place while we eat. I hate that I've had to increase security, but it's necessary after everything that happened. The security teams assigned to Bianca and Tatum are essential right now, especially till we find Jack and Dominic.

Once I'm satisfied that no one will spring an attack, I open the door and extend my hand to help her out of the car. One look at her, and the air is stolen from my lungs. She doesn't even have to try, yet somehow she is the most beautiful woman in the world. A man like me can have any woman he wants, but there's no alternative to Bianca.

She is the rarest diamond in the mine, and only she holds my heart.

We walk hand in hand through the front door, which is locked behind us at my request. If only I didn't have to look over my shoulder, waiting for a monster to leap out from the darkness and take her away from me again. I have to swallow down my anxiety, fearing it'll bleed over into our evening.

"I don't know why, but I feel like I have to whisper," Bianca admits with a soft chuckle as we're led to the only table set for dinner. The rest of the room is dark except for the candles on the surrounding tables, which give off a warm ambiance.

A bouquet of red roses that I ordered earlier sits at the center of our table in a crystal vase that sparkles in the candlelight. I wanted this evening to be perfect. It's been too long since the last time I took her out. I want to show her the benefits of being with a man like me, since all that's truly been seen are the downfalls.

"Callum!" Bianca gasps, "Red roses? Are these for me?" she squeals, leaning down to breathe in their flowery fragrance.

"They're your favorite, right?"

Her blue eyes sparkle in the light when they meet mine over the bouquet. "You remembered."

"I remember everything about you."

"You genuinely are amazing. I can't believe you thought of everything."

It wasn't really much. Only the result of a few phone calls and some careful planning. Yet to her, it's everything, which only reminds me further how important the small things are. A woman like Bianca deserves the world, and I'll do anything in my power to make sure she feels and sees how important she is to me.

"Everything... it's amazing." Before taking the seat I've pulled out for her, she leans over and gently kisses my lips. "Thank you for making me feel like a Queen. It's unnecessary because anywhere I am that allows me to spend time with you makes me happy, but it is appreciated."

"That's how I want you to feel always, forever. You're my Queen, and you deserve to be treated as one at all times." After getting her seated, I gesture to the young woman waiting by the kitchen doors, who approaches with a bottle of sparkling cider and a pair of champagne flutes. "Alcohol is off the table, obviously, but I couldn't let the night pass without a toast."

Once our flutes are filled, I touch mine to hers. "To many, many nights like this."

"Yes, and to a great future full of even more amazing moments together."

I grin, my own joy overflowing, "I hope you're in the mood for Italian."

"That's a joke, right? I'm always in the mood for Italian. I've been craving spaghetti. Just plain spaghetti. I have no idea why." Yes, and I heard her confessing that to Sheryl in the kitchen this morning, hence my choice of restaurant.

"That's easier than pickles and ice cream or ranch with mac and cheese."

"I always figured that pregnancy cravings were nothing but a myth, though I swear, I could shove my face in a bowl of plain pasta right now and be content." She looks down at herself and frowns, "It's sad. I won't be able to fit into this dress for much longer."

The thought makes my cock hard immediately. I can't wait to see her swollen with my seed, her belly bulging with life inside. Fuck, if I don't stop thinking like this, we won't make it through dinner. "I hope you're not worried about what I'm going to think or how I'll feel about you getting bigger, because if you're thinking that I'll be disgusted or upset, you're sorely mistaken. I can't wait to see your beautiful body swollen with our child."

"You mean you'll still want me even when I look like a whale?" She holds her arms out to the sides and puffs out her cheeks. The expression is adorable, but her fear of me disliking her body or size well into her pregnancy, or after, not so much.

"Are you kidding? If I don't stop picturing you round with our child, I won't be responsible for who sees you on this table with your legs spread wide open, your pussy on display for me to feast on. I'll have to let them know I don't need anything from the menu and that I'm already eating the most delicious thing my tongue has ever tasted."

A pink blush creeps into her cheeks. "I'd say there is no way you'd do something like that, but I'm not willing to take the risk so I have no doubt I'd find myself on my back in seconds if I disagreed."

"Do you want to find out? Because you know how I feel about your pussy, Bianca. I'll eat you until you beg me to stop and then I'll keep going just to prove a point." And I will. When it comes to her, I'm obsessed. Forever hungry.

"No, no. I believe you." She smiles, even though I don't miss the flickering flames of lust in her eyes as she denies it.

The waitress brings out the salad and the aromatic, freshly baked rosemary focaccia bread. "I know this is a strange question, but I want to get to know you better, see what makes you tick, and discover what it is you want out of life."

"Okay, so ask away." She grins.

"Well, what do you want to do with your life?"

She almost chokes on a mouthful of bread, then laughs. "Wow. Nothing like coming out with the big questions right away."

"I told you it was going to be a pointed question, but I genuinely want to know what it is you want to do?"

"This isn't a trick question?"

"Of course not." Smirking when she tips her head to one side, I add, "I understand why you would guess that, but trust me. We don't talk much about you, and I would like to change that."

"Okay." She seems to give it real thought while our server sets a platter of cheese and roasted vegetables between us. "You know, I always figured I had everything in place. I wanted to work in economics, get a stable job that came with a retirement fund, all that stuff." She drizzles honey over a piece of parmesan, then moans as she places it in her mouth.

"Careful," I warn, lifting an eyebrow. "I don't know how far my self-control will get us if you insist on turning me on with those sexy sounds."

"Sorry." The wicked gleam in her eyes tells a different story. We both know this will only lead to me ravishing her once we get home—if I can wait that long. I've already envisioned fucking her right here on the table.

"Anyway, it feels wrong turning my back on that." I keep my thoughts to myself, although I imagine good old Charlie drilling that into her head. "They always say hands-on experience is the best kind, and I have to say that's true. After spending time working in an office, I don't know if I want to do that for the rest of my life." I can almost feel her indecision when her brow furrows. "So many people would kill for a stable job like that though, so I feel…."

"That doesn't mean you have to want it. I think one of the saddest things in life is watching someone talk themselves into something they don't want, all because they think they should."

"Right, but I want you to know that this doesn't mean I want to spend the rest of my life hanging around the house or spending your money. I don't want you to think that."

What would ever possess her to believe I would think that? "Bianca, that is the last thing I'll ever think about when it comes to you. That's not who you are."

"Good, at least you know that. I don't want you to think I'm trying to take advantage of you." Her eyes close once she smears burrata on a piece of focaccia. Bringing it to her mouth, her teeth sink into the bread. "Oh, my God, this is heaven."

It's heaven to watch her enjoy herself. There's nothing like spoiling someone who deserves it.

"I know you better than that." Though considering my past with women—especially one in particular whose name I refuse to mention or even think of, if I can help it—I can understand why she would go out of her way to assure me.

"This might sound stupid, but I feel like I should have a better idea of what I want out of life."

"There is plenty of time to figure out what you want to do with your life. I don't know why society expects everyone to know what they want to do the second they turn eighteen. Most people don't even know what they want to do for a job until they're older, and then they've wasted years doing something they've hated simply for a paycheck and insurance. There's more to life than surviving. As you grow up, it's like you understand what you want most out of life."

"I know, but with the baby and everything..." She lowers the rest of her focaccia to the plate, and her dark brows draw together. I can see the worry lines creasing her forehead, and I want to kick myself for the direction this conversation has gone.

"That's the thing about having money. It gives you options. If you want to hire a nanny and work full-time? Go ahead. If you want to go back to school? Be my guest. If you want to be a stay-at-home mom and volunteer a few hours a week somewhere, that's fine with me. You can do whatever you want. I'll be here for you, supporting you, with whatever it is you decide to do."

"Wow." She sighs. "I'm sorry, I just never thought about it that way. There are so many options available."

"Compromising is a thing of the past." Eventually, I'm going to make sure she understands that. I never imagined the joy of being able to open up my world to someone else. Yes, there are risks with my job and the people I associate with but also benefits.

All at once her head snaps up, and a soft smile touches her lips. "This song. It was one of my mom's favorites."

I recognize the instrumental version of an old 80s love song coming from speakers somewhere in the dining room. The way she beams, paired with the candlelight and the flowers and the sense of there being nobody in the world except the two of us, leaves me doing something wholly out of character.

"Dance with me?" She blushes and lets out a giggle when I push my chair back from the table. I'm certain she's going to brush me off and tell me I'm crazy, but when I extend a hand to her, she places hers against my palm and stands.

"You're the most perfect kind of crazy."

I can't disagree. "It's a good thing you already knew that."

Her petite frame melts into mine when I place my hand against the small of her back and pull her close. The soft, gentle rhythm is easy to fall into, and soon we're swaying in time. I've never considered myself a romantic—more like the farthest thing from it. Still, I'd be kidding myself if I didn't acknowledge the magic of this moment.

If only she hadn't mentioned her mother. I didn't need a reminder of the dark cloud parked over my head. She casts a shadow on everything, all the time. I need to tell her. *Not yet. Not just yet.*

Let us have this night.

"Are you okay? Where did you go?"

I look down at her to find a puzzled, concerned look in her

eyes. "I guess I was thinking about how old it makes me that I remember when this song came out."

Disbelief shines in her pretty eyes. "You're such a liar."

"What? You don't think I'm that old? I'll do you one better. I remember watching a guy lip-sync this song on an old TV show, with girls in golden leotards dancing in a circle around him. The 80s were a different time. Kinda like you had to be there to experience it."

"You know that's not what I meant. I just... it looked... you looked at me like you were worried."

"My mind tends to wander sometimes. I'm sorry. I'm not worried, and you deserve my full attention, little bird." My grin must be natural enough to convince her since she lets it be and instead rests her cheek against my shoulder, letting out a happy little sigh that unlocks something in my chest. Something warm and sweet.

She keeps finding ways to crack me open and expose me to a more profound love than I've felt before. That love will never be enough to wash away my guilt, however. She deserves to know that I played a part in her mother's murder. I know I didn't pull the trigger, but I didn't have to, to know I was partially responsible for her death. I've stirred up trouble in Bianca's life for longer than I knew she existed, and I need to make things right. There needs to be a clean slate for us moving forward.

But not now. Not quite yet. I need to soak in her love a little while longer.

Her shining, dark hair smells of lavender when I lower my head to place a kiss on her temple. "I love you. No matter what happens, no matter who gets in our way. I need you to know that will never change. In my heart, this is who and where we are. The two of us, dancing like this. Forever."

"I wish this night would never end."

"We'll have to come back here. This can be our place. To hell with anybody who's got a reservation—they can come back another time. I want to be here with my girl."

"Hopefully, one day soon, we won't have to hide. Everything will be safe, and there won't be any fears of Jack or his men attacking us." I don't know that we'll ever have a day without any lingering fears of the enemy lying in wait, but I do know things will be better than they are now. *Eventually.*

"That day is coming. I promise." I hold her tighter, closing my eyes and sucking in deep breaths of her scent into my nose. Savoring her warmth, her body's soft curves, and the way it moves with mine. "This is us, here, in this moment. Nothing is going to change us. I refuse to let that happen."

I'm reminded then that there is no controlling Bianca. This is her life as well, and she deserves to have a say in what happens, so even if it kills me to lose her after my confession, I'll have no option but to let her go if that's what she wants.

"I love you." She lifts her head to gaze up at me, blissfully unaware of my worries. "And if the baby is a boy, I hope he looks just like you."

A son. "I hope he has your smarts, because if he has mine, we're in trouble."

"Don't sell yourself short. You're a pretty smart guy. I mean, how would you have gotten as far as you have if you weren't?"

No comment.

It hasn't all been about intelligence. There's also a degree of ruthlessness involved, and I would rather my son not have to take the steps I did. "Smarts is only half of it. It's no secret that I've made enemies in my line of work. I don't want this for our children. They'll have options, too. Choices. They won't have to do the things I've done."

"Our children can do whatever they want, be whoever they want to be." Bianca beams up at me.

Knowing how happy she is, and the hope resonating in her, leaves me feeling cautiously hopeful, as well. Like nothing but good things are coming our way. A future full of happiness. That is unless she decides I'm not worth the risk when she finds out her mother didn't have to know I existed in order for me to end her life. If that's possible, what's possible for the people closest to me? I want Bianca to know she's always safe with me, yet I can't help being reminded of everything her father said. All of it was horrible, but they were all true.

I'd love more than anything to bury the secrets, but Bianca deserves to know. She deserves to know everything.

BIANCA

"What about Harvard or Yale? We should start a college fund right away."

"Whoa, slow down. We need to do one thing at a time," I assure as we cross the front patio of the restaurant on our way out to the car. I love his enthusiasm, but we should focus on getting through this pregnancy before choosing a school. "We don't even know if it's a boy or a girl, and you already have them attending an Ivy League school."

"Nowadays, you have to plan far in advance. Trust me," he insists when I snicker. "I still wake up in a cold sweat when I remember those bills I got from the bursar's office, and you girls didn't go to an Ivy League school."

"I'm shocked. Even Mr. Torrio himself is worried about the cost of a university?"

He smirks, "Even people with money can experience sticker shock, trust me."

"Okay, well, let's wait until we have a due date before we start the college fund, okay?" Though I can't pretend it doesn't make me excited knowing he's looking forward to raising our baby. There I was, nervous he'd be upset and think it was too soon.

It's moments like this when I wonder if he's more excited than I am.

I wish he could be entirely in the moment, though. That's the one thing that would make tonight perfect. More than once, I felt like he was distracted, just as he is now. I know why, and I understand why he looks around before opening the car door. He's worried Jack or one of his men are waiting around the corner, looking for the perfect moment to attack. I hate seeing him so paranoid, but more than anything, I hate seeing him so afraid. A man like Callum having fears shows his weak spots, and we both know what Jack is willing to do to get what he wants. I can only imagine he wants to punish me—us—for what happened to Dominic. He was pissed enough when there was nothing but a fork involved. I'm sure he's feeling mighty murderous right now.

Callum seems to loosen up once we're in the car, pulling me in close for a kiss. Not the chaste sort of kiss he gave me in the restaurant. No, this is the sort of kiss that makes my toes curl and my core clench, especially once his tongue slides past my lips, tangling with my own.

On the one hand, I want nothing more than to lose myself in him right here and now. He's pretty much healed from his wounds, including the one he got from Dad. I still cringe–like, full-body cringe–when I remember the fear and embarrassment of that morning.

Judging from the steel hardness of his cock, he's feeling much better.

On the other hand, we're not alone.

"What are you doing?" I whisper when Callum reaches out to press the button that raises the privacy divider between us and the driver.

"What do you think?" All at once his hand is up my dress, his fingers dancing over my skin and setting it on fire. He pulls the crotch of my thong aside and chuckles against my neck, making me shiver. "Already wet for me, I see."

"We shouldn't..." But even I hear the weakness in my whispering, how half-hearted it is. He has a way of making me second-guess everything I believe. Like how it's probably bad taste to have sex in the backseat of a car that somebody else is driving.

My body doesn't care about any of that right now. It wants, it needs, and it's going to be satisfied.

I arch my back at the entrance of one, then two, of Callum's thick digits. His hot breath fans across my chest while my own fingers work through his hair, clutching him to me. All of my awareness travels south and tightens until there is nothing in this world except the delicious friction of the pounding of his knuckles against my sensitive flesh.

"Such a bad girl," he whispers, fingering me hard and fast. "This pussy is always wet and ready for me. My pussy. *Mine.*"

"Yours!" I pant, leaning against the seat, jerking my hips in time with his rapid strokes. When he adds a thumb to my clit, he sets off an explosion in my core. My body jerks, going motionless, before the tension breaks and leaves me shaking.

The shock waves still roll through me when he lifts his head, grinning at me. "That didn't take long." He withdraws his fingers, then lifts them to his lips, and I watch as he sucks them clean. There is nothing as erotic as this, watching him take pleasure in me. He doesn't try to hide it—no, he wants me to see. He wants me to know.

And now I want more. I pull him closer and find the bulge in his slacks, running a hand over it while teasing us both with light, playful kisses. He leans in for more, but I pull back, grinning at his frustration before giving him my lips. I taste myself on him, and something about it reaches that greedy, hungry part inside me. I want to experience everything with him, in every way.

My hands work his fly before I gently push him away to give myself room to kneel on the seat. "Oh, fuck," he groans, leaning back like I did now that it's his turn. I don't waste any time freeing him from his shorts before plunging my head down, taking him as deep as I can into my mouth. His satisfied sigh makes my pussy gush.

Juice, he picks up on his fingers once he hikes the dress over my ass and reaches around to stroke my smooth lips. "Ahh, so hungry for my cock, aren't you, little bird?" he asks while working the thong down to my knees so he can touch all of me. "Take me deep. Show me how much you need it. How much you love my cock in your mouth."

I hollow out my cheeks and press my tongue firmly against the underside of his shaft, clenching around him the way my pussy would. "Oh, fuck, yes. You're such a good girl when you're being naughty." His breathless grunts make my pussy ache painfully for him. This isn't enough. I need him inside me. "The driver's right there… Do you think he can hear us? Hear you struggling to take my cock in your perfect mouth?" His filthy mouth only turns me on more.

A couple of minutes ago, I almost froze in surprise at the idea of this.

Now, I release his dick in favor of discarding my thong, letting it fall to the floor. He doesn't say a word as I straddle him and take his rock-hard dick in my hand, guiding it to my entrance. I barely bite back a cry of pure bliss once he's inside me, as I lower myself and swallow him whole, all the way down to his balls.

Neither of us says a word. It's enough just to stare into each other's eyes as he grips my ass and pumps me up and down his shaft. *Hard. Fast.* I can't hold back the cries building in my throat no matter how I bite my lip and struggle against them.

"Careful little bird, you don't want the driver to hear how well you take my cock in that tight little hole of yours do you? How fucking good it feels to be on my dick?" I'm drowning in pleasure, the tension threatening to rip me to pieces.

Callum smirks, thankfully taking mercy on me as he clamps a hand over my mouth, watching my struggle, knowing how badly I need this "Scream little bird, let him know how good I make you feel and the sounds you make as you crumble on my dick knowing the only man who will ever get to be inside of you is me. Mine. Forever."

I do as he says. I can't help it. It's all too much, too good, and I let out a hollow scream against his hand showing him just what he does to me. I don't care about the driver, or that he might do just as Callum said later on. I scream as I come again while my whole world shatters into a million pieces that shimmer like glass. He uses me, making me take his cock faster and harder. I can tell he's close just by the heavy pants and how tightly he holds me to his chest, keeping me in place.

"God, it's so good! Such a tight pussy, my fucking pussy. With only my cum dripping out of it. Fuck, I'm coming!!" He growls, against my heated skin, filling me with his hot seed until I can feel it dripping out around his cock and down his base and onto his balls.

My body goes limp against his while we fight to catch our breath. His soft chuckle against my ear makes me lift my head to find him grinning. "And you were so shy about doing it," he teases.

I swat playfully at his chest before carefully climbing out of his lap. "It's all your fault. You're a bad influence on me."

"I would like to be a bad influence again once we're home." A glance out the window tells me it won't be long before that happens.

"Don't you have work to do when we get back?" I ask as we straighten ourselves out.

"No. Tonight's about you. Work can wait until tomorrow."

"I LIKE THE SOUND OF THAT." I wink.

"How about I run us a bath when we get home?" Callum holds me snugly to his side, like he's afraid I'll slip away if he doesn't.

"Yes! That sounds amazing."

Actually, it sounds heavenly. That's the one thing we've missed:

spending time together, just the two of us. Sure, there's the sex, which is amazingly earth-shattering and only ever seems to get better. I didn't know until now, though, what I truly craved was a night spent sharing dinner, a little impromptu dancing, and a hot bath together.

Although the sex was a big bonus.

Nobody would believe how much fun he is to spend time with. How funny he is, at least when he's relaxed, without the burden of work and the dangers involved weighing on him. I'm sure when people see us together—like the waitress at the restaurant, who at least did her best to hide it—they see a wealthy, middle-aged man and a much younger girl and immediately jump to all the wrong conclusions. They probably think there's no way for us to find any common ground with such a big age difference. And I'm sure the term *gold digger* gets thrown around.

They don't get it, and they never will. Not unless they find themselves in a similar situation, falling in love with a man who's wrong for them in so many ways that go beyond age and class. Callum's right for me in so many other ways, in all the ways that count, and he always wants what's best for me.

It's not a long drive back to the house, though I do sort of wish the driver had taken the long way. I want to stay in this happy little bubble for as long as possible.

After that fluke thunderstorm we had last week, it seems like Mother Nature is finally getting her act together. There's a slight chill in the air by the time we exit the car in the front courtyard, and I take a deep breath, savoring the crispness that signals the approach of the fall weather. "I can't wait for Christmas," I confess as we walk hand in hand through the front door.

"Why is that?"

"Well, one, I can't wait to decorate the house, and two cookies."

"It's funny that you mentioned that. I haven't really gone all out in years, not like the way I used to when you girls were younger." Yes, I remember when Tatum invited me to a

Christmas party here. We were ten or eleven. The house was decorated, like something out of a dream, with giant trees in every room, and lights strung up everywhere, the whole nine yards.

"I always remember that when I think of Christmas. We should do it again."

"We absolutely will. Whatever makes you happy." He places a kiss on my forehead as we enter the front hall. "Besides, after this year, we'll have a little one to decorate for." And I swear a happy tingle runs through me at the thought. I can hardly wait to see Callum holding a baby in his arms.

I come to a stop, forcing him to halt along with me, then take him by the lapels of his suit jacket and pull him in for a kiss. "Thank you."

"For what?"

"For giving me everything I ever wanted."

We're both startled when the door leading to Tatum's wing opens. Right away, I let go of Callum, even taking a step back. I don't know why that's my immediate reaction, but I can only guess at some lingering guilt. Tatum says she's okay with us being together, but that doesn't mean I want to rub it in her face.

It's not Tatum who emerges, and a glance at Callum reveals his frown of confusion. "Is everything alright?" he asks Romero, who stops dead in his tracks at the sight of us.

"Oh, yes. She's fine."

A question is on the tip of my tongue… are they? No, Tatum would tell me, but then why is he coming from her wing dressed in a t-shirt and sweatpants?

"It's not what it looks like. I only wanted to check on her," he explains.

I get this strange rumbling feeling in my stomach. Something's off here. "You know what? I'm going to check in on her," I tell Callum. "I'll be up in a little bit."

"Tell her I said goodnight." Callum starts up the stairs without another word. Usually, he'd go straight to his office, so he really does plan to take the night off.

Romero's still standing in the doorway as I approach. "Okay. Tell me the truth. How is she, really? Because I swear, I can't get a straight answer out of her no matter how hard I try."

He looks back over his shoulder toward her bedroom. Romero's known for his lack of emotion and feelings, yet I can see the concern etched into his features like stone. "She's been having nightmares."

I sigh, leaning against the door frame. "Of course she has been. Who wouldn't?" I've had more than my share of them in the past few weeks.

"I happened to check in a few nights ago, when Sheryl asked me to take her some tea to help her sleep," he explains. "I would've been on my way to my place otherwise. I'm glad things played out the way they did, or she would've been alone. She was sobbing in her sleep and let out a horrid scream when I woke her up."

"Jesus." And here I am, floating on Cloud Nine while she's suffering, slowly drowning in a pool of trauma.

"She doesn't want anybody to know. Not you, not Callum."

"I guess that would explain why she never told me, but I feel like she never tells me anything anymore." I frown, hating that I admitted such a thing to Romero.

"I've been sleeping in her office the past few nights," he confesses. "I'd rather you not tell Callum, please. I don't want him to get the wrong idea. He'd rip my balls off and shove them down my throat if he thought… "

"But he should know," I insist. "He needs to know. She's being so damn stubborn. How are we supposed to help her if she won't let us?"

"I don't have a clue." He runs a hand over his dark hair, sighing as he does. I get the feeling he cares more than he wants to let on. Maybe he feels sorry for her. Maybe if I wasn't here, Callum would have more time to put into helping her.

I can't do that to myself, but I can't help it, either.

"I'll go in and say goodnight," I offer. "Get a feel for how she's doing." Relief flashes in his eyes, and he nods, like he wanted to do that but knew better. While things have eased up between them—she's not ripping his head off the way she used to—there's never any telling with her. I've never seen anybody's mood change as quickly as hers does.

She's watching something on her laptop when I ease the door open, sitting with her back to the headboard. "Hey. Sorry if I'm interrupting."

She rolls her eyes and waves me in. "Another true crime documentary. I'm, like, addicted to them now. Women getting revenge."

"We should watch something together, in the living room. I'm not doing anything tomorrow."

Lifting a shoulder, she turns her attention back to the screen. "I feel more comfortable here."

The impulse to argue with her leaves me biting my tongue. I don't want to fight, and that's exactly what we'll end up doing if I push any harder. This room is becoming her tomb, full of used dishes. At least her hair looks like it's been washed recently, which is a step up, and she's wearing clean pajamas. Small miracles.

I wish I knew why she's so against talking to a doctor.

I also wish I knew why she insists on having the sapphire blue urn on her nightstand. She catches me looking at it. "It's pretty," she murmurs. "And her ashes make me feel… safer, somehow."

Her mother's ashes make her feel safer? If only I could understand where her head is right now.

"I'm glad you have them," I venture, crossing the room so I can sit on the edge of the bed. It occurs to me that maybe I should've changed before I came in here rather than walking around in a dress that cost more than I used to pay in a month's rent when I was living with Lucas.

"It's sad. She didn't even get a funeral or a service or anything.

They just took her body to the funeral home, and she was cremated by some shady guy who was paid under the table."

I doubt she had anybody in her life willing to attend a service. Tatum, maybe. I would've gone with her for support. Otherwise?

Still, memorials, funerals, celebrations of life, they're a sense of closure for the living and that's something she'll never get. "I could always put something together for her. Maybe scatter a handful of her ashes somewhere she loved to go."

Tatum snorts, "Like I would know where that is. She never told me anything about herself. I don't even know why I care so much. It's not like she cared about me."

"She was your mom, babe. I'd be worried if you didn't care." I place a hand on her shoulder.

"I know she got what she deserved." She wraps her arms around herself—jeez, she's so thin, she needs to eat more—before hitting me with a knowing, almost angry look. "And before you tell me one more time to talk to a professional, how am I supposed to talk about any of this? Gee, doc, my mom set it up so my best friend would get kidnapped. She wanted to ruin my father's life and help his enemy take control of his illegal businesses. Only she had her brains blown out, instead. Oh, and surprise, she couldn't even have a funeral because the whole damn thing needs to be kept a secret."

Okay, when she puts it that way, I can see why she's hesitant to talk with a doctor. "Okay, so you don't have to talk specifically about that," I murmur while a narrator drones on about the details of a grisly murder. "But you should at least talk about Kristoff and what happened in Europe. I'm not saying to go into specifics about how your mom died, either. You can talk about, you know, how strained your relationship was and—"

"Look, I get it. Okay? You don't have to beat a dead horse."

"I wasn't trying to." I've already pushed too hard. Damn it. There is no winning with her.

Her gaze flicks over my dress. "Did you have a good time tonight?"

"Yes, we went to dinner." I smile, though it feels strangely awkward to be doing so.

"That's good. It must have been a nice place if you're so dressed up."

"Your dad bought the place out for the night to ensure nobody else was there. Can't take any chances."

"No, you wouldn't want to do that. Not with the baby and everything."

I want to crawl out of my skin, I'm so uncomfortable. On the surface, there's nothing wrong with what she's saying, but I know her too well to be fooled. There's resentment dripping from every word; all I want to do is tell her I'm sorry. I'm not even sure what I'm sorry for or what it is that's really bothering her. Is it the baby on the way, the fact that I happen to be the baby's mother? The fact that I'm happy while she's sinking lower and lower? Maybe all of it combined.

I'm sure she wouldn't give me a straight answer even if I asked. I would have to be brave enough to ask first, which I'm definitely not. Not even close.

"Do you want to have a girls' day maybe tomorrow?" I probably know the answer already, but I have to try. "Maybe we could go shopping."

She cringes, "For baby stuff?"

"I was actually thinking more like clothes, and you know it's been a while since I went to the bookstore."

She nibbles on her bottom lip almost nervously. "I don't know. People and crowds mixed with me don't seem that appealing right now."

"Then we can hang around the house. Whatever makes you comfortable." The air is thick with tension, and I can feel her pulling away from me, but I don't want to let go. I can't.

"I don't need you hovering over me, all right? I'm just fine here, in my room, not bothering anyone. What's the big deal?"

"There's no big deal," I whisper. "Just, you know, I'm here. And I want to see you and spend time with you. I love you. You know that, right?"

Her head bobs up and down, only there's no light in her eyes when she finally looks at me. "I know. I love you, too."

Right now, that's probably as good as it's going to get. "Okay. I'm going to go to bed. I'll see you tomorrow."

"You know where to find me." I want to say something else—anything, so long as we don't leave things like this. But the moment is over too soon. She turns up the volume on the laptop, drowning out whatever I was wanting to say.

What bothers me the most as I leave the room, closing the door on her misery, is knowing I would've sailed straight up the stairs with Callum and not thought about her at all if it hadn't been for Romero popping up.

I can't blame her if she does hate me, but I also can't help her if she doesn't want me to, either. It's a double-edged sword piercing me through the heart whenever I think about her.

CALLUM

"We have to decide how you want to divide the Moroni businesses—if we do it at all."

"What do you mean, *if?*"

Romero looks up from his tablet, blinking fast like he's surprised. "If we divide up the businesses. What's wrong with my choice of words?"

"It's the uncertainty you're expressing."

His jaw ticks before he murmurs, "When. When we do it."

"We'll work it out." Checking the time leads me to shrug into my jacket. "Right now, I have an appointment with the doctor for Bianca."

I can't help gritting my teeth when he follows me out of the office, pecking at me like a fucking hen. "Costello will want an answer before he moves forward with tracking Moroni down. How much can we expect him to do without any idea of what he's getting out of this?"

My irritation only grows with every word that comes out of his mouth. This is supposed to be a good day. A chance to be happy for a few minutes, to look into the future and see every possibility, yet all I can think about is Jack Moroni.

Stopping, I turn to him. He falls back half a step like there's something in my expression that's startled him. "Work out the bottom third of his money makers. That's what goes to Costello."

"If he wants more?"

"That's why we're starting with a third. I'm willing to go up to a half, although that's my final offer." With that, I continue to the stairs and call up., "Bianca! We're going to be late."

"I'm right here." She's shaking her head and rolling her eyes on her way out of the kitchen. "Honestly, you act like I'm a lazy kid, sleeping in on a school day."

"You're certainly a smartass." I extend a hand which she quickly takes in hers, but it's Romero she glances toward. A look his way offers no answers. His expression is unreadable. "What am I missing?"

"Hmm?" Bianca's gaze snaps my way, her eyes wide. "Oh. Nothing. Everything's fine." It doesn't seem that way. It seems a hell of a lot like I'm the only one not in on a joke—though nobody's smiling, so it can't be good.

"It doesn't look that way from where I'm standing."

"We're going to be late, like you said." She tugs on my arm and I follow, shooting another look at Romero. I don't appreciate the sense that secrets are being kept from me. Romero wouldn't... no. He wouldn't dare. Anybody but him.

"What am I missing with the two of you?" I ask as we walk to the waiting car.

"It's nothing." She won't look up from the flats she's wearing, avoiding my gaze as she slides into the back seat.

It's nothing.

She couldn't have chosen a worse response if she had tried. *It's nothing* is the first step down a dark, twisted path. By the time I slide in beside her, I'm seething, prepared to grill her for answers. To hell with growth and trying to be a better man for her sake. This is what trying to be a better man gets you. You end up watching the person you love pull away from you, your love dying a slow and painful death.

Once I sit, though, I notice how she keeps her face turned away from me, she sniffles, and that sound alone makes the heat in my chest cool a few degrees. "What's really happening? What's with the secrecy? I thought we were past that point."

"I'm sorry." She wipes under her eyes, sighing before turning my way. "I'm not trying to be secretive, I'm not. It's just I don't know what to do."

"About what? Don't you know by now you don't need to go through things by yourself? That's why I'm here. Whatever it is, we'll find a way through it."

She blows out a long breath, puffing her cheeks. "Last night. You were wondering why I felt sort of bad after I came upstairs."

She's putting it mildly. She came upstairs a different person from the one I had dinner with. The girl whose hand I held as we walked into the house sparkled with optimism and dreams for the future. By the time she stepped into the bathroom, where I'd run a bubble bath for the two of us, the light was gone. The sparkle. It was apparent she fought to hide what she was feeling, but the damage had already been done. No amount of questioning—gentle, always—got me anywhere.

"You're ready to tell me about it?"

"Don't get on my case, please. I feel bad enough as it is." With another sigh, she looks me in the eye. "I think Tatum's upset about the baby, and she's pushing me away. Also, it's really creepy the way she spends all day sitting next to that urn. I'm sorry, but it's how I feel. And I'm worried about her."

She folds her arms, staring at her lap. "And then I told her we could spend time together today, but instead, we're taking this last-minute trip to the doctor. Yet another reason for her to resent me."

"I doubt she resents you. That's not how she operates."

"It's not how she *used* to operate. Nothing about her is the same as it used to be, except for how stubborn and pigheaded she is. I went in to see her, and she was distant and sort of cold. Here we are, happy and hopeful, and she's…"

She is unwilling to get help. That's the problem. "I'll talk to her."

"You've already tried. I don't think anything you say to her will be enough."

I know it isn't. I also know she refused to speak to the therapist I brought in last week and then refused to speak to me for five days afterward. I received a chilly *hey* yesterday, which sadly was a step up.

"You can't put this on yourself," I remind her as gently and kindly as I can. She doesn't need to be upset, not when she's already had more than enough reason to be. What she needs now is peace, protection. There's no choice but to swallow back the burning impulse to take control, which I know by now would only make things immeasurably worse.

"I can't help it. She's been a sister to me all these years. I want…" A tiny laugh bursts out of her. "I want to be excited over the baby without feeling guilty, but I can't because every time I look at her I feel like I'm rubbing that joy in her face."

Taking one of her soft, smooth hands between mine, I murmur, "You can't control anyone else's reactions. You can only give them space and time to adjust to change."

She quirks an eyebrow. "Listen to you. Did you hand in your criminal degree and go to school to be a shrink overnight?"

"I might have had a chat with the doctor, myself. In hopes of learning how to handle this all. I want to be supportive and help Tatum, but you can't help someone who doesn't want to help themselves."

Finally, she leans against me, and I stroke her hair. "I feel bad for being happy."

"In her heart, she wouldn't want that. I know it. I'm sure you do, too."

"I guess I do," she admits. "Still, it's hard because I see how sad she is, and how happy I am, so it just doesn't feel right."

"I understand, only let's try to focus on what a good day this should be. We get to see the baby, and maybe if we're lucky, we can find out if it's a boy or a girl?"

Bianca frowns, "I'm sorry, but I think it's still too early for that. Without a blood test, at least. I was looking it up online."

"Either way. I want to ensure everything's where it needs to be and that you're healthy. In time Tatum will come around." Now I'm talking out of my ass, because the fact is I can't guarantee that. I don't know what it will take to make my daughter happy again.

"This doesn't look like a doctor's office," Bianca points out when we pull to a stop in front of a small, nondescript building that could easily go unnoticed if someone wasn't looking for it. The rest of the office complex was once a part of what was torn down years ago, with only this single structure remaining.

"He works alone," I explain. "And he only sees a few private patients."

She looks at me, understanding dawning on her. "Is he some sort of shady doctor you pay off? Is that where we're going?"

"He's not shady. I trust him," I counter. "He's never steered me wrong, and he specializes in obstetrics. You'll be in good hands—I would never let anyone touch you if I didn't trust them. You know that, right?"

"Of course." Still, it does nothing to erase the anxiety in her features. What I don't want to mention, what I would rather not burden her with, is I'd rather not take her somewhere we could be spotted. Somewhere Jack might be able to pay off some dipshit nurse for Bianca's records. Is it likely that would happen? Probably not, but it is a possibility.

"Come in, come in." Doctor Oscar waves us into the small, outdated waiting room with paneled walls and faded carpet. Do I not pay him enough to renovate? After introducing himself and shaking Bianca's hand, he says, "I understand you're here for an ultrasound today, Bianca."

"That's what I've been told," Bianca jokes with a nervous laugh. True, this was my idea, but I hate seeing her so nervous.

He offers a grandfatherly chuckle that matches his general appearance and demeanor before patting her shoulder. "You'll be just fine. Nothing wrong with making sure everybody's healthy. Callum here wouldn't be the first father who wanted a little extra peace of mind."

We end up in a typical exam room: white walls, a tiled floor, a table complete with stirrups, and an overhead light. The machinery beside the table is, I assume, what will be used for the ultrasound. It's clear the money he hasn't put into renovations has gone to equipment, and I can't pretend to disapprove. The room might be cramped, but my little bird will receive good care and that's all that matters.

He gestures to the folded gown waiting at the foot of the table. "Take your time and make yourself comfortable. I'll need you to strip from the waist down, and you can use the gown for modesty. There's also a sheet you can drape over your legs."

"Thank you." She eyes me, but I shake my head. I'm not leaving her alone in here. Not with her looking so jittery and shifting her weight from one foot to the other while her gaze bounces over the instruction posters on the walls. The typical sort of thing you'd find in the doctor's office—anatomy and the like, this time focused on fetal development and the mother's health.

Is she overwhelmed? Still feeling touchy after the conversation with Tatum? No matter the reason, I'm staying with her. The doctor seems to get the hint, offering a small smile before stepping outside and closing the door. He can play the benevolent doctor all he wants, but he knows who pays his bills and keeps him in this office after his penchant for writing scripts for cash got him in trouble.

Once we're alone, she lets out a shaky breath. "I don't know why I'm so nervous," she confesses with a soft laugh, wringing her hands together.

"You're going to be fine. This is more for my peace of mind than anything. I know they said you were doing okay at the hospital, but I would like to be sure. And hey, we still don't have a due date."

"That's true." She goes through the motions of removing her shoes and leggings, then her thong. Once she's seated with the gown covering her, she stares down at her lap and fidgets, picking at her nails.

"Hey. Is there something you're not telling me? Some reason why you're so nervous?" I brace myself, expecting her to tell me she's been cramping or bleeding and didn't want to worry me. It would kill me to lose this baby, but I wouldn't be surprised with all the stress and trauma she's endured, either.

"I don't know. I'm anxious, I guess. I still feel guilty. And I'm afraid all our dreams will be for nothing if we get bad news here."

"We aren't going to." Standing in front of her, between her knees, I slip my hands beneath the sheet draped over them. "Take a deep breath. It's time to start expecting the best instead of the worst. All of that shit is behind us now."

"You're probably right." She won't look at me, though, her voice detached.

"How can I help? What can I do to relax you?"

"I wish there was something. I really do." The worry lines between her brows deepen when she glances toward the equipment that will soon be used. "What if there's something wrong?"

"There won't be." No amount of reassurance will fix this, that much is obvious. What else can I do to ease her nerves? Strange, the things that come into a man's head at a time like this.

"What are you doing?" She stares at me with mixed surprise and horror as I press her back, lowering her against the table.

"Shh." I hold a finger to my lips while placing her feet in the stirrups with the other hand. With her ass at the table's edge and her legs spread open on either side, I have a full view of her pretty pink pussy. "I'm going to need you to be real quiet for me, little bird. Can you do that? We don't want the doctor to come rushing in, now do we?"

"Callum... what are you doing?" she whispers, trying to sit up before I firmly lower her again.

"Making you relax." As I speak, I circle her clit with my thumb. "Just lie back, relax, and let me make you feel good.

"Callum, we can't do this." She arches her back slightly. "Oh god, this is insane."

"Your cunt is dripping—It doesn't seem like you think it's all that insane." And the aroma of her arousal draws me closer, making me pull over the doctor's stool to position myself between her thighs. I stare in awe, my mouth watering. I can't wait to feast on her. "I might need to buy something like this for the house," I muse, pressing a finger into her tight channel. I watch it disappear, pumping it in and out slowly. "A table like this, with stirrups, and a stool I can sit on. It would mean fewer stiff necks for me."

"So do that... but we should stop this..."

I begin to rub at her g-spot, and she can barely stifle the moan threatening to rip from her throat. "Are you sure about that?" I whisper while my cock twitches and strains against my zipper. What I wouldn't give to sink it deep inside her now. I doubt there's time for that, and besides, she's about to have an exam. The doctor will look the other way on a lot of shit, but I assume even he has his limits. Though, limits and boundaries were made to be broken.

"This is wrong," she insists, even as she rocks her hips back and forth fucking herself on my finger. "We shouldn't."

Her protests go silent the second my tongue sweeps over her clit. It doesn't matter if this is right or wrong when I can make everything else go away simply by touching and licking her. I add a second finger that's quickly coated in her sweet nectar, and slowly work her G-spot while my tongue moves in circles over the tip of her clit. If only I could torture her like this for hours, drawing it out, taking her to the brink and pulling back until she weeps for relief.

"My God... oh, my God..." She tosses her head from side to side and grips the edge of the table. She's the picture of abandon—my wanton goddess, always ready to accept the pleasure I want so much to give her.

"Such a dirty girl," I whisper, chuckling at her strained whimpers. "My dirty girl. It's good to know you have a thing for doing it in public, or is it just that you love being spread wide open, giving me access to lick your tiny clit, and finger-fuck your pussy whenever I please."

"Lick my clit," she begs, tilting her hips like she's offering it to me. "Please. Lick it until I come, and don't stop."

"Are you going to come? Fuck you're such a bad girl. Spray that sweet nectar of yours all over my tongue. I want your juices dripping down my chin," I growl against her folds and lick her from ass to pussy and back again.

There's a brief knock at the door followed by the squeak of hinges that makes her jump like she's been given a shock. I lift my head and bark, "Walk in here, and I'll fucking kill you right now." The door closes without the doctor saying a word.

"Callum." Whatever else she was about to say is swallowed by a moan when I return my attention to her clit, now sucking while pumping my fingers faster until the wet, sloppy sound of her arousal fills the room. *Fuck, her pussy is perfection.* Her body tightens, and her channel clenches around my fingers, squeezing me so tightly I wish it was my cock she was strangling. She lets out a soft sigh, her body going limp, teeth sunk into her lip to hold back her euphoric cries. My fingers are a dripping mess once I pull them free, and I bring them to my lips, licking them greedily before sucking all the juice she left on them.

"There." I stand, satisfied to look down at her limp, boneless body. "Now you're nice and relaxed, aren't you?"

"Mmm..." Her eyes open slowly. They twinkle, and I love the post-orgasmic look that fills them. "You're a very bad man threatening the doctor like that."

"Tell me something I don't know. All that mattered was I got to finish eating you out." While she sits up and straightens herself up, I wash my hands at the sink in the corner. Once she's ready, I open the door and call the doctor in.

He's noticeably embarrassed, avoiding eye contact with me and hurrying through the process of asking questions while I watch from Bianca's side. He makes a note of her answers—the details of her cycle, the fact that she hasn't had any cramping or spotting—before giving her a brief exam.

"Now, for the fun part." He wheels away from the table and turns on the ultrasound machine before squirting gel across her stomach. She's tense again, her mouth almost disappearing when she draws it into a thin line.

The touch of my hand against her hair makes her turn her gaze my way. *Relax*, I mouth with a smile. She nods, eyes wide. It looks like I'm asking for the impossible.

"Alright, Bianca. Let's see what we have here, shall we?" The doctor places the wand on her stomach, moving it back and forth across her gel-covered skin.

"Is that it?" she whispers when an image appears on the screen. I've seen this sort of thing in countless movies, TV shows. But this is real. This is my baby in front of me. Our baby.

"There's the baby," the doctor tells her while she grabs my hand. "Say hello."

"Hello, little baby." She practically glows with wonder, awe, hope. "Hi, there. I love you." She giggles softly as a tear rolls down her cheek.

"Does everything look okay?" I ask.

"Everything looks wonderful," he confirms. "According to what I'm seeing here, which aligns with the information Bianca's given me about her cycle, it looks like you'll welcome your bundle of joy within the first week of March."

"So everything is good?" The eagerness and relief in her voice is touching. She looks up at me, giggling softly, her eyes shining.

"Baby is developing well, and you're in great health. I'm very pleased with what I'm seeing here."

She squeezes my hand tight. "Thank you. That is a huge relief."

"Many first-time mothers go through the same concerns you have. It isn't unusual."

"Wow. March. It seems so far away, but I bet it will be here before we know it." I love the excitement in her voice, how optimistic she sounds. I can't wait to buy out an entire baby store and spoil this kid beyond all reason.

"Time will fly," he promises as he removes the wand from her belly. "I must say, it didn't take any time for you to conceive."

Her joyful expression turns to one of confusion before she looks to the doctor. "What do you mean?"

Fuck me. I know what he's saying, and I have to stop him before he spills the beans.

There's no time before he starts to explain himself. "The fertility shot. It must have worked like a charm if you're already this far along. I'm not really surprised since you're so young and fertile as it is. The shot just gave you an added boost."

"What? What are you talking about?" Bianca's gaze ping-pongs between us and I grit my teeth, rage simmering deep in my gut. I'm staring daggers at the doctor, thinking of all the ways I can murder him right now, when in reality the only person I have to blame is me.

BIANCA

I'm confused, and I'm sure Callum can see that as I look between him and the doctor seeking an explanation. He can't be thinking of the right patient. He's an old man. I wouldn't be surprised if he got his patients mixed up constantly.

Then why does Callum trust him if he can so easily get things mixed up?

The puzzle pieces start to click into place. The way Callum glares at him, like he's envisioning murdering him a million different ways. I've seen that look before.

Still, it doesn't make sense...

Fertility shot.

I got pregnant while on the pill.

Callum didn't seem surprised or shocked about the pregnancy.

Slowly, I slide my hand out of his grip and fold my arms across my chest, looking at the screen instead of him. *It's not possible, is it?* He wouldn't. He couldn't. Not to me. Not when we were supposed to have turned over a new leaf together. We're supposed to be honest with each other now. I'm supposed to be able to trust him.

He wouldn't go behind my back and try to get me pregnant on purpose, would he?

The doctor seems unaware of Callum's shift in mood, too busy turning off the machine before wiping the gel from my stomach. "I'll leave you alone so you can get dressed, and if you have any questions, I'm happy to answer them."

I mutter something—exactly what, I don't know. I can't hear myself think over the roaring emotions in my head. Here I was, blaming myself. So sure that he would hate me for getting pregnant, like he'd think I was trying to trap him. When all this time, he was trying to trap me.

I can't move at first, even after the door closes, and we're left alone again. I can't bring myself to look at him, either. I stare at the ceiling with its white tiles, frozen in confusion and pain. Not physical pain, although it might as well be. It feels like a fist is tightening around my heart, squeezing the life out of it.

The fact that Callum hasn't said anything, hasn't denied any wrongdoing only confirms fears. I struggle to suck air into my lungs; each breath comes heavier than the next. I was bubbling with excitement moments ago; now, all I feel is razor-hot pain. His gaze penetrates my skin right into the deep depths of my soul. He's watching me, yet I refuse to look at him. I can't.

"I want you to tell me something," My voice is a low whisper. "I want the truth. I don't want an explanation. I don't want a lie mixed with the truth. I want the fucking truth!" I release a breath and continue, "Did you tamper with my birth control so I would get pregnant?"

Silence. It drags on for what seems like an eternity. The longer he makes me wait, the worse it is. I don't even need to hear him admit it, for his silence is the biggest answer. However, I want him to say it. Tears fill my eyes and spill over my lashes while every second stretches like taffy, on and on.

"Let me explain."

"I did not ask you for an explanation," I whisper harshly. "I asked for the truth. *Yes or no.*"

His defeated sigh says everything. "Yes."

"Get out of the room. I want to be alone."

"Bianca—"

"I do not want to be around you right now!! Respect me enough to give me a few moments alone since you couldn't respect me enough to allow me to make a choice regarding my own body." I don't care if it hurts him. In fact, I wouldn't be upset if it did. Not after what he's done.

He hesitates, lingering like he's waiting for me to change my mind. That's not going to happen. It takes a slow count to ten, with me staring at the ceiling because I refuse to look at him right now, before he crosses the small room in a few steps and opens the door. He stays for a second longer, like he's considering what to say, but when I turn my face toward the wall, he walks out.

Immediately I cover my face with my hands and start to cry. He tricked me. Now, that word doesn't begin to cover it. *He lied. He manipulated me.* All so he could get what he wanted. It's not like he didn't tell me his plans to get me pregnant right away, but I didn't believe he would go to these lengths. I couldn't have made this up in my head if I tried.

How could he? He's supposed to love me. You don't trick the person you love. You don't tamper with their birth control to get what you want. That's not love.

But he got what he wanted. I'm pregnant with his child. What am I supposed to do now?

That's the worst question of all, the one that leaves me choking on my tears. I'm sure he's out there, listening, and I don't want him to hear. The idea of keeping a bit of my pride seems important. He's already taken my choices from me, so I won't let him take my pride away, too.

What do I do?

Lowering my hands, I sit up, then pull myself together. I have to think of the baby, first and foremost. What's best for it? After that, what's best for me? How do I live with this man, knowing what he's willing to do to get what he wants? It didn't matter to him that I had a life and goals of my own.

Were they really goals?

I shake my head at myself as I pull on my leggings. No, it's true, I was only living the life I thought I had to live. Getting the degree, the job, all of it. Still, if I wanted to change things. That should have been my decision. I should have had a choice. I shake my head with frustration. He's waiting for me out there, and soon enough, I will have to get in a car and go home with him. *What happens, then? What's my move?*

What's best for the baby? Because, in the end, that's what I have to focus on now.

On one hand, he's not the man he used to be. That much, I believe. The Callum I first fell in love with wasn't the man capable of going behind my back, messing with my pills somehow, or even giving me a shot. When did it happen? I guess it doesn't matter now.

Yes, he's changed since then, or he's trying to, but that's not an excuse for fucked up behavior. That's not enough to get me to forgive him or even trust him again immediately.

Do I still love him? That much I don't need to think about. If anything, this wouldn't hurt so much if I *didn't* love him. I can't imagine life without him. Even now.

Which means I need to find a way to get through this and somehow find it in me to forgive him. That's not going to happen today, however.

In fact, nothing has to happen today. I need time. To think this over and figure out what to do next. How I'm supposed to live with this man—who I still love—and be able to look at myself in the mirror every day.

First things first. Leaving this room and facing him. *Mom, please, if you're up there. Help me. Tell me what to do.* I don't expect an answer, obviously, but thinking of her is what gives me the strength to open the door and face the man waiting for me.

At least he looks remorseful. Actually, he seems downright distraught, with his hair mussed like he's been running his fingers through it, the pain hovering around his eyes, bracketing the corners of his mouth.

Here I am, knowing he betrayed me, and my first impulse is to comfort him. *I must be out of my damn mind.* The man tricked me into getting pregnant, and I want to comfort him. It's almost too twisted. I should want to scratch his eyes out, kick him in the balls, something that would make him regret even thinking about betraying me. But no, I want to smooth down his hair and cup the back of his neck while he rests his head against my shoulder. I want to tell him everything is going to be okay, when I don't even know if that's true.

"Did you have any questions for the doctor?" he asks as I rush past him on the way to the front door. I notice Doctor Oscar is conveniently nowhere to be found. Did Callum chew him out for letting their little secret slip? I can't even bring myself to ask.

"No," I snap, and push my way through the glass door without bothering to hold it for Callum, then walk straight to the car and climb inside before the driver has the chance to help me.

I'm tired of waiting for people to help me. I'm tired of many things I've gone along with to keep from rocking the boat. All it took was knowing how much of my life has been outside my control to see things through different eyes. All this time, I've been grateful to be part of this world and part of Callum's life, but I didn't realize this is my world, too. It's my life, too.

I need to start thinking about what's best for me and the baby instead of acting like I'm so lucky to be worthy enough to ride in a car like this, or to go back to a mansion in a guarded compound. I've been looking at this all wrong for way too long.

Callum slides into the car a few moments later, his body stiff, his features tight. Things couldn't be more different than they were on the way to the doctor's office. Instead of sitting close to him, we're on opposite sides of the back seat by the time the car rolls away from the little building in the middle of nowhere. I guess I shouldn't be surprised that a doctor who works for Callum is willing to be unethical.

"Will you at least speak to me, please?"

I'm almost stunned that he would ask me rather than demand I speak to him. It's obvious he's trying to do better, but better isn't good enough if the secrets of your past are never revealed. *Did he even plan to tell me, or was he going to let me think it was an accident all along?* I can't let this change my mind, but I can at least notice it.

"I have nothing to say to you right now."

"I only wanted—" I glance over at him and give him a glare that causes him to snap his mouth shut. He doesn't need to tell me. I know what he wanted. He wanted proof of what a virile man he is. He wants to see me pregnant—he's practically counting down the days until I start to show.

Either way, I'm not about to have this discussion in front of anyone else. Thankfully he takes the hint, and the rest of the ride passes in silence with me staring out the window the whole time I go through what my future could look like depending on the choice I make today. No more can I act impulsively, running away and hiding from him.

We're past that point of my having to find a way to handle the emotions and feelings I'm experiencing and learn to live with them.

A sense of dread builds in me as we close in on the front gate. Just last night, we came back from dinner talking about the future. There I was, fantasizing about the beautiful Christmases we'll have together. This morning is an entirely different reality, almost as if a bucket of ice water has now been dumped all over my dreams. How could I allow myself to forget that it's not so simple being involved with Callum Torrio. There's always a surprise waiting around the corner.

This latest surprise has me getting out of the car as soon as it stops in front of the house, heading straight inside, and walking up the stairs without so much as a backward glance. I'm not in any hurry—I'm not running, I'm not panicking, but I'm determined. He's not going to change my mind or sweet talk me or even threaten me into compliance now.

I'm his queen, the piece that stands beside him, his equal, and I'll stand for nothing less than that treatment.

"Please, Bianca. We need to talk about this." At least he waits until we're in the bedroom, alone, before he starts begging. "I can explain, and I will if you let me."

"I'm not interested in hearing your explanation, I already know what you'll be saying."

"That's not true."

My blood boils at his dismissal. "You told me you intended to get me pregnant as soon as possible. This isn't advanced physics, Callum. I know what you were doing and where you were coming from. It's as simple as one plus one."

When I go to the closet, grabbing a tote bag to throw a few things inside, he practically jumps on me. "You're not leaving. I won't let you. Not while you're carrying my child, and there are still—"

"You don't need to tell me about the risks and dangers that are out there. I know all about the danger I'm putting myself in from my association with you." He lets out a pained sound that both hurts and strengthens me as I throw clothes and toiletries into the bag.

"Then what are you doing?"

"I'm going to stay in another room away from you." When he refuses to take a step back so I can leave the bathroom after packing my shampoo and such, I slide past him.

"This isn't like you, Bianca. At the very least, allow me to explain myself. We've come so far, don't let this break us."

"I don't want to let you explain. Don't you get that? You saw what you wanted and went behind my back to get it as soon as possible. You wanted a way to keep me here with you, right? You knew if I was pregnant, you would have me under your thumb. That I'd be trapped, forced to stay with you, without another alternative."

"It wasn't as ugly as you're making it sound."

"Yes, it was, but that doesn't matter." Besides, I don't think I'm exaggerating where his head was when he did this. "And until you understand that this is the ultimate betrayal, worse than anything you've ever done to me, there is no chance of us returning to where we were before. I can't keep excusing your actions, because then you'll never stop doing them. I'm not going to let you get away with this so easily. I can't. I need to respect myself at least enough to take a step back and reevaluate the situation."

"That sounds a lot like a woman on the verge of walking out the door."

"You already said it yourself. I don't have a choice except to stay. Even if I wanted to leave, I'd be risking everything. My life, the baby's life. I have to think about my own safety." A bitter laugh slips out of me. "Congratulations. You managed to trap me the way you intended all along."

"Please don't say it like that."

"Why? It's the truth, isn't it?" I growl. "I'm sorry if it hurts you to hear it, although we both know it's true. That's what you wanted. You might not have known at the time how well it would work out, but I guess there's always an upside, right?"

"Bianca. I can't lose you."

"I guess you should've thought about that. I've changed, or maybe you've changed me. Or maybe there's only so far a person can be pushed before they start pushing back." I zip up the bag and throw it over my shoulder, facing him from the opposite side of the bed. I don't think I've ever seen him look so distressed, except maybe when it comes to Tatum. If I didn't know better, I would think he's close to tears.

Only men like Callum Torrio don't cry. I know better than to expect that. They just find another way to manipulate you, to make you think you've won when in reality you've gained nothing.

"I love you. Do you hear me, Bianca? I love you."

"I know you do, but it's going to take me a little time before I can trust you again. And until that happens, I'll be staying in one of the spare rooms down the hall. Please respect my decision, Callum."

I don't bother waiting for a response which I know will only end up being more of the same. The last thing I see before turning away and marching down the hall is Callum, his pale skin, the frantic fear in his eyes, and his beautiful jaw tight with tension. I hate seeing him so upset, but I remind myself with each step how much he deserves this. Nobody has ever deserved this more than he does. He took what should've been a decision belonging to me and decided I didn't get a say.

For once, he's going to understand the consequences of his impulse decisions.

Even if it breaks my heart to teach him that lesson.

CALLUM

*W*arehouse Fire: Three Structures "Total Loss" Says Fire Chief

The headline leaves me grinning in grim satisfaction, a grin that widens once I begin scrolling through the fiery images taken overnight. Damn right, they were a total loss. I'm not playing games here.

Tucking my phone away after perusing the headlines, I head to the kitchen for a fresh coffee. The breathtaking image of flames against the night sky plays at the edges of my memory and warms my heart. I'll be looking through those photos again before the end of the day, no doubt about it. What must Jack have suffered when he realized there was nothing he could do?

How did you like it, you bitch?

My heart stutters on entering the room, lighting me up with hope for a brief moment before I'm disappointed. *No Bianca. No Tatum.* Not that either would speak to me if they saw me. It doesn't mean I can't hope to catch sight of them and maybe exchange a word or two. They'll both come around eventually, Bianca most likely first. I'll lose my fucking mind if she doesn't.

It was one thing to be without her when she was at Charlie's;

when I knew better than to try to approach her. I have no doubt the man would have pulled a gun if I set foot on his front porch. It was my own personal torment, asking myself what she was doing, where she was, or if she was safe.

I don't have to worry about that now, with her here.

It was hard before, but now it's worse. Her proximity means I must concentrate harder than ever to stay away from her. The amount of self-control it took from me last night not to kick in the bedroom door, throw her over my shoulder and bring her back to *our* bed where she belongs, was excruciating. It would've been so easy to tie her down the way I did before– even told myself she liked it and had convinced myself that's what she's trying to get me to do now. That all she wants is for me to assert my dominance the way I did initially.

It's a nice little fantasy, but I couldn't give in the way the old Callum did. Giving into my baser instincts would only make things worse. I need to deal with it like a logical person would, not a psycho, even though my love for Bianca is borderline psychotic. Unfortunately, this means I've hardly slept the past week, but I've had plenty of work to keep me busy.

Moroni is lucky he lost nothing more than a trio of warehouses last night. The time I need to fill, combined with my murderous attitude, could very well leave him with nothing by the time this is over.

"Did you see the headline?" It's the first thing Romero asks when we cross paths on the way to my office. He can't pretend the news didn't thrill him, and I wouldn't ask him to. He may shy away from showing that side of himself, but we both know the beast is lurking right below the surface.

I shake my head, clicking my tongue in mock sorrow. "I did. They're saying it's a total loss."

"Did you confirm the payment went through?"

"I did. Our firebug friend will be pleased."

"He'll be even happier once we move to 'phase two' of the

plan and need him again." Setting my coffee down, I open the document we compiled between us. I can check off step one now, knowing the warehouses have burned to the ground and all the items inside along with them. It's low-level, and I know it won't hit Moroni in the wallet as hard as it will hit his pride. He can afford to lose pallets of stolen goods, electronics, clothing, etc. This was less about money and more about sending a message.

He wants to play dirty? I'm already in the mud, waiting for him.

"I have a few things to discuss with you, but Costello called me directly this morning and fucked my plans." When I look up from the checklist, Romero's wearing a sour expression. I'm used to nothing less when it comes to Sebastian.

I need his shit like I need a hole in the head. "I don't have time for an impromptu meeting. If he's not happy with our offer, he can cry about it while sucking my dick."

"He was fine with that. He said there's been a change in plans—sounded almost manic."

"A change in plans? These aren't *his* plans to change."

"He's probably worked up because those warehouses were supposed to go to him."

"Considering nothing's set in stone, he's crying over spilled milk."

All Romero does is smirk, lifting a shoulder. "You can tell him that when he gets here. I'll stand back and watch."

"He's young and will soon realize it was nothing except a strategic move."

"I agree, but you can be the one who explains that to him. Nothing I say to him will leave much impact."

"Fine, fine." I wave a hand, hardly giving a shit what the kid thinks he's owed. Considering he hasn't done anything yet to earn what he believes should be his, he has zero room to complain. "And we're fully manned, otherwise?"

"We have double the guards on duty at the club, at the restaurant, at the warehouses, and all of them are working six-hour shifts to ensure they're fresh in case something goes down."

It doesn't feel like enough. We knew when we went into this that Moroni would be chomping at the bit to get back at me, however, having men working in shifts at my various businesses doesn't leave me feeling secure. "I'll ask Sebastian to provide additional men to keep an eye on things."

"If he's trying to change plans because he's pissed over what he thinks he's owed, I doubt he'll feel generous.."

"He doesn't have to feel generous. He only has to care about his own self-interest."

Our eyes meet when the phone rings, and we both know who it is without looking. I pick up the phone and tell Henry to let Sebastian through. "I didn't think he meant he was on his way already," Romero mutters, shrugging into his suit jacket.

"He's young and impatient. It's not a surprise." Frankly, I'm glad for it. Every moment I spend without something to occupy my mind is a moment spent in agony. Where is she? What will she do today? Has she commiserated with Tatum yet? For all I know, this could be what brings them back together, something for them to relate over. They can join together in their hatred of me and everything I stand for.

Romero steps out, and I assume he means to greet Sebastian. Instead, he gets no more than a few steps from my doorway before his voice rings out. "This is unusual. Guests don't normally show themselves to Mr. Torrio's office without being greeted first."

"Can we please drop the bullshit?" I look up from my computer in time to see Sebastian shoulder past Romero before marching into my office. Usually, he's the definition of collected, almost annoyingly so, though not today. Today, his eyes glitter like a man who stumbled over a gold mine. Romero's right. He looks as manic as he sounds. "Been here before, and I'm not some beggar looking to kiss the ring."

I sit back, hands folded, sizing him up in a single glance. "You're in quite the mood today. To what do I owe the pleasure of you strolling in here without waiting to be greeted?"

"I'm here to make sure you don't hear chatter and get the wrong idea."

I blink, waiting for more. When he merely stares at me, his shoulders rising and falling as he jogs from the car, I lift my brows. "Care to elaborate?"

"The warehouses. That could only have been a message."

"A message to Moroni. Not to you." Why do I feel like we're speaking two different languages? "Why would I send you a message?"

He blinks rapidly, stammering, color rising in his cheeks. Romero observes all of this from the doorway, frowning in puzzlement. "I thought… I mean, I assumed you heard and wanted to take away part of what you promised me."

I didn't promise a damn thing. It was an offer. This kid still has lessons to learn, but I'm more concerned with what he's hinting at. Lesson time can wait. "What are you talking about? Sit down, for God's sake, and take a breath."

He rakes both hands through his hair before sinking into a chair. "I had planned on telling you, but since he hasn't committed either way…"

"Since who hasn't committed?" The hair on the back of my neck is beginning to lift. I've never enjoyed being the last to know.

"I've been attempting to negotiate a deal." He draws a breath, grimacing. "With Moroni."

"You what?" Romero makes a move for the gun I know is tucked in his waistband. A slight wave of my hand signals him to stand down, which he only does reluctantly.

My blood is simmering, and everything around me begins to go red. "I'm giving you a chance to tell me what you're playing at before you learn what happens to people who go behind my back,"

I murmur, fighting for control over the rush of rage brought about by the mention of the man's name.

"It's not what you're thinking. I have a plan."

"Really. It sounds more like you're double-crossing me."

"If it's a double-cross, he's the one getting fucked." His gaze bounces to Romero like he's looking for support—he might as well try to get blood from a stone. "It's not what you're thinking, I swear. I had planned on sharing this with you, although as I said, he hasn't committed. He's dragging his feet."

"On what?" I grit out.

"I know how to hit Moroni where it will hurt a hell of a lot worse than anything you pulled last night. And when he agrees to my terms, you can have him."

"I'm looking forward to hearing this," Romero announces before closing the door. He's right, of course. I would rather the girls not venture by and overhear any of this. The least I can do is keep them out of it.

Sebastian merely turns to stare at him for a beat before looking my way again. "Dominic isn't Jack's only offspring."

Consider my interest piqued. "He isn't? What, is there a love child tucked away somewhere? Some leverage we can hold over his head?"

"Not quite. They were born out of wedlock, two girls who were one and two, before Jack's wife kicked the bucket."

"He's got two daughters?" I exchange a glance with Romero, who looks gobsmacked. "You knew nothing about this?"

"I'm not in the habit of keeping information from you," he reminds me. To his credit, he doesn't look offended, but I can only imagine it stings to know he missed something this big.

"They're twenty years old and currently living with their mother's family upstate. He rarely ever goes to see them but provides for them financially. Word has it he wants to keep them as far away from his work as possible."

"Sure. I bet it has nothing to do with them being girls rather than sons," I muse. That sort of mentality is far from foreign in our world.

"What do you plan on doing with this information?" Romero questions, lifting an eyebrow.

"I know one of the girls was recently engaged to a kid from an upstanding family. They're in politics on a small scale yet have plans to step things up and have plenty of profitable business interests. They consider themselves the next Kennedy family, and she'll make a good wife for a future senator." His smile spreads slowly. "I think she'd do better married to a man like me."

There's a moment of silence, a long one, and I expect Sebastian to laugh. When he doesn't, I look at Romero and find hesitation in his eyes.

"What are you saying?" he finally asks.

"What does it sound like I'm saying? I'm reaching out to him, offering an alliance in exchange for an arranged marriage with his daughter." Another long pause. Part of me wonders if he's really serious, only the expression he's giving me shows no hint of humor.

"You're serious?"

"I've already booked a room at Niagara Falls," he snickers. "Do people still honeymoon there?"

"Why?" My anger is receding in the face of curiosity and disbelief.

"I have my reasons."

"Not a good enough response," Romero seethes. This time, I don't signal for him to stand down. He crosses the room and comes to a stop beside my desk so we can both glare at the kid.

Sebastian shrugs. "That's as much as I can tell you. I want her. She's going to be mine. And in return, he'll think he's getting my backing. He needs all the help he can get, especially with his warehouses mysteriously going up in flames. You might have inadvertently pushed my plans forward, come to think of it."

"If they're sisters, why not ask for the other one instead?"

"No. That won't work. I don't need my sister-in-law marrying into a political family. If they had ties in our world, then it would be different. I could use that. But they're above that kind of thing." He rolls his eyes. "Trust me. I've done my research."

Something about this isn't clicking for me. It's clear from Romero's pensive expression that he's going through the same process of trying to put things together. "And you said Jack's not going for it? How long have you been working on this?" *Without telling us.* He leaves that part unspoken, though it's hanging over the room.

"Not long. It's been a little over a week since I reached out to him."

Romero grunts his disgust, even as I manage to stay calm. "You should've come to me first."

"That's not how I operate, and it's not how my father operated. I do what I feel is best–and I'm giving you the heads-up out of respect while also making sure you don't think I'm crossing you. I'm as committed as ever to eliminating that bastard, but I want something from him first. Once I get it, you can take whatever you want." Sitting back in the chair, he shrugs. "I don't care."

"You don't want any of the assets we discussed splitting?"

"I wouldn't say no to a nice chunk of cash, but it's the girl I'm most interested in."

Usually, his cavalier attitude is something I chalk up to youth. He wants respect he hasn't yet earned. Except this is a little much. "What is so special about her?"

"That's my business. I didn't come here to be interrogated."

At first, I'm stunned into silence. Never in my wildest dreams would I have spoken that way to someone in my position when I was his age. "Listen, and listen good," I murmur, lowering my tone. "You're in my house now, kid. I was willing to overlook you walking in here like you own the place, but I won't be insulted in my own home."

He holds my gaze, unblinking, until it's clear he gets the message as I glare right back at him.

"If you want to be considered a partner in this, you need to lay all your cards on the table," Romero informs him. The tick in his jaw and the slow, measured rise and fall of his shoulders tell me he is fighting to control himself. "We need to have trust for this to go forward, and right now, you're anything but trustworthy."

"Are you in the habit of letting him speak for you?" Sebastian asks me, jerking a thumb in Romero's direction.

Be calm. Don't take the bait.

"Romero is my second and trusted confidant. He knows what this empire stands for, and he knows the sacrifices that must be made. I think negotiating a deal with Jack is taking things a little too far." I remind him, my voice icy.

Anyone else would be pissing their pants by now. Not this kid. He stands, palms on the desk, leaning down. He wants to loom over me, to overshadow me. To intimidate me. "No, that's the problem here. I don't think I've gone *far enough*. You don't get to burn down shit that you said would be mine without consulting me first, and then tell me how to conduct my business. You want this fucker wiped off the map? So do I. Although, first, I'm going to get what I want."

"And what if he never goes for it?" Romero asks, folding his arms. "He could find a political alliance more beneficial than anything you're offering."

"Not with you burning his shit down. Don't you get it?" He barks out a laugh. "He's going to start getting desperate. He'll want all the help he can get. You just made things easier for me. I can almost feel the wedding band around my finger."

"And once Jack thinks he can use your money and your men to fight us, then what happens?"

He lifts a shoulder. "It'll be a disappointing day for him, won't it? And if he threatens to hurt me for crossing him, I'll remind him of the pretty, soft, luscious girl he handed over to me. It would be a real shame if anything happened to her, wouldn't it?"

"Would you follow through on that?" I murmur, watching him closely.

"By then, she'll be mine," he reminds me with a sigh. "Mine to do whatever I want with."

"And if he never agrees?" I ask even though I know the response.

"Then I'll take her anyway. I'd rather do things properly, with her father's blessing and all." His lips twitch in cold humor. "But desperate times call for desperate measures."

"You can be a fucking psycho on your own," Romero fires back, and Sebastian only blurts out a laugh. I don't approve of the choice of language, yet considering the unhinged note in his laughter, he might not be far off the mark. "But that's not how we do business."

Sebastian looks Romero up and down, wearing a cocky grin. "What are you going to do about it? Come and huff and puff and blow *my* house down this time? Warning you now, it won't end well for you."

"You think? You're so fucking green, your balls have barely dropped," Romero growls. "Mr. Torrio here has gone out of his way to be respectful towards you, but I don't owe you shit."

"You think so?" Sebastian takes a step toward him, shoulders thrown back like the cocky, insolent little prick he is.

Romero mimics his posture, taking a step of his own. "I know so."

"Maybe we should take this outside."

"Nothing would give me more pleasure." Romero slips off his suit jacket, tossing it on the chair Sebastian left vacant. He starts undoing the buttons of his shirt and rolling up the sleeves on his forearms. "I've been thinking for a while now about kicking your ass since clearly you need a lesson in respect."

"Alright, that's enough." Before they can leave the office and do something truly stupid, I step between them. "You're not fighting each other. This isn't a goddamn middle school playground or a pissing contest."

Sebastian snorts, leading me to turn his way. "Don't eyeball me like that," I growl, and it's gratifying to watch him fall back a step instead of glaring at me like he was. It's time to set him straight on a few things—maybe past time. "There's no negotiating. I want nothing to do with bringing innocent girls into this. Dominic is fair game since he's part of the life—same thing with their crew. Nonetheless, we do not involve women or children. End of story."

"That's where we differ."

"Your old man wouldn't have done it this way, either."

Something close to frustration crosses his face before he wipes it away, lifting his chin. "I'm not my old man, am I?" There's a silent challenge in that question. For all his swagger and bravado, what he wants most is to prove himself. It's clear as day.

Behind me, Romero snorts. "That's an understatement."

"Fuck off," Sebastian snarls, lunging forward until the hand I place against his chest holds him still. He might chomp at the bit to take a swing at Romero, but he's not stupid enough to do the same to me. The wild, crazed look in his wide eyes says he might give it a shot, in any case.

"You should've listened better when he tried to teach you," Romero taunts. "Or maybe there was just no getting through your thick fucking skull."

"How thick is your skull?" In a flash, Sebastian pulls out his piece, pointing it at the ceiling while glaring at Romero. "You think it's thick enough to stop a bullet?"

"That's it. Put the fucking gun away and leave. You've said your peace, you have your answers, and now it's time to go." Gripping him by the shoulder, I guide him toward the door, opening it before taking him down the hall. I snap my fingers when I catch sight of a guard at the other end. "You're still welcome here, but not until you calm the hell down. Don't you ever pull a gun in my fucking home again. I'm letting this go one time only out of respect for your late father, however that's as far as my generosity goes. Next time I'll let Romero kill you where you stand."

The guard reaches us, and I give Sebastian a slight shove in his direction. He straightens out his jacket, concealing the gun again. "Take Mr. Costello out to his car."

Sebastian turns and points a finger toward my office. He's trembling with rage that leaves sweat beading at his temples. "I'm going to need an apology from that prick if you expect us to do business together."

It'll be a cold day in hell. "I'll pass on the message." A jerk of my chin gets the men moving, and I watch until they round the corner to the entry hall.

So much for that. If I can't trust an associate, we don't do business. He might still be helpful, but he's coming nowhere near my inner circle unless he makes amends. I will need a gesture of some sort to convince me he's worth trusting.

"Don't start with me," Romero warns without turning to face me when he hears me enter the room. He's standing at the window, watching Sebastian's progress while breathing hard, his fists clenched, shoulders rising and falling quickly.

"Maybe Sebastian isn't the only one who needs to be reminded of who he's speaking to."

He releases a long breath before lowering his head. "And now, do you understand my feelings on that asshole?"

"I always did."

"Do you think he'll go through with it? The girl, I mean?" He glances at me over his shoulder, his eyebrow arched.

"I don't know, but I don't want any part of it. All I'm worried about is making sure it doesn't blow back on us, since he has no idea who he's fucking with. He'll only get so far on his family name." Especially once word starts to spread of how unpredictable he is; nobody wants to do business with a loose cannon. Those types have a way of suddenly disappearing without a trace.

"I'm sorry I lost my cool." He turns away from the window, still scowling, but his fists have loosened.

"That better be the last time I have to keep your brains from getting splattered across this room."

"I'll make a note of it." He rolls his head from side to side, shaking out the tension in his shoulders. "That ignorant kid." An ignorant kid who got under his skin the way I've rarely seen anyone do.

I can't spend the rest of the morning talking about this. We need to get off the subject. "Didn't you say there was something you were planning on discussing this morning?"

His brows draw together in time with the pressing together of his lips. Not that I expected great news, but this doesn't bode well. "Right. It took some digging, but I got one of my contacts in the police department to draw up a list of people they knew were taking money on the side around the time Mrs. Cole was murdered."

I'd think this would brighten his mood. We've been trying to get our hands on names for weeks. "And? Are we looking at a lot of names?"

"A considerable amount," he tells me, pulling out his cell phone and handing the device to me. "Although there's one in particular I thought would interest you. I looked into all of them, and… it's him."

The name might as well be written in bold print. It leaps out at me, carrying the sort of ramifications I hadn't considered until this very minute. My heart sinks as the enormity of the situation becomes clear. *Ken Miller.* "You're sure it's the Ken we know?"

"Positive. I wanted to be sure, so I did some internet searching. It's him." The man her father trusts above all others. A crooked cop. The perverse part of me is almost gleeful, imagining how this would shatter the last of that sanctimonious asshole's illusions.

This isn't about him. Not entirely.

"We can't let her find out," I murmur, handing the phone back. *Why do I feel numb?* "It would crush her."

"Finding out her father's best friend was in on the take?" He sighs, shaking his head. "Damn right, it would. And you know Charlie can't find out about it. They're still friends."

"Right." No way the great white knight would stand for that. As soon as he confronts Ken, it would mark the end of him being useful to us. Hell, Charlie might blow his brains out–he's that unhinged.

"We don't know yet who was paying him, though, so we've got to keep that in mind."

The thing about reaching my position is you don't get there without sharp instincts. Instincts can't be turned on and off at will, especially not when a man doesn't want to face reality.

I have to face the possibility of a time when the last of my little bird's illusions shatter. I hate to imagine being the one to shatter them—but it might be better coming from me, come to think of it.

Not yet, however. I need more information before I can do anything with this. "Let's dig deeper and find out who was paying him."

"Will do." Romero heads to his office while I sit back in my chair and rub my tired eyes, hoping for Bianca's sake that her mother's killer wasn't someone she was supposed to trust.

BIANCA

I honestly didn't think Callum would give me the space I needed. Sure, I asked for it. I physically removed myself from the bedroom. I've gone out of my way to avoid him—sneaking around the house when I know he's busy in his office, basically pulling a Tatum otherwise. I've done a lot of reading and caught up on a lot of shows that I've been meaning to binge. The nights are tough, especially since I've gotten used to sleeping next to him and being alone isn't easy. I doubt it's any easier on him.

It sort of gives me hope, in a way. He's not trying to push himself on me the way he would have done before. There's no begging or forcing. He's not chasing me through the house or seducing me--which I have never, ever been able to fight back against. It's like my Achilles heel, the sexual chemistry between us. Only he hasn't taken advantage of that.

I wish I could believe this means he's genuinely turned over a new leaf, but a big part of me can't help but be suspicious. Is this his way of yessing me to death? Playing along to keep me from walking away for good?

Thank you for being so understanding. I skim the rest of the email to make sure there are no typos, then send it off to my manager.

The fact that I still have a job is a miracle. No, I don't really want it, but that doesn't mean I want to be a total jerk and no-call, no-show. This latest leave of absence would probably get anybody else fired, but everybody seems understanding.

If I didn't know better, I'd think Callum was behind all of this.

Wait. Who am I kidding? I don't know better. I'd bet he called somebody and fixed things for me. The more I think about it, the more obvious it looks. If I had any desire to speak to him right now, I'd march downstairs and tear him a new one for once again interfering where he wasn't invited.

The thing is, I have no desire to speak to him yet. It's been a week, and I still have nothing to say that wouldn't end things immediately. That's not what I want—out of everything, all the confusion and sadness, and even with the sense of betrayal still fresh, I still don't want us to come to an end. I can't live without him.

I just don't know how to be with him right now, that's all. A week of thinking about it hasn't helped anything. I doubt a month would. Our entire relationship has been a puzzle. Why would things change now?

One thing I do know: I need to get out of the house. Acting like a hermit might work for Tatum, but I need something more than the same four walls, or I will start going out of my mind. It can't be healthy for the baby, either, lying around when I don't need to. Sneaking up and down the stairs while listening to make sure Callum isn't nearby. Dreading the *slap slap slap* of his shoes against the hard floor, knowing the second I set eyes on him, I'll want to give in. That's no way to live.

Yet, here I am, refusing to go. No matter how many times I turn the situation around in my mind, I can't get any closer to making sense of it. I should go. This should be the end. Nobody would put up with this sort of shit–and if I was on the outside of this situation and listening to a good friend tell me about the kinds of things I've been through, I might tell her to go. For good.

However, there's a difference between standing on the outside and being on the inside. I understand that better now than I ever did before. I understand *him* and why he does what he does. And damn it, I love him. I can't walk away from somebody I love. Especially when I'm carrying his child.

Yeah, I definitely need to get out of this house. After pulling on a sweater and leggings, I add a pair of sneakers and go to the door to listen for any signs of him. I'm not afraid. That much, I know. He won't hurt me. No, I'm afraid, as I tiptoe down the hall with my heart in my throat, that if I see him, it's over. My anger will melt into a puddle. A puddle I'll slip in and inevitably land in Callum's arms. I get the sense that if I don't hold out and make him understand what he did and why it hurts so much, I'll never get another opportunity again.

The upstairs hall is clear, as is the vast, winding staircase. I remember back when this house felt foreign to me. It took forever to feel comfortable walking around on my own, no matter how many times Tatum told me I could. Compared to where I grew up, this is a palace.

Now, here I am, jogging down the stairs, leaning over the railing occasionally to see if anyone is coming my way. It's ludicrous, and I know it, but that's not enough to stop me. I don't need anybody asking where I'm going and reporting back to Callum. Besides, I'm not sure where I'm going. Away from here, that's all I know for sure.

I reach the bottom of the stairs, and my gait slows a little when I look toward the door leading to Tatum's wing. She used to leave it open sometimes, back when we were younger. Now, it's always closed. She lives in her own world of pain and loneliness. I don't even know if she's up or dressed or anything. I don't even know if she'd want to spend time with me if I asked. How is it that we've drifted so far apart?

When footsteps ring out, I have no choice but to either leave now or risk getting caught up with Callum and probably arguing about whether it's okay for me to go out alone. I'm not trying to take a massive risk. I know better than to parade myself around after what's already happened. That's not going to fly with Callum though, and I know it.

So instead of approaching my best friend and asking her to take a drive with me, I bolt, scurrying outside. It doesn't feel right, running from the house like this, even so, I can't face him now. I'm still too conflicted.

On the other hand... I can't risk anything happening while I'm out on my own. Already my conscience is plaguing me, but it's for the right reasons. There's a guard patrolling nearby, rounding the side of the house and approaching when he finds me standing by my car.

"Nathan?" I call out when I recognize him.

"Everything alright?"

"It's fine. I have to take a drive and wonder if you'd come with me." When he glances toward the front door, I know what he's thinking. "I'm sort of in a hurry. We won't be long, and you're armed. Right?"

"Right." But it looks like he wishes he hadn't found me out here, just the same. Better somebody else get in trouble.

"Come on. I'll drive." When he scowls, I add, "It's been weeks since I had the chance. You can drive back if it makes you feel better... or you can stay here and be the one who lets me go off on my own." Sort of a shitty thing to say? Maybe, but nevertheless, it gets the point across. He rounds the car and slides into the passenger seat while I text Callum to tell him I'm leaving and am not alone.

There's a sense of something close to confusion when I get behind the wheel. It's not like I forgot to drive or anything, yet the last time I did was the last time I went to work. The last time I opened the door, it was with the expectation of going out with my best friend and having dinner.

Instead, I was kidnapped, and from there, it only got worse.

EMPIRE OF PAIN

I shake off my nerves and start the car, pulling out before there's a chance of getting lost in my thoughts. I still don't know where I'm going to go. I only know I love the freedom surrounding me, a freedom that I wasn't aware I had missed so much. I still don't have anyone to talk to, to honestly talk to, but at least I can choose my own adventure for a little while.

At first, it's enough to simply drive with a silent Nathan watching out for any threats beside me. I'm almost amazed at the way the world keeps turning. People are eating their lunches in the park the way I used to do sometimes. Kids riding on bikes, couples holding hands as they go for an afternoon stroll. I wonder how many of them understand how suddenly everything can change. It's almost enough to make me want to shout out the window and tell them to get as much out of the good times as they can.

It's not like my life is inherently bad or anything like that, but I know how it feels to lose. That nauseating shock when everything changes all at once. I've been through enough of that to last me a lifetime.

I don't know if my thoughts guide the car or what, but before I know it, I'm rolling slowly through yet another tall, iron gate. This time, it's not the gate in front of the Torrio compound. This place is much more peaceful and holds more meaning. Nathan only grunts softly as I drive along the wide, gravel road that cuts through the heart of the cemetery.

I can't remember the last time I visited Mom's grave. All I know is that she's the one person I wish more than anything I could talk to at this moment. All my questions and worries about the baby, and myself. About what to do next, and how to build a life with a man willing to go as far as Callum went and will undoubtedly continue to go. I've never wished so hard that I could sit next to her, maybe put my head on her shoulder like I used to, and have a good cry. I'm not little anymore, but I guess we all need to act like little kids sometimes.

It's a beautiful day, full of sunshine and the promise of a stunning autumn around the corner. The sky is so blue it's almost unreal, and there isn't a cloud to mar its perfection. The leaves are still green, but they won't be for long. I'm sure the towering yet graceful trees will burst out into a riot of color in another month or so.

I pull up close to Mom's plot on the south end of the cemetery and step out of the car, noticing the various bits of evidence that plenty of people visit their loved ones more often than I do. Flowers in different stages of decomposition, wreaths, and decorations adore the other headstones. Other graves sport weeds around the base of the gravestones. Some of the plaques in the ground are covered by overgrowth. *Are those people forgotten?* Maybe their loved ones are all dead and gone, too, or perhaps they never had any, to begin with. What a sad thought.

"I'll, uh, wait by the car and keep a lookout," Nathan offers as I start walking toward Mom's grave. He seems even more uncomfortable now than when I strong-armed him into coming with me. Some people don't like cemeteries, I guess. Even big tough guys who carry guns.

My sigh of relief sends birds fluttering from the nearby trees when I find Mom's headstone in good condition. There are dandelions and clumps of overgrown grass around the base, but for the most part it looks alright. I wonder if Dad's been here recently as I drop to one knee and begin pulling the weeds. I feel like I need to do something to prove I care.

Once everything's cleared away and there's nothing to do but sit with my thoughts, I settle back on my heels with my hands folded in my lap.

"Hi, Mom," I whisper, cringing at how awkward this feels. Do people usually speak out loud to their dead loved one's graves? It feels better than doing it in my head, plus there's nobody around to look at me like I'm crazy. "I'm sorry I haven't been here to see you as much as I should," I continue. "I hope you know it's not because I don't think about you. I still do. I think about you all the time. Right now, there's not a day that goes by when I don't think of you and remember who you were and wish you were here. In fact, I think about that now more than ever. With a sigh, I look up, taking in my surroundings. "This is a pretty place. Some of the trees were just saplings back when we first buried you here. I was just a little girl then, right? And now look at me. Your baby is going to have a baby."

A baby she'll never hold. A baby who will never know their grandmother–and Callum's mother has been gone for a long time. He rarely mentions her, but I know his father raised him alone.

Closing my eyes, I try with all my might to imagine Mom as she would look now. There might be gray at her temples, lines at the corners of her eyes, and around her mouth. *No, definitely.* She'd have deep laugh lines after another fifteen years of filling the room with her bawdy laugh. I've never heard anyone laugh quite that way since, with their entire body.

I smile at the memory while a soft breeze stirs the hair at my temples. I can almost make myself believe it's Mom doing it. Like she's brushing my hair back with the tender touch I didn't get to enjoy nearly enough of when she was here. Comforting me the way she was so good at doing when I was younger.

"It's so unfair, and I know life itself isn't fair, but I didn't get enough time with you. I mean, I guess there's no such thing as enough time, really. You could have lived to be eighty years old, and I still would have wanted more time with you. But I feel cheated." The thought tightens my chest until it's hard to breathe. It isn't sadness. It's anger. I'm fucking angry that somebody took her away from me–from us. Dad's never been the same, and only now do I understand why. He didn't just lose his wife. Somebody took her away, and he's spent every day since then clutching me tighter to keep the same thing from happening again.

I reach down, plucking a long blade of grass before trying to remember how to whistle with it. She taught me when I was little, but it's been too long since I've tried. All that comes out is a burst of air, which somehow stirs my anger again. "I don't want to forget the little things about you," I whisper and start twirling the blade between my fingers until it blurs, thanks to the tears in my eyes.

The last thing I want is to break down weeping at my mother's grave, so I blink them back and wait for the wave of emotion to pass before speaking again. "Maybe it makes me think about when my baby will start forgetting things about me. It's scary. I never thought about that sort of thing before. Is this what happens when you become a parent? You start questioning the things you used to take for granted?"

I toss the grass aside with a sigh. "God, I wish you were here. I have so many questions, and I'm so scared. I know you would make me feel better, the way you always used to. I've never needed you more than I do now, and yet somehow, even though you've been gone all these years, you've never felt so far away. What should I do? Where do I go from here? I can't tell Dad about what Callum did—I'm honestly afraid he would kill him, or at least attempt to. That would cause more problems for him. And I don't want to tell Tatum, since she's already messed up enough over everything that's happened. She no longer needs knowledge of how crazy her father is, and the lengths he's willing to go to keep me at his side."

My voice starts to wobble. Despite that, I continue since I need to get the words out. I need to let go of some of the weight dragging me down. "I feel like a terrible friend. I feel like an awful, ungrateful daughter. No matter what I do, somebody is always going to be unhappy. Is it too much to ask for everybody to get along and be happy?"

That sounds so immature. It's impossible for everyone to be happy, except this goes beyond that. "I don't know what to do, Mommy," I choke out just before the tears start to fall. Hot, stinging tears that roll down my cheeks and drip off my chin land like heavy raindrops on the grass. "I just don't know what to do. I have to keep the baby safe—that's my biggest concern, but after that... I'm lost. I don't even know how to be a mom or if I'll even be a good one." I sigh, "Did you ever feel that way?"

Her light gray headstone offers no answer, and neither does the singing of birds in the trees above. I'm alone. There are no answers. Just the wind and this heavy gray headstone in front of me.

It seems like all I can do is kneel here and water the grass with my tears, praying for answers to my questions. Answers that will never come.

CALLUM

I know that what I'm hearing isn't the alert beeping on my phone. There's only one reason for that alert to go off the way it did when I tested the software of the app, now flashing a notification across my screen. I know Bianca is not stupid enough to do something irrational, or at least I hope not.

Yet there's no ignoring the notification. *Vehicle in motion.*

I'm alone in the office while Romero digs deeper into the Ken situation, leaving me no one to growl at in frustration and disbelief while I open the app to see what the fuck is happening. There must be a bug in the app. Probably a malfunction or something because there was no way she would leave the house without bothering to tell me.

The blue dot moving across the map confirms my biggest fear. She's on the move, and she left without letting me know. No, that's not true–checking my messages, I see she sent a text.

Bianca: I'm going for a drive and will be back soon. Nathan is coming with me. Don't worry. I just need some air.

Because there's no air out by the pool or elsewhere on the property? Damn it, she should know better than this. After everything she's been through, she's going to drive around for no reason? And why the hell didn't Nathan tell me?

I'm out of the chair and on the way outside before there's time to think. This is not a situation where thinking is a luxury I can afford. I need to find her now. A call to her phone gets me her voicemail, which leads to me slamming the car door closed before sending gravel flying in my wake as I start the engine and fly down the driveway.

The dot is still moving. She's a few miles away. Where could she go in the early afternoon? What was so important she couldn't think twice before putting herself and our baby in danger?

I'm less than a mile from her when she comes to a stop… in the cemetery.

Some of the burning pain in my chest subsides, though not all of it. She went to the cemetery. "How am I supposed to protect someone who refuses to be protected?" I growl, hitting the gas when the light turns green. I follow the route to where my insolent, stubborn little bird decided she had to be today.

The lack of other visitors is a plus. There are no other cars besides mine and the familiar Corolla parked up ahead. I slow down to avoid being spotted right away. If she's in a jumpy mood, she might decide to run, and there's not much I feel less like doing than weaving through headstones to catch her.

Nathan looks like he swallowed his tongue when he spots me from his position beside her car. No doubt he remembers that broken nose–it hasn't been too long since I broke it. We'll have a talk later about reporting to me rather than making me chase Bianca around. This could have been avoided if he'd communicated with me. For now, it's enough to find out why she had to come here so suddenly.

There she is.

My heart thunders in my chest. She is kneeling on the ground, wearing a yellow sweater that makes her stand out against the blue sky and greenery. Might as well paint a target on her back and blow a whistle to attract the attention of anyone looking to hurt me by hurting her.

Any hint of anger evaporates once I see her covering her face with her hands. If an artist tried to capture the essence of grief, they couldn't do better than what I see once I climb out of the car and watch from over the roof. There she is, my little bird, crumbling under the weight of her pain. Her slumped shoulders shake with unfathomable emotion. Nobody needs to tell me whose grave she's kneeling at.

She can't know about my connection to Jessica's murder. She can't. Only Romero and I know about that, and we're still working with theories. There's no solid proof of who pulled that trigger. Still, my heart clenches in fear that takes time to ease. I'm being paranoid, imagining ghosts in the shadows. This isn't the time for my imagination to run away from me.

What would bring her here? That's a stupid question which doesn't take much thought to answer. She's missing her mother, probably now more than ever. There must be questions, along with fears and concerns, she doesn't feel comfortable bringing to me—or wouldn't if she was speaking to me, which she still isn't.

I've never carried a baby and was shamefully absent for most of Amanda's pregnancy. We lived under the same roof, but I was too busy building what would become my empire. I couldn't be bothered with doctor's appointments and shopping for furniture, aches and pains, or cravings. Tatum owned my heart the moment we locked eyes, however. Still, before then, I didn't think much about everything that went into bringing her into the world.

That's on me. That's something I will have to live with, along with so many other mistakes and oversights.

Even if I had been more present, there's no substitute for first-hand experience. I don't know how it feels to carry life the way Bianca can. I can't relate to what it means, bringing a life into the world that she wasn't ready for. This should be a joyful, happy time in her life, and I took that away from her—that and so many other things. In my life, I feel guilty for very few things, for if I allowed myself to feel remorse for all the things I've done, it would kill me.

Nonetheless, the guilt I feel for hurting Bianca. Nothing touches that pain. It's one I feel with every beat of my heart, every breath of air into my lungs. I did this to keep her at my side, but inevitably it was the one thing that pushed her the furthest away.

I can't help how my feet automatically take me to her, carrying me through the thick grass. She can hate me all she wants, but there is no chance of me standing by and watching her suffer without at least letting her know I'm here. I'm finally starting to understand I can't take the pain she feels away, but I can ask her to lay some of it on my shoulders.

I have rushed into buildings knowing a gunman could be waiting for me to enter. I've faced virtually every form of threat known to man. All that was nothing compared to this, approaching the woman I love with every ounce of me. There's no guarantee of how she'll react or if following her here is the last straw. I would have to accept that if it is. She's not going to get me to change my fundamental nature.

I don't know what alerts her to my presence. There's no snapping of a twig, no sudden disturbance to make her lift her head and look around. I'm standing downwind, so I doubt she picks up the smell of my cologne. Whatever it is, it leaves her staring at me, her expression bleak, tearful.

"What are you doing here?" she asks with a soft, defeated sigh. There's no surprise, no attempt at defending herself as I slowly approach.

"Following you."

Another sigh. "Of course you were." The disdain in those four words leaves me bristling, while at the same time I feel roughly two inches tall. How does she manage to do that?

"What do you want me to do?" All she does is turn her face away, which is relatively harder to deal with than if she had hurled insults at me. "In case you've forgotten—and I know you haven't—you were kidnapped recently. And all you were doing was something as innocent as going to work. Excuse me if, in the days after that, I overreacted and installed a tracking system on your car."

"Once again," she seethes, still looking away, "you did it without talking to me about it."

"I did what I thought was right. The only things that matter to me are you, our baby, and the safety of you both."

Those magic words send her head swiveling around, eyes blazing. "That isn't the point, Callum. Don't you get it? I'm not even arguing the idea of having you track my car. I understand why it makes you feel more secure after what happened. And honestly, I wouldn't mind you always knowing where my car is when I leave—even though I don't necessarily love the idea of you being able to follow me around. Besides, tracking my car wouldn't have helped things."

"You're right. That does make sense."

Her gaze narrows. "You're just saying that."

"No, I'm not. What you said makes sense. I didn't think of it that way."

"This wouldn't be an example of telling me what I want to hear just to make things better between us, would it?"

"Not even close." However, I can admit to myself how good it feels just to be in her presence. Hearing her sweet voice, even when there's a note of sarcasm winding its way through her words like an invisible thread. Anything, so long as I can look at her, speak to her, connect with her, even on a simple level like this. I'd say damn near anything for her to keep talking.

"And you're not just saying that because I was crying?" An interesting use of past tense, considering there are still tears cutting a slow path down her cheeks. She pulls one of the sleeves of her sweater down over her fist and uses it to mop up the wetness.

"What do you want me to say, Bianca? I'm trying. For you, I'm trying."

She releases a shuddering breath, turning her face toward the headstone bearing her mother's name. "I know."

I could double down now while she's quiet and accepting. I could drill into her head the importance of her safety and how I don't trust my enemies to lay low for long. What could have happened if one of Moroni's men was out here and found her? I'm sure she thought about that before she left, and somehow it was still important that she get out of the house. That she ventures here to her mother's grave.

"It isn't easy to accept there's something you can't get from me." The words come out so slowly, and each one is a struggle. She deserves to hear this, though, just as much as I need to say it. "You would rather kneel here by your mother's grave and speak to her headstone than speak to me, the man who loves you, who would do anything for you. That's not an easy thing to wrap my head around."

"You know exactly why that is."

"I do. I know this is my fault, which doesn't make it any easier. If anything, that makes it more impossible to bear."

"I don't know what you expect me to say to you. I'm not going to comfort you and tell you that I'm sorry and everything is going to be okay."

"I don't expect you to, and I don't need you to. Anything I'm going through right now, I set into motion. I see it, and I want you to know I see it. And no," I'm quick to add when her mouth opens, "I'm not saying that just because I think it's what you want to hear. I mean it from the bottom of my heart. I understand and know what I did was wrong. I'm sorry."

"Why was it wrong?"

She will not be satisfied until she has me by the balls and twists them off. Right away, my old instincts flare to life, crowding my thoughts. Nobody speaks to me this way. Nobody demands I explain myself. I'm a Torrio, a man of power and money.

That's childish. The result of fear. If there's any hope of us lasting—and we have to, there's no other way—I can't afford to blindly give in to those impulses anymore. I need to be the man she needs me to be.

Which is why, instead of lashing out or dragging her to the car kicking and screaming, I settle for a deep breath to steady myself. "I was never anything but open about what I wanted from us. It was wrong because I took your choice away. You deserved to decide when you were ready to start a family, and I should've given you a say in the matter."

"Yes. You absolutely should have."

"The best I can promise is to try to do better, to be a better man, and to consider you in every choice that is made regarding us." This is fucking torture, but the expectant lift of her eyebrows tells me she is waiting for more. Fuck me. This isn't going to end until she's damn good and ready. "Even if it kills me, I will give you as much space as I feel is necessary while maintaining your safety," I stress the words so she'll understand.

"It was not safe for you to go off on your own without telling anyone in the house your plans. There will always be parts of my work and world that I have to keep from you. It's not because I don't trust you, but because the less you know, the more protected you are. There are a lot of moving pieces in motion right now, and I can't have you getting caught in the middle of it all. Go where you want, but for God's sake, take someone with you. Someone who knows how to use a gun and can protect you. That's all I ask. I'm trying to meet you halfway, but I can't do that if you don't do the same."

She purses her lips but eventually nods. "I understand, and from now on, I'll make sure somebody's with me. I don't want to take any chances, and I appreciate you letting me know things are still dicey." Dicey is hardly the word for it. Regardless, I don't want to increase her stress. I won't get anything out of scaring her; she's been through enough because of me.

"Thank you for that. That will give me peace of mind."

"And in return...?"

This is the woman I love. This is the woman I plan to make a life with. She's carrying my child. She is the last person I need to alienate. No matter how it makes me grind my teeth when she looks at me the way she is now, I know there's no denying my next sentence.

"In return, I'll run things past you before I make any major decisions. I'll trust you."

She doesn't flinch or lash out when I move closer, which I take as a good sign. Eventually, I'm close enough to crouch beside Jessica's headstone, putting me at eye level with her daughter. "I think that's what I need you to understand now more than nearly anything. For years, I haven't been able to trust anyone. There I was, with the best prize I could ever receive: you. Somehow I still couldn't trust that you would stay, and I was so desperate to hold on to you, and I did something I shouldn't have."

"You violated my trust." The quivering of her chin makes me want to look away, but I can't. I won't. I deserve to witness this.

"I did. And it was wrong. Still, I'm never going to change the man that I am at my core. I'm going to always want things my way. I will be impatient much of the time, and there will still be instances when I jump at the chance to do what I think is best. I'll act on impulse, but it will only ever be out of love."

My fingers itch to touch her, to trace her features, and hold her in my arms. It's been too long since I indulged in the almost unnatural softness of her skin.

Reaching out, I stroke her cheek. She doesn't flinch or stiffen, and I let myself go further, tracing the line of her jaw. "I love you, Bianca, and that's why I'm going to work like hell to give you everything you need. I only need you to understand that you can't ask me to change who I am."

"I don't want you to change," she whispers before a fresh tear hits my fingers. "I love you the way you are now, even though you drive me crazy and make me doubt everything I thought I knew about myself. I love your craziness, your obsession, and your need to be near me."

Her gaze drifts back to the headstone, and her brow furrowing leaves no question of her feelings. "I wish you could've known her."

"I do, too. She sounded like a good woman. I haven't known many in my life." I crane my neck to see what's etched on the gray stone.

Jessica Cole. Beloved wife and mother. Gone too soon.

Isn't that the truth?

"Mrs. Cole," I murmur before chuckling to myself. "It would be too awkward to call a woman my age by her last name, so Jessica. There's something I want you to know."

"What are you doing?" Bianca whispers curiously.

"You have a smart, beautiful, loving daughter. I know she must have gotten most of that from you—no offense to your husband." Bianca snickers softly at this. "She's shown me the sort of happiness I didn't think was possible for a man like myself. She's helped me become a better person and makes me want to work hard to become the sort of man she needs."

Glancing at Bianca, I add, "There's a question I want to ask her, but I thought I'd ask you first."

"Okay, what are you actually doing?" she asks again, standing and brushing off her knees.

I stand, too, gazing down at the headstone representing the life of a woman who was cruelly taken from the people who loved her most. People who still love her. "Jessica, I want to marry your daughter. May I please have your blessing?"

"Callum," Bianca's choked whisper drags my attention back to her. I hold her upright when I do, snaking an arm around her waist. For a second there, she looked like she was ready to drop to the ground.

"I mean it." I pull her closer, savoring her warmth, sweetness, and the way she trembles against me. "I want you to be my wife and carry my last name. I want our child to know their parents are devoted to each other—our baby deserves that."

"This is a lot," she whispers with a shaky giggle. "Do you really mean it? For real?"

"Do you think this is all a game? I've known all along I was going to marry you. You were meant to be my wife, and there's nothing I want more in this world than to spend the rest of my life loving you. All I need is a single word from you."

Her gaze narrows as she eyes me wearily. "This isn't your way of getting me to stop being mad and hurt, is it?"

"No. Not even close. I have other ways of doing that."

"I want you to know that this doesn't change anything. I'm still hurt, and we still have a lot of things to work out."

"I have all the time in the world for you—and us."

This time, the tears sparkling in her eyes seem to carry hope and happiness. "Callum, you know I love you. I want us to have a life together."

"So… it's a yes?"

"It's a yes."

Thank you Lord. I'm not sure what I would've done if she said no.

BIANCA

I can't pretend it isn't a huge relief to be back in Callum's bed. No, *our* bed. I need to stop thinking of it as my bed, my room, my home. We're supposed to be getting married, after all.

Married. It's been less than twenty-four hours since he proposed, so I'm nowhere near used to the idea yet. It will feel more real when I get a ring—not if, since I know Callum better than to think he wouldn't give me one. Once I have that, I'll feel like an engaged girl—a fiancée.

The rush of excitement that floods me when I think about it dries up reasonably quick when my brain keeps moving. It's not enough for me to lie here, basking in sunlight and love, feeling happy. Right away, Tatum's face flashes in my mind. How will she feel about it? And Dad. I don't need to wonder about him. It's going to take a while for him to come around.

I don't want to think about any of that right now. I want to be happy for a little while. To live in the moment instead of thinking two steps ahead all the time.

When I get out of my own head and back into bed with my fiancé—nope, still not used to it—there's a sense of everything being the way it's supposed to be again, even if I still feel guarded. I told him his proposal didn't change things, and I meant it.

Now that we're back together like this, I only want to forget everything and start again. It would be easiest that way, for both of us. I don't want to fight. I want to look forward to the future with hope.

That's not how you fix problems, though. It would be the same as telling him that what he did was okay. That in the end, all it will take is a few days of being apart for me to come around and go back on all of my principles. It's no way to build a relationship. If my time with Lucas taught me anything, it was that it was way too easy for me to forgive simply because it was easier not to fight. I didn't want to be that girl anymore. I wanted to be the one who stood up for what she believed in and had her thoughts and wishes respected.

The pleasant ache between my thighs is a reminder of the way we spent last night. The twisted sheets and pillows strewn over the bed are another reminder. By the time we finished making up, I was as frantic to make up for lost time as he was. Even a few days may as well have been a lifetime when you crave someone the way we do each other. We didn't get much sleep. However, I don't think either of us would complain much about that.

"I think I want to quit my job."

Callum lifts his head from where it's been resting on my stomach for the past few minutes. He might even have started to doze, yet my sudden announcement seems to have woken him up. "Pardon?"

"I think it's the best thing to do." I didn't know I was thinking about it, not seriously. Saying it out loud, though, crystalizes the idea and makes it real.

"How so?" I have to give him credit for not rubbing his hands together like the evil villain who's getting his way. He must be thrilled since he already wanted me to quit once, but now he's trying to do the right thing and be supportive.

"Well, for starters, there's the fact that I really should be getting up and getting ready to go into the office right now," I explain while stroking his hair. "I can't help but lie here feeling guilty, because I have a job and a degree. If I'm being honest, I don't want to return to that job or even that field of work."

"There's nothing wrong with that."

"There is when you consider how many people don't love their job. But they still go, don't they? They don't use it as an excuse the way I am."

Callum gives me a knowing look, "I think you've had more than enough reasons to be out of work lately."

"I know, but things are better now."

It's apparent before he even says a word that he disagrees. It's becoming easier to read his facial cues, primarily when his eyebrows draw together and his mouth screws up in a frown yet he doesn't say anything right away, I know he's weighing his options. Trying to figure out what to say without upsetting me. "I don't know if I could handle you leaving the safety of our home to go to work every day. I think I'd need to make sure you have a bodyguard with you at all times."

That's funny. Right away, I want to tell him no. That I would be safe and he wouldn't need to worry. I don't want him always hovering over me, concerned and obsessed with my safety. Except, that's a lie. The Moronis are still out there, and I'm not going to lie to him and say it wouldn't give me all kinds of anxiety to go back to work, to park in the same garage where Tatum and I were taken. "Truthfully, I don't know if I want to play with that kind of anxiety. I mean, with the baby and everything."

"That's understandable."

"Still, I refuse to let this rule my life. I don't want to turn into a recluse who hides in her home, never going anywhere or doing anything."

"I would never ask you to do that. I know I talk a lot about wanting to keep you here, however you need to be able to leave the house, to go out and do things." It's refreshing to hear him say that and to know that he sees me, that I'm not just a precious jewel meant to sit on his shelf.

"It's not all bad. I wasn't ever really happy there."

"I understand, and that's even more of a reason to quit. Whatever you decide to do for work should be enjoyable. Life is so much more than clocking in and out and waiting for the weekend to come. Take it from me, the years pass quicker than you think."

A bubble of laughter escapes me. "You're talking like you're seventy-five."

He wiggles his eyebrows at me, "I feel like it sometimes, and if I were, I'd be highly impressed. Seventy-five and catching a woman like you. That's not even mentioning the fact that I still have swimmers capable of knocking you up."

"Oh my god, stop." I playfully smack his arm. "Back to what I was saying, I feel bad keeping the position when I never go in. Someone who really needs a job could be working there."

"You're right, but I've got to be honest with you. I feel like you're trying to convince me more than you're trying to convince yourself, and we both know I'd rather have you home than anywhere else.."

"Does that make me come off as a spoiled brat?"

"Is that what's bothering you?"

"A little bit," I admit. "I was raised to appreciate the things you're given. Not to shit all over them and act like you're above others."

"While I understand the sentiment," he murmurs, propping himself up on one elbow, "I think you're being too hard on yourself. I've never seen you act boastful or full of yourself, and you're not some spoiled brat who thinks the world owes her something. You're someone who's been through a hell of a lot, and you need time to process that. We both know you don't really need the job, although somebody else might, someone without a safety net."

A safety net. That's an intriguing way of putting it. "I don't want to become spoiled and ungrateful."

"I've never met anyone less spoiled and ungrateful in my life, and I'm not saying that lightly." He places a gentle, lingering kiss on the back of my hand that warms my heart... along with other places. "I've never met anyone as sincere, hardworking, and determined to do the right thing. In every way you're the opposite of what you fear."

"You're only saying that because I'm your Baby Mama."

His laughter rings through the room. It's infectious, and I soon start to laugh as well. What a shame so few people have ever heard him laugh or even smile. "I love you. Of course, I'm going to see all your best attributes. Remember, I'm realistic too. I'm not in the business of blowing smoke up anybody's ass—not even an ass as delectable as yours." He playfully rolls me onto my side and whistles at the sight of it.

"Look all you want now," I warn with a groan. "It's going to get all fat and droopy soon."

"There still won't come a day when I don't want to grab it when nobody's looking." His teeth sink into my ass cheek, just enough to still be playful before he purses his lips, his eyes pointing toward the ceiling. "Actually, it doesn't matter if anyone's looking or not. I'm still going to want to grab it."

"I hope you don't end up getting tired of me."

The mischievousness in his features twists, and he hits me with an apprehensive look that makes me wish I hadn't said that. "Where's this coming from? I've told you before there is no getting tired of you. Wanting you in the first place had nothing to do with danger or how wrong it was for us to be together. It's you, Bianca. Everything about you. There won't be a day when I don't want you. Crave you. Fantasize about you how a dying man fantasizes about having one more happy, healthy day."

Warmth stirs in my core as he sweeps his tongue over my skin, as it always does at times like this. I know what he means about craving—I crave him, too, constantly. No matter what I'm doing, he's always there, lurking in the back of my mind like some prize I get at the end of the day—something to always look forward to. Even when I was sleeping down the hall, lost, hurt, and confused... I wanted him. He was the reason for my pain and the only thing that could take it away.

Once he's finished his slow tour and we're face-to-face, I make a point of casting a look toward the clock on the nightstand. "It's getting late. Romero will be up here any minute now wondering why you aren't already at your desk."

His groan leaves me chuckling while I run my fingers through his hair. "Way to go and mention him at a time like this."

I look down between our naked bodies to find his thick cock jutted out and hard as steel. "It didn't seem to do anything to him," I point out, brushing my fingertips over the mushroom head, grinning at his heavy sigh.

So needy, and only I can give him what he craves.

"That's because he has a one-track mind."

"Funny. I thought you were the one with the one-track mind."

"Don't tell anybody." He winds his fingers around mine and gives me an insistent tug until there's no choice except to follow him out of bed. "He does a lot of my thinking for me."

"I figured that much." It's not like I can complain or act like I don't want to get in the shower with him—any excuse to be close for an extra few minutes before real-life stuff gets in the way.

Soon it's Callum's hands I'm more focused on, how he gets right down to the business of lathering me up with my lilac body wash. The flowery scent fills the shower, just one more pleasurable thing for my senses to pick up on, along with the pleasure of being touched. Wanted. Treasured. Things might not be perfect between us—we have a long way to go—but we can always come back to this.

"Let me do your back." I turn and face the wall, bracing my forearms against the tile while he lathers my neck, then my shoulders, before working his way further down. "You have the most perfect skin. It's unreal." He slows, his touch becoming more deliberate.

What's unreal is the sudden electricity in the air. How does he do it? It's his soft, seductive voice. The throb of desire running through it. How his hand lingers a beat longer than necessary when he soaps my legs, or how his fingertips skim my ass cheeks until I tremble. By the time he's finished, I'm one big, pulsing nerve ready to beg for release.

I have to credit him for taking as long as he does before his body begins sliding against mine. "Are you my shower sponge now?" My chuckle is cut off by the touch of his hand between my legs, caressing my already swollen lips. How is it so easy for him to turn me into a whimpering, needy animal whose only goal is to come?

"I'm afraid I'll only be able to get you dirty." His breathing is harsh and heavy in my ear, and he exchanges his dick for his hand. The touch of his thick head against my clit is the added friction I needed, as I spread my legs wider and bear down to increase the pressure while he slips through my wet folds.

"Am I complaining?" No, instead, I arch my back to give him better access to my pussy.

"Mmm..." His hands grip my hips, almost as if he's testing to make sure I can handle what he's going to give me. Then he releases his grip and slides them up my sides before cupping my breasts, his fingers gently pinching my pink nipples, hardening them. "Somebody's in a hurry. Did I not give you enough last night?"

That's the thing, it's never enough. There never will be when it comes to him.

"I need more," I whimper and grind my ass against him in hopes of urging him on. "Give me more."

"Whatever you want, little bird." It only takes a slight adjustment to line himself up with my dripping hole. Slipping the thick head inside, he drives himself forward, flattening my boobs against the wall with the force of his first stroke. My eyes flutter closed, and I give myself over to him, knowing he will give me what I need most. I'm safe with him.

"Fuck little bird. Your pussy is so tight, and perfect. I love the way you struggle to take every inch of my cock inside it." His grunts of pleasure only deepen what's going on inside me thanks to the way he works his thick cock in and out of me, at a slow and steady pace. The frenzy of last night has turned to something slower, sweeter, but just as toe-curling.

"Your pussy loves my cock, doesn't she? She loves the way I fill her with my cum, and let it drip out. She loves the way I alternate between fucking her hard and fast, and slow and steady," he rasps against my ear before taking the lobe between his teeth. "She loves it when I fill her up with my cock, stuffing myself so deep inside there's no way to tell where you start and I end, doesn't she?"

"Yes," I whine, pushing back against him. "Yes, oh god, it feels so good." Right then he pistons his hips forward, and his tip brushes against a bundle of nerves that make me tremble.

"Oh shit, you're tightening little bird." His strokes become harder, and my muscles tense. I'm so close, only a little more. "You're going to make me come inside you. Fuck... my balls ache to release inside of you and I know you want it. You're my good girl, my little cum slut, aren't you?"

Every word gets me hotter, making the tension mount, making me whine helplessly. The sound of my moans fills the shower along with the steam rising up from the hot spray. "Callum, oh god... I'm...!"

"Be a good girl and come on my cock," he demands, breathless, grunting every time our bodies crash against each other. "Then I'll fill you with my cum as a reward."

I don't have a choice. It's all happening at once. The wave slams into me, the power of the orgasm is so strong the air in my lungs stills, and I'm drowning, being pulled down into blissful darkness where Callum's grunts are barely audible over the pounding of my own heartbeat.

"Fuck, fuck, fuck..." Callum growls, his grip on me tightening. "God... I'm coming. I'm filling your pussy up for being my good girl. I want you to hold my cum inside of you. Hold it in, and don't let any slip out."

All I can do is nod, the blissful pleasure still overtaking me. He pounds into me almost mercilessly and with one last hard stroke he explodes, his entire body vibrating. I can feel the warmth of his release spreading through my pussy, and tightening my muscles, holding his cock and his release inside me.

"I swear to god your pussy is going to suck every drop of semen out of my balls."

All I can do is laugh and let out a sigh as he gently pulls out of me. I hate the emptiness that follows after he pulls out. Sometimes I wish he'd stay inside me all the time, but let's be honest that's not realistic.

He makes up for the loss by peppering gentle kisses against my neck and throat. "I'll never get enough of you." I can feel his heart pounding against my back and each tremor that works its way through him. My pussy aches from the punishment his cock has delivered two days in a row and I slowly feel his release slipping out of me, getting washed away by the water.

"You better not," I warn with a giggle. "I'm not going to forget what you asked me yesterday. It would suck if we got married and you decided I bore you."

"Never." He pulls away to quickly wash himself while I clean myself up. "Which reminds me. Do you think we should announce our plans?"

All at once the water feels cold. Only for a second, only as long as it takes for me to shake off the surprise. "Do you want to?"

"Are you kidding? I can't wait. I want the world to know you're mine."

"I was just thinking maybe we should tread lightly. Get a feel for how Tatum will take it." I hate talking about my best friend this way, like I have a secret I'm keeping from her. It wouldn't be the first time, though. I fought like hell to keep us a secret while she was away. She only ended up finding out, anyway.

I'm still thinking it over as I dry off, and pull on a t-shirt and jeans. What if she sees this as a form of betrayal? I don't know what's going on in her head right now and I'm afraid I'll only end up ruining our friendship if we blurt out the news all at once.

"I'm ready to follow your lead on this," Callum decides once we're finished getting dressed. "I want to take out a full-page ad announcing the news, but I don't want you to be uncomfortable." Every word sounds like he's struggling to get it out. He's trying so hard to make me happy.

I can't help but smile as I sit on the edge of the bed and watch him put himself together. Not a half hour ago, we were in this bed, and he was warm and naked and wrapped up in me. Now, he's the stern, commanding boss and all I want is to strip that suit off him and fall into bed again.

Instead, we leave the bedroom together, walking hand in hand down the stairs. "Let's feel Tatum out on it," I decide. "I mean, it doesn't have to be a huge secret, but I don't want to make it look like we're rubbing it in her face. She's been through enough and I don't want her to think she's losing me as a friend."

I wasn't wrong about Romero. He's pacing in tight circles at the foot of the stairs. I can't help but giggle when he very obviously checks the time. There can't be many people with the balls to boss Callum Torrio around.

"Should I know better than to schedule morning calls from now on?" he asks, watching our progress.

"I was distracted. Sue me." Callum slides an arm around my waist. "It's something you're going to have to get used to."

"I'm already doing my best." He looks from one of us to the other with his brows drawn together. "Wait a minute. Are you saying what I think you're saying?"

"What do you think I'm saying?"

"It sounds a lot like you're telling me you're engaged." There's no hint of how he feels about it, though I guess in the end it doesn't matter. Or it shouldn't. I need to get better at ignoring what other people think. Maybe I'll learn to breathe underwater while I'm at it, since the idea seems about as possible.

"We're trying to keep it quiet for now," Callum explains while beaming from ear to ear. "But yes. Bianca agreed to a lifetime of being driven crazy by me."

"Congratulations. Sincerely." Romero offers me a genuine smile before shaking Callum's hand. "We could use all the good news possible. Do you have any idea when the wedding will be?"

"When what will be?"

No. Not like this. Not while Tatum stands open mouthed in the entry hall, so surprised she drops her muffin on the floor. All she was doing was getting breakfast, and now she has to deal with this.

"Tell me I'm imagining this. Last I knew you just got together, now there's a baby, and you're getting married?" I never thought my own best friend could look at me with so much anger and even disgust. We might as well be strangers.

Before I can come up with anything to say, Callum lets go of my hand and gestures for Tatum with a crooked finger. "In my office. Now. We have a few things we need to discuss." All I can do is watch with a sinking heart while she marches off behind him, fists clenched like she's ready to fight.

"So much for trying to ease her into the idea," I whisper, and all Romero can do is frown. Maybe he feels sorry for all of us.

CALLUM

"It's time we talk about this, and you're not going to shut me out anymore." I gesture for Tatum to enter my office, which she does before I follow her and close the door. I don't know whether or not Bianca followed us. She's perceptive enough to know this needs to be a one-on-one discussion.

"Oh wow, now you want to talk to me about the happy day? All of a sudden, it matters what I want?" She barks out a laugh, crossing the room and standing at the window with her back to me. "You care what I think now?"

"It was never about not caring what you think." I pause, and when she says nothing, I decide to take my life in my hands. "What do you think?"

That earns me a filthy look thrown over her shoulder. If I didn't know better, I'd think I was in the middle of a fight with her mother. Somehow, she manages to project the same disdain. "You can't be asking me that question right now. It's a little late either way."

"Did you think this was all a joke? Bianca and me being together? We're having a baby. What did you think was going to happen next?"

"I don't know what I thought." She looks downright defensive when she wraps her arms around herself, and the way her chin juts out tells me this isn't going to be an easy, straight-line conversation.

"You thought this was some crazy, midlife crisis thing, didn't you?" When she looks at the floor, I know I'm right. "I hate to disappoint you, but this is the real deal. I know what I want. And I am so terribly sorry if it hurts you, sweetheart."

"That's easy to say when you're not on the receiving end."

The amount of bitterness in her voice leaves me recoiling. "It's the truth."

"Well, it does hurt."

"Then let's talk about it, for God's sake. Do you know how long I've wanted to have an honest conversation with you about this?" She scoffs, turning her gaze toward the window again. I'd throw something through the fucking window if I thought it would help. Anything to break through this wall she built between us. It wasn't always this way, but it's not like I've done anything to improve it, especially not in the past couple of months.

I lean against the desk, shoving my hands into my pockets while I fight to find the right words. No matter what I say, it'll be a mistake. There's no way of getting through this without shedding blood, figuratively or otherwise. "Tatum, it's clear you're suffering. No amount of pretending you're fine will fix things. I don't want to hurt you, but I won't know what does or doesn't hurt you if you don't talk to me."

"This hurts me," she whispers, hunching her shoulders. "We grew up together. We're the same age, and now you want to marry her?"

"She's having my baby, sweetheart."

"I know, but that's one thing. I could live with that. These things happen, but deciding to get married? That's so much more. And I have to say, I really wish you would have come to me and let me know what you were thinking about before all of this."

"To be fair, I didn't plan on asking her this soon. It sort of... happened."

Her head tips to the side before she turns slowly and hits me with a very knowing look. The sort of look that cuts through me and might as well be delivered with a blade to flay my skin. "Dad. Nothing just sort of happens with you. You plan out every step. You deliberate over every choice. This isn't the kind of decision you make on the fly. Especially not a man like you."

At first, all I can do is chuckle. "Sometimes I forget how perceptive you are. It's been just the two of us for so long."

"Don't do that. Don't make it sound like we were the two musketeers or whatever. That's not how it was, and you can't rewrite history."

"I can accept that," I murmur. She's seemed like an unsolvable riddle for so long, but now I see she's an onion. Each layer I peel back reveals more layers beneath, and those layers are marinated in grief, anger, resentment, and betrayal.

"I'm not saying you weren't a good father. You did your best, and I always felt safe with you. I felt like you wanted me around. Most of the time," she's quick to add while her lips tighten in disapproval. "When you weren't consumed by work."

"Which I was a lot of the time. I know."

"But at least you wanted me around, unlike my mother." My heart aches when her voice trembles on the word. My poor, wounded child. I wish I could take the pain she feels away.

"I want you around now, too."

"Are you sure about that?"

"Loving Bianca doesn't mean I love you any less. I don't feel like I should have to say that out loud, but I will in case it helps." How much have I failed her if she truly needs me to explain that?

"I know you love me. But it's just weird, Dad. I can't pretend it isn't. You used to complain that we made too much noise when she slept over. And there was that one time when we were kids, and I had the pool party for my birthday. Do you remember that?

She changed into a two-piece once she got here because she knew Charlie wouldn't let her wear it, and you gave her so much shit over it. Do you remember that?"

I do, and I can see where her discomfort is coming from. "She's not that little girl anymore, and neither are you. You're both grown women."

Her hip pops out to the side, telling me I walked into a trap with my eyes wide open. "So you would be okay if I started dating Charlie? The two of you are pretty close in age."

"That's a different story."

"How so? Explain it to me. How is there any difference in me, a grown woman, deciding I want to be in a relationship with a grown man? Why is it so different for you two? It sounds a lot like a double standard."

"Come here." I have to pretend it doesn't hurt when she shrugs away from me when I reach for her. Does she resent me that much? I force myself to push down the anger that instantly flares to life when she tries to avoid me. "Tatum. I just want to sit down with you."

She sits on the leather sofa against the wall opposite my desk, her arms still folded, her walls still intact. I perch carefully beside her, giving her space when I really want to gather her in my arms. It was so much easier to do that when she was little. So much easier to make everything right back then, so much simpler. Even her wildest tantrums—and God knows she went through them—were easily calmed compared to the vast chasm of pain between us.

It isn't easy, going against my natural paternal instinct and pointing out how she's clearly not taking care of herself. Her hoodie and yoga pants are more like sails swallowing her thin frame. Her golden curls are frizzy, lifeless, and pulled back in a scrunchy while thick chunks hang around her face and the back of her neck. She looks like she just rolled out of bed even though it's early afternoon. She's nothing like the girl she used to be, even if she looks the same on the outside.

"Honey. Look at me." Tension appears in her jawline, but she slowly turns her head. My God, she's haunted. I've seen photos of refugees fleeing war that now come to mind when I find the pain in her eyes. There's no light anymore, not the way there used to be. "Why won't you let me in? Why won't you let me help you? You have me at a loss. I'm not used to standing on the outside, hoping and wishing for a chance to make a difference. I normally barge in and do what I think is best."

"Yeah. I know."

"I can't do that now. All I want is to help you, and I don't know how. I need you to let me in. Tell me what you need. You know I would do anything in my power for you. But I'm flailing around in the dark. Please, give me a clue. Let me help you through this."

At first, I'm sure my words have fallen on deaf ears. I watch as she chews her lip, her eyes darting over my face before finally looking away. My heart sinks with certainty that something has broken between us, something that can never be fixed. Not if she refuses to take the first step.

Finally, though, she releases a long sigh. "It's so sudden."

"The marriage?"

"Yeah. I don't want you to rush into this and get hurt."

"Do you know something about Bianca that I don't? Because—"

"No, no. I didn't mean it that way. There's a reason she's my best friend and probably one of the only people I trust."

"I thought so."

"But she's already run off on you a couple of times now, and I'm not saying she didn't have a reason to. She had a really good reason to; you're a bit unhinged at best. What happens if you guys fall apart again? What's that going to do to you and to her? This is a huge step, and I know you love her, I do. I know she loves you, too. But are you sure this is the right step? I mean, it's almost like..."

When her brow creases, I know I have to tread lightly. "Go on. You can say it. I'm listening. You don't have to be afraid."

"Like you were waiting for Mom to die."

I thought it would come down to Amanda somehow, considering the presence of her urn on Tatum's nightstand. But I didn't know hearing it come from her lips would feel like a slap to the face. "Please believe me when I say this, Tatum. I didn't want your mother to die," I whisper, shaking my head. "Honey, I need you to believe that. I wanted her to move forward with the divorce, yes. We both know she was dragging her feet, and if she were still alive, I'm sure she would try to stand in the way of this, but that doesn't mean I wanted her to die."

All she has to do is arch an eyebrow for a flood of memories to come rushing back. All the times I so casually announced what a relief it would be if Amanda stopped breathing. What a waste of oxygen she was. How I wouldn't shed a tear if she dropped dead.

"You're old enough to understand that people say things all the time in a moment of anger or frustration. How often did you tell me you wished I was dead when you were a teenager who wanted her way? You were downright nasty."

"That's different. I was young and just coming into my feelings."

"All I'm saying is, did you really want me dead? If you said that one night and woke up the next morning to find me gone, would you have regretted saying it? I think you would have. Now, the situation with your mom and me was somewhat different. She made it her mission to make me miserable, and if I hated her, it was because of her actions. That still doesn't mean I was waiting for her to die or happy when I found her dead. Believe me. Nothing could be further from the truth. I was horrified and sad. I'm still sad. I might not have loved your mom at the end of her life, but I loved her once. Enough to have you. What she went through, the experience, it was a terrible way to go—and even worse because it meant you never got the chance to build a better relationship with her."

It damn near breaks my heart when she scoffs. "Yeah, well, she didn't want me anyway. She made that very clear when she was alive."

"But there's nothing wrong with hoping she would one day. I would never judge you for that." This time, she doesn't pull away when I reach out to touch her shoulder. "And it makes me sorry for her, so sorry. She's the one who missed out. You have been the one singular bright spot in my life since the day you were born. And every day I've spent watching you grow has been a privilege. I'm in awe of the woman you've become—no, really," I insist when she rolls her eyes. "I'm not just saying that. I mean it with all my heart. You're the one good thing that has ever come out of my existence."

"Until now, right? You have another chance at a family. You can start over."

"You've been my family all along. My relationship with Bianca isn't meant to fill in some imaginary gap in my life. I'm not trying to replace you, not with her, and not with another baby."

Her nose goes red first, and I know what that means. Tears are on the way, no matter how hard she tries to blink them back. "I don't know where I belong anymore. Nothing feels right anymore."

"Oh, sweetheart." To hell with giving her space. What she needs right now is to be held by someone who loves her. Her head hits my shoulder the instant my arms encircle her trembling form. "What I wouldn't give to take all this away from you. All my money, the business, everything. So long as it meant you could be happy again."

"I don't know if I can take it anymore."

"Take what?" I ask, rubbing her back. Damn, she's so thin. I know better than to comment on it, but feeling her ribs through her sweatshirt leaves a sour taste in my mouth.

"Everything. All of it. I feel so broken. I can't even remember who I used to be. It's like that person doesn't exist anymore, like she never did."

"You're still Tatum. You're still my beautiful, brilliant girl."

"But I'm not, Daddy. I'm not her anymore."

"Then we'll get you back to that place. We'll find a way. A map to guide you back to where you want to be. I know I haven't done a great job of helping you so far. I'm flailing around just as much as you are. I don't know exactly how to help you or what would be best. But we have to try, both of us. I need you to meet me halfway. I need you to try even if you don't feel like it. Or else nothing's ever going to change. You can lead a horse to water, but you can't make it drink."

"I know."

"And you can do that on your own time," I make sure to add so she doesn't feel like I'm pressuring her. *Am I doing this right? Am I making a hopeless disaster of the whole thing?* I wish I knew. If there's one thing fatherhood has taught me, it's that there's no instruction manual. And as incredible as she is, she's never made it easy.

"I'm only making things miserable for you and Bianca." She pulls her sleeve down to wipe her nose, sniffling. "I don't want to be a burden on you guys. You deserve to be happy and have so much to look forward to."

Slowly, the meaning behind her words sinks into my brain. "What are you trying to say?" The hand rubbing her back goes still.

"I mean... I've been thinking... And maybe I should leave, go off and do my own thing."

"No. Honey, I want you here. We both do."

"I'm just in the way. I'm so damn tired and sad and scared all the time—every day. And I see you guys, and I see how happy she is, and I think to myself she's been through a lot of tough shit, too, and she's not falling apart the way I am. Something must be wrong with me. Why don't I get to be happy, too? Where's my happily ever after and knight in shining armor?"

"Honey, there's nothing wrong with falling apart. We have to fall apart sometimes. It's how we grow and become resilient to the shit life throws at us. You'll find happiness. I know it's hard to believe at the moment, but you will. There's a man out there for you and a future and happiness."

"I'm sorry, Dad. I really am, but every day I see you together, and every time there's a new announcement like there was today, it makes me feel worse." Slowly, she detaches herself from me. "This is what I want. What I need."

This is the worst possible idea she could come up with. If she can't keep herself together while she's under my roof, and in my care, how the hell is she going to do it by herself? Then again, is it cruel to force her to stay when I know how unhappy it makes her to be here?

It's the hope shining in her teary eyes that makes the decision for me. I can't extinguish that. Not when it's the first time I've seen hope in her eyes in weeks. Months, even.

"This is something we're going to have to work out together," I decide, speaking slowly, choosing my words carefully. At any other time, under any other circumstances, I would shut the idea down immediately and leave it there. That's exactly what I want to do now. My first impulse is to say no, but I know that would only push her further away, and I don't want to lose her, not any more than I already have.

The surprise in her raised eyebrows confirms how out of character this is for me. "Seriously? You mean it?"

"I do. I'm not going to keep you prisoner if you don't want to be here, but I'm telling you it would make me a lot more comfortable if you would stay. I would prefer you stay for as long as you need to until you feel secure getting on your feet, but I respect your choice, and your need for space, and if you decide to come back, the door is always open."

I have to laugh at myself, especially since she's looking at me like I've grown a second head or something. "I'm trying, kid. I'm really trying. But don't be surprised if I call you every day and ask when you're coming back—if you decide to leave."

"She's really good for you, isn't she?" A faint smile plays at the corners of her mouth. "She's changed you."

"I've had to make myself change for her, not in a bad way, and not because I don't want to. It's just hard, but I'm sure it'll be worth it."

"I love you." And all at once, she's a little girl again, throwing her arms around my neck and squeezing like her life depends on it. It's the most life she's shown in far too long, so I won't ask her to let go. I would rather soak this in for as long as possible.

If I've learned anything recently, it's how suddenly everything can change. How fast you can go from holding someone tightly to fearing they might be dead.

BIANCA

I feel like a stalker, sitting in my car, parked a few houses down from my father's. There aren't many cars parked on the street this early on a weekday afternoon with everybody at work, yet I still feel like I should hang back. His car is parked on the street, meaning he's home, though I didn't want him to see me. I'm not even sure why.

We haven't spoken since that day at the house. It's driving me crazy not knowing how he has been handling life since our argument. I figured Ken would contact me if there was an emergency. Otherwise, I waited about as long as I could before curiosity forced me to come up with a reason to show up here.

Maybe some people can deal with being shut out, but not me. He's still in too dangerous of a place to leave him on his own. Add to that a grandchild I would like him to meet someday, and I didn't see how this could continue. Waiting for him to come around and get in touch with me didn't work, so I resorted to a peace offering by grabbing groceries in case the kitchen's in shambles again.

All that's left is getting out of the damn car. Taking a breath, I open the door and pull the two brimful bags from the back seat.

What am I going to find? I shudder to think about it. He could have spiraled worse than ever after that fight or taken it as a sign that he needed to turn things around. I know better than to assume the latter, but I can still hope, right?

As I approach the house, I can tell the front porch has been swept recently—a good sign. I press my finger to the bell and squint, trying to see through the curtain hanging in front of the glass cut-out. There's movement on the other side, and before I can step back, the lock clicks and the door opens. I hold my breath. Waiting. Hoping.

On the other side, I find my father. He's showered, shaved, and dressed in a clean t-shirt and jeans. His eyes are clear rather than bloodshot and glassy when they travel over me from head to toe. "What are you doing here?"

At least his snappy question crushes the emotion swelling in my chest, or else I may have burst into tears of relief at finding him looking better than he has in weeks. "I'm going door-to-door with bags of groceries, seeing if anybody wants to take them."

"I really don't need the sarcasm."

"Dad, obviously, I'm bringing groceries to ensure you have what you need."

"You don't have to do that."

"I know, but I want to."

"When did you get it into your head that I need you to take care of me? No, don't answer that." He shakes his head, scowling. "Is this really what you think I am? Some hopeless loser who needs his daughter to bring food to him?"

"You're putting words in my mouth that weren't there, Dad." I make a big deal of craning my neck to look over his shoulder. "And unless I'm interrupting something, maybe I could come inside and unload some of this food? I got your favorite ice cream and those frozen waffles you like. They're thawing out as we speak."

"I'm a sucker for rocky road." He steps aside to let me in. It's a relief to find the house looking good, neat, and clean without so much as a beer bottle in sight. I didn't tell him I was on my way, so it's not like he tidied up for my sake.

Could he have turned a corner?

One thing I can't do is make a big deal out of it. I pretend not to notice, heading straight for the kitchen. "Have you eaten lunch yet?"

"I have a more important question for you." He makes a big deal of checking his watch, and right away, I know what's coming. Just need to brace myself for it.

"Okay, alright, I know what you're going to say. Why am I not at work at one o'clock in the afternoon."

"That is roughly what I was concerned with, yes." He leans against the counter, his arms folded, while I continue to put away the groceries. "I'm waiting."

"I am not working there anymore."

"Knew they would have a problem with all these absences. Not that I'm saying it's your fault."

"Honestly, no. That's not what happened." With the freezer door open between us, I close my eyes and take a deep breath. After closing it, I force myself to look him in the eye. "I quit. I walked away."

"You what?" His wide-eyed, open-mouthed expression is pretty close to what I expected. The cherry on top is the way his face begins to flush. He brings to mind one of those old Bugs Bunny cartoons where a character's good and mad—and once the color reaches the top of their head, their hat flies off or something like that. He's not wearing a hat. I hope his head doesn't explode.

"Let me explain, at least?"

"What is there to explain? You're throwing your entire future away a little bit at a time. One poor decision after another."

"Don't make me regret coming here, Dad," I whisper while my chin quivers as I fight back tears. "Please. I don't want to fight."

"Okay, okay," he grumbles, holding up both hands. "I don't want you crying over it."

"It's like I can't predict my emotions anymore."

"Yes, I guess you would be fighting with that right now. I remember your mom's mood swings." Then, his brows draw together and his hands close around my arms. "What are you not telling me? Is everything alright with the baby? Is that why you quit your job?"

"No, no." I shake my head, touched at the sudden change. Though I am sorry his mind went in that direction. "I'm just fine. I went to the doctor last week, and he said everything was right on track. You'll have a grandbaby in March."

That's not enough to distract him, unfortunately. "And my grandbaby is going to have an unemployed mother."

"I wouldn't be the first."

"Bianca…"

"They're called stay-at-home moms, by the way."

"You know what I'm saying. I don't appreciate you making jokes about it."

I can't count how many times I've picked up his spirits by joking around, making sarcastic comments, teasing him a little. It looks like that's not happening today. "Dad. Please, hear me out." I sink into one of the chairs at the table with a heavy sigh. "It's not what I wanted. I never wanted that job. I know it was what you wanted for me, and I'm sorry if you're disappointed, but I have to do what's best for me."

"Honey. It's not about having the perfect job, not all the time. Do you know how many kids graduate college and end up taking the first job that comes their way for the sake of experience? That's what your first job is about. You work your way up to what you actually want to do."

Considering he went right from high school to the police force, I have to wonder how he manages to sound so sure of himself. "I understand that. And I could have stayed—they were happy to let me stay on. I just... couldn't see the point." It sounds pretty lame when I say it out loud. Unlike me, or rather the me I used to be. I can see why he'd be confused.

"Not when you already have a meal ticket, right?"

"Please. I will need you to stop saying or doing things like that." His head snaps back a little like he's surprised—and he's not the only one. I didn't mean to come out sounding so stern. Then again, he's done plenty of things in the recent past alone that is enough for me to get an attitude over. Maybe he has it coming to him. Maybe he needs to hear what a jerk he's being.

"I would think you'd know by now that you raised me better than that," I continue once the first rush of anger passes. "I'm insulted that you would even speak those words."

"Yes, but then you've done a lot of things lately that have left me scratching my head and wondering if you're the kid I raised."

"Trust me. I am still that same person. And I'm sorry that my life isn't turning out the way you hoped. I'm sure when the time comes, I'll have the same hopes and dreams for my child."

"Yes. You will." He releases a chuckle, running a hand over his head before taking a seat of his own. "You're going to learn pretty fast what it feels like to stand back and watch your kid make a mistake. You can try with all your might, but there's no changing their mind."

"I'm sorry I've put you through that."

"You don't seem very sorry."

"I am. But being sorry isn't the same as changing my mind to make you happy. I'm starting to learn, finally, that I need to be able to look myself in the eye every morning when I get out of bed. That I'm the person whose opinion matters most. And right now, I can tell you that if I went back to that office and wasted my life sitting in a gray cubicle, going blind, staring at tiny columns of numbers all day, I'd lose it. It wouldn't even take that long."

"So you'll find another job. I don't want to see you waste your education."

"And I will find another job. But it's going to be something I actually want to do."

All it takes is seeing his lips draw together and his eyes narrow to know what's coming next. "And what does *he* think about it?"

"*He* has a name."

"Don't split hairs with me right now. What does he think?"

"Callum wants me to do whatever I want to do."

"Right, I know what that means."

"Oh? Please, enlighten me. I haven't had a good laugh all day."

"I'm going to pretend this sarcastic attitude is a result of pregnancy and let that go."

"You don't get to make comments like that and expect me not to fire back a similar response. What do you think it means when I say he wants me to do whatever I want?"

"He's going to keep you home. That's where he wants you. You'll be the Carmela Soprano from "The Sopranos." Spending endless amounts of money, keeping an eye on the kids, and letting your intelligence go to waste."

The thing is, I can't even tell him he's wrong. I'm sure that is what Callum would want if I allowed him to have his way. "That's his knee-jerk reaction," I say, choosing my words carefully and trying to ignore the smug look on my dad's face. "My happiness and what I want is important to him. I'm not pretending to know how good I have it, because being freely open to walk away from something that makes me unhappy is extremely lucky. Let's face it, it's not like I'm fulfilling my potential by checking spreadsheets all day, either."

"I'm telling you, that wouldn't be forever. Not for a girl as smart as you."

"No offense, Dad, but the workforce has changed. It's not all about putting in the time with the company anymore. There are no guarantees. I would rather spend my time feeling fulfilled."

"You've made your decision. And at least I don't have to worry about you getting kicked out on your ass when you can't make rent."

"That's true." I reach out, covering his hand on the table with my own. "You don't have to worry about me. I mean it. I'm fine. He wants to take care of me."

"That doesn't make me feel better."

"He'll take care of the baby. That much, I know for sure."

He grumbles while withdrawing his hand, then standing and walking over to the fridge. "Did you have lunch? I should've asked."

"I ate a little something before I went to the store to make sure I didn't overbuy when I arrived."

His laugh is genuine, even light. "Your mother's tried-and-true technique. She used to carry protein bars in her purse just in case." The way he transforms when he talks about her both warms my heart and makes me indescribably sad. He's a young man still, and he's nice looking—he's my dad, but I can look at him objectively.

He could find somebody to love him. Somebody who makes him happy. It's a shame, the thought of him spending the rest of his life only loving the memory of my mother.

"You only ate a little?" He leans into the fridge. "What about a sandwich? Turkey? Bologna?"

My stomach growls at the word. I didn't even feel that hungry until now. "Bologna and American? I brought a loaf of rye."

He grins over the top of the door. "And I have brown mustard. Just the way you like it."

"I had no idea that was exactly what I wanted until you said it."

I get the feeling he misses taking care of me. If I wasn't hungry, I'd pretend to be if only to see him looking glad for a minute, even whistling under his breath as he smears a thick layer of mustard on a slice of rye. "Has Callum forgiven me yet for what I did?"

I had no idea he'd want to talk about that, now or ever. And I was more than willing to let it go, if only to avoid the discomfort that makes me shift in my chair. "You'd have to ask him."

"Don't be cute."

"I don't think he holds a grudge," I relent. "At all."

"How… about you?" He slides the sandwich in front of me before returning to the chair across from mine. It's obvious he's going out of his way to avoid eye contat with me, as he examines a scratch on the table instead. He's probably looked at the thing a hundred times.

I should've known he was more worried about me. "I don't like to hold grudges, either. They're a waste of energy. And I wouldn't have shown up with groceries if I was angry."

Even so, the memory of that day makes me feel a little sick, causing me to set the sandwich down for a second. "You must know it hurt me to watch you beat him like that. Is this what I have to look forward to? It'll make for a hell of a Christmas party."

"I didn't want to hurt you. I was trying to—"

"Help me. I know."

"I was doing everything I could to protect you." He grimaces when our eyes meet, then quickly looks away. "I did everything I could think to do. I found that damn camera and I saw red."

"I know. I was upset when I found out about it. I didn't talk to him for days." That wasn't quite the truth—that wasn't why we didn't talk for days, but he doesn't need to know that. He never needs to know that. The thought of how he'd react is almost enough to make me regret eating when my stomach tightens.

"I won't say what I'm thinking."

"I would appreciate that." Not that he has to say a word; he wants to point out that a few days of the silent treatment isn't enough. Nothing will ever be enough. He's my father, and that's how it'll always be. He'll want what he feels is best for me, regardless of what *I* actually want or need.

I'm halfway through the sandwich when another thought bubbles up to the surface. I'm too curious to let it go, though I know I should if I want this visit to end well—or at least amicably. Any normal, concerned daughter would ask the question that threatens to get stuck in my throat. "What are you doing? I mean, with your time? Do you think you could get your job back?"

"I'm not sure I want my job back." The instant, guilty glance he shoots my way says I don't have to point out the irony of him basically saying what he gave me shit over not just five minutes ago. "I know somebody down there is on the take, so how am I supposed to work beside that kind of person?"

"I get it. I wouldn't want to look at any of them." The memory of walking through and feeling the weight of their stares is still fresh. Wondering which one of them was dishonest, which one stood back and let my father suffer. I'd go crazy if I were in his shoes. "But you do have skills. Training. I'd hate to see it all go to waste."

"It just so happens I'm putting those skills to work at a new job." He holds up a hand when I can't help reacting with excitement. "Don't go overboard. It's employment, and I'm glad to have it, but let's not act like I achieved something special."

"What are you doing? Where is it?"

"Overnight security at an office building downtown. Nothing too strenuous, but the pay is good and it's quiet."

"Do you like it?"

He frowns but nods. "I guess I do. It's nothing special, though it's a good living. I'm sure I'll start reading a hell of a lot more."

"That's great! I don't have to worry about you anymore." And when I say it out loud, I realize how true the statement is. I don't have to worry about him. He pulled himself together—as much as he could, anyway. He's still got all kinds of questions and confusion hanging over his head, most of which has to do with Mom, but he's taking steps to move forward after almost burning his whole life to the ground.

Once I've finished eating, he takes the plate and washes it. "I have something to show you. Something I've been working on."

"Oh?" If he takes me down to his office to show off that nightmare of a corkboard, I might scream.

"Upstairs." Okay, at least that rules out his office. "Come see."

He seems happy... ish. Upbeat. It's enough to keep my anxiety from growing out of control as I follow him from the kitchen to the stairs. I have to stop worrying about him, but then again, it's not like he hasn't given me any reason to.

He leads me to my old bedroom, where I pull up short in surprise at what I find inside. "When did you—" Of course. This is why he was going through things and found the camera.

Running a hand over the crib that now stands in the corner where my bookcase used to live, he explains, "I pulled out the baby furniture from the attic. Your old crib, the changing table, the rocking chair."

"I can see that." The bed and dresser are still in their place, but the rest of the room looks more like a nursery. "What brought this on?"

"I thought you might want to bring the baby around for a visit occasionally." There's hope in his voice, small and shy but undoubtedly present. He straightens out the cheerful flowered sheet in the crib, then props a teddy bear up in the corner. "I wanted them to have someplace to sleep. I'm looking forward to meeting them. I want you to know that. This baby is going to have a lot of love around them."

"Oh, Dad." That's as much as I can choke out before I throw my arms around him. "Thank you. I was so worried you would have weird, mixed feelings about the baby because of Callum."

"Let's just say I never saw myself getting linked to him in such a permanent way." He chuckles, chagrined, while stroking my hair. "But this baby is a blessing. And I want nothing but the best for both of you."

"Thank you."

"Keep in mind I plan to spoil the hell out of this kid."

I close my eyes as the last of the tension I was holding drains out of me. "I would expect nothing less."

CALLUM

"That's three shipments overhauled in the past week." Romero arches an eyebrow when he turns away from the window. "I think you've made your point. We'll be lucky if the bastard doesn't blow us up."

"It's not enough." I push back from my desk, where we've wrapped up a call with our trucking contact. They recently sent a crew to intercept a shipment of electronics which now belongs to us. "Not until I hold that fucker's beating heart in my hands."

"You want to move on to step three, then?"

"Hell, yes." The thought makes me smile. "I hope Moroni isn't too attached to his fleet of trucks."

"This is going to put that warehouse fire to shame. Sixty trucks, five garages?"

Yes, and it's a way of proving to Sebastian that I'm willing to sacrifice what was supposed to go to me once the smoke clears. We're still not on what anyone would call friendly terms after he pulled a gun on my right-hand man in my home, but we don't need to be friends to work together. "It'll get the point across."

Romero checks his phone, frowning. "What's taking him so long? He seemed to be in a hell of a hurry when I called him after our call started wrapping up. He said he'd be here as soon as possible."

"I'm sure he's moving as fast as he can. Maybe with one of those dome lights on his roof."

"There's a chance he could decide not to tell us a damn thing, you know."

"I know, except I have a feeling I can get through to him." I'm going to do everything in my power. After what we've learned since Romero pulled together that list of cops in on the take, I'm pleased we've uncovered the full story of what happened to Jessica Cole. I want to hear it from Ken, however. I need to, since he allowed his best friend to continue hating me for years and even watched him beat the shit out of me when he knew the truth all along.

"You're sure this is the right thing to do? What if Bianca comes back early?"

"Please. Charlie will keep her there for hours. Knowing him, he'll spend the whole time trying to convince her to stay for good."

As soon as Bianca announced she was paying him a visit, I knew it had to be today. Otherwise, she would've been hanging around the house, and there would've been no discussing this. I don't want her to know yet, not until I figure out a gentle way to break the news—if there is such a way of breaking it.

"Besides," I add, "the app will let me know once she's moving." I tap my phone that's sitting on the desk, where the app tells me she's parked by Charlie's house.

Henry's call from the front gate sets Romero in motion while I sit at the desk and brace myself for what's to come. It's sort of a last-ditch effort, calling Ken in for an emergency meeting, but I'm tired of tiptoeing around the issue. I want answers, and I want them now. Until I know for sure what happened to Jessica Cole, there's no moving forward with Bianca. The guilt and uncertainty are acting as barriers between us whether she knows it or not.

Eventually, she will and clue into the way I hold part of myself back from her.

Ultimately, I'll have to tell her about my connection to the murder, but I can't leave it there. I need to be able to follow that up with the rest of the story. I need to provide the answers I promised.

I hear Ken's deep, strident voice before I see him. "Is Bianca here? Is she alright?"

"She's fine," Romero tells him. "This doesn't have to do with her."

"Tell me Charlie hasn't pulled some crazy bullshit again." He looks and sounds beside himself when he enters my office, his angular face flushed, his skin shining with a thin layer of perspiration. He's in the typical detective outfit of a shirt-and-tie combo, his badge hanging from a lanyard around his neck. "What's happening? Why did you need me to come right away? Tell me he's not tied up somewhere in this house."

The idea makes me laugh a little. "I wouldn't go that far. No, Charlie isn't here and hasn't been since the last time you and I saw each other. As far as I know, Bianca is visiting with him right now."

"Jesus Christ." He comes to a stop in front of my desk, hands on his hips, lowering his head as he attempts to catch his breath. "Do you know how many ugly thoughts can go through a man's head when he gets an urgent call?"

"I do apologize, I didn't mean to make you anxious. We need to discuss something else, and I didn't want Bianca here for it. She hasn't gone out on her own much lately, and I had to take advantage."

"What's going on? Is there anything I can help with?"

"I'm thinking there is something you might be able to help us with. Please, have a seat."

He reminds me of a wary animal now, eyes narrowing slightly as he sits. "What's going on?"

"I'm going to cut right to the chase, for there's no point in wasting time." Looking him in the eye, I fold my hands on the desk. "I have it on good authority you were in on the take."

His face drains of color all at once, as suddenly as if I flipped a switch. "I'm using past tense because I would like to give you the benefit of thinking you've moved on from that, however who's to say? At any rate, you were taking money from outside influencers around the time of Mrs. Cole's death."

"Who did you hear this from?" His head swings around until he finds Romero standing by the window. "Where are you getting this information from? Because they're full of shit, whoever they are."

"From what we've learned," I continue, ignoring his outburst, "you were in with one particular family. It so happens I was in the middle of brokering a pretty big deal with that family at around the same time. And, of course, Charlie was a dog digging for a bone, determined to put me and anyone I did business with in prison for a long time."

He's fighting hard to keep it together, only that doesn't stop him from trembling, no matter how he tries to laugh everything off. I've watched men spiral through the different reactions of getting caught red-handed. This is nothing new.

"I still don't understand what this has to do with me," he insists. "For one thing, it isn't like guys on the take announce it to the rest of the department. How would anyone know for sure?"

"Ken. You realize I could have taken this information directly to Charlie and let him do what he wants with it? I brought you here out of respect and with an understanding that this is a very complicated situation. The least you can do is man up and quit the bullshit."

"I cannot believe I came here to be insulted." He blurts out a bitter laugh as he stands. "This is insanity. Are you this desperate to show Bianca what a decent man you're trying to become? It's going to backfire, big time."

"I confirmed it with his son," I murmur, freezing him in place. "Sebastian Costello. He was here the day Charlie kicked my ass. You saw each other."

"And I noticed the way he looked at you," Romero adds, his voice so low I could almost call it apologetic. "Like he had seen you before."

"And when I asked him," I continue, "he confirmed having seen you in his father's office more than once when he was younger. Many times, I believe he said." Romero's head bobs up and down slowly in confirmation.

He's trapped. He knows it. It's in the way his face sags and his shoulders slump before he lowers himself into the chair once again. "I know it's early," he mutters, "but do you think I could have a drink?"

I give Romero a slight nod, and he goes to the bar, pouring two fingers of whiskey, which he hands to a shaking Ken. "Listen, I'm not here to give you shit over taking the money. We've paid our fair share to different contacts in the department over the years. And if a man could make a decent living in law enforcement, he wouldn't have to rely on... other sources of income."

"I needed the money," he murmurs, staring down into his glass. "My wife didn't recover well after she gave birth to our second kid. The bills piled up and I was drowning."

"As I said, I get it. And Salvatore Costello must have seemed like a safe bet. He had a reputation for being a decent guy. It's a big part of the reason I got into business with him in the first place. He wasn't a hot-tempered sort of guy. And he lived by a code."

"That's what I told myself," he mutters before sipping his drink. "If I had to get into bed with somebody like that, I wanted it to be someone who wasn't out there shedding blood and destroying families."

"But he did destroy a family, didn't he?"

His head snaps up. "I don't—"

"Ken, what did I say? Don't waste my time, and don't fucking lie to me. When I think about it, it makes perfect sense. I'm not saying you had anything to do with it."

"I didn't. I swear to God, I didn't."

"But he did have her killed, didn't he?"

His jaw ticks before his eyes fill with tears. That surprises me. I didn't expect the tears. The excuses, yes, but tears, definitely not. "It was supposed to be Charlie. He knew Charlie was after you and didn't want to get caught up in any of it. He paid me to…"

"He first approached you to get Charlie off my back, didn't he?"

"Yeah." He snorts before throwing back the rest of the whiskey. "Look what a good job I did. I begged him so many times. To think about Jess and Bianca. To think about his job, to try to nail all the other bad guys out there."

"You were unsuccessful," I sigh. "So Sal decided to go ahead and take care of things."

"I swear to God, if I had known…" He places the glass on my desk before bending forward, elbows on his knees, his head in his hands. The slight shaking of his shoulders tells me what I need to know. He doesn't want me to see the tears he can't hold back.

"She took his car that day, didn't she? And the gunman had no idea."

"I don't know the details." His voice is thick with emotion, shaky. "But as soon as I heard, I knew what happened. I went to Sal as soon as it felt safe and told him I knew what he did. I'm surprised I made it out of there alive. I was half out of my mind, horrified, grieving. She was my best friend's wife; she had a little girl. She was a special person. It shows he wasn't a total fucking monster at his core, or he could have had me executed."

"Did he give you any idea of how he felt about it? The mix-up?"

"He swore he was sorry, and part of me believed him. He didn't want to kill an innocent woman. That's not who he was."

"So why did his guy go through with it?" Romero demands. "I can see running the wrong car off the road, but he had to walk up to that car, open the door, and blow a bullet into her skull. He knew she was a woman when he did it."

"He gave me some story about his guy panicking because she saw him. And she was badly injured. He figured she would be dead either way, so he wanted to be sure in case she made a miraculous recovery and identified him."

I can see that happening. I might even do the same thing in that guy's shoes, whoever he was. Sometimes you do what has to be done to ensure your safety rather than leave anything to chance.

"I begged and pleaded for it to end there." When he lifts his head, his face is wet, his eyes red-rimmed. "I told him Charlie would take it as a warning to back off—and if he didn't, I would see to it that he did. And I kept my word. I was the one who convinced him to back off. He didn't do it all the way, but he wasn't as determined anymore."

That's the truth. There was a shift in Charlie's attitude after his wife's death. I didn't realize it at the time—Tatum and Bianca hadn't met at that point, and I was unaware of what went on in Charlie's personal life. Although when I look back at the timeline and piece things together, there's no denying he backed off after that point. Not entirely, as Ken said, but a great deal.

If he hadn't, Sal wouldn't have gone through with the deal. When Charlie backed off, Sal's confidence grew.

"If it weren't for me, Bianca wouldn't have either of her parents," he insists. There's an edge of panic that creeps into his voice. "You can't kill me for this. I did everything I could."

A glance at Romero tells me he's as confused as I am. "Nobody said anything about killing you, and while I don't particularly like Charlie, I know Bianca cares for you. It would hurt them both if anything happened to you."

"Are you going to tell her?"

"There's a reason I had you here when she was out, remember?"

He lets out a deep, shuddering breath. I can imagine his relief. "Thank you. I couldn't take it. Charlie is like my brother. I couldn't... I can't... If he knew..."

"I was the one who needed to know. I needed confirmation. All these years, he thought I was the one who did it. And you sat back and let him believe that because it didn't matter then, right? I'm an asshole, so why not let him believe I would murder his wife to get back at him?"

A fourth voice chimes in from the doorway. "No. It's worse than that."

Shit.

My stomach drops at the sound of her voice. I glance down at my dark, silent phone before glancing to the doorway, where Bianca sways slightly, her eyes as big as saucers.

How the fuck did she get here without me knowing? I was either too engrossed in Ken's story to notice the alert when it came through or the app failed.

Fuck me. Fuck everything. She wasn't supposed to find out this way.

"Bianca." Ken's chair almost tips over when he stumbles to his feet before lurching toward her. "Kiddo, what did you hear? It wasn't my fault, I swear. I never. I wouldn't have ever—"

She cuts off his panicked rant with a sharp slap that snaps his head to the side.

BIANCA

My hand stings.

I let it fall back to my side, where it throbs in time with my fast, pounding heartbeat.

I can barely look him in the eye, so I focus on the palm print I left on his cheek. It stands out redder with every second, while the rest of his face is as white as a sheet.

"Bianca..." Callum's somewhere behind him, though it's like everything around me is muffled, like I'm underwater.

"How could you do it?" I don't feel anything besides the stinging in my hand. There's no anger, no rage, no grief. I'm cold. Disconnected.

"I didn't have a choice."

And I used to respect him so much. I looked up to him the way Dad did. Now, here he is, crying and shaking, a fucking blubbering mess. I can feel it coming. He's going to start begging for me to forgive him. I don't know if I can handle that. I really don't.

"You didn't have a choice?" I whisper. "You had no choice but to let him believe he was going crazy? You had no other choice?"

"Bianca." Callum pushes Ken to the side and reaches for me. "You don't need this added stress."

Something in the way I look at Callum makes him back down. I can't imagine the expression on my face, but whatever it is, it makes his features pinch like he's pained. "Come, sit down. At least sit, please."

I shake him off, though, because sitting is not what I need most. What I need is answers and damn good ones. "What's your excuse for that, huh? All this time, everybody treated him like he was some sad joke. You could have stood by him at the very least."

"I did! I was the only friend he had left in the department." His voice cracks.

"Some friend," I snicker. "You let him believe he was making things up since that made it easier for you."

"How much did you hear?" Callum asks.

"I heard enough. Now I know who the real snake in the grass was this entire time."

"You've got it all wrong. I did everything possible to get him to walk away from the case."

"You gaslit him." Whatever holds me frozen in place must loosen, because now I can walk. Each step I take sends Ken scrambling backwards. "You watched him fall apart a little at a time, cracking slowly, pieces of who he was being chipped away. Yet, all along, you knew the truth. You knew he was right, that she was murdered, and you still made it seem to everyone else that he was broken by grief. Like he couldn't think for himself."

"And the autopsy," Romero interjects. "Are you the one who altered the report?"

My God. It keeps getting worse.

"He was looking too deep into things. He was going to get himself killed, so I had to step in."

"You hid the truth from him and made him think he was crazy."

"You don't get it. You don't know how it was. That man would have killed your father the way he did your mother. He would never have let it go if Charlie knew somebody had shot her. I did that to protect him. To keep him from walking headfirst into danger—"

"Don't. Stop trying to make yourself the hero."

"It's the truth. And if you think about it, you'll see I'm right. I convinced him to back off. You would have lost them both if it hadn't been for me."

"You could have told him the truth," I counter. "If you had been honest about what truly happened, he could have moved on by now. Could have told him it was for my sake, that he needed to back off for me so I wouldn't lose him, too. But no, why would you do that? That would mean admitting you were a crooked cop. Right?"

He wants to argue with me. I can see it in the way his eyes dart back and forth like he's a cornered animal. Only he can't come up with anything to say, because he knows I'm right.

I see everything now. I see him for the snake he is.

"You're a coward," I whisper as tears fill my eyes. "You took the money and told yourself you were doing the right thing, but all you did was make him a joke in the department. Again and again, you told him to let it go, but it meant acting like he was a fool. Like he was crazy. You sacrificed him to protect the image he had of you."

"I would have lost my job," he whispers.

"Oh, you mean the way he lost his?"

"I never told him to lose his fucking mind over this! Did I encourage him to use department resources to research? To forget all his other work, his caseload, everything else? Every damn day I tried to steer him back on course, and every day he ignored me."

"Poor you," I whisper, shaking my head as the tears fall. "You poor thing. The man was haunted. Everybody told him he was crazy when he was the only one who wanted to know the truth."

"You need to calm down." Callum wraps an arm around my waist, and even though it is comforting, it's not enough. Nothing will be enough. When I think back on all the years he could have told the truth and helped my dad find a way through it...

"I'm so disgusted and angry. I don't even want to look at you."

"It would be better if you left, Ken," Callum announces.

"You're not going to tell him, right? You can't tell him. He'd never forgive me. Please, Bianca, think. Think about what they will do to him."

"Oh! All of a sudden, you care what this will do to him? No, Ken, all you care about is what he'll think of you when all the lies are revealed. You can't stand to have him believe anything other than you being the good, honest guy he always thought you were. Funny, you had no mercy for my father when he needed it, but now you're standing here begging me for mercy."

"Please, it would be like losing my brother. You might not understand, but everything I did was for him, and for you."

"No!" I bark. "You did it for yourself!! Don't you dare say you did it for me. You don't get to rewrite history now that you've been caught."

"Please. I couldn't take it." Throwing his arms out to the sides, he releases a choked cry filled with anguish. "What do I have to do? Do you want me to beg? I'll get on my knees and beg you. I'll do whatever you want. All I ask is that you don't tell him. He can never find out."

"Even if it means finally getting closure, that's what he needs more than anything. He needs to be able to move on with his life. And he can't do that with the way things are now."

"As I said, Ken, you need to go." Callum tries to turn me away from Ken, and I know he wants to make this better. He wants to help, but this is something I'm going to have to do myself.

"Wait a second." I look up at Callum. "Do I get to decide?"

"What do you mean?"

"You invited him over, so I guess this is between the two of you."

"You do what you need to do. I was always going to leave it up to you after I broke the news."

It's up to me. I'm not used to hearing that.

What should I do? How do I handle this? I know what I want to do. I can see myself spitting on him, kicking him, making him feel as small and as hopeless and friendless as my father has felt all this time, yet who would that help? What would it accomplish? It wouldn't make me feel any better in the long run. I would only end up feeling as small and pitiful as Dad has felt.

"I won't tell him," I decide, ignoring the way Ken shudders with relief while his legs sag. "I'll let you live with that guilt for the rest of your life. What I am going to do is tell him what happened, because he deserves to know the truth." More than that, he needs it.

"But you won't say anything about me?"

"I won't. You can live with the gnawing guilt." Dropping my voice to a whisper, I add, "But if I were you, I would make it a point to stay away from me, because I don't know if I could hide how I feel about you in front of Dad."

"I understand." He looks to Callum, who nods, stepping aside.

"You heard her. Get out of here," Callum orders. Ken gives me one last sorrowful look before leaving the room, Romero following close behind him.

At first, I can't move. All I can do is stare at the spot where Ken just stood and remember all the times he had the nerve to grieve beside my father. All the times he sat with him, talked with him. The way he wept at my mother's graveside on the day of the funeral.

He knew exactly what happened to her. All the time. He held the truth right in the palm of his hands, and he never told us.

"Now, will you please sit down?" I'm barely aware of Callum guiding me to a seated position on the sofa. I hardly feel the supple leather beneath my hands.

"Why did you ask him to come here? How much did you know?"

"It's complicated."

That's not the answer I want to hear. Not after everything we've been through, not after discovering the truth.

"Can you just give me a fucking answer, Callum!! How much did you already know?"

"I promised I would find answers." I nod, waiting. "Romero finally put it together when he noticed how it seemed like Sebastian recognized Ken the day he and your father came to the house. We dug a little deeper, and Sebastian confirmed Ken took money from his father years ago."

"Why?"

Callum's voice is edged with hesitation. "Bianca... Are you sure you want to hear this?"

"For God's sake, I'm not a child, and just because I'm pregnant doesn't mean I'm some delicate flower incapable of handling big emotions. Tell me."

"Salvatore Costello paid Ken to keep your father out of our business. We were in the middle of working out our first deal at the time. He didn't want the extra complications. When Charlie wouldn't back down, Sal decided to get rid of him. I was completely unaware of it, I swear. I didn't know anything about you, your mother, or any of it. And for what it's worth, Ken probably did his best. You know how impossible it is to make your father listen."

"Okay." That's not true at all. I don't see a damn thing. "How long have you known?"

"I didn't want to tell you anything until I knew the whole story."

"That's not an answer, Callum!"

"Weeks. I've known for weeks. It seemed obvious the autopsy was altered, which then got me asking questions. I didn't have anything to do with her death—not directly. I was afraid you would blame me once you found out."

"I'm not stupid. I know you couldn't have done anything to stop this. And I understand you were trying to protect me." A sudden sob erupts from my chest before I cover my face with my hands. "My poor dad. All this time. He trusted Ken. He's been suffering alone, no one believing him, wondering who he could trust, and the one person he believed in…"

I can't do it anymore. My heart is going to break.

"Come here." Callum pulls me closer until I'm in his lap, and resting my head on his shoulder while the tears continue to fall like rain. "If it helps, I do believe Ken was trying to do what he thought was best. He was afraid of telling Charlie the truth. I can understand why. Costello paid him to do a job, and he needed the money. He thought he was helping Charlie. I'm not trying to defend him," he murmurs, rubbing my back, his breath stirring my hair. "However, I can see his side of the story."

"He let my father believe it was you who killed my mother all this time."

"And I'm sure that would have worked just fine if it hadn't been for me falling in love with you."

"That's not fair to you."

"You think Charlie Cole is the first person who ever hated me? Please. I can handle that. What I can't handle is knowing how that gets in our way now."

"I have to tell him the truth, somehow, except I don't have the first idea how to do it."

"It's good that you don't have to do anything right now. Take your time. Figure out what feels best. You don't necessarily have to put a time stamp on when you tell him."

How tempting, the idea of pretending this never happened. "No. He needs to know he was right. He needs closure. Or else he will spend the rest of his life stuck in one place. I can't let that happen. I don't want to hurt him in the process, though."

"I understand." The touch of his lips to my forehead is sweet, comforting. "Although you know, it would be alright to admit this hurts you, too. It's a betrayal. He betrayed both of you, even if he thought he was doing it for the right reasons."

"The villain isn't supposed to be the person closest to you."

"No, but sometimes the people who hurt you the most are the people closest to you, and usually they're fighting an inevitable battle between right and wrong. Not everything is black and white. Sometimes you do things to protect the people you care about, even if it's a decision that would hurt that person if they ever found out. Caring and loving someone makes you do crazy things."

That's true, only I don't think I have a bone of forgiveness inside me. Every time I think about it, all I see is the despair my father went through. He loved his job and lost it. He was so consumed with finding my mother's killer. And all along, Ken had the information.

"Whatever you decide to do—even if you never tell your father the truth about what happened—I'm behind you. I'll support whatever you choose." Callum squeezes me tight to his chest, and I snuggle deeper, wanting to escape reality.

"Thank you, and thank you for keeping your promise. You said you'd find out who killed her, and you did. Hopefully, Dad can move on, and there won't be so much tension between the two of you."

His lips twitch like he wants to laugh, but lucky for him, he's smart enough not to. "I won't expect such a miracle to occur."

CALLUM

Being playful doesn't come naturally to me. I imagine anyone who grew up the way I did would have the same problem. It has nothing to do with my choice of profession. Maintaining an image. None of that matters when I'm in my own backyard, sitting by my pool. This is where I get to be myself. Life didn't give me many opportunities to kick back and enjoy myself. In my younger days, I was always working, hustling. Fighting to claw my way to the top. There's very little room for fun in that sort of life.

And it goes without saying that my time with Amanda didn't exactly lend itself to laughter and good times.

I want to try for Bianca's sake, which is why I suggested we come out for a swim after announcing I was taking the rest of the day off. Sure, Romero looked at me like I had grown another head, but I didn't expect him to understand.

My little bird has been feeling depressed since she came in at the worst possible time a couple of days ago, and I'm trying like hell to make her feel better. Damn shame it doesn't seem to be working. Rather than swim with me, she's laid out on a lounge chair with a book. Judging from the number of pages I've seen her turn since she picked it up, she might have it finished by New Year's.

"There isn't going to be another day like this until next summer. Why don't you come in the pool?" I splash her a little and chuckle when she glares at me. "The water's the perfect temperature."

Her mouth is fixed into a tight frown as she sets down her book. "I don't know."

"Bianca. You have to stop punishing yourself."

"It's just that—"

I hold up a finger, shaking my head. "I know what you're going to say."

"Oh, you do?"

Yes, because it's the same thing she's been saying for two days. She hates the feeling of lying to her father. "He wouldn't want you to punish yourself like this." There aren't many positive things I can say about Charlie Cole while keeping a straight face, but that's one of them. I don't doubt how much he loves his daughter. "And you look really hot in that new bathing suit."

She looks down at herself, as uncomfortable as I would expect from someone who still has no idea how beautiful they are. "It's just a plain old one-piece."

Maybe that's what I like about it so much. It hints at everything beneath it without giving too much away. "You're driving me crazy. So either get in this water now, or I'll come out there and throw you in. You're too far away from me for me to remain sane."

There's a lot of love in the way she shakes her head, wearing the smile women wear when their men act like little boys. "Okay, okay. Whatever makes you happy." It doesn't make me happy to see her the way she is now, but at least she's smiling as she gets up from her lounge chair and makes her way down the ladder and into the water.

"Okay, you're right. This feels incredible." Once she's halfway down the ladder, she pushes away from it, floating on her back.

"I told you. It would be a shame to waste this beautiful day sitting on the sidelines." It's enough to watch her float around lazily for a short while, her face turned toward the sky, eyes closed. She's more peaceful now than she's been in days. I don't want to break that, so I settle for paddling around, enjoying the simplicity of being together.

"I'm sorry I've been such a downer."

"I would never call you that, and you don't have to apologize."

"But nobody wants to be around the girl who can't get her shit together."

"It just so happens I fell in love with a woman who feels things very deeply. I knew what I was getting into." That's not entirely true. There was no preparing myself for her, or for all the ways she would challenge me to be better than I was.

She sighs before rolling onto her stomach and slowly swimming toward me. Her body cuts through the water like she was born into it. Once she reaches me, she takes hold of my shoulders, draping her arms over them and tucking her head in close to my neck. "I just wish I knew how to process everything. I can barely sleep. I'm thinking about it so often."

I know. We share a bed, and I've never been a particularly deep sleeper. However, she's been tossing and turning, and when she does sleep, her night is full of dreams that only make the tossing and turning worse.

Last night was the final straw for me when she whimpered a single word: *Mommy*.

I couldn't spend a day in my office, away from her. I might not be able to take her pain away, but I can make myself available to her at the very least.

"Let's talk it through," I suggest. She joins me at the side of the pool, both of us folding our arms on the concrete edge.

"I'm not sure what there is to talk about. I just need to figure out some way to live with the truth." She kicks slowly, sighing as she rests her chin on her arms. "How do I do that?"

"Life is full of these moments. Trying to decide if it's better to let things go or to possibly hurt someone you love with the truth."

"Like with Tatum," she murmurs, her lips setting in a tight line.

"She's coming around." She's trying, anyway. "We have had dinner together the past three nights, and she seems a little better than she's been lately, right?"

"That's true. She actually spoke to me and appeared happy when I asked her to be my maid of honor."

"She did." For a moment, it looked like everything was back to normal. My daughter's bubbly personality leaked through, and there was a sparkle in her eyes. It gave me hope that things are finally beginning to turn around.

"But if she hadn't walked in on us talking with Romero, I wouldn't have told her yet. Is that normal?"

Hitting me with the heavy questions today. "I know a little something about keeping things from the people I love most, because I know it's better for them in the end. That's a burden. It's one I wish you didn't have to carry."

"Nobody ever said life would be easy all the time, right?"

But that's all I want. To make her life as easy as possible. She's a lot smarter than I am when it comes to this. More realistic. "You don't have to tell Charlie the specifics. He never has to know about Ken if you think it would be better for him not to."

"I can't do that to him. I don't know if he could handle it."

"Still, he can still know he was right. You can give him closure, or whatever you think he needs."

"And you would be okay with that?"

"This doesn't have anything to do with me. I would like him to know I didn't have anything to do with your mother, but that's as far as it goes. Even then, I've lived long enough with him hating me so I'm sure I could continue on the same way."

"If anything, it would make things better. He would be able to trust you more."

"Well, I would hope so." Nevertheless, I'm not going to hold my breath.

"I wish he could understand how normal our lives are." Then she smirks, looking around, taking in the pool and patio. "Maybe not normal. More like a lot nicer than normal."

"You mean, he probably imagines me sitting on a throne made from the skulls of my enemies?"

"Something like that," she says with a sigh. "He still has too many crazy ideas."

"Why don't you invite him over for dinner?" The words are hardly out of my mouth before I have to ask myself what the hell I'm thinking. *Charlie?* Sitting down at my table, in my house? If anyone's going to thaw the cold war between us, somebody has to make the first move. Besides, I wouldn't mind looking like the bigger man.

Her eyelids flutter for a second before she swallows hard. "Did I hear that right?"

"I think you did." I grin.

"Do you honestly want Dad to come over here for dinner?"

"Yes. I do." I don't, but I will do it for her sake.

"Is it going to be like a *Godfather* sort of situation? Are you going to shoot him halfway through his veal parm?"

"I think you've watched too many movies, babe." I can only shake my head when she doesn't return my smile. "Do you honestly think I would do something like that? That's a straightforward question. Why would you marry me if you thought I was capable of shooting your father at the dinner table right in front of you?"

She arches an eyebrow. "I haven't married you yet."

"You know what I mean." I can't go another moment without reaching for her. Taking hold of her waist, I pull her close. Right away, all interest in any conversation flies out the window thanks to her enticing body and its curves which fit so well against me. "I love you. You do know that, right?"

"I do."

"I want you to have everything you need to be happy. Your father means a lot to you. I would never want your relationship with him to suffer because of me. Invite him for dinner, maybe have a talk with him. Let's show him there are no hard feelings and that I want him to be part of our baby's life."

"Thank you." Her eyes start to well up with tears, and she wraps her arms around me, hugging me. "I can't tell you how much it means to me to hear you say that." If that's the case, it will be worth putting up with the sanctimonious prick for a couple of hours—anything, so long as my little bird has what she needs.

"Perhaps I can make something," she suggests, pulling back with excitement in her eyes. "Something he likes."

Yes, that's exactly what my life needs—more time in front of a stove. Keeping my happy expression in place is becoming more of a challenge. "Sure. Whatever you want."

She can barely stifle a giggle—and soon, she stops trying. "You'll crack a tooth if you don't stop grinding your teeth together. I love you."

The woman can see right through me. If I didn't trust her the way I do, it would be damn terrifying. Her legs wrap around my waist, drawing a surprised noise from me. "I love you too, now be careful there," I murmur when my dick instantly responds to the contact. "You know what happens when you get him started. No matter where we are or who's watching."

"You're right, you're right." Yet when she tries to disentangle us, she meets resistance in the form of my arms wound around her back.

"Did it sound like I was complaining?"

"We can't out here," she whispers. Her eyes sweep the patio while she bites her bottom lip seductively. "Somebody might see us."

"Sheryl is off for the day, and I made it clear we were not to be disturbed out here." Even if there was a chance of being discovered, it would already be too late for me to change my mind. As usual, my body's needs are impossible to ignore.

And once I caress her ass cheeks with both hands, she melts against me. She can't ignore her body's response to me, either. "You are incorrigible," she whispers in my ear as I back her into the corner of the pool farthest from the house. The sun warms my skin, however it's the warmth between her legs that I'm more interested in.

"Kiss me," she whispers, taking my face in her hands, her tongue probing the seam of my lips before I part them and let her inside, her tongue sliding past mine and lighting up every nerve ending in my body.

Our kiss deepens as her nails dig into my flesh until I'm sure she's pierced the skin—I nip her bottom lip in response until she starts to whimper. That needy little sound goes straight to my balls, making them ache. Just knowing she's as ready for this as I am is enough to drive me insane.

I break the kiss, trailing my teeth and lips over her jaw before laving at her throat. The sweetness of her skin and the faint taste of sunscreen and chlorine shouldn't excite me the way it does, but with Bianca there is a never-ending level of excitement.

The way her eyes scan the house over my shoulder shouldn't excite me, either. "Scared of being my bad girl?" I taunt, running my tongue over the thundering pulse in her throat. "Afraid somebody's going to see you getting fucked out here?"

I love that she's still a good girl deep down inside. All of the darkness she's experienced from my world hasn't tainted the sweetness that initially enticed me.

I lift her, taking her covered nipple between my teeth, nipping at the peak until she squirms and rakes her nails down my back again.

"Quick," she pants, tugging at my shorts.

"Now you're in a hurry?"

"Yes." She grinds against my dick, panting heavily in my ear. "Hurry up and fuck me."

Nothing could stop me at this point. Reaching down between us, I pull the crotch of her suit to the side to position herself over my thick head. "Oh, God," she moans as she slides down my shaft. Her head falls back as her eyes close, the image of a woman losing herself to lust. I give her a moment to adjust and nearly come out of my skin at how tightly she grips me.

"You are so fucking hot," I growl, moving her up and down without effort, thanks to the water. "I love how you come apart on my cock."

"Feels so good." She lifts her head and crushes her mouth against mine. "So fucking good," she pants between deep, sloppy kisses that have our teeth clashing.

This is how I like her best. When she lets everything she thinks she needs to do and who she needs to be fall to the wayside. When she gives herself fully. No apologies, no questions. Nothing except sensation.

Her grip on my cock tightens, and her strangled cries get higher in pitch.

"Callum... Callum... oh, yeah..." She uses her legs to pull me closer, grunting every time she hits my base.

"That's right. Be a good girl and make yourself come on my cock."

The tingling in the base of my spine promises my release—I don't know how much longer I can hold on with her hot, tight pussy gripping me like a vice.

"Fuck, your pussy is sucking the release out of my balls. Come with me, baby." Our foreheads touch, her eyes meeting mine before they close. A broken cry stirs in her chest—I catch it when my mouth covers hers, absorbing her ecstatic moans while her muscles flutter around my shaft, massaging. Milking me.

There's no choice except to follow her, filling her with rope after rope of cum before she collapses in my arms and shudders against me. "I love you…"

I love you. Nobody ever told me how much it would mean to hear a woman whisper those words at a moment like this—not that it would have mattered if they had. It's the sort of thing that needs to be experienced firsthand.

I thought I'd seen it all, done it all, that all I needed was a warm, wet hole. Feelings and all that shit weren't worth my time.

She's turned me into a believer. She's made me understand how much better it can be when you're with someone you love.

"Now that you got off…" She's wearing a wicked grin when she unwinds her body from around mine. "Are you still sure about dinner?"

"Shit. I didn't know changing my mind was an option." She swats at me and I laugh before we start to climb from the pool.

"It isn't." She tosses me a towel before squeezing the water from her dark locks, then wraps a towel around her chest.

"I'm sure, and just so you know, this wasn't a ploy to get in your suit. I just love fucking you that much."

"Good. I'm going to go give him a call." The way she happily scampers into the house, her phone in hand, tells me I made the right decision. She already looks cheerier than I've seen her in days, maybe weeks. The strain of Charlie and me being at each other 's throats can't be easy for her to live with.

That's fine. Let him come to my house as a welcome guest. Let him see how civilized and generous the criminal he's hated for so long can be.

Once I'm dried off, I follow her inside, taking a bottle of water from the fridge. I'm sure Sheryl has the pantry more than stock, so there won't be any reason to go out for groceries unless Bianca's set on fixing something out of the ordinary. I can't imagine Charlie being too difficult to please. He doesn't strike me as the complicated type regarding food choices.

"Boss?" Romero leans into the room, looking around before

finding me seated at the island. "I heard Bianca come in, so I figured you'd be around here somewhere."

"Yes, she's inviting Charlie over for dinner tonight."

"Dinner? Here?"

"That's the idea."

"And you were okay with that?"

"I'm the one who suggested it." I drink my water, savoring the cold that spreads through my chest almost as much as I savor Romero's shocked expression.

He manages to compose himself, clearing his throat. "Here's hoping he doesn't decide to continue what he started the last time he was here."

"Don't remind me."

When it appears like he wants to keep bringing up reasons this won't work, I shake my head before he can say another word. "Listen. If this is what it takes to make her happy, I'm willing to do it. You've seen how she's been ever since Ken was here. Now, she's smiling and seems to be more hopeful. If I have to grin and bear it through dinner with that asshole, so be it. It's worth it."

"Fair enough."

"Feel free to take the night off," I add as an afterthought. "I've been working you like a dog lately."

His arched eyebrow leaves me scowling.

"What?" I snap.

"I was just thinking to myself, what a shame you didn't find her sooner. With Bianca here, you're able to focus on more than work."

"Yeah, that's a good thing. You might have time to develop a hobby or two."

He doesn't see the humor in that—in fact, he scowls while his gaze drifts toward the empty patio. "I have a few things I'd like to take time for."

Something about the way he said it strikes me as ominous. "Is there something we need to talk about?"

Before he can answer, Bianca pops into the room, one hand over her cell's speaker. "Is seven tonight okay?"

"That's fine." She just about beams before turning away, murmuring into her cell.

Romero wears a faintly sarcastic grin as he backs away. "You are going to have your hands full tonight," he reminds me, shaking his head. "No offense, but I wouldn't want to be in your shoes. Although I would definitely like to be a fly on the wall."

BIANCA

"Where's the ricotta?" I could have sworn I pulled it out of the fridge while gathering the rest of the ingredients.

"Right here." Callum slides the container my way. "How can I help?"

It's sort of adorable that he wants to help, so I don't want to turn him down. And with my nerves as fried as they are right now, I could use the help. If I'm not careful, I'll end up knocking the baking dish on the floor instead of putting it in the oven. The thought of tomato sauce splashing across the white tile and shiny stainless steel makes me wince—Sheryl would never forgive me if I didn't leave this kitchen looking better than she left it. I love her, and she seems to like me a lot, but there are lines you don't cross.

"Can you please crack two eggs and stir them into the ricotta?" I wish I had a written recipe, but Mom never worked that way. Everything she cooked, she eyeballed. A meal could taste totally different depending on her mood that day, but it was always delicious.

Noodles are boiling on the stove, along with marinara sauce

Sheryl made a while back and had kept frozen. That's thawed now, bubbling slightly beside a pan of browned sausage. Everything's in place. So why am I so nervous?

Oh, that's right, because depending on how things go between a pair of stubborn, pigheaded men, this could be the final meal for one of them. I'll have to keep them from clawing each other's throats out.

"Stir the noodles, please?" I feel like my head's going to explode from everything buzzing around inside. I have to prep the vegetables to layer with the cheese and sausage and make sure the noodles don't get overcooked—there's not much I hate more than mushy pasta.

He dips a pair of tongs into the boiling water, stirring gently. "Do you want to hear something that will shock you?"

I blow out a breath, "Oh god, I don't know, yes, maybe."

Callum grins, and I swear I'll never get over how devilishly handsome he is. "This is kind of nice."

"You're right, I'm shocked." Somehow I manage to take a break from stressing out to kiss him. And it is nice. It's the sort of thing I would always like to do. Working as a team, watching as he does his best to be helpful and positive. I know I'm being a real pain in the ass, freaking out, wanting everything to be perfect. He's been nothing but patient even though I know he can't be looking forward to having dinner with Dad.

"Did you ever do any cooking for yourself?" I ask while finely chopping herbs to be mixed in with the ricotta.

Shrugging, he says, "I mean, I had to eat, so yeah."

"That's not what I meant. Do you have any signature dishes? Something you fall back on?" Ugh, did he ever make something special for Amanda? I'm starting to wish I hadn't asked.

"If you count cereal and instant ramen, sure." I slow my chopping, looking at him. Finally, he shrugs. "We didn't have any money when I was a kid. I told you that."

"Yes, I remember."

"So I made do with what we had. Once I was on my own in the world, I didn't have much money either. What do they call that? The salad days?"

"I have no idea what that is but sure."

"Every penny I made went to survival, and that's what food was then. I ate because I had to if I wanted to live. There was nothing about pleasure or enjoyment." He snorts, and I notice his gaze moving around the spacious, gleaming kitchen. "Hot dogs chopped up in a bowl of ramen noodles was as fancy as it got."

"That doesn't sound too bad, actually."

"When you live on it for a week straight, you might feel a little differently." He's smiling about it, so I guess it's easy to smile when you're on the other side.

Once I've declared the noodles a minute shy of al dente, he drains the pot and rinses the pasta according to my instructions. There's a salad already prepared in the fridge and garlic bread waiting to be placed in the oven once the lasagna comes out.

"I have to hurry," I fret once I start putting everything together. "The lasagna needs to sit for a while to set up, or else you slice into it and it falls apart."

"I'm learning so much tonight." He pours himself a glass of wine from a bottle he opened for the occasion. "However, you need to take a breath. No matter what you make him, he'll love it."

"How would you know?" I ask with a breathless laugh.

"It's part of being a father. I know what I'm talking about."

His choice of words stirs my curiosity as I ladle sauce into the bottom of a casserole dish. "Did Tatum tell you where she's going tonight? I told her about dinner, but she said she already had plans." I can't put my finger on it, but something about that doesn't seem right. She's spent weeks festering in bed, locked in her rooms, and now she has plans she doesn't want to share with me.

"No, she didn't want to give me any details, but she seemed happier than she's been lately, so I didn't want to give her shit about it." He kisses my temple, probably because he sees my worries written across my face. "She's a big girl. I learned a long time ago which battles to pick, and this one's not worth it. So long as she's starting to get out in the world again, that's all that matters. Plus, I have Romero tailing her for her safety."

He's right. I need to stop worrying about everyone else and their lives. I have more than enough on my plate, anyway.

* * *

"Everything is perfect." Callum shakes his head and whistles in appreciation once he pulls the lasagna from the oven. "It's nice that you made this, but what did you make for you and your father?"

"Stop flattering me." I give him a look, placing my hand on my hip.

"That is not true. This is the most gorgeous lasagna I've ever seen." I have to admit he's right, it's perfect, and the aroma of garlic hangs in the air once the garlic bread starts baking in the oven. Just a few minutes ago, I was too nervous to even consider eating, but now my stomach is growling.

I run both hands over the front of my polka-dotted dress. It's cute, simple enough for a family dinner. "Do you think I should have set the dining room table? Is eating in the kitchen too casual?"

"Relax, or I'll make you relax, and you know how that works." He cups my shoulders and gently kisses my forehead. For his part, he looks gorgeous in a white polo shirt that sets off his tan skin and dark hair. "We could always eat in the dining room if you want, but if we're trying to convince Charlie of how normal things are around here, the three of us sitting at a table built for eighteen might seem a little much."

"That's true. Good thinking." He's right. I just need to take a breath. It would probably be easier to do that if I were sure of the kind of attitude Dad would have when he gets here. He seemed pleasantly surprised at the invitation and asked if he could bring anything. I told him to bring an open mind. He didn't seem to think that was funny.

"I think we make a pretty good team," Callum announces, setting the salad on the table along with a small plate of cured meat, cheese, and olives. "I should give Sheryl the night off a few times a month. It'll give us the chance to cook together."

"Nothing would make me happier." And I mean that with all my heart. I could never have guessed we would come this far, happily fixing a meal together while music plays and we plan for the future. It almost feels too good to be true, and it's easy to imagine a time when our children will run around underfoot.

Please, Dad, don't ruin this.

Henry already knows to expect him, so there's no call announcing his arrival. There's only the ringing of the doorbell at ten minutes to seven. "He loves to be early," I explain, untying my apron and heading for the front door. My heart's pounding, and my palms are slick with nervous sweat, but I somehow manage to plaster on a smile when I open the door.

He looks good, like he wants to come off as presentable tonight. His blue polo matches his eyes and looks brand-new. So do the gray slacks he's wearing. Actually, he looks like he got a haircut too.

"I hope you're hungry," I tell him after kissing his smooth-shaven cheek. "I made enough lasagna to feed an army."

His lips stir in a faint, almost disbelieving smile. "Lasagna. Your mom's favorite."

"Charlie. Thanks for joining us tonight." Callum plays the part of the charming, gracious host, extending a hand to shake. Here we go. My heart's in my throat, and I'm afraid I might throw up as I wait to see what Dad's reaction will be.

He hesitates for a split second, then extends his own hand for a firm shake. "Thank you for having me. I appreciate it."

"After all, we have someone in common, don't we?" He raises an eyebrow. "Would you like a tour of the house?"

"No, thank you. That's not necessary." The way Dad makes it sound, Callum just invited him to have a root canal.

That's my cue. "Dinner's ready. The lasagna is cooling slightly, but we have salad and antipasto."

"That sounds terrific." Callum leads the way to the kitchen while I sneak one look after another toward Dad. He doesn't have to say a word—I can read how his eyes move and his jaw twitches. He's looking around at all this luxury and thinking about how the money was made. When he catches me looking at him, I grimace and fold my hands like I'm begging him.

Please, don't mess this up for me.

"What can I get you to drink, Charlie?"

"I think I'll have water with dinner or iced tea if you have any."

"I made sure there was some in the fridge." Callum pours the drinks while I sit down with Dad, who's still peering around, taking everything in.

"This is a beautiful home," he observes in what, for him, is a neutral tone of voice. "Very nice."

"Your daughter is comfortable here," Callum says, placing a glass of iced tea on the table. "And safe."

"I sure hope so." Their eyes meet, and I hold my breath. Dad only takes a sip of his tea and keeps his thoughts to himself.

By the time we settle in with our salads, some of the tension has dissolved. I guess when you're eating, there's less time to be angry or resentful. "Did Bianca ever tell you about the first time she tried to make dinner?" Dad asks out of nowhere, looking my way with a twinkle in his eye.

"Oh, my God, can we not tell that story, please?" I groan while glaring at him.

Callum sets down his knife and fork, grinning. "Okay, now I must know."

"She wanted to make spaghetti," Dad explains. "Mind you, she had never cooked before and had only ever watched her mother."

"I was seven years old," I grumble, spearing a cucumber with a bit more force than necessary. "What did I know?"

"Anyway, in case you couldn't tell, we're both fans of Italian food. So she wanted to make sure there was enough spaghetti for both of us and figured a pound per person would do the trick."

"No!" Callum practically hoots with laughter.

"Add in that she forgot to put a lid on the sauce, so that started bubbling and spitting all over the stove, counter, and backsplash."

I slide down into my chair and wish for the floor to swallow me. "I did my best."

"Needless to say, we had pizza that night." Dad casts a fond smile across the table. "She's not lying though, she's always done her best. Always thinking she had to take care of me, even when she was seven. Then again, she always has been an old soul."

"I used to feel that way about Tatum," Callum agrees. "There were times when she would look me in the eye with so much wisdom, it was almost scary. Here's this little kid imparting wisdom and common sense. It was rather humbling."

"That's a good word for it," Dad agrees.

Meanwhile, here I am, wondering if I should pinch myself and refusing to, because let's face it, I don't want to break the spell. If I'm asleep, I don't want to wake up. This is nice, watching them get along and finding common ground. Even if it means taking a little teasing.

By the time we start on the lasagna and bread, they're talking about football and playoff chances. I don't know much about that, so I tune them out and settle for appreciating how much they seem to have in common once they set aside their differences. I hope it can always be this way, but I'm not naive enough to fully believe that. I'm not going to wish for a miracle. I need to work on appreciating the good moments rather than hoping for something even better.

"I am absolutely, painfully stuffed." Callum pats his stomach before pushing away from the table after what felt like a lifetime of football talk, staring down at his clean plate. "I don't know where I put it all. If I didn't know better, I'd think you slipped something into that. It's addictive."

"It looks like I learned to make something the right way," I retort, smirking at Dad.

"I'm going to go get myself a drink." Callum turns to Dad. "Can I interest you in anything?"

Dad clears his throat, suddenly looking a little embarrassed. "No, thank you. I... have stopped drinking."

I have to grip my chair to keep myself from falling off. "Like, entirely?" I ask.

"You don't need to make it sound so surprising," he says with a gentle smirk. "Yes, entirely. I figured now is the time to get a grasp on it. I want my grandchild to have good memories of me—and I would like to be able to remember spending time with them, too."

"Wow, I'm... I'm so happy to hear that." I reach out and cover his hand with mine. *Do not cry. Don't be a complete dork about this.* There's nothing worse than somebody making a big deal over an issue he would rather they not. I don't want to embarrass him.

Callum leans down and kisses my forehead in passing. I lift my eyes to meet his and see the silent message he's sending me. *Do it now. For both of you.* I know he's right. I just don't know how to approach the subject.

"Let's go outside for a minute," I suggest, groaning as I stand. "I need some fresh air to help me digest all my food. Remind me next time not to take seconds."

"You're eating for two now," he reminds me.

"Tonight, I ate for four," I joke as we head for the doors leading out to the patio. The unusual warmth from earlier today has given way to something closer to what I'd expect in late September, and I shiver a little before rubbing my arms.

"I have to admit, this is impressive." Dad heads straight for the outdoor kitchen, as I knew he would. "What I wouldn't do for a grill like this."

Then, it's like he catches himself, lowering the lid carefully. "Within reason."

"Lighten up a little," I whisper. "Maybe you could come over sometime, and we'll grill together."

"I'm doing my best," he murmurs, shrugging.

"You're doing great, and I'm so happy you're here." I wind an arm around his and rest my head on his shoulder. "It means a lot to me to have you here, and I want you to be a part of my life."

"That's all I want, too."

"And Callum wants you to be part of things." I can't pretend I don't notice the way he stiffens up at the mention of Callum's name. "It was his idea to invite you over tonight, since he knew it would make me happy. That's all he wants, for me to have the things that make me content. And you're one of those things."

He absorbs this in silence as we walk the perimeter of the pool. Night has fallen so the automatic lights shine under the water's surface. When a faint breeze stirs the otherwise still water, the light ripples across his pensive face. "It's not easy to drop a habit you've had for years."

"You mean the habit of hating him? I'm going to have to ask you to try."

"I am."

"Can I tell you something? Something important."

"Always."

I can do this. I can make it through this. "Remember I told you he was going to help find out what happened to Mom." His jaw tightens before he nods.

I come to a stop and turn to face him, taking his hands in mine. "He found out. We know who killed her."

His eyes move over my face. "You're serious? You aren't just telling me what you know I need to hear?"

"I'm serious. He guessed it had something to do with his business—someone who wanted to clear the path and make things easy for them to strike a deal. I don't know any of the specifics. He doesn't tell me those things, and I honestly don't want to know." I pretend not to notice the way he scowls. "But he followed that hunch and asked around."

I have to fight against the sudden tightness in my throat, being that this is where Ken comes in. But I won't tell him. I can't. It would break his heart. It's already broken mine enough.

"So? Who was it?"

"It was a man named Salvatore Costello."

His expression hardens. "I know that name."

"Salvatore ordered a hit," I whisper, speaking slowly, ready to stop if he can't handle it. He seems to be holding up pretty well, so I add, "I'm sorry, Dad. It was supposed to be you, not Mom. It was a mix-up. Callum didn't know anything about it—remember, I didn't know Tatum then, and now, Costello is dead. I'm sorry, but there's no way to make it right. I wish I had better news."

"And you believe this is all true?"

My eyes sting from the tears welling up in them. "I do, Dad. I know it's true."

Please, don't press me for more. Please. You don't want to know how I know.

"So it was supposed to be me." His face drops, his voice thick with emotion. "Well, I always knew that had to be a possibility."

"I'm so sorry."

"You know what's funny?" he asks with a bitter laugh. "I don't know what I expected. Finding out the truth doesn't change anything. She's still gone. I thought it would heal me somehow, but I don't think it will. I can stop blaming Callum," he admits. "In the end, that's a good thing. But it doesn't change anything, does it? The damage was already done."

"Maybe now you can move forward," I suggest. "I know she would want you to, seeing that she loved you, just like I do."

"Oh, honey." He wraps his arms around me and sighs, pressing his lips to the top of my head. "I know I need to move on with life. I've been thinking about it a lot —mostly thanks to my unborn grandchild. It's the same as with drinking, I believe. I want them to have the sort of grandfather they can love and be proud of. I don't want to miss a minute with them. I have more to live for the now rather than let the past eat away at me further."

I can't help it. The tears start to flow, soaking into his polo. And, for a minute, I cling to him like I'm a little girl again. Like, I think he's big enough and strong enough to take care of all the bad guys and make all the bad stuff disappear.

"Don't cry," he whispers, stroking my hair. "I know I've been hard on you, and I'm so sorry. I wish I could go back and do everything over again. You didn't deserve half the shit I put you through."

"It's okay."

"No, it's not. I was paranoid and scared. I couldn't stand the thought of losing you. And there I was, setting it up so I would lose you by pushing you away. I'm surprised you want anything to do with me now."

"Don't say that." I lift my head to find him crying, too. "I know you did your best. There's no instruction manual for that kind of thing. All you can do is try."

"I want you to know something." He holds my head between his hands, smiling through his tears. "Regardless of everything, your mother would be so proud of you. You have become a wonderful woman, loving and kind, and generous. Exactly the way she always hoped you would be."

"Really?" I manage to choke out.

"Really. I look at you, and I see so much of her—all of the good parts. And to think, I could have missed out on that, because I was too busy worrying about you and trying to control what you did and who you saw. I can't take it back, but I can tell you here and now that it's going to stop. It's all going to change. If you are happy, I'm happy. That's all that matters."

"I love you so much." I wrap my arms around his waist and press my forehead to his chest while he touches his chin to the top of my head. Together we take a deep breath and let it out slowly; with it goes all the years of pain and sadness.

I genuinely believe we will start over again and be the family we were always meant to be.

CALLUM

I can't remember the last time I had to load a dishwasher.

If Romero caught me being this domestic, there would be no end to the sarcasm. There's a reason I wanted us to be as alone as possible tonight. That meant giving almost everyone the night off except for the guys down by the gate. Not that I'm afraid of getting caught scouring a pan, but I need my crew to respect me. I don't know that they could if they caught me up to my elbows in soap suds.

That's what I get for trying to give Bianca and Charlie a little space. Neither of them needs me hanging around while she navigates this impossible conversation. I keep an eye on the patio, ready to jump in if it looks like things are going south, but I need to give her father a little more credit. It's not like he would hurt her—that much, I know for sure. Nonetheless, I wouldn't put it past him to throw furniture into the pool when he can't control his rage.

Maybe I'm projecting my anger management issues onto him.

Finally, the table is clean and the sink spotless while the dishwasher hums quietly. There's nothing left for me to do except check on them. Drying my hands, I head for the door, watching as Bianca presses her face to Charlie's chest. They're both in tears, and with good reason, but at least there's no fighting.

For years, they were all each other had. I can relate to the feeling. Amanda was MIA for virtually all of Tatum's childhood, only popping in when she wanted something before breezing out again. Half the time, she asked to meet somewhere besides the house. She was that determined not to set eyes on her daughter.

I can only imagine how difficult it must be for Charlie to step back and allow someone else into her life. I'm witnessing the final moments of the two of them existing on their own—the two of them against the world.

He lifts his head, wearing a smile, and Bianca is beaming when she looks up at him. The last of the tension that's plagued me all night loosens, and I can finally breathe as I slide the glass door open. "Everything all right out here?" I ask while stepping out.

Bianca wipes her eyes with her hands, still smiling as she crosses the patio to give me a hug. "Everything's fine," she announces, then murmurs, "He'll be okay."

After much sniffling and clearing his throat, Charlie slowly approaches me. I'm not going to take the lead on this. He knows what needs to be said, and considering his pained expression, he knows it, too.

"Say, Callum. I, uh... well, you see..." He scrubs a hand over his short, dark hair before rubbing the back of his neck while grimacing. "I'm having a hard time deciding what to say."

No shit. "Take your time, whatever it is." Bianca squeezes me a little, even growling under her breath. Let her growl. I've waited a long time for what's coming. I refuse to rush things.

"I'm sorry," he finally announces. "I'm sorry for a lot of things. I was wrong, and I made many mistakes. I can't promise I won't make more, but for now, thank you for going out of your way to help with..."

I'm not a completely heartless bastard, so I throw the man a lifeline. "I understand. I'm sorry there was nothing more I could do."

"What else could have been done? As I told Bianca, it doesn't change anything beyond showing me how wrong I was and how much I have to make up for."

"All that matters now is that we can all move forward and perhaps put some of this behind us."

"I would like that." I'm not fooled. I see the way his jaw works as he grits his teeth before extending a hand to shake. It's not going to be as easy as putting everything behind us. However, for now, it has to be enough that we're both willing to meet halfway for the sake of the girl in my arms.

A girl who releases a shuddering sigh when she watches us shake hands. "I'm a mess," she announces, unwinding her arms from around my waist. "If you'll excuse me, I'm going to clean myself up."

"Don't take too long. I'm not sure if I can trust myself around the tiramisu that's in the fridge."

Charlie perks up. "Tiramisu? Now I wish I had saved a little room."

"It was one of the few things she didn't insist on making from scratch," I murmur once she's in the house. "I managed to convince her to pick some up at a bakery. It meant a lot to her for everything to go well tonight."

"After all the shit I put you through, I'm amazed you let me through your front door."

"Let's be fair," I offer as we follow in Bianca's footsteps, returning to the kitchen. "I'm no angel. We both know that. Although, I am willing to put all that behind us for her sake and our family's sake." His jaw ticks at the word *family*, yet he's gotten better at keeping his thoughts to himself. Maybe there's hope of all of this working out, after all. Stranger things have happened, I'm sure.

"I have to say, if there's one thing I never expected, it was one day being part of the same family."

"That makes two of us." As I reach into the refrigerator to pull the pink cardboard box from its shelf, another box that the velvet box in my pocket reminds me of a conversation I want us to have. With Bianca occupied in the powder room, this might be the perfect time.

Right away, my pulse picks up speed and a cold sweat covers the back of my neck. I've brokered deals with men who tortured people for fun, and I can't find the words to ask a man for his daughter's hand.

"Charlie, I—" It's the ringing of the doorbell that cuts me off, and I grunt under my breath at the interruption. "Who the hell would show up at this time of night?"

He follows on my heels, chuckling. "I would expect you to have somebody answering the door for you."

I'll choose to take that comment at face value and not read into it. "I gave almost everyone the night off. I wanted it to be just the three of us tonight."

"I appreciate you trusting me that much."

"As we said, we're putting all that in the past." Still, I can't help but scowl at him when he falls in step beside me. "And I know you wouldn't do anything to upset Bianca."

"Good point." To my surprise, he grabs my arm as I reach for the doorknob. "You're sure it's safe?"

"I still have men down at the gate. They wouldn't let anyone up who couldn't be trusted." Still, I'm slow to open the door, scanning the area before looking down to find a plain cardboard box on the doormat. I glimpse up to find a brown truck rolling down the driveway, its taillights disappearing before I bend to pick up the package.

"Probably something Tatum ordered," I murmur, checking the label and finding her name. "Sure enough. I'm starting to think she's collecting mailing labels at this point."

"How is she, by the way?" he asks as I close and lock the door.

"She seems to be getting better. She's been going out more, which is a big step up from locking herself in her room day and night." I toss the box onto the table beside the door, where she can pick it up once she gets home.

"I'm pleased to hear that."

And here we are, awkwardly staring at each other for lack of anything else to say. "Were you going to ask me something before we were interrupted?" he prompts, sliding his hands into his pockets, lifting his brows.

"Yes."

From where I stand, I can see the powder room door. It's still closed, and the faint sound of running water tells me she's busy washing her face. If I'm going to do this, I need to do it now. Here I am, a man some have called heartless, brutal, and countless other names on top of that. Nevertheless, I can't find the words to express what's in my heart. Especially not to this man, who already thinks so poorly of me no matter how hard he tries to hide it.

"I'm going to say it all at once, since it's not easy for me to talk about these things. I love your daughter very much. She is the most important thing in my world besides my own daughter—and the baby, of course. I would stop at nothing to make her happy. While she's with me, she will never know anything but love. You can be sure of that."

"I believe you."

"Thank you. I know we haven't done things the traditional way, but I want to make things official with the baby coming and with me already sure of my commitment to her."

He looks like he regrets he ever stopped drinking, his eyes widening as he gulps. "I see."

The ring box is heavier than ever. I've looked at the ring so many times since picking it up from the jeweler that I see it clearly in my mind's eye. The pair of delicate platinum bands wound together into something more substantial, symbolizing the way our lives have intertwined. The brilliant cut, four-carat diamond that I would swear holds fire in its center—I've never seen a stone throw off the sort of light it does.

And engraved inside, the words *Forever Mine*. I'm aching to slide it onto her finger.

"I wanted to do this right," I explain while my fingers itch to pull the box free. "I want to marry your daughter. I hope for your blessing—or at least your acceptance, if your blessing is too much to ask for right now."

We turn in unison when the powder room door opens and Bianca emerges, fresh-faced, looking happy and content until she sees us standing together. "What happened?" she asks, freezing like a deer in headlights.

"Nothing. Just a delivery." I jerk my chin toward the kitchen. "And that tiramisu is calling my name."

"Thank you for cleaning up, by the way. I noticed when I walked through the kitchen." She winks at Charlie, giggling. "You're full of surprises."

"I do know how to use a sponge," I retort as the three of us stroll down the hall. "And I'm fairly sure I even remembered to put soap in the dishwasher. You're supposed to use the stuff in the bottle on the sink, right?"

"Ha, ha." Then she looks at me, frowning. "You're not serious, are you?"

"No. That's what's called a joke."

Charlie heaves a sigh behind us. "Somehow, my daughter got it into her head that men are all helpless."

"Gee, where could I have gotten that idea from?" she fires back, smirking as she lifts the cake from its box.

"You want some coffee?" I ask Charlie, who nods eagerly. Anything, so long as I have something to do, something to distract myself. It's amazing how a situation like this can make a man forget everything he knows.

Do I do it here and now? Should I wait? I don't know if I can wait. The days since I picked up the ring have been utter torture. No matter what I do, all I can think about is presenting it to her. Getting down on one knee, the whole thing. Making us official. It's the least she deserves.

If anyone ever told me I would end up brewing coffee for Charlie Cole in my own kitchen after asking for his blessing to marry his daughter... Life is full of surprises.

"Are you going to do one of those baby registry things?" he asks Bianca while she slices the dessert.

"I don't know. I hadn't really thought about it," she admits while licking cream and cocoa powder from her thumb. "I guess? I'm not even sure what we need."

"Don't look at me," I say with a shrug when the two of them do just that. "I'm sure they've come up with at least another dozen must-haves since Tatum was born."

"Maybe that's something we could do together," Charlie suggests, meeting my gaze over the top of her head. Why do I feel like this is a test? Probably because it is. He wants to be sure he has a place in all of this, that I won't shove him out of the way.

"I'm sure you would be much more helpful than I ever could," I admit, handing him a steaming cup. He makes a point of holding my gaze, inclining his head ever so slightly. That subtle gesture encompasses a thousand words.

I passed the test.

"Before we eat..." Oh, I'm doing this. It felt like the moment would never come. Bianca gives me a quizzical smile when I take her hands, turning her away from the table.

"What's up?" She looks at Charlie. "What's happening?"

"There's something I need to say." And now that the time has come, everything I rehearsed in my head vanishes in a puff of smoke. I don't have the first idea where to start. How do you tell someone their existence makes yours worthwhile? How can I ever express the way she changed me?

The thing is, with her father here, I'm not sure how I want to go that deep. Certain things are for her ears only. Rather than stumble my way through, I cut to the chase by getting down on one knee and reaching into my pocket.

"Oh, my God." She covers her mouth with one trembling hand, her eyes as wide as saucers. "Is this really happening?"

"It really is." I open the box and hold it up, offering the ring since I can't pull out my heart and offer that instead.

"I love you," I murmur as my heart pounds out of control. This woman has complete hold over me, body and soul. She'll never understand how wholly she owns me. My entire existence hinges on this moment. Her answer. Three letters. I know what she's going to say, since she already has, but that does nothing to lessen this profound moment. "Will you be my wife?"

"Oh, Callum," she chokes out before the tears begin to flow again. "I—"

Whatever she's about to say is cut off by an ear-splitting explosion that rocks the house.

BIANCA

There's a ringing in my ears and a high-pitched squealing that makes it nearly impossible to hear anything. I can vaguely make out Callum's shouting. My father shouts something back, but I can't make out the words. It's like trying to listen to someone speak while you're underwater.

The smell of smoke tickles my nostrils. What is burning? Callum rushes towards me, his hands cup my cheeks and I want to tell him I'm okay but I can't hear my own voice.

What happened?

The look on his face is pure terror, and his hands wrap tight around my arms as he pulls me through the kitchen, my Dad close behind us. Once outside, the fresh air helps a little, but I still can't put the pieces together on what happened. All I know is that my heart's pounding out of my chest, and I think I'm going to throw up.

"Are you alright?" I can read Callum's lips even if it sounds like he's talking to me from behind a closed door. He runs his hands over my arms, torso, face, and neck. "Were you injured?" I shake my head hard and he touches his forehead to mine for a moment before letting me go. My Dad gathers me in his arms.

"Are you okay?" he asks, his voice muffled. My head bobs up and down, and I lean against him when he wraps me in a protective hug. I can't get my body to stop trembling.

A minute ago, Callum was on one knee, looking up at me with so much love I didn't know how I could take it. I was overwhelmed, overjoyed, and blissfully unaware of what was about to happen. Everything was finally clicking into place; my happy ending was within sight.

Now, Callum paces like a caged animal, shouting into his phone. He even kicks a patio chair into the pool in his rage.

"What happened?" That's all I can say, over and over, while thin wisps of smoke begin drifting out through the partly opened sliding door.

"An explosion," Dad says close to my ear. "Something exploded."

"That fucking package!" Callum roars.

"What package?" My question is swallowed up by Callum's continuous shouting. I've seen him like this before. He is ready to kill someone.

"There was a package." Dad is probably shouting, too, since his ears are probably ringing as bad as mine are. "It came when you were in the bathroom."

"I want you back here now!" Callum bellows into the phone. "Right now, immediately, and on the way, call everybody in."

Then he stops in his tracks, looking at me. "You still have eyes on Tatum, right?" he asks the person on the other end—I'm guessing Romero. I tense up, gasping, and Dad's arms tighten around me.

"She's fine," Callum tells us before turning his attention back to the phone. "Get her here, now."

He then puts his phone away, lacing his fingers together on top of his head. "I should have known. I should have fucking known!"

"What the hell is going on?" Dad demands. "What the fuck did you get her into this time?"

"Dad, don't," I beg, but he doesn't want to hear it.

Callum throws Dad a steely glare. "Not now." He reaches for me, yet Dad refuses to let me go.

"Please," I plead. "I'm okay. Are you?" He looks fine, uninjured like Callum and me, although he's shaking from head to toe. I can only imagine what must be going through his head.

"I'm going back in there," Callum decides.

"No, don't!" On impulse, I try to follow him, but Dad refuses to let me go no matter how much I twist and fight to escape his grasp. "Don't go!"

"Let him do what he needs to do," Dad insists.

"I don't understand!" Though now that the shock is starting to clear from my mind, I think I get it. Somebody bombed the house. Somebody's still trying to kill us. Trying to kill my baby.

I should be afraid—and I am. I'm scared to death that there will be another explosion while I stand here trying to make sense of the madness. I'm terrified of losing Callum. What if he never comes back through that door? There's a thin line between fear and rage. The rage is taking over, turning the terrified pounding of my heart into something murderous.

They tried to kill my baby, again.

And I don't think it's any mystery who's behind it.

"We have to get away from the house," Dad decides, pulling me along the patio, and around the pool until we're standing at the far end. "Jesus, why do you want any part in this family?"

I ignore the question once Callum emerges, waving at us. "Come on. I want you to get her out of here."

"Is it safe?" Dad asks.

"The box was destroyed. There's nothing left to detonate." When Dad doesn't move fast enough, Callum charges at us, taking hold of me. "I mean it. I want her out of here, and you have to be the one to take her."

"I'm not leaving you!" I may as well be talking to myself for all the good it does. Callum pretty much ignores me as he rushes me through the house, where the alarm is still shrieking. It's like an ice pick drilling into my eardrum. We hurry down the hall from the kitchen, where plaster dust is drifting through the air and the acrid smoke from a small fire flickering in what's left of the entry hall.

The sight of it stops me dead in my tracks. The windows to either side of the front door are blown out, and the table next to it is in pieces. The artwork blasted off the walls, and a glance toward the living room shows the same thing happened in there—even the big flat screen was knocked off its mounting and is now on the floor.

All that rushes passed me in a blur as Callum sprints through the house with me in tow. I don't think I take a breath until we're outside again, where Romero's car is flying up the driveway.

"What the fuck happened here?" Tatum jumps out of the passenger seat while Romero barely has the car in park before flinging the door open.

"Where were you?" I can't believe that with everything going on, that's the first question I have as Tatum runs toward me.

"I was just out." After hugging me, she stares through the open door into the house. Her mouth hangs open briefly before she whispers, "What happened?"

Callum clamps a hand over her shoulder and turns her toward him. "Were you expecting a package tonight?"

Her brows draw together, her gaze darting to the destruction again and again like she can't make sense of it. That makes two of us. "Yeah? I think so. It was supposed to come today."

"Where was it from? Where did you order it from?" Callum barks.

"Are you accusing me of doing something wrong?"

"That's not what he's saying," Romero insists as he joins us, standing at her side. "Whoever sent it either made a big mistake, or they always intended to send you a bomb."

"A bomb? I ordered a couple of bras, for fuck's sake!"

It's Dad who cuts through the growing panic. "It's obvious what happened." A change comes over him—his eyes go narrow, unyielding, and now I see the longtime detective. Like he slid back into the role. "Whoever did this must have intercepted the UPS truck. It would be best if you had your men search nearby. They could have killed the driver and left the body somewhere. They placed the explosive in the box and left the mailing label intact to make it look legitimate."

With his hands on his hips, he turns in a slow circle. "You can't see this place from the street. They could have used a timer, or someone might have remotely detonated it after a certain amount of time. How long would you say it was?"

Callum shrugs. "Five minutes?"

"That sounds about right. Was the box heavy?"

"Not very. You saw it. I practically tossed it onto the table." His eyes close, brow furrowing like he's in pain. "I fucking tossed it." My blood runs cold at the thought. What if it had detonated then and there? I could have lost the two most important men in my life.

"Who would do this?" Dad demands.

"Who do you think? The same fuckers who took them."

Callum must not see the effect his words have on us, but Dad does. He wraps an arm around me, draping the other over Tatum's shoulders. She wraps her arms around herself and tucks her body close to his while I do the same.

By now, Callum's men are swarming the house, searching for any signs of further damage. The two men posted to the front gate come running up the drive, both shouting excuses before they reach us. "It looked legit! The guy had ID and everything!"

"It was a regular UPS truck," the second guard insists. Both of them look scared to death, pale-faced and jumpy.

"Oh, it looked legit? Did the person have an ID?" Callum's fist collides with the second man's jaw, knocking him on his ass. Tatum lets out a whimper while I flinch at the sound of bone crunching. I'm surprised Dad doesn't react, but then he looks like he wants to take a turn throwing fists, too, his nostrils flared beneath steely cold eyes.

"Come on, beating the shit out of these guys isn't going to help." Romero pulls Callum back while he snarls and curses at the two guards. "We've got to think about what to do next. Whoever did this, they'll be in the area. They're going to want to see the outcome."

"A fucking bomb. They sent a fucking *bomb*! To my *home*! These motherfuckers. I'm going to skin them alive." Callum takes Romero by the shirt collar, pulling him close. "And you're the one who wanted to be cautious. You're the one who thought I was moving too fast."

"Dad, stop!" Tatum begs. "It's not his fault!"

Callum shoves him away, snarling, but Romero only brushes himself off. "Blame me all you want, but that won't change what needs to happen now. We need to make sure they're safe." He nods toward Tatum and me.

"I'm not going anywhere." I don't know where that came from—the words poured out of me before they were a conscious thought.

"You can't stay here," Dad growls. "Either of you. This place isn't safe right now."

"I don't want to leave," Tatum weeps. "Dad, it's happening again. Why is it happening again?"

That's what does it. That tearful, pleading question snaps Callum out of his enraged haze. He is absolutely in anguish as he turns our way, and for a split second, I think he's going to cry, too. I know him so well I can practically read his thoughts, and he is blaming himself for this.

"Charlie's right," he announces. "You and Bianca should go, at least for the time being. Not forever, just for now."

"Should they be together, though?" Romero asks.

Tatum and I exchange a glance. I don't want to leave without her. It's bad enough I have to leave at all. This is where I belong, with the man I love. I didn't get into this life to run away when things get bad—I might have before, but that was then. I've changed. I know where I belong. But I also can't be selfish. There's a life growing inside me, and until my baby can make their own choices, I have to do what's best for them. They come first, then me.

"You're right," Callum decides. "Charlie, I'm going to give you the address of one of our safe houses."

"What about me?" Tatum whispers while her eyes well up again.

"I'll take you to a separate house," Romero offers. "You'll both be safe."

Safe. I'm starting to wonder if that word means anything. I've heard it so many times, but once again, the illusion has shattered. I don't know if I will ever feel safe again.

Dad pulls out his phone for Callum to rattle off an address which he programs into his GPS. "It's twenty minutes away. I'll get her there in fifteen," he vows.

"I'm scared. I'm scared for you."

Callum takes my face between his hands and touches his forehead to mind while I whisper frantically. "Come with us. Please. Let your guys take care of this. I need you with me. Our baby needs its daddy."

"I'm going to be alright." He presses a quick, fervent kiss against my lips and wraps his arms around me. I can feel his thundering heartbeat against my own. "I have too much to live for. I'm going to be fine. I'll be better and able to think clearer knowing you're safe. Your father will protect you until we're together again. I believe that."

That doesn't stop him from looking over my shoulder toward Dad. "Are you carrying?"

"I have it in the glove box."

"Hopefully, you won't need it, but I'll feel better knowing you have it."

Dad tugs my elbow. "Honey, we should go now. This won't be forever."

Right now? This second? Though I know it's the right thing to do, my feet don't want to move. "My things! I don't have anything with me!" I might as well be talking to myself as Dad drags me away toward his waiting car.

"As soon as it's safe, I'll send somebody with a bag," Callum vows. "Everything's going to be okay." He wraps his arms around Tatum, who I wave to before Dad practically throws me into the passenger's seat. I can't stop the sobs from tearing themselves from my chest as Dad gets in the car and turns it around, pointing it toward the road.

I twist around in my seat, desperate for one more look at Callum before the driveway bends, and I lose sight of him, of them. *When will I see them again?*

"It's going to be okay," Dad grunts while he navigates the winding, gravel path. "We're going to get you through this. Everything will be fine."

If I wasn't crying so hard, I'd ask who he's trying to convince, me or himself.

CALLUM

*T*here she goes. There *they* go. She's taking part of my heart with her. I doubt I could live through sending her away with anyone else. Romero, maybe, but that's as far as it goes. Charlie better hope he hasn't gotten rusty during his time away from the job, because if anything happens to her, I will paint this town in blood.

A cold breeze blows over me, chilling my skin. Tatum shivers in my arms. "Dad?" Her soft voice brings my thoughts back to her. "What should I do?"

She needs me to pull my shit together. I can't upset her by blowing up now. As calmly as possible, I respond, "I want you to go to your room and pack a few things while Romero and I make plans. Okay? Can you do that for me?"

"Okay. Is it safe in there?"

I turn to the pair of men exiting the house, my brows lifting in a silent question. "All clear," one of them announces. "We got what was left of the device out through the back."

"Go ahead–but don't waste any time." With a kiss on her forehead, I send her inside with one of them while Romero mutters into his phone. I haven't seen him this intense since our time at the hospital. He ends the call and turns to me. "I just sent out word that we want Moroni. Both of them."

Hearing the name twists my guts until I'm sure I'll be sick. Sick with rage, disgust, and disbelief. "A fucking bomb. Just when I think he can't stoop any lower."

"He's a fucking animal." Romero's face is a mask of rage once we enter the house, and he gets a good look at the damage. "He's going to find out how fucking animals die."

I still can't make sense of it. "There was no way of knowing who would pick up that package," I muse. There are bits of cardboard on the floor, most of it charred. At least the alarm has been silenced, allowing me to hear myself think. "How long do you think it would take to get an idea of the sort of device they used?"

"I'm sure I know somebody." He looks at his phone again, scrolling through his contacts. "Though I have to say, I don't know how much good it will do. I doubt we could track whoever manufactured it, and it isn't like we have any doubt of who's responsible." He checks the time, grunting in frustration. "She needs to hurry. I'll feel better once she's out of here. For all we know, they're planning to send guys in here now, while we're all running around like chickens with our heads cut off."

And there I was, prepared to propose. Ready to eat dessert, drink some coffee, and bid my future father-in-law goodnight before taking his daughter upstairs. I was going to spend the rest of the night basking in the warmth of her love.

The thought stirs my memory, and I dart to the kitchen, where I dropped the ring box when the bomb went off. A short search reveals it's lying under the table. To think, I had been moments away from placing the ring on her finger. The symbol of my devotion to her.

Now she's on her way to a safe house, because being too close to me is a liability, and I let Moroni go too far. I underestimated him, thinking he was nothing more than a useful idiot. I've done some unforgivable things in my life, but that underestimation has to be the worst.

"Boss? I have Costello on the phone."

Sliding the box into my pocket, I join him in the hall. Sebastian's voice filters through the speaker loud and clear. "A bomb? Was anyone hurt?"

I exchange a look with Romero, that tells me he believes the concern is real. "No, everyone's fine. There's damage to the house but nothing severe."

"I'm glad to hear that. It's a good thing Moroni's a fuck up, or else it might have been worse."

"If you know anything…"

"I swear, I didn't know a thing. I would've warned you immediately if I had. I assumed it was Moroni because, you know. Everything that's been going on."

I'm going to have to take his word for it. "Does he still consider you a friend?" I can't bring myself to say the bastard's name.

"He's dragging his feet on the deal, but we're cordial."

"Call him up. Tell him you heard there was an explosion, but you don't have any details on the extent of the damage. I want confirmation, and I want to know where the fuck we can pick them up and yank their beating hearts from their chests."

"Got it. I'll get back to you as soon as I know something."

Romero locks eyes with me upon ending the call. "Do you trust him?"

"You heard him. He was ready to piss his pants." My answer seems to be sufficient enough, as he nods before moving on to the next phone call.

It's only been a few minutes since I watched Bianca drive away. The fear in her eyes, the worry flashing at the forefront of my thoughts when I need to focus on ending this shit. *Ending them*, both of them, father and son. All the while, though, I receive updates from my men and wonder what the hell is taking Tatum so long.

My thoughts keep returning to my little bird. Is Bianca glad she didn't have the chance to give me an official answer before the bomb went off? I can't afford to think that way, yet I can't help it. She has the baby to think about now, as do I.

But while I want nothing more than to keep her close, she could very well decide this is the final straw. I believe she loves me, that she knows as well as I do that there's no killing what's between us.

However, she's also a realist.

Get it together. Whatever she's thinking, we can work it out, but not until I know both Moroni men are dead and buried six feet deep. I won't be taking chances with my family again.

"Where's Tatum?" Romero mutters between phone calls. "I would like to get out of here with her like five minutes ago."

"I'll light a fire under her." I have no doubt she understands how crucial it is to leave now. If I were in her shoes, I'd be packed and out the door by now. This is not the time for her stubbornness.

"Tatum! Let's go!" Her bedroom door is open, and I hear the argument going on inside as I approach. "What is taking you so long?" I demand, entering the room.

"I'm not leaving without her."

Craig scratches his head, groaning. "I don't know if you can keep it safe. It's better to leave something important like that here for now."

He reaches for her, and she jerks herself away. "I'll cut your fucking hands off."

"What the hell is going on?" I bark, startling them both. "We don't have time for this, Tatum."

She whirls on me, holding Amanda's urn, clutching it to her chest like a shield. "I'm bringing this."

For fuck's sake. Nobody has ever less deserved this level of devotion.

My jaw aches from the effort of grinding my teeth. "Honey.

He's right. What if something happened to it? It's safer to leave it here. And it isn't like you'll never return."

I shouldn't be surprised when she barks out a disbelieving laugh. "How do you know? There's no such thing as protection."

I need this like I need a hole in the head. "Fine," I grit through my teeth. "Take it with you." The moment Craig grimaces, the look I give him clears it up on the spot. This is not the time for him to be squeamish.

"Where am I going?" she asks, trotting beside me down the hall. With her bag slung over one shoulder and Amanda's ashes still clutched like a teddy bear, she's never looked so much like a little girl. A lost, confused little girl.

"Romero will take care of everything." At a time like this, I hate to lose him. However, there is no one else I trust more guarding my daughter. "Just do me a favor and go along with what he says. No arguing."

Romero's still on the phone. He looks her up and down—no reaction to the urn—before jerking his head toward the courtyard. "Go wait in the car. I'll be out in a minute."

"Is this really necessary? What, are they going to bomb the house again?"

"Listen to me." I grab her by the shoulders and even shake her a little because, damn it, I need her to understand. "I can't do what I need to do if I'm worried about you being here. I don't know what their next move is, that's the problem. Having you safely tucked away somewhere is the only way I can focus on what needs to be done. Do you understand? I don't ask much from you, but I need you to do as Romero says. Get in the car, and we'll talk it out once you come home."

Her angry snarl drops away before her chin starts to tremble. "I'm afraid for you. I don't want to leave you."

"I know." It's a struggle to stay calm for her sake when what I want is to push her out the door. "It's not easy for me to send you away, either. I need to trust that things will be alright—and they will. You have to believe I'm doing this for the right reason. Can you do that for me?"

"Yes," she decides, squaring her shoulders. "Can you do something for me?"

"What would that be?"

"Kill them."

"That's my plan." Satisfied, she finally follows Romero's orders, walking out the door with her head held high.

Now that she's out of the way, my thoughts return to Dominic and Jack. Sebastian has been wrong about many things but made a good point earlier. We're lucky they are both a couple of fuck ups. That bomb could easily have destroyed the house, and all of us with it.

Couldn't it?

"I'll stay in contact," Romero promises. "The minute I hear anything, you'll be the first to know."

I hardly hear him over the thundering in my ears. Something's wrong with all of this. We've been too busy reacting in a panic to step back and look at the entire situation. "It didn't do much damage, did it?"

"What are you saying?"

Looking around at the cracked plaster and broken glass, I murmur, "It didn't do as much damage as it could have, the bomb."

"Yeah, and good thing."

He's practically halfway out the door before I grab hold of him, forcing him to listen. "You're not hearing me."

"Alright, alright. What are you thinking?"

"One thing about this doesn't make sense." I walk up and down the hall, toward the stairs, toward the kitchen, following the path of the damage. "There's not an impressive radius to the damage. Did you notice that?"

"I haven't had time to pull out my tape measure just yet."

"Listen to me. Hear what I'm saying. The bomb wasn't very powerful." He's still looking at me like I've grown two heads. I wouldn't normally have to explain myself like this, but this is hardly a normal situation. "A powerful bomb could have torn this place to shreds. It didn't."

Understanding dawns on me all at once. "Why didn't it do more damage?" he whispers. "Why set off a bomb that was never meant to kill anyone?"

His phone rings, and he answers without looking at it, too busy staring at the house like he's seeing it for the first time. "Yeah?" he barks before hearing something on the other end that makes him turn on the speaker.

"It's a fucking trap." Sebastian, his voice tight, the words coming so fast they almost overlap. "Dominic did it. It was a distraction. He's out there somewhere, nearby. You've gotta stay where you are and keep a watch out for him. I can send my guys to help."

There's another bomb—the one that's now going off inside my head, tearing everything I thought I knew to pieces. It's all so fucking obvious now that the panic has worn off. "He knew I would send her away. Fuck!"

All it takes is one look exchanged between us before I bolt, running for the car and throwing myself behind the wheel.

This is what he wanted. He wanted her away from the house. He was looking to flush her out much in the same way we've been trying to flush him out all this time.

And as I tear down the driveway, I can almost imagine Dominic sitting in a car down the road, watching everything unfold. Waiting for the truck to return, counting down the seconds before detonation. After that, it was only a matter of time before I sent my little bird to safety.

I fumble with the phone, eyes on the road as I swing the car around. Tires squeal, and I almost lose control before righting the vehicle and flooring the gas pedal.

Bianca's phone rings with no answer. "Pick up!" My roar fills the car with no one to hear it except me. Fuck, did she even bring her phone? Was it on her when Charlie took her away?

I know he's got his phone, since I gave him the address and he plugged it into GPS.

Yet it, too, keeps ringing. Every unanswered ring is a knife to my chest.

The gas pedal is almost touching the floor by the time I reach the interstate. The blaring of horns fades to the background as I weave from lane to lane, the cars around me blurring while I speed past them.

They're out there somewhere.

Possibly caught in the trap set for them.

A trap I pushed them into in an effort to protect her and our unborn child.

BIANCA

"This isn't easy for me," my father rambles on as we reach the interstate and merge into traffic.

It's not very heavy at this time of night, and I hope we don't end up getting stuck in a jam somewhere. The sooner we are at the safe house, the sooner I'll be able to breathe easier. Not easy, but easier than I am now, with my heart in my throat and a sense of dread drumming in my head.

"You think it's fun for me?" I counter. "I don't like this any more than you do."

"You have a choice. That's what I need you to get through your head. You don't have to go through this." His hands tighten around the wheel, his shoulders rising as he takes a ragged breath. "He doesn't own you. You get to make your own choices."

"I realize all of that."

"Are you sure?"

The anger bubbling in his voice tells me I need to take a breath and smooth things over before we steer this conversation into dangerous territory. What I need most at this point is his support to keep me centered, and that's not going to happen if we're sniping at each other and hurling ugly words.

"I know it sounds crazy," I begin as calmly as I can.

"I can think of a few other adjectives for it."

My teeth sink into my tongue. *Don't take the bait. Don't let this devolve any further.* "I'm sure you can, and I don't need to hear them."

"I don't know what else I can say to get through to you."

"It's not a matter of getting through to me. Would you please stop? I'm upset enough as it is."

Captain Last Word won't let it go at that. "You don't need this. That's all I'm saying." Before I can argue, he holds up a hand and shakes his head. "Listen to me. I understand I was wrong about Callum. But that doesn't make him a good guy. Even if he was, he's involved with too many people who aren't. And they want to hurt him."

When all I do is stare out the window, still biting my tongue, he sighs. "You know that old saying? You don't just marry a person. You marry their family. That applies here, too. You are looking to get involved in this entire world, and you're carrying a child. Do you want them exposed to this?"

"It's not like I don't see your side of things," I murmur, choosing my words carefully. If anything, this is something to think about besides the explosion and the fact that Callum could be under attack at this very moment for all I know. "And I'm not saying it doesn't matter. It does. But I love him."

"Bianca…"

"I do. And there's nothing I can do to stop it. You don't think I tried? You don't think I told myself so many times this couldn't possibly end well? Trust me, Dad. I know."

"And yet you walk into it with your eyes wide open."

"That's just my point. There's nothing else I can do. I can't force myself to stop loving somebody. Could you force yourself to stop loving Mom?"

"I don't appreciate you throwing that in my face."

"I'm not. I'm only trying to show you my side of things. If there was any way I could get through this life without Callum, it would be different. I might be able to walk away. But that's just it. There is no going through life without him. That's the only way I can think to describe it."

Silence falls between us. It doesn't feel cold, and it's not tense either. I wish he would say something. I wish I could think of something else to say, anything that might help him understand where I'm coming from.

"I can't stand watching you walk headfirst into this," he finally admits. "That's all. I do want us to have a better relationship. I want us to be a family. But you can't expect me to be okay right now. I'm driving you to a safe house. Doesn't that seem out of the ordinary?"

"You know it does. But I'm not running away ever again. I know where I belong." And when I say the words out loud, when I feel them on my tongue and hear my thoughts being given a voice, I know I'm right. I'm doing the best thing for me and my baby. I've chosen this life and everything that goes along with it.

"So long as you're sure."

"I am," I whisper. He sounds so despondent. No matter how much I want to tell myself otherwise, his sadness is going to weigh on me. It's going to color every interaction we have until the day finally comes when he can move past this ugly, horrible night.

Maybe around the time the baby graduates high school, I guess.

"These new headlights…" Dad's grumbling stirs me out of my brooding.

Before I can ask him what he means, I flinch away from the intense glare in the side mirror. "I hate those things. They make it a pain to drive at night."

"It doesn't help that this guy is up our ass." He speeds up a little to put space between us and the offending car. "Nobody behind us for a mile, but he has to ride our tail."

Of all the times for me to laugh… "I remember you teaching

me to drive. You always drilled that into my head. Leave at least five car lengths between me and the vehicle in front of me."

"And do you?" There's a tiny bit of humor in his question, thank God.

"I hear your voice in my head all the time, so yeah."

He doesn't laugh—he's too busy raising a hand above his eyes now that the headlights coming from behind us are blinding him. "What the hell?"

Sometimes a lifetime's worth of understanding can pass through a person's head in the time it takes to gasp. Like a sudden download. So many things materialize all at once, so fast you think your head will split open.

That's not a random driver.

Wouldn't this be the perfect time to come after me?

They were counting on this.

This must have been how she felt once she figured out somebody was on her tail.

"We have to get off the road!!" I twist in my seat, looking behind us with a hand shading my eyes. It's no use. Those headlights blind me to everything else. I can't make out the car or who's behind the wheel.

"What do you mean?" My father peers out the rearview mirror.

"I have a very bad feeling." The GPS says we're ten minutes from the safe house. "I don't think—"

The car lurches when we're tapped from behind hard enough to make the phone tumble from my fingers and into the back seat. "Shit!" Dad grunts out as he fights to regain control of the vehicle.

"We have to get away from this car." I try not to sound as panicked as I'm feeling.

"You think?" His voice is tight, like a wire pulled taut enough that it could snap any second. He sounds like the cop he used to be. "Face forward and make sure your seat belt is secure."

"Dad?" I can't find the breath to finish whatever it was I wanted to say.

"I know. Just hold on—and if I tell you to get down, get down."

From the corner of my eye, I watch his gaze dart back and forth between the windshield and the mirror.

"This son of a bitch thinks he's dealing with an amateur."

"Please, be careful," I squeak. It's amazing I can take a breath with my throat tightened to the size of a pinhole.

The car lurches again when the driver hits the right corner. This time we swerve to the side and turn halfway before Dad steers us over to the center lane.

Dinner's churning in my stomach and my life is flashing in front of my eyes. There are only so many close calls a person can have before they've had one too many. What sucks is there's no way to know which one is the last until it's too late to do anything about it.

I'm too young to die. I have too much to live for. Everything was finally starting to click. I was a heartbeat away from officially being engaged. I was about to plan a shopping trip with Dad. He was finally coming around on so many things and looking forward to being a granddad and, damn it, I need more time.

A single thought rings out loud and clear—so clear I can hear it. More like a prayer than a thought.

Mom. Help us, please.

Is this how she felt? Seeing that car bearing down on her, panic rising in her throat, the combination of fear and survival instincts making her foot heavier against the pedal.

No. In her case, it was worse. In her case, she was alone. She went through all of this by herself.

"I can't shake this son of a bitch!" Dad jerks the wheel to the side while barely avoiding sideswiping a truck. I'm unable to bite back a breathless scream and I can't help but wonder if she screamed too.

But there was nobody there to hear it…

We weave around a few cars whose drivers lean on their horns.

They do it again once our pursuer passes. "Dad, I'm scared." It doesn't need to be said, but I can't hold it in either.

"I know, baby." He jams on the gas and the sudden burst of speed presses me against my seat. "There's a police station two exits down, just off the ramp. We can make it there."

Two exits? No way whoever is driving that car is going to let us make it that far. Not when they're up our ass again, the lights getting brighter, bigger.

"God damn it!" Dad shouts as he pulls into the right lane, where we swerve onto the gravel at the side of the road before swerving back into place. The car follows us.

When the phone starts ringing in the back seat, frustrated tears fill my eyes. I know who it is—call it instinct, or maybe a mental connection forged over the past few months. It has to be Callum. Maybe he's calling to see if we've arrived yet.

My body moves before my brain knows what it's doing. I start to turn, to look for the phone, but the car jerks forward and I'm tossed back.

"Face forward!" Dad barks as he fights to regain control.

"It's probably Callum! We need help!"

"What is he going to do?" he demands, almost leaning over the wheel. The speedometer reads eighty-five but the needle keeps drifting toward ninety. Of all the times for there to be no cops on the road, why is there no one out here to help us?

The question is still running through my head when the pursuer veers to the left, then starts inching closer like he wants to come up alongside us. "Dad, he's coming!"

"I see that. Hold on."

Meanwhile the phone continues ringing, and ringing, and all it does is remind me of who's waiting at home. How will he ever get over this? He will never stop blaming himself. If I could only reach the phone, but every time the car swerves from one side to the other my cell slides along the back seat.

I glance over my shoulder and now that the lights aren't

directly behind us, I can see inside the other vehicle. It doesn't surprise me to find Dominic Moroni behind the wheel, and it looks like he's laughing. I could be imagining that, but I don't think so. I know he's crazy and that's exactly what he would do.

He takes his eyes off the road for a second, no more than that, and our gazes lock. He sees me and he knows I see him. All it takes is the slightest turn of the wheel to bump us, hard enough that we skid off the road.

"Motherfucker!" Dad shouts while I scream, bracing myself as the car speeds toward the woods alongside the road.

Everything goes through my head at once: Callum, Tatum, the ultrasound, Mom and Dad, Mom's funeral, even Lucas. The good mixes with the bad, all of it overlapping in the short time it takes us to tear through the overgrown brush bordering the tree line while Dad slams on the brakes.

Then it's all over. The car crashes into a tree, the impact stopping us in an instant. At first I'm stunned when the airbag hits my face and chest, but I shake it off, pushing the deflating bag away and looking into the passenger side mirror once it's visible. He's not back there—the road is quiet. I doubt he could come to a dead stop all at once, as fast as he was going, but he's coming. I know it deep down in my gut.

"Dad. Are you okay? Oh, my God." My heart's still pounding when I turn to him. It feels like I'm moving in slow motion as I clear the deflating airbag away and find him knocked out cold. "No, no, Dad. Wake up. Come on, wake up!" I don't want to shake him too hard, though, since I don't know if he's injured. All I know is he's slumped over the wheel, but when I hold my hand up close to his face, I feel his breath on the backs of my fingers.

I unbuckle my belt and turn in the seat, scanning the area through the rear window. There's smoke rising up from the front of the car. *What should I do?* Should I try to get him out in case there's a fire? I don't know if the smoke means something's already burning. I'm not sure I could move him or whether I should even try. I don't know anything.

One thing I can do is finally reach the phone. Once I have it in my hand, I decide to dial 911. Until it occurs to me I have no idea where we are, exactly. I wasn't paying attention to the mile markers and I don't know the number of the exit we were approaching. But none of that matters, not when Dad needs help.

My eyes flick up to the road, searching for some kind of landmark, and land on a car as it backs its way down the shoulder of the road. A car with damage to its front passenger side. A car that comes to a rolling stop.

"Oh, god!" I drop the phone from my shaking hands and reach for Dad. "Dad! Please, wake up! Help me!"

It's no use. I might as well be alone, and again, I can't help the thoughts of Mom that flood my mind as the car door opens, then slams shut.

He's coming for us. He's going to kill us...

All at once, a sense of calm washes over me. Everything comes into sharp focus. It could be the sight of Dominic sauntering around the car, his silhouette lit by his headlights, before he begins strolling across the soft ground torn up by speeding tires. He acts like he's on a leisurely walk.

Mom might have been alone and defenseless, but I'm not, because driving isn't the only thing Dad taught me how to do. Twisting around, I open the glove box, where the gun he told Callum about sits. There's a round in the chamber when I check.

Please, Mom. If you're there, if you can help, I need you.

"Anybody alive in there?" he taunts, laughing like the maniac he is.

Any lingering nerves or questions about whether this is the right thing to do vanish when I hear that menacing laugh. *He wants to kill me. My father. My baby. No fucking way.* If it's a choice between my life and his, I'm choosing me. My first instinct is to jump out of the car and start firing but I have to be smart about this. The element of surprise is what's going to give me a leg up.

I open the door a little, then keep my right arm pressed to my stomach with the gun tucked under my left. "Please... Don't do this..." I moan like I'm injured. I raise my right foot and step out, planting it firmly on the ground. "Please, Dominic. I think he's dead."

"Boo-fucking-hoo," he retorts. "That's the entire point. If you get out of the car like a good girl and don't fight, I won't have to hurt you. But if you pull the shit you did back at the basement compound with that knife, I can't make any promises."

"I'm coming. Just, please, don't hurt me." I climb out slowly, my body hunched over and my once racing heart now beating normally. There's no fear. No doubt. Only the certainty of what needs to be done. He must die.

"Look at you. Not so brave now, are you? No knife for you to pull on me, huh?"

"You knew this is what would happen, didn't you? It was your plan all along." I don't know why I ask the question. It's not going to change anything but it will confirm how fucked up he is, and give me another reason to blow him away.

"Your precious Callum likes to play dirty. Well, we can play dirty, too. My father told me what he would do, because he's so fucking predictable. Create a distraction, a way to split everyone up. It's the oldest trick in the book, and he ate that shit right out of my hand. All he cared about was getting his precious Bianca out of harm's way. Funny enough, he sent you right into it. It's a shame he won't get a second chance at being a father.``

I turn to him slowly, ensuring he's close enough for a clean shot. The last thing I want is for the bullet to miss him. I don't know if I'll get another chance. Straightening my spine, I lift the gun and point it directly at his chest. I don't say a word. I only take a moment to savor the smug expression he wears.

"What do you think you're going to do with that?" he laughs.

"I'm going to make certain you never fuck with me or my family again. I'm going to end your life." Everything happens in slow motion. The look of shock on his face, the step he takes towards me, his body hunching over and reaching for the gun. I release all the air in my lungs and squeeze the trigger.

My fingers squeeze the trigger and the smell of gunpowder fills my nostrils. The bullet zips through the air, hitting its mark. The center of his chest. He stumbles back with a strangled cry before landing on his ass. "My father will kill you for this. You're all dead." He scrambles backwards on his hands, while I slowly advance on him.

What kind of person does it make me to be able to watch him die? To see the light slowly seep out of him.

He gasps, flopping around on the ground like a fish out of water. I wonder how he likes it? Drowning on his own blood. What a shame his death couldn't be more drawn out.

We've taken too many chances with these monsters. We've left them too much room to come back at us again and again. I'm not doing that anymore. And that thought is what has me taking aim a second time. My story won't end the way my mother's did. I pull the trigger, my mind numb and my sole focus on my target. Another bullet lodges itself in his chest and I look from his face to the advancing headlights that sweep across my body.

Relief washes over me as I watch him take his final breath. *Dead. He'll never hurt anyone I love again.* I raise my left arm to shield my eyes, and all at once, reality comes rushing back.

I killed a man. I killed him.

What if I can't prove it was self-defense?

"Bianca!" I've never heard anything sweeter than the sound of Callum's voice calling my name. He stops the car and flings the door open, running to me with his arms outstretched. When I'm finally wrapped in his embrace, I melt against him and let everything else fade away. I killed someone. I should feel shame, or guilt, but neither of those emotions come.

All I feel is relieved.

"He's dead," I whisper, almost in disbelief. "He's dead and I killed him. I killed him. He's dead." My teeth chatter and suddenly I'm so damn cold.

"Shh, little bird. I know. It's okay. You did what you needed to do. You protected yourself."

"...Bianca?" Dad's voice—soft, groggy—sounds from inside the car. He's alive. He'll be okay.

I'm so thankful he's alive. We both made it. My knees buckle and I end up on the ground, sobbing while Callum holds me.

Everything's going to be okay. I just know it.

CALLUM

There is no sense of peace in the house. No hope of calm. Not while it's crawling with guards at all hours. Not with Jack out there somewhere, plotting how he's going to blow my world to pieces for taking his son's life.

I sent Romero home an hour ago against his wishes. He needs sleep–we both do, but I can't imagine willing my mind to quiet down long enough for sleep to catch up to me. I would only toss and turn and wake Bianca. One of us needs to be sharp, meaning he needs a break while I pace my office or check in with the guards down at the front gate walking the perimeter. Watching. Waiting.

If this goes on much longer, I don't know how my nerves will stand it. A man in my position can expect to spend sleepless nights. I've lived with strain, stress, tension, to the point where I thought I was impervious. But this? Everything that's ever mattered is at stake, and at the moment, I can't do anything but wait for Jack to show his face. Romero's exhausted his extensive contact list. We have guys combing every square mile between this compound and the property Jack's been living and working out of.

We even have eyes on his Miami residence in case he flew down there to regroup.

Where is he? What's his next move?

A whiskey might dull the incessant pounding in my head, but I can't risk dulling my senses. I can only grind my teeth and push through, ignoring the bar cart while I pace for lack of anything else to do. Patience has never been one of my virtues.

The ringing of my phone pierces the silence. I pounce on it, snatching it from the desk. The sight of Sebastian's name, especially at two in the morning, takes my already rapid pulse and sends it into overdrive.

"This had better be good," I murmur without greeting him.

"Of course it's good. Why else would I be calling you at this time of night? I did it. It finally happened."

My grip on the phone tightens. "What are you talking about? I'm not in the mood for games."

"This isn't a game."

So why does he sound so jumpy? Almost hyper. "Tell me you have good news."

"Excellent news. And if you want what I know you want more than anything, you will meet me at the address I'm about to provide."

Easy. Calm. I can't afford to leap without looking first, especially when it sounds like the kid is on speed. His breathing erratic, the words pouring from him in a rapidfire stream.

"Is this about what I think it's about?"

"You'll find out when you get here."

"I'm going to need more than that, Sebastian."

"Do I have to spell it out? I have something you want. This merchandise isn't the kind I can let out of my sight. So either you can claim it, or I'm going to have to. Either way, it needs to be dealt with."

"How many men am I bringing with me?"

"None. You won't need them. This is the part where you trust me."

Trust him? My heart is about to tear its way out of my chest. If he has Moroni, why won't he use his name? What's with speaking in these cryptic codes?

"Give me the address," I grunt, scribbling it down on a notepad before tearing the page free.

"It shouldn't take you more than twenty minutes to get here. I'll be waiting." With that, the line goes dead, leaving me staring at my phone while the sound of my heartbeat fills my ears.

Why was he so cryptic? That's what bothers me, the question that rolls around in my head as I leave my office and stride quickly down the hall, to the staircase. I take the steps two at a time before rushing down the hall as silently as I can, slowly opening the bedroom door.

She left the lamp on the nightstand burning, and a book is open on her chest. She fell asleep while reading. I can imagine her waiting for me as long as she could before there was no fighting sleep anymore. Considering she blew a man away three nights ago, she's taken things well. No outbursts beyond the breakdown at the scene. I'd be worried if she hadn't at least wept after what she went through. Beyond that, she's been strong, and resilient. She knows what needs to be done now and can accept it. Yet another example of her belonging at my side. She was made for me, for this ruthless world. My queen.

For a moment, I take in her peaceful beauty. The dark locks fanned across the pillow, the hand curled beside her head. *My little bird.* She got damn lucky, escaping the crash without a scratch. It was Charlie who ended up with a concussion and a broken arm, and even that seems mild when I think of how bad it could've been.

Now she's dreaming, unaware of the current battle waging a war inside my head between trusting Sebastian and possibly losing a golden opportunity. When I look at her and think about the life growing inside her, there's no choice to be made.

Whatever it takes, I'm going to protect them, and that means following Sebastian's instructions.

I walk into the closet as quietly as possible and push all the clothing out of the way, typing the code into the safe built into the wall. *Weapons.* I need a gun or two and maybe a knife. I strap a knife to my ankle and grab one gun, placing it at my back. Then I close the safe and walk out of the closet, my gaze lingering on Bianca for a moment longer. I'm tempted to kiss her goodbye, but I don't want her to wake up and question where I'm going. Lying to her is not an option, and I wouldn't want to anyway. We're partners in this.

I choose against it and slip out of the room. After closing the door carefully, I jog downstairs and straight out the front door. The trio of armed guards standing in the courtyard cast quizzical looks my way. I ignore them, heading straight for Romero's cottage. I'm not surprised to see the light on in the front window — he hasn't gone to bed yet. It's as much of a challenge for him to relax and let go at a time like this as it is for me.

The door swings open practically in sync with my knock on the door. "I saw you coming," he explains. He's in flannel pants, and a plain white T-shirt, so at least he made the effort to prepare for sleep.

By the time I finish rattling off all the details of Sebastian's call, his brow is lowered to the point where I can barely see his eyes. "You trust him? When he sounded half out of his mind?"

"You know how he is. He can be… theatrical at best."

"To put it mildly."

"If he's holding Moroni for me, I can't afford to pass up the opportunity. Like he said, there's only so long you can hold a guy like that before people come sniffing around. This isn't like Kristoff. There's no keeping him indefinitely."

His sigh is heavy. Resigned. "You're going to go, aren't you?"

"I can't afford not to. I need him dead. We all do." I point at the house, my hand shaking with anticipation. "Those lives in there? They're all that matters. If I don't end him tonight, I'm going to regret it. One way or another, I'll regret it."

"Give me five minutes."

"I never said you were coming with me." I'm talking to the empty living room by now. He's already getting changed in the adjoining bedroom.

"I swear you're out of your damn mind. Why would you think I'd let you go alone? You might trust that little shit, but not me."

There's no use in arguing, so I don't bother. I want to get this done and over with. I pull three men together. "I want a man posted at my bedroom door, and one at Tatum's. We'll be back as soon as we can. Romero will keep you posted."

I look over my shoulder to find him leaving the cottage in dark jeans, a leather jacket, and his T-shirt. "Do we have an address?" I hand him the paper and wait as he plugs the address into his phone. "A warehouse. No surprise. It's in Costello territory, at least. Did he ask Jack for a meeting there?"

"I don't know. I didn't ask questions," I tell him. I'm halfway to the car, which I'll be driving. I can't sit passively for another minute. I've done enough of that the past few days to last me a lifetime. This is it. I've waited so long, craving the sensation of grinding the man into dust under my heel. That craving has only intensified until now, I want blood. Knowing I'm this close to achieving what I've waited for is a heady sensation that translates to a heavy foot on the gas pedal. I'm so close. This ends tonight.

"I'll take the lead." Romero's voice is quiet, low. "Just in case. Stay back until I give you the all clear."

When I don't answer, he turns toward me. "Boss. I need you to agree with me."

"We have nothing to worry about."

"I'm going in first." When I scoff, he slaps a palm against the glovebox. "Let me do my job. I'm not going to watch you walk into a trap. I need to check and make sure it's safe."

"Do what you feel is best." I'm not going to fight over something this inconsequential when I prefer imagining Jack's agony. He kidnapped my little bird. He could've killed my daughter. He took her mother from her. He tried to use my unborn child against me. There is nothing painful enough for him—but that won't keep me from trying to make him feel that pain.

The warehouse sits in a quiet part of town surrounded by tall, boxy buildings with darkened windows. They cast long shadows over an empty street, and I swear I taste foreboding in the air. I couldn't have chosen a better location for what's about to happen. I know it is. I feel it. He's nearby, and every breath he takes is one closer to his final gasp. I slow the car to turn into the fenced-off lot.

We're a few dozen feet from the warehouse when I roll to a stop. Neither of us speaks as we study the scene: five dark cars sit empty and the wide door leading inside the brick structure sits slightly ajar beneath a bare light bulb.

"I don't see anyone out here," Romero muses before removing the Glock from his waistband. "That's a lot of cars to have nobody posted outside."

"I'll call him." I look away from the door long enough to pull up the last incoming number and place the call. When he answers, I mutter, "I'm outside."

"Come in." The door swings open, and Sebastian appears. He looks around for a moment before spotting my car, then waves his arm. He's smiling like a man greeting long-awaited guests.

"He's either insane or... no, I'm going with insane." Romero opens his door, and I do the same. Sebastian eyes the gun visible in Romero's hand—his brows drawn together with concern, but he doesn't say a word. A good sign. If this was a trap, he'd tell us we don't need to be armed. It's what I would do.

I can barely hear over the heavy thud of my heart by the time we stop in the circle of light thrown off by the overhead bulb. "I told you to come alone, but I figure you two are joined at the hip, so it doesn't matter." Sebastian looks Romero up and down, smirking.

"What's this about?" I demand. "Tell me he's waiting for me in there."

He's still smirking when he jerks his head toward the door. "See for yourself."

"Wait." Romero throws out an arm, blocking me. "I'd like an explanation. There's a lot of cars out there for only a few people to be here."

"They won't be driving home. They won't be driving anywhere. There are two people from Moroni's side still breathing: Jack, and his oldest daughter." His eyes gleam while a satisfied smile stretches his lips. "Congratulations are in order. I'm getting married."

"He agreed to your deal?"

"Big time. He was so desperate to end you after Dominic, he would have agreed to anything. He gave me his daughter, and I was supposed to give him the men and the money to get to you." He lifts a shoulder. "Whoops. I guess I lied."

I can't stand waiting any longer. "I'm going in."

"One second." Sebastian's jovial smile slips, revealing the cunning animal underneath. The sight makes my hackles rise. "I'm going to need a little more than we first discussed when we made this deal."

"Why am I not surprised?" Romero mutters, shaking his head.

"Out with it," I urge, ignoring the comment. "What do you want?"

"Everything. I want all of Moroni's holdings."

Romero barely stifles a laugh, but I find no humor in this. My impulse is to agree, to give him everything and anything he wants so long as it means putting an end to this. Instead, I think back on the information we compiled on Jack's finances, his holdings, the properties scattered over the East Coast. Compared to my empire, it's nothing. An anthill in the shadow of an armed fortress.

But there was a reason I didn't want the kid to get his hands on everything all at once. The fear of him becoming too powerful, too fast. Thinking back on the sum of Jack's meager little portfolio, I feel better about the prospect. "It's yours."

Romero's head swings my way. It's either wisdom or shock that keeps his mouth closed. Not that I need to hear what he's thinking. This is my call. This is my family. My well-deserved vengeance. "Now. Can we proceed?"

"Be my guest." He steps aside, wearing a victorious smile, and I move forward into the brightly lit space. Instead of a massacre involving my men and my ex-wife, it's the sight of a prone Jack Moroni that catches my eye. He's curled on his side, hands bound behind his back, ankles bound, and a gag in his mouth. Sweat coats his skin and soaks through his suit. The blood spattered on his jacket most likely came from the dead man lying a few feet away. He's not the only one, either, which explains the metallic tang hanging in the air. I count four dead bodies in all.

"Please... let him go..." The soft, pitiful whimpers catch my attention, drawing my gaze to a girl whose red face is swollen and slick with tears. A pair of men flank her, one hand wrapped around each arm. "Just let us go, please!!" I recognize one of the men as Damien, Sebastian's brother.

"What do you want us to do with her?" he asks, appearing almost annoyed.

"Shhhh, we'll be leaving as soon as we finish here," Sebastian assures her in an offhanded way. She flinches before a broken sob tears its way out of her. "Just keep ahold of her while I help our guests out."

I turn my attention to Jack. He's the reason I'm here after all. "Hello, Jack," I murmur, coming to a stop in front of him. "It's been too long. How's the family?"

His eyes are bloodshot, making their already icy color stand out in sharp contrast as he glares at me with pure, seething hatred. Good. Let him hate me. Let him reflect on the pain he's endured so far. I crouch slowly, my gaze locked with his. "There's something I want you to remember for the rest of your increasingly short life: everything that's happened to you so far is your doing. You chose to turn this into a war. You hijacked my shipments and attacked my business. You partnered up with Amanda. You kidnapped Bianca and my daughter. You set all of this into motion. There is no one to blame but yourself for what is about to happen."

I break eye contact only long enough to look over my shoulder at the weeping girl who will soon become a Costello. "You lost your only son as a result, and you were desperate enough to hand your daughter over to a man who double-crossed you. Look at all you've lost. All you threw away."

His face is beet red, and the hatred radiating from his eyes intensifies as I stand. "Get him in a chair. I want him sitting up for this."

"Dad... no..." The girl tries in vain to fight against her captors, straining and tugging against their grasps.

"Take her out to the car," Sebastian orders his brother. "I'll be out when it's over. No one touches the girl, or I'll cut off their hands." The girl's cries echo through the warehouse as the men drag her out, fading until they go silent when a car door slams outside.

Romero pulls up a wooden chair for Sebastian's remaining men to haul Jack off the floor and drop him onto it. I circle him slowly, savoring the rapid rise and fall of his shoulders. "How do you feel right now, Jack?" I ponder aloud. "Maybe you feel the way Bianca did when you held her captive. Then again, no. You don't have a life growing inside you that you're hoping to protect."

I blurt out a laugh on coming to a stop in front of him. "You couldn't even protect the kids you already had. But then it was always about you, right?"

His head snaps to the side when I backhand him. "Every day, I've imagined what I would do to you once I had you in this position. I've had a lot of time to come up with elaborate scenarios involving jumper cables and waterboarding and… well, it got graphic. In the absence of those props, we'll have to settle for a good, old-fashioned beating."

I backhand him again, then tighten my hand into a fist, crashing against his cheekbone. His eyes. His nose. Blood pours from it by the time I'm finished, coating his mouth and chin before dripping onto a shirt that used to be white.

"He's suffocating," Romero observes in a flat voice. He might as well be commenting on the weather. "He'll need to lose the gag unless you want to end this soon."

No fucking way. I'm just getting started. I yank the gag free, and he gasps, sucking in as much air as he can. "You… made your point… fucker."

"Not even close." I bend to free the knife sheathed at my ankle, then hold it up for him to see. "We're just getting started."

His chin quivers while he stares at the blade. Let him pretend he's not out of his mind with terror. "How does it feel, knowing your life is almost over?" I wonder aloud. "The way Dominic knew once that first bullet pierced his chest that it had to be the end. He died on his back, flopping around and gasping for air with nobody around to comfort him in those final moments. Bianca told me all about it. I wish I could've seen it for myself."

"You made your point." He spits out blood before lifting his split lip in a grotesque snarl. "Kill me. Get it over with."

"Oh I plan to." I grin.

He doesn't scream, not at first, when the blade slices through his pants and sinks inside something soft between his legs. It takes a moment for his brain to catch up to the sensation, but once it does, a shriek unlike anything I've ever heard fills the warehouse, the echoes overlapping until I'm surrounded by the sweet symphony of Jack Moroni's agony. The dark-red spot that quickly spreads across his crotch and down his thighs heightens my pleasure until I can't help but sink the knife in again. When I back away, his blood drips from the chair and begins to pool beneath it.

His voice is nothing more than a weak croak once his screams die off. "Just... end it..." he sobs, his head hanging, the sweat that drips from his hair mixing with his blood.

I take a handful of that hair in my hand and yank his head back until we're eye to eye. "Oh no," I whisper, beaming down at his anguished face before dragging the bloody blade along his cheek. "You're going to suffer until you bleed out. This is nowhere near over."

For Bianca. For Tatum. For my baby.

"I'm going to teach you the meaning of pain and regret before you die," I promise, savoring his agonized sob before making my next slice.

I won't stop until he's unrecognizable, until he's dead at my feet.

BIANCA

I don't know what stirs me awake. There's no loud sound, like a gunshot. There's nothing but the beating of my heart, racing now that something startled me.

I haven't even dreamed about shooting Dominic since the night it happened—an ugly, awful night full of all the darkest parts of my subconscious. All the what-ifs. What if I hadn't been able to get the gun, like if I was injured the way Dad was? If we had both been unconscious when Dominic found us, that would've been it. We'd both be dead now. What if we had crashed hard enough to kill us? What if Dominic had killed Dad while I watched? Oh yes, I went through all the scenarios in vivid color.

But that was it. Like once it was over, it was over. No more need to dredge up the memories.

I don't wake all at once. It's not one of those sudden, eyes flying open things. At first, I'm confused. There's light coming through the windows, faint and pale, like the sun hasn't risen yet but will soon. Right away, I reach out without looking, hoping to find Callum, but all my fingers touch are his empty half of the bed. The sheets are cool, telling me he never came up to bed, or if he did, he's been gone for some time.

But he must have at some point. The lamp on the nightstand is off, and my book sits next to it. I can't remember putting it there.

It's when there's movement out of the corner of my eye that I jump, my heart in my throat. "Who's there?" I whisper, staring at the open bathroom door.

The sight of Callum's familiar face lets me release the breath I was holding—but that doesn't last long because I immediately notice the dark-red splatters of blood across one cheek. "Oh my God," I gasp, scrambling out of bed, ready to run to him.

"No. It's not my blood. I'm fine." The heaviness of his voice, the fatigue in it, brings me up short. What in the hell did I miss last night? What went on while I slept?

I'm too worried to put my thoughts into words, but I don't need to. "I didn't mean to wake you," he murmurs, taking one step to his left so his body is visible. My mouth falls open. I don't even try to stop it because I can't think. Not when the sight of his blood-soaked clothes is all I can focus on. It's dried to a dark, rusty brown. Whoever was bleeding did a lot of it.

"Romero?" I finally whisper with my heart in my throat. If it was Tatum, I don't think he would be calmly undressing in our bathroom. Then again, he might not if it was Romero, either.

He shakes his head, and when I look into his eyes, I can see now how they shine. No—they glitter. There's a strange, almost manic sort of light in them. "It's over. He's gone."

There's only one person he could be talking about. The person who's consumed his thoughts since the night of the explosion and everything that came after. I almost don't want to believe it. I'm afraid to, afraid this is still a dream. I never woke up; I'm still sleeping.

"Jack?" I whisper, hating the sound of his name. But I need to know this is real.

He nods. "You will never have to fear him again. You don't have to be afraid of anything. I took care of it. You're free, my little bird."

It's instinct, I guess, the way I want to run to him. He did it, and he came home safe. With my arms outstretched, I take a step, but he shuts me down with a stern expression. "You don't want to touch me right now." He looks down at himself and slowly pulls the stiff shirt away from his skin. It's actually stuck there, and he winces as he detaches it from his chest and abs. What do you have to do to a person to make them bleed that much? Actually, on second thought, I don't want to know.

"I'll turn on the shower." There's so much I want to know, and at the same time, I would rather he never tell me. I can imagine it all, anyway. What he must have done to Jack to make him bleed that way. If the body had a drop of blood left in it, I'd be surprised. He's already taken off his pants, which sit in a blood-crusted heap next to his shoes. Even they are painted red.

He killed Jack. Jack is dead. I know he did it for me and for the baby. He did it so we don't have to be afraid anymore. I can look forward to having my baby without wondering in the back of my head how Jack might destroy everything. He's so good at that.

Was. Past tense. It's going to take time to get used to that.

By the time Callum finishes undressing, the water runs hot, and I'm already pulling my T-shirt over my head. He doesn't say anything, and neither do I. This is what I need to do. There's a force inside me that's pushing me, an instinct. He went out and slayed the dragon for me, for all of us. He was willing to risk everything—even his life—to make sure no threats were hanging over us anymore. Now, it's my turn to take care of him.

I pull him in with me, placing him directly under the showerhead. Right away, the blood starts to loosen, and by the time I've soaped up a sponge, the water around his feet has a red tinge. I tip his head back with one hand, letting the water run over his face, while with the other, I begin sponging his skin. I want to erase every last trace of that monster. He'll never be anything more than an ugly memory, a scar. But scars fade. We get used to them. Eventually, we don't even have to think about them anymore. That's how it's going to be. We are never going to think about him again, just like his blood will be gone by the time the shower is over, the water running down the drain. All that's left of him in our lives will be gone forever.

I run the sponge across his chest and over his shoulders. Once or twice, I look up to find him watching me, but I can't read his expression. The light I noticed before has faded into something less intense, but a fire still burns behind them. Relief? No, he's victorious. He's the warrior who came home to his woman. He avenged us.

I even wash his hair, running my fingers over his scalp, making sure every last trace of what happened overnight is gone. And every touch comes from the love in my heart. There I was, thinking it would be impossible to love Callum more than I already did, but little did I know. My heart is so full right now, it might explode. My protector. My hero.

By the time I start to rinse his hair, his arms have found their way around my waist. His heart's strong, steady beat reverberates in my chest while I run my hands over his head, rinsing off every last trace of shampoo. "Thank you," he whispers, gazing down at me.

"Thank you," I whisper back before reaching up to touch my lips to his. It's gratitude in that kiss, it's relief that he's safe and back with me, it's wonder at the lengths he's willing to go to if it means protecting what's his.

And instantly, the fire ignites. He takes the back of my head in his hand and holds it still, his tongue forcing its way into my mouth. I part my lips eagerly, my skin warming not because of the water but because of the fire he ignites deep in my core. I'm helpless against it. I want him to take me away, to wrap me up in his love.

I offer no resistance when he pushes me against the wall, pinning me with his body against the cold tile. His rough kisses bruise my lips, but a part of me welcomes that. I want my lips bruised. I want the evidence of him all over me.

He's the one who backs off with a grunt. "I don't want to hurt you," he growls, trembling. "The last thing I want is to hurt you. But oh, little bird..." His hand travels down the length of my side, to my hip, where his fingers press in hard enough to make me wince. "I need to take you. I need to be inside you and take you. I don't want you to think I don't... that it doesn't matter..." He bares his teeth, breathing hard, while his erection presses against my stomach. I move slightly and slide my skin against it, making him release a shuddering groan.

All I do is part my legs, hooking one over his hip, silently welcoming him. He needs this, too, just as much as I do. The connection. A return to what's real and true.

It's obvious how he's straining to control himself when he enters me in a single sharp thrust, making me hiss through my clenched teeth. He makes a sound—regret? Concern? I don't know. I only shake my head so he knows I'm all right, that he didn't hurt me.

He lifts me off the floor so I can wrap both legs around his waist and hold him close, right where I need him to be. Where the fire has turned into an inferno that will burn us both to ash even with steaming water spraying over our bodies. I've never needed him more than I do now, when something dark and dangerous swirls behind his blue eyes. Something I should shrink away from but instead melt into.

"Bianca..." He drives himself into me, and I close my eyes to focus on the sensation. "Bianca... little bird..." His fingers weave through my hair, and he wraps the locks around his fist before pulling my head to the side, burying his face in the crook of my neck, breathing me in. My hero. The man who killed for me and our child.

"That's right," I whisper in his ear, pulling him deeper with my legs. "Give it to me. Give it all to me, Callum. All of you.

Everything. I want to feel whatever it is you're feeling. Let it out."

"I love you…" His tender words are almost lost under my ecstatic cries as he pushes me higher with every stroke. "My love. My all…"

"My hero."

Our gazes collide, and he's still moving inside me, our mouths almost touching. "No matter what… you have all of me." His eyes flutter closed when my nails rake across his back.

"Callum… oh God…" I'm so close, but I don't want this to end. I want to stay here, suspended in time. He drives his hips upward, and the tip of his cock touches something deep inside me.

"And if anyone tries to hurt you." His eyes snap open, and I shudder at the way they gleam. "I'll end them. I would burn down the world if it meant keeping you safe for a single day. To see you smile, to hear you laugh, to touch your body and make you moan my name."

"Callum…" I moan.

"Because you're mine." Our foreheads touch, both of us gasping for air as we come close to the end. "You are mine always. Forever. I will never let you go, and I would give my life if it means protecting yours."

I want to tell him I'm his. I want to tell him I'll never go away again, that my place is at his side. I hope we have a boy he can raise to be as strong and protective and loving as he is. I want to say all of it and so much more, but I can't when I'm this close to detonating.

"Oh God, Callum!! I'm going to come," I whine, clutching him, almost afraid of the intensity of what's building in me.

"Come for me, come now." I can't cry out that it's already happening before he covers my mouth with his, almost devouring me, plunging his tongue inside and claiming it along with the rest of me. I'm his, completely.

Sheer bliss explodes in my core and pulls me under, where

everything is dark and sweet, and nothing but pleasure radiates through my body and my soul. By the time he breaks our kiss and leans against me, my head spins, and I'm limp... but satisfied. Triumphant, even. We won.

And here is my prize, cradling me tenderly, kissing my neck and shoulder and face. "My love," he murmurs. "My queen. My everything." There's no one else I would rather be than his, forever.

Once we're dried off, he climbs into bed. "I'm only going to take a nap," he promises as he lowers his head to the pillows. "It's been a long few days, and I haven't slept for shit."

The fact that he's asleep before I've finished getting dressed tells me this might be more than a nap, but then rest is exactly what he needs. I stroke my hand over his damp hair and smile down at him, my heart swelling. With Jack finally dead, we're one step closer to our happily ever after.

CALLUM

"I don't care that he thinks it's charity. The man's car was totaled, and the least I can do is make sure he gets a new one. It's not like I'm buying him a Mercedes. It's a goddamn Acura, for fuck's sake." To think. Charlie Cole, refusing my generosity.

Who am I kidding? This is entirely the sort of thing he'd do. The man will cut off his nose to spite his face if it means accepting something from me. "I hope he enjoys driving a rental for the foreseeable future, then."

"I know, I know. You should talk to him about it yourself. He's not listening to me."

Right, because that's something I want to do. Arguing with Charlie Cole over whether or not I owe him a new car. "I'm doing it, end of story. If he doesn't like it, he can go through the trouble of returning it to the dealership."

"Okay. I'll tell him and then I'll be on my way home."

"Don't take too long."

Her giggle warms my heart like few things ever have. In the week since she blew Dominic Moroni away, she's handled things better than I dared to hope. "Believe me. I love him, but spending the afternoon shopping for the baby so he wouldn't be here when the car arrives is more than enough time together."

"I don't know how you do it."

I'm no fool. I'd be standing at Bianca's grave if it wasn't for his skillful driving. He did his damndest to protect the most precious thing in my life. I'd buy him a Benz if I thought I could get away with it. That doesn't mean he's not a stubborn prick when he wants to be.

"Secretly, he loves it. He'll come around." She lowers her voice to a whisper. "I love you."

"I love you. Now tell Nathan I want you back here pronto." Because she's going nowhere by herself. Not ever again. Even with Jack and Dominic out of the picture, I'm not taking chances. She has a driver now.

Romero enters the office when I call for him and winces at the high-pitched whine of equipment being used in the entry hall. "I'm popping ibuprofen like candy. Good thing they're supposed to finish today."

"The car arrived with no issues."

"Good. And Charlie?" He snickers when I scoff. "Told you he'd be pissed."

"And Sebastian? Has he reached out to you?"

"No. I can only imagine he's on his honeymoon, if you can call it that." He sighs, rubbing his temples while sinking into a chair. The strain of these past several days shows on his face—the noisy construction work isn't helping. "I don't want to touch that situation. Besides, there's something else I wanted to discuss with you."

Leaning back in my chair, I raise my eyebrows. "Shoot."

"That might be the wrong choice of words—you're the one who may want to shoot me."

Dread takes root in my gut and starts to grow even as I try to fight it off. Here I am, my problems solved. No more threats, no more plotting. I don't even have to worry myself with absorbing Jack's businesses.

I should know better by now than to think there's such a thing as relaxation. "Go ahead."

"It has to do with Tatum." That does nothing to ease my dread. Far from it. "She hasn't wanted to tell you about it, but Jefferson Knight has been calling and texting her the past few weeks."

Jeff Knight. Son of a bitch, I wrote him off. When he never called back to ask about Kristoff, I let him and his rapist son fade to the back of my awareness. I had much bigger fish to fry then.

Now he comes rushing forward. "He's been harassing her?" I growl, picturing him in my head. The smug expression he always wears, as if managing businesses left to him by his old man is some incredible feat. "For how long, exactly?"

"Four weeks." I turn at the sound of Tatum's voice. She's leaning against the doorway jam, hands tucked into the pockets of her hoodie. "He's been reaching out to me for four weeks, demanding I tell him what happened to Kristoff and asking why he never came home."

"What the fuck—" The widening of her eyes stops me from finishing the process of blowing up on her. Damn it. I'm practically shaking but somehow manage to control my volume. "Why did you wait until now to tell me?"

"I was ignoring him at first. I figured he'd get tired of bothering me if he never got an answer."

"I want to see your phone." Holding out my hand, I make a *come hither* motion with my cupped fingers. "Let's see it. Now."

"Here." Romero taps on his phone. "I sent you the screen shots."

I fucking hate this. Sputtering, fighting to keep up. Learning there's been secrets I wasn't privy to. "Why the hell does he have screen shots and I'm only hearing about this today?"

"Can we not make this a federal case?" she asks with an exasperated sigh.

"Why?" I insist. "Tell me why I'm the last to know."

"For one thing?" She waves a hand in front of me, scowling. "This whole thing you've got going on now. I didn't want to deal with it. And you obviously had other things on your mind."

Right. And she's developed a habit of suffering in silence. Regret lances my heart–I wouldn't be surprised to find blood spreading across the front of my shirt. "Have you responded at all?"

She tips her head to the side, shrugging. "How can I, when I don't know what happened?" Smartass. She suspects. She'd be a fool not to, and my daughter is no fool.

"Good point." I open the message app on my phone, and find a dozen screen shots from Tatum's app that Romero sent. In the beginning, Jeff was almost cordial.

Jefferson: Tatum, I need to speak to you. It's important to have details of Kristoff's mental state and the people he was spending time with in Italy. You are my only hope.

Jefferson: I would appreciate a phone call as soon as you're free. My son is missing and I haven't heard from him in weeks. Please, get in touch with me.

It didn't take long for him to drop the thin veneer of civility. After a week of being ignored, he got real, and each progressive message carried heavier threats.

Jefferson: I have been as patient as possible. If I don't hear from you shortly, I'll have no choice but to take legal action.

Jefferson: The fact that you refuse to engage with me only points to an awareness of something you don't want to reveal. I have to wonder if there's guilt involved here.

Jefferson: Is that it? Are you guilty of something you would rather not share?

Jefferson: What happened in Europe???

"You were dealing with this on your own?" The man is damn lucky I don't blow his brains out this instant for harassing her like this. Threatening her with legal action. "Who the fuck does he think he is?"

"Can you believe I actually considered telling him what he wants to know? I mean, about what happened?" She laughs bitterly, though the sound is a little too high-pitched for my liking. Her nerves are strained as it is. She doesn't need this shit heaped on top of it all.

"I doubt he would want to believe it."

"What, his precious little boy?" Again she laughs. "Yeah, right. There's a reason he ended up the way he did, and it's not because he was ever held accountable for his bullshit."

"I could put an end to all of this very quickly, if you want."

"What does that mean?"

"You should know better by now than to ask me a question like that. You might not like the answer."

"You can't kill him. It would look pretty obvious, wouldn't it?"

The breath catches in my throat while Romero sounds like he's choking at her sudden bluntness. "Oh, come on," she sighs. "What else could you have meant? Let's be real. If anybody knows he's after me, it'll look bad if he suddenly disappears."

"Last I checked, I don't need you giving me advice on how to run shit around here."

"But you know I'm right."

"I wasn't going to kill him." Though I would like to shake him up a little. Show him what happens when you bully a defenseless girl. The apple didn't fall very far from the tree, did it? If Jeff's not careful, he'll end up like his dead kid.

Tatum exchanges a glance with Romero–guilty, hesitant–before clearing her throat. "I think... it would be best for me to go the way we talked about before."

"You can't be serious. If anything, this is exactly why you shouldn't. What happens if you're off on your own and he decides he's tired of only sending messages?"

"Dad, I can't rely on you for the rest of my life. I can't hide behind you. I need to face this on my own." On her own, but something tells me she'll be living on my dime the way she always has. The girl has never truly been on her own in all her life. She's always been able to fall back on me, and I wouldn't have it any other way. I would rather she lean on my generosity than, God forbid, rely on strangers who might not have her best interests in mind.

"I can't pretend the idea makes me happy." I'm too busy pretending I'm not fighting the impulse to tie her up somewhere so I know she's protected when I pull her in for a hug. "Where will you go?"

"I don't know yet."

"And how will I know you're being looked after?"

"Dad, I'm not a little kid anymore. I don't need to be looked after." We'll only end up fighting if I remind her how much help she's needed over the past couple of months. I would rather not permanently damage our relationship.

"I'll feel a lot better if I send someone to look after you."

"A watchdog?"

"If I feel like it, yes. A watchdog. That's actually a very good idea—thanks for putting it in my head."

"I don't want to live that way."

"With all due respect, you don't have a choice."

Finally, Romero decides to speak up. "If you don't mind, I have an idea."

I turn to him, expecting him to back me up—and in a way, he does. "I could go, and watch over Tatum."

Instantly, I'm bombarded with memories of the two of them at each other's throats. "And run the risk of this one spending all her time coming up with ways to kill you in your sleep?"

"This one? I have a name." She extricates herself from my grasp and makes a big deal of brushing herself off and straightening out her clothes. "And I might have been like that before, but I've grown up a little. Maybe a lot. Also I'm not stupid. I don't want to be walking around with a target on my back with nobody to protect me."

"It's obvious you've already talked about this behind my back." Otherwise, there's no way she would accept the idea so quickly.

"Come on." She looks worn, tired, as she shakes her head. My little girl, so tired. "He has the screenshots. You think I didn't give him any context? I knew you wouldn't let me go on my own."

She's got me over a barrel, a position I've never much enjoyed. She already wants to leave, and I can't force her to stay, but it means losing my right hand in the process. At the same time, he's the only one I'd trust alone with her. I doubt I would sleep a single night for fear of what she might be doing, seeing, or going through. I know I can trust Romero to provide regular updates and he'll protect her with his life.

"Maybe it would be for the best," I have to admit even though it pains me like I can't describe to think of letting her leave. "We'll work out a way to get him off your back, and in the meantime, you can lie low."

"It would mean taking her somewhere secret," Romero murmurs, as if I haven't already realized that.

"I know, and together we can decide where that will be."

"And you're still okay with it?"

"Do yourself a favor and quit while you're ahead," I advise my daughter with as close to a smile as I can muster. Besides, I have an idea of where she could go and be perfectly safe, somewhere I could find her if I needed to. "It's for the best right now—that does not mean I expect this to be permanent. You will be coming home. This is where you belong, with your family."

"I know. And I'll come back for the baby. I promise."

Romero and I have a lot to talk about, and the look I give him conveys this. That can wait until later. "You'd better," I tell Tatum, holding her a little tighter before steering her out to the hall with an arm around her shoulders. "Or else you'll have to be the one to explain it to Bianca, because I'm not sure she'd want to hear it from me."

"Don't want to hear, what from you?"

Sound travels very easily in this place. It doesn't hurt that Bianca stands at the other end of the hall, frozen stiff.

Tatum pulls up short, sighing unhappily. "Let me explain."

"Explain what?" Her head swings back and forth as she searches for an explanation. "I was just coming in to say hi and let you know I made it back okay. What did I miss?"

Tatum looks up at me, pleading silently. I have too much to do, making arrangements for her safety, but it looks like that will have to wait a while. "Tatum is going to be leaving us for a little while—Romero, too."

She comes our way slowly, dragging her feet while her mouth hangs open in disappointment. "What? Why? Where are you going? What about the wedding and the baby and all the things I was hoping we would do together?"

"It's complicated," Tatum tells her, reaching out like she wants a hug. Her arms drop when Bianca backs away. "Don't be mad."

"Don't be mad? You've practically been a stranger for weeks. I keep getting the feeling you resent me. Now you're running off with no warning?" The color rises in her cheeks, darker with every word. "How am I supposed to keep from getting mad?"

The quaver in her voice gives away the sadness hiding beneath her anger. Something tells me there's much more of the former than the latter.

"At least hear her out," I murmur. There's a line between wanting to help and getting too involved. I've never been good at navigating this sort of thing but I can't stand back and watch them hurting. "She has a good reason, and I've agreed it's the best way to go."

"Until things calm down," Tatum promises. "I didn't want to worry you, but Kristoff's dad has been on my ass for a while now. I just need to get away from everything. Get my head straight."

Bianca's mouth pops open. "So it's not because you don't want to be here?"

"Not even close."

"You were supposed to be my maid of honor." Tears fill her eyes. "I'm sorry. I know it's selfish of me to bring that up but I'm disappointed. Damn that jerk, making you run away and miss everything."

"I think I know a way around that." Not quite, but an idea begins to form. "Would you mind having a smaller, intimate ceremony at first? Something we could put together here, on the property?"

Bianca's eyelids flutter. "Oh. I—I don't—"

"You don't have to go to the trouble for me," Tatum murmurs, watching her friend. "I know you want the whole shebang and you shouldn't have to sacrifice that just to have me with you when you get married."

"No, no, I think that's a great idea." A smile begins to stir at the corners of her mouth. "I was surprised, that's all. We could do a smaller ceremony here to make things official, and once things have calmed down and you're feeling better, we could have a bigger party."

I didn't realize until this moment how much it would mean to have my daughter with me while I commit my life to the woman of my dreams. "That sounds wonderful."

"We have so much work to do!" Like magic, Tatum snaps into planner mode. "We might be doing this here at the house, but that doesn't mean it can't be special. You need a dress and shoes, and we'll need flowers and rings and you'll have to get your marriage license, and maybe we could get something set up on the grounds —like a floral arch or something where the two of you can say your vows."

It's the most life she's shown since her return from Europe, and the dazzling—if dazed—smile Bianca wears tells me she sees it, too. "I'm following your lead," she tells Tatum, who takes her by the arm and leads her down the hall while making lists of everything that has to be done.

Something tells me even an intimate ceremony can end up costing an arm and a leg, especially when my daughter is involved. The price doesn't matter. It'll be worth every penny.

BIANCA

"Everything's all set." Tatum comes flying into her room, a tablet balanced in one hand.

The past few days, I would swear that damn thing was permanently attached to her. It contains her many lists, phone numbers, email addresses, and schedules. There's even a spreadsheet complete with a cost breakdown for Callum to review.

I would never complain. She's her old self again, vibrant and alive and bossy. Seeing her like this, hearing the strength and excitement in her voice, reminds me how much I've missed this side of her.

"You really should consider being a wedding planner." I grin at her in the mirror when she finally looks up from the device and rolls her eyes. "I'm serious. You'd make a killing at it."

"Eh. I don't know if I would care half as much if the wedding was for a couple of strangers."

"I want you to know I appreciate all the work you've put into this. Seriously, everything you've put together in a week?" I'm still not sure how she did it. Though I did overhear her bullying the hell out of some poor florist and reminding them of the rush fee they charged.

I guess she had a point. When you pay a rush fee, you expect results. And the results are stunning—I've only gotten a few glimpses of the archway they constructed on the lawn off the patio, but what I saw was breathtaking. Like our bouquets and boutonnieres for the men, there's an array of cream, red, orange, and yellow roses to fit a fall theme. My bouquet is entirely cream, while hers is red, and both are so lush and fragrant I can't help but take a sniff every time I get a chance.

"How are you feeling? The dress isn't too tight, is it?"

I run a hand over the bodice of my white satin dress. Its lace overlay conceals the fact that I've gotten a little thicker around the middle—I haven't popped yet, but I'm starting to put on a little bit of weight. "It's great. If we had waited another week, that might be a different story."

Standing, I take in my reflection in the full length mirror behind the bedroom door. The sleek, sleeveless satin flows over my body like it was poured in liquid form. The overlay's sleeves run the length of my arms and the entire piece features pearl and glass beads that shimmer ever so slightly when I move.

Tatum adds another pin to the elaborate updo created by the stylists who came in earlier. It's studded with beads matching those on the lace, and it makes me feel regal. *Me. Regal.* "I swear, I keep thinking I'm going to wake up and this will all have been a dream," I confess as she inserts the comb attached to a short, lace veil.

She then gently wraps her arms around my waist and grins over my shoulder. "I'll pinch you, if you want. *Stepmom.*" That is so strange to hear, and I know she only says it to tease me. I might technically be her stepmother once the ceremony is finished, but she's always going to be the best friend who defended me against a bully the day we met. I'm just glad she's not angry and would rather tease me over my new position in her life.

"No, thanks." Turning, I can't help but admire how beautiful she looks today—and much healthier than I've seen her in a long time. I'm not going to fool myself into believing all she needed was something to take her mind off things. I mean, that could be true, but that would also mean that once the wedding is over, she could go back to her depression. I don't want to imagine that happening.

Instead, I'd rather take in how the burgundy A-line dress sets off her blond curls and makes her green eyes sparkle. "I think we have a problem."

Right away, her brows draw together. "What? I figured everything out down to the last detail. Don't tell me somebody decided to fuck with my plans."

"More like you're too pretty to be my maid of honor," I giggle while she gapes in shock. "You'll upstage me."

"I could strangle you." She appears to think about it, though, and shakes her head. "No, then this will all have been for nothing. And I've already threatened to strangle my father twice today."

"How is he doing?"

She blows out a frustrated sigh. "Please. He wants to act like this is all no big deal, but he's been on edge all day and can't stop double checking every single detail, like I'm suddenly an idiot."

"Oh! I thought he was feeling relaxed with you in the driver's seat."

She lifts a shoulder, sighing. "He wants everything to be perfect for you, just like I do, but he's not exactly, you know, skilled at sharing his true feelings."

"No way. I'm shocked." When we laugh together, it feels like the old days. Like I have the old Tatum back. I hope that's true. I don't want to think of spending the rest of my life without her. It's bad enough she's running off with Romero first thing tomorrow morning–but she'll be back. And we can be a family, finally.

The soft knock at the door sends her scurrying to stop whoever's on the other side. "You can't see the bride before the wedding, Dad. We talked about this."

"I'm a dad, but not that one."

She throws the door open, laughing. "Oh, that's okay, then." She whistles in appreciation, giving Dad a thumbs up. "I have to say, you look good in a tux, Mr. Cole."

He chuckles and brushes invisible lint off his shoulder. "Thank you, Tatum. You look very nice tonight."

She steps aside to give me a full look at him, and right away my throat clogs with emotion. He does look good—very good, almost like the young man from his wedding pictures. He's come a long way from the mess he became. Pride swells in my chest when I think of how much it must take for him to look as genuinely happy and hopeful as he does today.

His breath catches when he sees me, and right away his eyes start to water. Tatum clears her throat, offering me a meaningful look before saying, "I'd better get outside. God only knows how things might fall apart if I'm not around to keep everybody in line."

That leaves Dad and me alone. "How do I look?" I whisper, doing a full turn for him.

"Like a princess," he chokes out. "I told myself I wouldn't get emotional, but that was before I saw you in that dress. You're so grown-up, and stunning."

"Thank you."

"I'm only telling you the truth."

"That's not what I meant. Thank you for being here. Thank you for loving me enough to care as much as you do—even when I've disagreed with you, I know you were coming from the right place. I need you to know I understand that."

"And I need you to understand I'm always going to care first and foremost about you. I see how happy you are today and I know this is the right thing. This is what you need. I'm just glad I get to be a part of it."

He makes a move like he wants to give me a hug, but holds himself back. "I don't want to ruin you."

"I don't think you could." I wrap him in a tight hug, eyes closed, hoping to hold this moment for as long as possible. No anger, no resentment, no fear. Just the two of us together one last time before I become an official Torrio.

"Are you ready for this?" he asks and he lets me go.

"Very." And I mean it. I mean it with all my heart, with every fiber of me. I'm ready to be Callum's wife. I want the world to know we belong to each other, that I'm by his side no matter what.

It's nearing seven o'clock, go time. I touch up my makeup once more before Tatum hurries into the room. "Everything's ready. Are you good?"

I only hand over her bouquet. "Let's do this." Dad takes my arm once we step into the hall outside Tatum's room, and with her leading away we walk through her wing to the exit closest to the backyard. It was either this or go through the kitchen, but that seemed like a bad idea with Sheryl finishing the wedding dinner we'll eat after the ceremony.

At first, I stop short of stepping out into the night. "Whoa." It's like something from a fairy tale. I knew Tatum worked miracles, but I didn't expect this. There are white fairy lights strung in the bushes and trees. A white runner starts at the door and leads to the arch, flanked on both sides by flickering pillar candles on stands. There are rose petals strewn the runner's length, leading to the spectacular floral arch and the dozens of lights and candles arranged around it. The sun is setting, the last streaks of pink and purple on the western horizon, and altogether the effect is breathtaking.

It's all beautiful but there's nothing more breathtaking than the sight of the man waiting for me under the arch. I've never seen him look as handsome as he does in his black tux with its cream rose to match the flowers in my bouquet. Romero stands behind him, and even he is smiling in a way I've never seen before. Like a genuine, happy smile. Yet another miracle.

It's Callum I can't take my eyes off of as Dad walks me down the makeshift aisle. This is it. Everything's been leading up to this very moment. It might feel inevitable now, but I can't pretend there weren't moments when I wondered if we'd ever reach this place. So many reasons why this moment might never have come—close calls, fights, lies. Maybe that's what makes this so sweet now, the sense of our happiness being earned. We both fought hard to get to this place.

I wonder if Callum is thinking the same thing as we approach slowly while the wedding march plays through a speaker hidden somewhere. I wonder if he's thinking back how far we've come. Either that, or he's reflecting on how he knew all along that this was where we would end up. That's the thing about him. He always knows exactly what he wants and stops at nothing until he gets it.

How lucky am I that it was me he decided he wanted? Dad says I look like a princess—I feel like one, too, practically floating over the rose petals under my feet. I almost want to look down to make sure I'm even touching the ground.

This is it. No going back now. Not that I want to. Not when I finally know exactly where I need to be, now and always.

My heart is practically pounding out of my chest once we reach the place where Callum waits expectantly. He and Dad exchange a handshake and a few murmured words I can't hear before Dad steps aside, taking my hand and placing it in Callum's. He kisses my cheek, then takes a second to look at me one last time before he steps back.

"You look breathtaking," Callum murmurs after I hand my bouquet to Tatum. "Thank you for being the most exquisite bride a man could ask for."

I'm so overwhelmed, so completely floored by the amount of love coursing through me, that I can't respond. I'm not even sure I could put into words exactly how I feel right now. Maybe someday I will.

We have the rest of our lives for me to do it.

The judge says a few words that I can barely make out over my excitement, not to mention how hard I'm trying not to cry. I guess this would be emotional enough without all the pregnancy hormones wreaking havoc on me.

"I'm very happy to be here," the judge begins, smiling at us both. "It's an honor to officiate the union of two people so clearly in love, so deeply committed to each other. After speaking with you both prior to the ceremony, it's clear you've had your challenges, like any couple, but that you've also grown stronger in your love and commitment through those challenges. That's what this is all about. Growing together." He chuckles softly. "I don't normally make a speech like that—but I wanted to let you both know how glad I am to bear witness to your union, and that I hope the years to come are full of nothing but joy for you both."

I'm humbled by his words until he slides an inquisitive look toward Tatum, who from the corner of my eye gives him a slight nod. Just like her, micromanaging things to the point where she told the judge to make a speech. I only love her more for it.

"Now that I've gotten that out of the way," he continues with another chuckle, "I understand you would like to share vows you've written for each other."

It's the one part of the whole event Tatum left up to us. I was more than willing to go along with her ideas, but I had to shut down her well-meaning suggestions on what I should say.

"Bianca, ladies first."

I turn to Callum, placing my hands in his. He's smiling at me, love radiating from his eyes, eyes which seem to stare into my soul. It's almost enough to make me forget what I had planned to say.

"You know something," I begin, "until a few seconds ago, my hands were shaking. Not out of fear or anything like that. I've never been so sure of anything in my life as I am right here and now standing in front of you. I guess I'm just excited. And I'm not used to people looking at me the way they are now." I look around, smiling at our small clutch of witnesses. "But you know what? You touched my hands, and the shaking stopped. Like it never happened. All of a sudden, I remembered I had nothing to be nervous about. Nothing to fear. You have given me everything I could ask for, as well as a few things I didn't even know I needed. You've taught me to be strong, and brave. You taught me to have faith in love. You've shown me I'm capable of so much more than I ever thought possible, and that I should never, ever settle for second best. I'm glad I didn't, or else I wouldn't have you now. Because you are the best, and even through our challenges, I have never doubted your love. All I can do now is hope to love you as well as you love me. I promise I'm going to spend the rest of my life trying my best to be the wife you deserve."

I can't believe I got all of that out without shedding a tear. I didn't plan on starting off the way I did, but the general message was always going to be the same. Every time I've tried to run through it, I ended up bawling my eyes out.

He's staring at me, his eyes widening, before he finally releases a gentle laugh. "How am I supposed to follow that?" The rest of us laugh along with him, though I'm pretty sure I hear Tatum sniffling behind me. "Bianca, you honor me beyond words. With your love, your gentleness, your patience."

We both have to chuckle at that one. "I won't pretend I've always made things easy, but for some reason, you're here. And I am never, not for a minute of my life, going to take that for granted. You are everything to me, and you have already made me the happiest man alive. I'm sure I don't deserve you, but I don't want you to ever doubt for a moment that I plan on spending every minute of the rest of my life earning you. And even then, when I take my final breath, it could never be enough. Thank you for helping me believe in love. I was in a dark place when we found each other, and you showed me the light."

Well. Just when I thought I could make it out of this without crying my eyes out. Tatum's sniffling has gotten louder, too.

Callum pulls out a handkerchief and dabs at my eyes and cheeks. All I can do is accept his gesture, smiling through my tears.

"Do we have the rings?" the judge asks.

That's Romero's cue. "I knew better than to misplace these," he murmurs. "I didn't want Tatum to kill me."

"I can hear you," she whispers back.

I'm fighting giggles as Callum extends his left hand for me to slide the titanium band over his third finger. He said he wanted the titanium as a symbol of how unbreakable our bond is. All I know is as I place it on his hand, I'm almost swept off my feet by a wave of pure love. It's the most profound thing I've ever felt except for the first rush of joy that ran through me when we saw the baby together during the ultrasound.

I switched my engagement ring to my right hand for the ceremony, leaving my ring finger free for the exquisite platinum band set with tiny diamonds. It sparkles like crazy, catching the light no matter how I turn my hand. "Like this ring," Callum murmurs, "there is no beginning or end of my love for you. It goes forever."

"I had no idea you were so good with words," I whisper.

"I guess you bring it out in me." Once the ring is in place, he kisses my hand. "Mine forever."

"Always," I whisper.

"Then by the power vested in me, I declare you husband and wife. Callum, you may kiss your bride."

Not just yet. Give me a second. Let me be in this moment just a little while longer, this last moment before we seal it with a kiss. Let me savor this just a moment more.

I could swear he hears my thoughts, taking his time, holding my face between his hands and staring deep into my eyes. "Are you ready?" he murmurs, and I don't think he's talking about the kiss. He's asking whether I'm ready for everything life has in store for us.

There's only one answer. The only answer. "Yes." And I mean it with all my heart.

EPILOGUE

BIANCA

I'm pretty sure we're in paradise.

I'm not sure what part of the resort I love the most. The staff falls over themselves to make sure we're happy. I wouldn't complain if I had to fall asleep to the sound of the ocean every night for the rest of my life. The weather is absolutely perfect. There's a gentle warmth in the air, absolutely no humidity, sunny skies, and balmy breezes.

Like the breeze that stirs the sheer white curtains that hang on each side of the sliding door that leads out to the private pool. After a morning of swimming together—among other things I'm glad nobody else could see, thanks to the discrete walls between our suite and the ones adjoining—we managed to climb our way out of the pool, rinse off in the shower, then collapse into bed for a nap.

I'm smiling when Callum's gentle kisses against my temple bring me back to reality. A reality sweeter than any dream. "Can we just move here permanently?" I murmur, drowsy and happy.

"You know you've asked me that at least twice daily since we arrived."

"I guess I keep hoping the answer will change."

He pulls me closer, the big spoon to my little spoon, and I fit my body against his. "It's a very tempting idea," he finally admits, his lips grazing my ear when he speaks. "But somebody's got to run things back home."

My impulse is to tell him to leave it to Romero. I guess it's going to take a little more time to remember he and Tatum are... wherever they are. It's safer that I don't know, and I understand that, but I don't have to like remembering them leaving the morning after the wedding without so much as a hint to their whereabouts. This is my best friend's life, her safety. I'm worried for her, but if even Callum thinks it's for the best that she not be with us for a little while, that's gotta mean something. I know he hates her being gone as much as I do.

"What's the point of being the boss if you can't say fuck it and take off to parts unknown?"

"I would hardly call a luxury Hawaiian resort *parts unknown*."

I can only scoff. "Semantics."

"Anyway, we'd get bored with it."

"I would like to test that theory."

It's so good to hear him laugh. The days we've spent here, in our little honeymoon haven, have loosened him up, to put it mildly. I've never seen him look so happy, almost carefree. No matter what we're doing—sitting on the beach, swimming, eating some of the most incredible food I've ever tasted—he's playful, funny, lighthearted. He needed this after months of strain.

"Don't act like your father wouldn't be on the first flight out here if he found out you weren't coming back." He follows that with a groan. "And here I am, thinking about Charlie Cole while on my honeymoon."

"If I didn't know better, I would think he's the one you're interested in, not me."

"You got me. This has all been a ploy to spend more time with your dad."

I roll over to face him, and at first, it's enough just to look at him. His skin is more tanned than ever, thanks to all the sun we've gotten. There's a faint scruff on his cheeks, and he appears blissfully happy. He's the most beautiful thing I've ever seen. "All kidding aside, this is better than I could have ever imagined. Thank you."

"None of it would be worth a damn without you. I'm the one who's grateful."

It's not a surprise, the hand he begins sliding up my thigh. Like a creeping spider, only I don't want to shoo him away. I start to melt against him before I can help myself. His touch has become as necessary as breathing, the most natural thing in the world. I close my eyes and soak in the pleasure of his love. It's moments like this I find it hardest to believe this isn't a happy dream I concocted.

But, no, it's real. The slight breeze and the sound of waves hitting the sand and the impossibly soft sheets against my skin tell me it's real. And we've earned it. We deserve it.

"As nice as that is," I murmur, groaning when he caresses my ass, "if I don't get some food in me soon, I won't be good for anything, and we do have dinner to think about." The light is already starting to get thinner, dimmer, telling me night will be falling any time now. No wonder my stomach's starting to growl. I love not having to live by a clock.

"Even on my honeymoon, I have to wait to have you," he grumbles, but it's a good-natured sound.

Rather than remind him of how we spent the late morning and early afternoon wrapped up in each other's arms, I give him a playful shove. "Hey. We have to keep this baby fed, right?"

His humorous scowl softens, and now he strokes my belly gently, almost reverently. "Since you put it that way, we'd better get moving. What's the baby want for dinner tonight?"

"Anything, so long as there's a lot of it."

"You know..." He rolls away from me and stands, and for a second, I can only lie back and soak in his beauty. Everything about him, from his chiseled muscles to his easy grace as he walks around the room, still fascinates me. I doubt I could ever get tired of looking at him. "I was reading during the flight over, and they say if you're carrying a boy, he requires more calories than a girl."

"Really?"

"Something like a third more than a girl would."

"Or maybe I'm just using the baby as an excuse to finally let loose and pig out a little."

"I'm telling you," he insists with a grin as he pulls on a pair of shorts, "it's a boy. Mark my words."

"Whatever you say, doctor." I know he'll be happy either way, but for his sake, I hope it is. And I can't help but imagine what it would be like to watch Callum raising a little boy. The idea warms me inside like few things can.

* * *

"Right this way, Mr. and Mrs. Torrio." The hostess leads us to the table closest to the water, positioned at the far end of the outdoor dining room overlooking the beach. Lit torches and the lights hanging overhead give everything a romantic glow—or maybe that's because I'm feeling romantic. Who wouldn't on their honeymoon, especially in a place like this?

Once we're seated, Callum flashes me a roguish grin from across the table. "Mrs. Torrio. I love the sound of that."

"I love it more." And I mean it.

"Remind me to keep you pregnant forever."

"Oh? You think so?"

"You're absolutely glowing."

"It's a trick of the lighting," I tease. "That, and I've gotten more sun than usual."

His dark eyes flare with desire. "Just the same, you're lucky we made it out of the room."

"Since when is that anything new?"

We have to put the conversation aside once our server approaches, but we can't help giving each other sly looks as we order our entrees. I love the sense of always having a fun little secret. Though, considering the way Callum keeps eyeing me, it's probably not that much of a secret. We're on our honeymoon, after all. I'm sure we're not the first couple to lust over each other in public.

There's a band playing on the beach, and by the time our mahi-mahi arrives, several people have finished their meals and wandered down to the sand to dance. As time goes on, the crowd grows until there are a few dozen people having fun while I take the last bite of the light, buttery fish.

"You know," I muse as I push the plate away before the impulse to lick it clean is too much to handle, "there's one thing we've never done together."

Right away, Callum perks up. "Oh? I'm all ears."

"I was going to say dance, you horn dog."

His brows draw together. "I don't dance, at least not in front of people."

"There's a first time for everything."

"Bianca..." he groans like I asked him to castrate himself or something equally as awful. "You can't teach an old dog new tricks."

"You're not old." I stand, holding out a hand. "Let's at least go down and listen."

"We can listen from here." But it's obvious from the way he fights back a grin that he's only teasing me. Soon we're hand in hand, wandering down the beach. There's a half moon hanging in the night sky, and its silvery light paints the waves that crash up ahead. I could plop right down and stare at it until dawn. It's magical.

A strong breeze stirs my hair and the flowy, ankle-length dress I'm wearing. "You smell incredible," Callum growls in my ear.

"Your desire for me is incorrigible."

Still, when his hand grazes my bare back, a delicious shiver runs up my spine and goosebumps pebble my skin. Maybe I'm just as bad as he is. I can't get enough of him either. That being said, I want there to be more to our honeymoon than falling into bed.

After a few songs, it seems as if even Callum's getting into it when his head starts bobbing up and down in time with the beat. I wonder how long it's been since he loosened up and let himself have fun. Years, probably. He always has too much on his mind.

"See? I knew you'd get into the spirit once you got over yourself."

His scowl makes me laugh before I start to sway to the irresistible rhythm. I haven't touched a drop of alcohol since I found out about the baby, but there's this natural buzz flowing through my veins.

"Now, this I can get into," he growls, inching behind me and placing his hands on my waist while I move my hips. "Watching you dance. I'll need a private show back in the room."

It's no surprise when he pulls me closer and a familiar bulge presses against my ass. Another shiver runs through me and there's nothing to do in response by wiggle against him until he groans in my ear. Now we might as well be the only two people on the beach.

"You are so fucking hot." His hands run up and down my sides while he grinds against me, his hot breath fanning across my neck with every ragged grunt. "Watching you move, feeling your body, I could fuck you here and now, in front of all these people."

Right now, I kinda wish he would. I'm so hot and wet, my pussy throbbing with every beat of my heart. I can imagine him forcing me to my knees and taking me from behind while everybody watches. Like a couple of animals with no choice but to take each other no matter where we are, or when. I can imagine him fucking me until I howl loud enough to drown out the music, and my pussy drips at the thought.

He finds my hips and grips them hard, pulling me against his raging erection while his lips graze my skin until my skin sizzles. I can imagine his fingers leaving bruises but I don't care. I want him to. I want to wear the proof of how deeply he craves me. I can feel the power surging in his body and something in me responds to it in the most intense way. I'll die if I don't have him inside me.

I let my head drop back against his shoulder and turn my neck to murmur in his ear. "Take me back to the room. Now." I'm surprised he doesn't throw me over his shoulder and charge up there—as it is, we're practically trotting. We can't move fast enough for me. I need him too much.

Rather than walk through the hotel, Callum uses the key to the gate that opens onto our personal patio and ushers me through it before pulling me close for a deep, searing kiss that takes my breath away and makes my knees go weak. By the time he lets me up for air, I'm clinging to him to keep from collapsing.

With his arms around my waist he lifts me off my feet, carrying me through the sliding door and only putting me down once we're next to the king size bed. But instead of lying back and letting him take me, I undo his belt, staring into his eyes as I do. Neither of us says a word as I open his fly and let his slacks drop.

"Oh my God," he groans, sighing when I cup his balls through his boxers. I take my time, teasing him, letting my thumb graze his head in slow circles while his breathing quickens and his helpless moans grow louder, more needy. He's always in control... but not now. I can't help but want to draw that out as long as possible.

Once there's a growing wet spot on the front of his shorts, I whisper, "What do you want me to do with this?"

"What do you think?" He places a hand on my shoulder and presses down firmly. I drop to my knees on the tile floor, staring up at him as I do, then hook my fingers around the waistband of his boxers, lowering them all at once. His dick bobs in front of my face before I take him in my hand and run my tongue around the ridge of his swollen, purple head.

"Fuck, yes," he sighs, sinking his hands into my hair, massaging my scalp while I lower my head, taking him deep.

The salty taste of his precum fills my mouth, and I savor it as I bob up and down, drawing more and more of it from him. I'm wetter than ever, the slickness coating my inner thighs by the time he begins moving his hips.

"I love seeing you on your knees, my cock in your pretty mouth."

My clit is almost painfully swollen now, throbbing, and there's nothing I can do but hike my dress up and wedge a hand between my legs.

"Fuck, yeah," he mutters once he realizes what I'm doing. "Such a dirty girl. I can see your pussy weeping juices onto the floor. I want you to make yourself come for me. Come with me in your mouth."

It doesn't look like I have a choice. I was already so close, and now with the motion of my fingers against my hard nub combined with his filthy words, the tension suddenly breaks and there's nothing I can do but moan wordlessly while he continues thrusting. My body shudders in relief, trembling by the time he pulls back and falls from my lips.

He takes himself in one hand, stroking his slick shaft, while he pulls me to my feet and turns me away from him with the other, before pushing me against the bed until I fall across it with my feet still on the floor. All it takes is the touch of his hands against my legs while he works the dress around my waist to set off my hunger again. Not that it ever went away, even after coming. All that did was whet my appetite and deepen the primal need coursing through me.

He wastes no time yanking down my thong, pausing to drag his head through my sopping slit before plunging inside. "Yes!" I cry out. There is nothing in the world more satisfying than the feeling of his thick cock stretching me the way only he can. I'm happy to hand control back to him, moaning when he takes me by the hips and pulls me against him in time with his deep, sensual strokes.

Now there's nothing but sensation. Sweet, hot, addictive sensation that rolls over me like the waves crashing beyond our door. I give myself over to it, losing myself the way only he can make me do.

"Fuck, you're such a good girl. My good girl. My wife," he whispers between thrusts. "I'm going to fill this tight little hole up. Do you want that? Do you want me to come inside you? I want to see your pretty pink pussy dripping with cum."

As he speaks, he pushes the dress up further, and I quickly pull it over my head before propping myself on my palms to thrust back against him. "Yes! Come inside me. Please come inside me," I moan.

Callum's filthy mouth will get me to agree to anything, I swear.

He cups my breasts, massaging and tweaking my nipples until all I can do is whimper my approval as the tension in my core builds. He fucks me hard and fast. The friction and pleasure rising with each thrust. He's rough but sensual, enlivening parts of my body I didn't know existed before him. I have a lifetime of this to look forward to, being ravished, worshiped. What's better? I get to worship him in return.

"Callum... it's so good!" My skin is slick with sweat by the time he loses his rhythm, pummeling me with sharp, deep strokes that make me gasp and squeal each time he slams into me. Every slap of his balls against my clit sends me higher and higher.

"Milk my cock, baby," he commands before sinking his teeth into my shoulder. "I want to feel your muscles quiver and flutter around my cock. Don't let me down. Squeeze my cock until my eyes roll to the back of my head."

The sudden burst of pain intensifies my pleasure and before I know it, I'm clenching down on him, my body going stiff before I scream out my release. "Callum... I'm... coming!" I let out a possessed scream, so it probably carries outside. I don't care. Let the resort know Callum Torrio fucks me so well. Let them envy me for having a husband like him.

"Fuck yes, you are…" He slams into me over and over again, owning my body, my pleasure. "Oh, fuck…" he growls. "Here I come, baby…" Then he explodes, and the warmth of his release spreads through my core. By the time we collapse in a sweaty heap on the side of the bed, I'm laughing breathlessly.

"How long did we manage to keep our hands off each other this time?" I ask between gasps for air.

He checks his watch, squinting at the face before smirking. "Three hours and twenty-three minutes. That's a new record. I hope you're not getting tired of me."

"Tired of you?" I can only smile at the love of my life while considering the idea. "Never."

His handsome face lights up when he smiles back at me. "Good, because we've got a lifetime ahead of us."

I know, and I can hardly wait.

* * *

The End

Thank you so much for reading and being a part of Bianca and Callum's love story. If you're interested in reading bonus scenes and hearing more about them, as well as future books please sign up for my Patreon: www.patreon.com/AuthorJLBeck
Read on for an exclusive look at Tatum and Romero's book called Dark Knight or preorder here: https://amzn.to/3pL2lEG

TATUM

Ten Years Ago

There's only one thought that races through my mind as soon as I blink my eyes open.

Summer vacation.

After nine months of school, it's finally summer. The thought that I won't have to do a single sheet of homework, that I won't have to go to bed early, and that I can wake up whenever I want is thrilling at least for the next three months. Freedom, it's so pungent I can almost taste it. I already can't wait to spend the whole summer out by the pool soaking up every last sun rays. The plan is to be a nice tan shade come fall when school starts again, and not this ghostly pale white that I am now.

The reminder that Bianca, who is my best friend will be here in a little bit sends me over the edge.Her dad doesn't usually let her do sleepovers unless it's a birthday party or something else special. He's the kind of dad who always has to know where she is, what she's doing, and who she's with. I'm sure it must suck, having a dad that is overbearing. My dad always wants to know those things, too, but he still lets me visit with my friends, and go shopping. Not alone of course.

When I go out, I always have somebody with me, and it's almost always somebody Dad pays since he's too busy to do things like take me to activities or drive me to the movies. Maybe that's what Mr. Cole doesn't like about Bianca coming over here. Dad is here, but he's usually working in his office, so we pretty much have the whole house to ourselves. The only people to keep an eye on us are the guys my dad pays for security. And there's really not much they can do—so long as I'm not, like choking to death or drowning or doing something that could cause injury, they sort of look the other way.

With Mr. Cole being a detective and all, I guess he knows how messed up life is. That's what Bianca says, anyway. The excitement of Bianca's impending arrival is what gets me out of bed and into the shower even though I could have slept another hour or two.

I didn't know kids had chores and stuff until I got to know Bianca better. I'm not stupid. I know not everybody has staff around the house to do the cooking and cleaning. I figured parents took care of that stuff, but for Bianca it's different, she always has to keep her room clean and do her own laundry and even some of the cooking and house cleaning since it's just her and her dad. Like me, she doesn't have a mom in her life, though in her case she can visit her mom in the cemetery. I don't know where my mom is most of the time.

Hanging out with Bianca made me realize that I could at least make my bed and keep my bathroom clean, so after I'm done in the shower I tidy up my room. Once I move my things to the unused wing of the house, like Dad promised I could once I start high school, I'll have more responsibility.

It's one of his rules, so I might as well get in the habit and show him I'm serious about wanting to take care of myself. I'm not a little girl anymore. I'm getting older and I want him to see that.

Once finishedI have the rest of my day to look forward to. It's already almost eight-thirty and Mr. Cole has to be at work by nine, so Bianca will be here any minute now. I grab a green one-piece suit that matches my eyes—Dad won't let me wear a two-piece yet no matter how much I beg him. *"I'm paying for it, so you're going to wear what I think is appropriate."* It's times like that I wish I had a mom that was willing to step in for me and take my side, but I can't even get her to answer the phone when I call. I'm pretty much on my own when it comes to talking to Dad.

I can feel the sticky misery and sadness that thinking about her brings on invading my mind and I squeeze my eyes shut and push the thought away. I'm not going to let her abandonment bother me today, not on the first day of summer vacation. Instead I pull on the suit, then add a pair of cutoffs on top before pulling my blonde curls into a bun on top of my head. *Perfection.* I give myself a once over in the mirror. I'm tall, and thankfully my body is finally starting to fill out. I was worried for a little bit that my arms would always be longer than my body but thankfully I grew. My skin is pale, and sickly looking and since Dad hardly ever lets me wear make up-which is going to change this year-I always look this way. A Casper The Friendly Ghost look-alike.

Whatever, with all the sun I'm going to get this summer it won't matter. I'm halfway down the stairs when I hear my father's voice. I might be able to say good morning to him before he locks himself inside his office for the remainder of the day. I wonder if I can get him to go swimming with me sometime. He can't work all the time, can he? It seems unfair that grown-ups don't get summer vacation the way kids do. Maybe I need to remind him that there are other things in life besides work.

Right away, I smile, since he's not usually around. Maybe we can have breakfast together. Or if he's busy and on his way to the office down the hall, I can bring him some food. I want to spend a little time together this summer before I start high school. I know I'm going to be super busy with activities and studying once Fall comes, and I miss just sitting and talking to him.

"I'll have keys made for you," he says, his voice getting louder the closer he comes to where I'm standing while the dress shoes he almost always wears during the day snap against the wood floor. "You can come and go as you please, though it will be better if you stay on the grounds as much as possible. If you need anything, let me know and I'll arrange for orders to be made and delivered. It's important that you lie low for a while."

"I understand."

I'm at the bottom of the stairs when I hear that second voice. It's deep. I don't think I've ever heard it before. Whoever it belongs to is going to have keys to the house. *A new guard?* The idea makes me roll my eyes. There's enough of them wondering about the grounds.

I'm still standing on the bottom step, confused, when Dad walks out of the unused east wing. His eyes widen when they land upon me. "Good morning," he says before he looks over his shoulder at the stranger behind him. It's strange, but he's worried or nervous.

"Good morning, Daddy. Can you come swimming with me and Bianca today?"

He steps aside, and I get my first look at the man he was talking to.

I really wish Dad would let me have a two-piece suit. I also wish I was wearing something nicer than cutoffs right at this moment. I peer up at the man, who has to be the most gorgeous man I've ever laid eyes on. Even cuter than Johnny Townsend. The mysterious man is tall, around Dad's height, with thick, black hair, and dark blue eyes that scream leave me alone. They look like they could burn a hole through anything he stares at and I'm intrigued.

Unfortunately, he doesn't stare at me. Instead, he looks at the floor, walls, and ceiling like he's mad at them. His full lips are pulled up into a sneer, and he looks like someone made him really mad. I've never met anybody who looked angrily at objects just because they exist. His hands are huge, and he runs one through his dark hair—which could use a cut, not to mention a wash—and jams the hand into the pocket of his black jeans.

A dark knight if I ever saw one in real life. That's who this man is. Rugged, dark, and mysterious. Butterflies take flight in my belly. While heat creeps up my neck and into my cheeks. I stare intently at the stranger trying to figure out who he is, and what makes him tick but all I can seem to observe is anger.

Dad clears his throat, dragging my attention back to him. "Romero, this is my daughter, Tatum. Tatum, this is Romero. He's going to be staying with us for a while."

"What? Not in there I hope?" I nod toward the open doorway they just walked through. "You said I would get to move my stuff into that wing once I start high school in the fall."

"I said maybe," he sighs, narrowing his eyes. I know that look. It means whatever patience he had has suddenly vanished. "I know you wanted to move your stuff in there but that's hardly the most important thing right now. Romero needs a place to stay, and rather than give him a room near yours, I think he would do better to have his own separate wing. Eventually, I might move him out to one of the cottages on the property."

My chest aches, my heart tightening in my chest. Forget the mysterious knight, the jerk just ruined everything, and yes I know it's just a room, and I shouldn't feel this let down over something so small but I was really looking forward to it. Like another step in my new high school life, but I already know there's nothing I'll be able to say to change his mind.

My father is a businessman in every aspect of his life and once he's made a decision, that's it. Since I don't want to look like a spoiled baby in front of a cute boy, even if I'm disappointed I grit my teeth and choose to swallow it down. Does it really matter that I was looking forward to having all that extra space, plus the added privacy? I guess not. I'll eventually get over it, just like I get over everything.

"Okay," I mutter, digging my nails into my palm instead of lashing out like I want to.

"I see you're dressed for swimming," Dad points out like he didn't hear me inviting him to join in the fun.

"Yeah, Bianca's coming over."

"Oh. That's nice sweetie." His attention drifts and he turns it back to Romero, and suddenly it's like I was never here to begin with. "In this house what is mine is yours. Anything you want, you only have to ask. We have a cook who comes six days a week. She takes off Saturday nights and all day Sunday, but always makes sure the kitchen is stocked."

They pass me on their way out to the kitchen and all I can do is stand there and stare at them. It's not like I expect to have a say in anything, because I never do. Not really, but I can't deny the anger that blooms inside my chest at his clear dismissal. Obviously, whatever Romero's story is, Dad wants to help him and that's cool, but at the expense of breaking another promise to me?

I reach the kitchen in time to hear Dad introduce Romero to Sheryl, our cook, and she's as kind to him as she's always been to me. "Can I fix you something for breakfast?"

"No, thanks," he mumbles his gaze on the floor, his voice thick and raspy. "I'm not really hungry."

"That's fine, but be sure to stop back whenever you want." She notices me hanging around and gives me one of her bright, kind smiles. "Good morning, Miss Middle School Graduate. I fixed your favorite: french toast and bacon, plus fresh orange juice."

"Oh. Thank you." And now Romero knows I just graduated middle school, which means he knows how old I am. Cue the embarrassment. He probably thinks I'm a dumb kid. I have to open the refrigerator door to abate the way my cheeks heat up.

Behind me, Dad speaks up. "You should really eat something."

I'm almost jealous of the concerned tone that fills my dad's voice. Yes, my father loves and cares about me, but he never seems concerned, not like this. It's more like he's especially interested in Romero, like he cares if he eats. Why? Who is he? And what about him would my father care so much about?

"I've made plenty," Sheryl adds. "It's only a matter of pulling an extra plate from the cabinet."

Great. He gets the wing I was supposed to move into, and now Shyrel is making him a plate of my special breakfast. I have to bite my tongue as I pour orange juice into a glass without asking if Romero wants any. He can get his own since he obviously lives here now.

"I'm really not hungry." The edge in his voice becomes sharp, like he's angry. Why is he mad? Because people are being kind to him? That seems ridiculous.

"Fair enough," Dad murmurs in that gentle, caring way. "So long as you know everything you need is here. You don't have to be shy. Why don't I show you around the grounds, and then you can get settled into your room?"

Nothing hurts worse than the hand he places on this strange, rude kid's shoulder as they walk out of the room. If I thought he'd give me the whole story, I'd think to ask Dad later why Romero is here and how long he'll be staying, but I know my father. He'll tell me to go hang out with Bianca or go swimming, or shopping. Whatever it takes to keep me out of his way.

Especially now that he has the son he always wanted.

I don't know where that thought comes from, but it takes away my appetite until I have to force my way through finishing the rest of my food. Sheryl went to all the trouble and I don't want to insult her the way Romero did. Not that she seems to mind—she's busy humming to herself as she pulls produce from shopping bags and washes it in the sink.

"Tatum?"

My spirits lift immediately when I hear Bianca's voice echoing through the entry hall. "In the kitchen!" I call out, and a few seconds later she hurries in, all flushed and wide-eyed.

"Who is that boy outside with your dad?" She flashes an embarrassed little grin at Sheryl, who just laughs.

I give her a look that means we'll talk about this privately while getting up from the table and leaving the dish next to the sink. "Do you want anything?" Sheryl asks Bianca, who politely refuses before I pull her by the arm out onto the back patio. It's already hot and sticky for this time of morning, and I can practically feel my curls frizzing thanks to the humidity in the air.

"What's going on?" Bianca's carrying a backpack over one shoulder and a beach towel in the other arm, both of which she sets down while I pace the ground in front of her. I'm not mad. I'm... bothered, actually annoyed.

"First of all, he's moving into the empty wing," I whisper before grinding my teeth. "I don't even know him, but somehow he's so important my father gives him the bedroom that he promised me."

"Ugh, that's crappy." She sits down, shaking her head. "I know you were looking forward to moving all of your stuff into that room."

"I was. And it's just I don't know. The guy showed up five minutes ago, but it already feels like I don't exist anymore." I have to laugh at myself. "Not like I did before this morning, but still, it's less now."

"That's not true. Your dad was just as happy as any other dad at graduation, and he took us out to dinner and everything." She makes a sour face. "Sorry, my dad was so weird about trying to pay."

I wave it off because men are generally weird, and I was surprised he even wanted to go to dinner with us in the first place. I've always got the vibe he didn't like my dad, though he's always been nice to me. "It's okay, men are weird, but that's the thing. Last night, Dad cared about me. He actually paid attention to me. This morning? It's all about Romero. No explanation. Not anything. Just like, *hey, here's this guy who's going to live with us now. Have a nice day by the pool.*"

Bianca shrugs, "It could be worse. He could be gross and ugly looking."

She's not wrong about that. Even though he's kind of a jerk, I already can't wait to see him again. "He's older than us. Maybe sixteen, or seventeen. I don't know, Dad didn't tell me, of course, and for the whole five minutes I met him he stared at the floor like he was pissed off. I doubt he'd talk to me anyway, that's if I even wanted to talk to him."

"Besides," she adds with a giggle, "it's not like your dad would let you hang out with an older guy."

"Ugh, also true." To think, I was in such a good mood when I first woke up. "Happy first day of summer vacation, I guess."

"It's all going to be okay. Don't let this get you down." She hops up from her chair and takes off the sundress she wore over her white suit. "Come on, let's enjoy the pool and try not to think about them. We'll play some music and start on our tans."

She's right. I know she is. I don't have to pay any attention to Romero. He can be another one of Father's guards, or whatever it is he pays them to do to keep us safe from whatever it is he does for a living. I'm not supposed to know about any of that.

I do know one thing, though. The first chance I get, I'm buying myself a two-piece suit. If Dad's going to ignore me for this guy, whoever he is, I'm going to start doing what I want.

Preorder your copy here: https://amzn.to/3pL2lEG

ABOUT THE AUTHOR

J.L. Beck writes steamy romance that's unapologetic.

Her heroes are alphas who take what they want, and are willing to do anything for the woman they love.

She loves writing about darkness, passion, suspense, and of course steam.

Leaving her readers gasping, and asking what the hell just happened is only one of her many tricks.

Her books range from grey, too dark but always end with a happily ever after.

Inside the pages of her books you'll always find one of your favorite tropes.

She started her writing career in the summer of 2014 and hasn't stopped since. She lives in Wisconsin and is a mom to two, a wife, and likes to act as a literary agent part time.

Visit her website for more info: www.beckromancebooks.com.

To stay in touch with J.L., subscribe to her newsletter here. If you'd like exclusive, early access to ebooks, paperbacks, and other exclusive content subscribe to her Patreon. You can read the first couple of chapters of the next book there now!

facebook.com/AuthorJLBeck
instagram.com/authorjlbeck
patreon.com/AuthorJLBeck